THE
TURNING
POINT

Freya North is the author of fourteen bestselling novels which have been translated into numerous languages. She was born in London but lives in rural Hertfordshire, where she writes from a stable in her back garden. A passionate reader since childhood, Freya was originally inspired by Mary Wesley, Rose Tremain and Barbara Trapido: fiction with strong and original characters.

In 2012 she set up, and now runs, the Hertford Children's Book Festival. She is a judge for the CPRE Rural Living Awards, and also an ambassador for the charity Beating Bowel Cancer.

To hear about events, competitions and what she's writing, join her on Facebook, Twitter and her website.

'A richly drawn, romantic weepy' *Sunday Mirror*

'A moving tale about never taking life for granted'
Stylist

'An emotional tale about finding love in unexpected places' *The Herald*

'From the initial spark and through the unfolding drama, it is joyous but understated. And the great cruelties that life harbours are not forgotten, either . . . full of . . . *.ady*

ALSO BY FREYA NORTH:

THE
TURNING
POINT

freya north

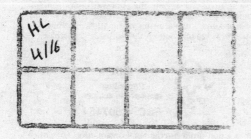

HL
4/16

HARPER

This novel is entirely a work of fiction.
The names, characters and incidents portrayed in it are
the work of the author's imagination. Any resemblance to
actual persons, living or dead, events or localities is
entirely coincidental.

Harper
An imprint of HarperCollins*Publishers*
1 London Bridge Street
London SE1 9GF

www.harpercollins.co.uk

This paperback edition 2016
1

First published in Great Britain by
HarperCollins*Publishers* 2015

A catalogue record for this book is
available from the British Library

ISBN: 9780007462308

Typeset in Meridien by Palimpsest Book Production Ltd, Falkirk, Stirlingshire
Printed and bound in Great Britain by Clays Ltd, St Ives plc

MIX
Paper from
responsible sources
FSC® C007454

For Maureen Pegg and Jo Smith - my MoJo indeed.

I would always rather be happy than dignified.

Jane Eyre, Charlotte Brontë

La musique commence là ou s'arrête le pouvoir des mots.
(Where music starts, words cease.)

Richard Wagner

SCOTT

Alone in his truck on an empty stretch of road in the middle of Thompson Country, Scott cursed out loud though no one could hear him. For the previous half an hour, as he drove from the belly of Kamloops and through the entrails of its suburbs, his phone signal had been off and the radio had played crystal clear everything he wanted to hear. His own personal playlist, beamed telepathically back through the radio, providing company and a soundtrack to the three hours remaining of the journey home. And now, as the road climbed and the scenery most deserved a rousing score, the music had gone and, instead, the cell-phone networks were polluting this immaculate part of British Columbia. His phone rang, his voicemail beeped, his phone rang again, his voicemail beeped. The sound wasn't dissimilar from some god-awful plastic Europop. A barrage of text-message alerts now chimed in like a truly crap middle eight before the calls started again. The phone was in his bag, in the footwell. Whatever risks Scott had taken in his life, he'd only ever driven with two hands on the wheel and both eyes on the road ahead. He pulled over. What, for Christ's sake, what?

The voicemail icon with its red spot as angry as a

boil. The envelope signifying text messages bursting with four unread. Missed calls. Managing his phone was the only thing in life that Scott was prepared to multitask, because to minimize the time spent on it, was time well spent. He accessed the voicemail whilst clicking into the texts. Before he'd heard a thing he knew what was wrong from Jenna's two words:

I'm fine x

But by then, a recorded voice was filling the car with the details.

'Hi Scott – it's Shelley. I've been trying to contact you – Jenna's had a seizure. She's OK now but it lasted near enough five minutes. She hit her head, she has a concussion so they've taken her to Squamish just to be sure. It's just gone two. You have my number so feel free to call me.'

Scott only vaguely listened to the later messages, all from Jenna's friend Shelley repeating the information in different tones of voice: tired, upbeat, reassuring, pseudo-medical. He stamped on the gas and drove fast, without looking at the view and with the radio off. There was no quick route. Too many mountains in the way.

When he opened the door to the hospital room, Jenna was still sleeping. Four hours later she woke, groggy and bashful. She always looked that way after an episode – not that she had any control over them. They had lingered over her life, a storm cloud, a menacing smudge on an otherwise blue sky and she never sensed when they were about to cover the sun.

'Neil Young, Jimmy Reed, Prince,' said Scott.

She looked at him as if to say, Really? I have to do this now?

'Joan of Arc,' she said. 'Dickens and Dostoyevsky.' She knew why he did it, this roll call, to make her feel less ashamed, less alone. She was part of a club, a member of epilepsy's renowned society – but it irritated her.

Actually, Scott did it to gauge her responsiveness.

'They glued me,' she said lightly. 'See?' Her finger hovered tentatively over the dark maroon splice above her brow.

'Very Harry Potter,' Scott said, thinking to himself that if he was a religious man he'd want to thank God for medical glue, for the fact that she was OK. But he wasn't a religious man because he just couldn't reconcile a God figure smiting someone so beautiful, so vital and harmless, with such an affliction. He sat down and put his hand gently over her wrist.

'I'm sorry,' she said. 'It just happened.'

He hated the obligation she felt to apologize. He hated God for that too. Why burden the victim with guilt as well?

'I know, sugar, I know.'

'I thought we had the meds pretty much sorted.'

Quietly, they both felt suddenly foolish for having had so much hope in the new cocktail and doses.

'You're booked in for your EEG next month?'

Jenna nodded. 'Can I come home tonight?'

'Doc says tomorrow.' Scott looked at her and assessed in a glance the new scar she'd be adding to her collection. And then he shrugged, his signature gesture when he'd assessed all the pros and cons in a split second. Jenna had suffered a seizure but see, she's back.

'It's been a while,' he said, 'since you had one that's ended you up here.' He tucked her hair behind her

3

ear. But Jenna didn't nod and he found he couldn't look at her. 'Tell me it's been a while.'

Jenna could do neither half-answers nor white lies.

'They've been, you know, *manageable*. And, as you say – they haven't put me in here for a good while.'

Scott was appalled. 'Why didn't you tell me?'

'Because you'd react like this? And blame yourself? And worry too much?'

The accusation was fair but it irked him.

'I kept a note – so I can discuss it with Dr Schultz next month.'

'You should have told me.'

She looked pale and exhausted. 'No driving for me, I guess,' she said. 'That's another six months wasted, hoping for normality.'

They both thought of her little red car in the driveway at home, which had hardly moved in two years.

Back home the next day, Scott settled Jenna into the armchair and built a small fire though it was May.

'I can cancel England next week,' he said.

'Are you crazy?'

'They can do it without me.'

'No, they can't – you won't let them anyway. You *have* to go,' Jenna said. 'That's what they pay you for.'

'The team there is great – they know me, I know them.'

'I'm not having this *thing* do this to me – to you. You have to go. It's your career. You need the money.'

They sat and reflected quietly, independently, together.

Scott went to the kitchen and took something out of the freezer. This *Thing*. Jenna's epilepsy was indeed just that – an incendiary entity that would grab her when he wasn't there, that would fight him for her when he was. All these years and he was no closer to finding any peace, any acceptance that this affliction held Jenna hostage right in front of his face and he just couldn't rescue her. A long time ago, he'd decided that if he couldn't rescue her, then he'd be right there with her, alongside her in captivity.

He rooted around for potatoes and onions, he clanged pans against pots, he clattered cutlery and muttered inanities under his breath but loud enough to fool Jenna if she was listening. All the while, he tossed the concepts around, like a juggler throwing machetes. It didn't necessarily follow that though she'd had a bad seizure another would recur any time soon – so if he did cancel England next week, say she was fine? And then, say the next time she *wasn't* fine when he was abroad? But how many times had there been recently that he hadn't known about? She'd said a couple – did she really mean only two? And define 'recently' Jenna. How long are we talking about?

England. Would she come with him? But she had work. Anyway, she wouldn't want to – she'd been there and done that and they both knew he'd have little time for anything other than sleep and work. Her life was here. If only the Thing would do them both the courtesy of some kind of schedule, better warning signs, softer landings. But when had it ever done that? The only predictable thing about most of her seizures was just how unpredictable they were. Scott thought about it as he sliced and chopped and steamed and fried. There was no magic solution, no cure, and still it made him furious.

Jenna was dozing when he went back through with a tray of food. He lifted a strand of hair that he felt was too close to her new wound. He had no appetite. He pushed his tray to one side and kept watch while she rested.

I'll always be here. I'll never leave you, baby. His oath was as solemn now as twenty years ago.

FRANKIE

Alice Alice Alice.

Frankie paused. She'd been here before, waiting for Alice. There was little point expending emotion on it. She'd just chant Alice's name again, in case she was creeping up on her, unseen.

What are you up to this time? Frankie asked quietly. Where are we going, youngling – you and I?

She thought she could hear her, in the distance. A snatch of a giggle, the arrhythmic scamper of small footfalls over twigs and leaves, the sound of joy that propelled a leap into the air.

Alice? Are you coming?

Frankie! Frankie! Can you hear me?

Sort of, but you're very muffled. Come closer, you little minx. Come closer so I can catch you.

Can you see me, Frankie? I'm *here*. Look!

Yes! There you are! Hold on – wait for me.

And then the back door opened with a creak and closed with a slam and all that Frankie had to show for her day was a stark, staring whiteness. A blankness that was as confrontational as it was empty. A sheet of white paper, with absolutely nothing on it.

'Hi Mum.'

'Hi darling.'

'Are you Alice-ing?'

'I thought I was.' Frankie smoothed the paper in front of her as if it was as creased as her brow. It wasn't. It might as well have been ironed flat, such was the pristine sharpness to the edges, as if potential paper cuts were its *raison d'être*.

'Haven't you done *anything*?'

'Almost.' Frankie looked at her son and glanced away. 'No.'

'Mum,' Sam sighed.

'It's so hard –'

'– there's no crisps.'

It was this that was the cause of Sam's concern, and it made Frankie flinch. Just then no crisps was worse than no Alice.

'Have crackers,' she said with forced brightness, 'with butter. That's what I had for lunch.' She gauged her son's response and she thought, when I was thirteen, would I have dared roll my eyes at my mother? And then she softened. My son with the hollow legs. 'I'll make them for you. Homework?'

'Chemistry and maths.'

'How awful.'

Sam thought about it glumly. Then he perked up. 'I can show you how to do a mind map on the computer – it's the best way for organizing ideas. It can cure your Writer's Block. I swear on my life.'

Frankie looked at Sam, looked at the pages in front of her, woefully devoid of a single word or image. Her body felt compressed and inert from the effort of spending all day creating nothing.

'OK, but you still have to do your homework.'

'I'll do it later. This'll only take me ten minutes to show you. It will change your life. I swear to God.'

'Sam – if I can plan my next book in ten minutes, *I'll* do your homework for you.'

'Sick! Promise?'

'No.'

He rolled his eyes at her. 'Can I just check Instagram?'

'No. And don't roll your eyes – it makes you look like you're having a fit. And that's not funny.'

Forty minutes later, Frankie was still flailing about with the technical demands of on-screen mind mapping. Her son truly wondered whether she was pretending to be so thick or whether it was an avoidance tactic because she didn't actually want to do another Alice book. One time, he'd watched her clean the inside of the dishwasher rather than write.

'Sorry darling – about the crisps.'

'Annabel will be far angrier than me. You promised her, remember.'

For a hideous frozen moment, Frankie could not move.

'Oh shit – not again.'

Listening to his mother fulminate her way through the house, tripping over her own shoes strewn in a doorway, hunting for keys tossed goodness knows where that morning, Sam thought to himself that resurrecting the swear jar might be a very good idea indeed. He and his sister would be rich in a matter of days.

Frankie backed her car down the driveway. Today, it infuriated her that she'd bought a house with a driveway but with no space to actually turn a car. Every day, it cricked her neck. Added to that was the headache of being really late already and now she found she was going to need to wave and wait and wave again at Mr Mawby. The elderly farmer next door was manoeuvring his tractor from the road into his yard as cautiously as if it was a Ferrari he wanted to keep pristine. Oh God please don't get out of the cab, please don't come over. Get back in the cab, Mr Mawby. No time for a little mardle today.

It did occur to her that she hadn't had time last week either.

'Hi, Mr Mawby, hi.' She wound down her window but kept her car creeping along. 'Are you well? Mrs Mawby too? I have to go – I'm late for Annabel.'

And Mr Mawby thought, When will that girl slow down and bed in?

Over the last few months, it had struck Frankie that the sharp bends on these empty and stretching country lanes were every bit as taxing as heavy traffic in the city she'd left nine months ago. As she drove, she suddenly felt nostalgic for the crafty back-doubles she knew off by heart around the roads of North London. There didn't seem to be any short cuts to Annabel's school. Or perhaps there was a clever route she didn't know about because she wasn't yet local enough.

Even from a distance, she could see that Annabel was glowering at her. One of the few children in After School Club and now the last child in the playground.

'I'm so so sorry,' Frankie called out in general, as lightly as she could, as she approached. 'Oh dear.' She was so out of breath she couldn't even swear under it. 'Mrs Paterson, I am so sorry – I was writing. And the time – it just . . .'

'That's all right, Miss Shaw. Annabel and I were having a very interesting conversation.'

Frankie didn't doubt that.

'Good afternoon, Annabel.' Mrs Paterson said goodbye with a formal handshake.

'Good *night*, Mrs Paterson,' Annabel said.

'Sarcasm is the lowest form of wit,' Frankie told her daughter as they walked to the car.

'That's what Grandma says,' said Annabel. 'I don't know what it means exactly – but I do know that you say *oh God I sound just like my mother* like it's the worst thing in the world. So I wouldn't say that one, if I were you.'

Sometimes, thought Frankie, there really is nothing you can say to a nine-year-old who has all the answers. She took Annabel's hand, persevering until, after snatching it away twice and then turning it into limp lettuce, her daughter finally furled her fingers around her mother's.

'Not much more than a year, then it'll be better. When you and Sam are at the same school, same bus.'

'But I don't want to leave my school,' said Annabel quietly.

Frankie looked at her. 'You like it here, don't you?'

'Yes,' Annabel said. 'I've only been here two and a bit terms but I like it much more than my old school. In fact, I hardly ever think about London.'

'Nowadays we have the sea,' said Frankie.

'And a big garden,' said Annabel, 'and a room of my own.'

'I'm truly sorry I was late, darling.'

'Sometimes I really hate Alice.'

'Why? What happened? Shall I speak to Mrs Paterson? Hate is a terrible emotion.'

'Not Alice in my class, Mum. *Your* Alice. She's like this stepsister or something. It's like you favouritize her. What's for supper?'

'Baked beans, chips. Tomato and cucumber. Possibly.' She paused. 'I didn't have time to go to the shops. I was working.'

'Does that mean there are no crisps?'

'I'm so sorry, darling.'

It was Annabel's forlorn silence, the way her little fingers slackened as if sighing, that made Frankie feel suddenly useless at everything. She knew Annabel blamed Alice. But Frankie had no one to blame but herself.

'Come on – let's go via Howell's and I'll buy you two packets and one for tomorrow.'

But then she realized she'd come out in a rush without her purse. And she wondered, does nine months living here warrant credit at the local shop?

* * *

Alice & the Ditch Monster
Alice & the Ditch Monster Hatch a Plan
Alice & the Ditch Monster Brave the Storm
Alice & the Ditch Monster Save the Day
Alice & the Ditch Monster Go for Gold
Alice & the Ditch Monster Halloween Howls
Alice & the Ditch Monster Wonder What the Fuck
    They're Going to Do Next

Children quiet in bed, one asleep, the other reading. A glass of Rioja to hand. The paper is still stark white

12

and glaringly empty in front of Frankie. It's raining outside and it shouldn't be. All that relocation research done quietly in Muswell Hill over a two-year period was proving pointless, the websites and books were inaccurate. North Norfolk in May should have lower-than-average rainfall. It should be neck and neck with Cornwall in terms of daily sunshine hours and be the driest county in England. But look at it out there – streaming and soaking and that huge sky dense with more to come. She'd overheard Sam calling it Norfuck yesterday.

Alice – we have a book to write.

But there was neither sight nor sound of Alice. Frankie trickled a little wine onto the page, folded it in half and vigorously rubbed her hand over it. She opened it out and stared hard. It looked nothing like the butterflies or strange beings that the children had created with poster paints at nursery school all those years ago. Even Freud – or whoever it was who'd used the exercise in therapy – would have had a hard time reading anything into it. It was simply an amoebic splodge and a waste of wine.

Alice and the Ditch Monster Do Absolutely Nothing

PART ONE

MAY TO JULY

t's Daddy!'

Momentarily, Frankie's heart ached for her daughter who was so used to fathers coming through the post that she brandished the envelope like it was a missive from royalty, running it in a lap of honour around the kitchen table before placing it carefully in front of Sam.

'Can you tell where it's from?'

Sam looked at the stamp and the franked mark. 'Ecuador,' he said as if it was some tiresome general-knowledge quiz set up by his father.

'Ecuador,' Annabel marvelled. 'Is that the capital of the equator? Is Daddy at the centre of the universe?'

'South America,' said Frankie.

'Open it then,' said Sam.

Frankie's heart creaked again as she watched Annabel slip her little finger into a gap and serrate the envelope as carefully as she could as if in anticipation of its contents bettering a golden ticket to Willy Wonka's. You never knew what Miles would send the children. Previously, they'd received a torn label from Israel which said Coca Cola in Hebrew, a wrapping from a ready meal in Japan called SuShitSu, a beer mat from Tasmania, a shrivelled-up floral lei from Hawaii, something from

Venezuela they had thought was a dead beetle but turned out to be some type of bean that they'd planted without success. Occasionally, there were notes, mostly not. Usually there were months between letters but then again Miles might bombard the children for a while, like friendly fire. These days, Sam was inured to all of it, whereas Annabel's life still depended on them.

Annabel eased out of the envelope a slim, rectangular piece of paper. It was torn carelessly from a Barclays Bank cheque book. Attached to it was the smallest yellow Post-it note imaginable.

Kids!
It's amazing here!
I've struck gold!
Give this to your mother.
Dad xx

Annabel wasn't bothered about the cheque addressed to her mother. All she cared about was that her father had travelled to the equator for her, had dug for gold and found it. She peeled off the sticky note, placed it on her fingertips as if it was a rare butterfly, and left for her room.

'Four *thousand* quid!' Sam was hard-pressed not to love his dad just a little bit more just then. He passed it to Frankie. 'Look.'

Four thousand pounds, made out to her and signed, legibly, by Miles.

'Sick!' said Sam, leaving the table. 'Four grand.'

'Sam – please, no tweetering or facebookgramming about this.'

'Seriously?' His mother's terminology wasn't even amusing, just annoying.

'Yes *seriously*.'

'But you're not on Twitter.'

'That's irrelevant. It might buy you a few more followers – but not friends. Anyway – it's vulgar to talk about money. And anyway – it's private.'

Sam huffed his way out leaving Frankie alone in the kitchen with all that money. If there's four grand in your English bank Miles, God knows what you have squirrelled away under your Ecuadorian mattress. And not for the first time, Frankie thought, whoever you're in bed with this time, I hope there's a gun under your pillow. And then she thought, this autumn, we'll have been divorced for seven years. These days it was strange to consider that once she'd had a husband and even odder to think that the husband had actually been Miles.

'Frankie?' Peta assumed her sister had phoned for a chat, yet she was doing all the talking.

'Still here,' Frankie said. Peta's impassioned tirades against politics in the PTA, unfairness in the rugby club, Philip's long hours, the boys' adolescent mood swings and stinky bedrooms had wafted over Frankie quite soothingly, like a billowing sheet.

'So – what's been happening in the Back of Beyond?'

'I don't live in the back of beyond.'

Peta laughed. 'Burnham Market it ain't.'

It was just under twelve miles to Burnham Market but Frankie had to admit quietly to herself that her sister had a point. Renting a holiday cottage in the popular market town had inspired her move from London to Norfolk. But like most holiday romances, reality rendered the fantasy obsolete. Property prices in any of the Burnhams were beyond her means. The type of home she envisaged for her family, that which she could afford, took her further afield. Or, as Peta would have it, in the middle of a bloody field.

'And the kids?'

'They're brilliant,' said Frankie. 'Loving school. Loving the outdoors, the sea. Dressed crab from a shack. Scampering.'

'And you? New friends?' Peta worried that Frankie's choice to have a limited social group in a city was one thing, but to move miles away from anywhere was quite another.

'There's Ruth,' said Frankie.

'The reiki woman?'

'Alexander Technique,' Frankie said. 'It's about balance and posture, rest and realignment and it's helped with my headaches already. She's definitely becoming a good friend.'

'She's not a lentil-munching happyclappy hippy is she?'

'Peta you're terrible. She's chic, sassy and my age. She's much more Jäger-bombs and a secret ciggy than mung beans and wheatgrass shots.'

'Thank God for that. But you can have more than one friend you know.'

'You're not going to tell me to join the PTA are you?'

'No but too strong a belief in self-sufficiency can be isolating. Lecture over – how's work?'

Frankie paused. 'It's back. The block. I can't hear Alice. It's really worrying me now.' She misread Peta's ensuing silence and leapt to the defensive. 'Just because I write for kids doesn't mean it's child's play.'

'Whoa – whoa. But it's happened before – when

you've struggled with the story. Have you told your editor?'

'No. He keeps leaving messages. And I daren't tell the bank either.'

'Are you strapped?' Peta asked. 'For cash?'

Frankie thought about it. She had only to ask her sister. She'd done so in the past and Peta had been generous, keen even; as if the money she'd married into had value only when she could give it to others.

'It's OK, Peta. Guess what turned up today? Not so much a bad penny – but four grand. From Miles.'

'Oh dear God that man. Where is he?'

'Ecuador.'

'Doing what?'

'God knows. Being Indiana Jones.'

'Bank it – before it bounces. And go and drink wine with Ruth. Or join the school mums for a coffee morning.'

'I don't have time – I have to write my book.'

Frankie decided she'd try and fool Alice into appearing. She left her pencils and paper all spread out on the kitchen table like a fisherman's nets but instead, she drove to Wells-next-the-Sea directly from dropping Annabel at school. It was all part of her plan. She went to the bank and was told it would be five working days before Miles's cheque appeared in her account. She went to the newsagent, bought a plain notepad and a clutch of pencils that she wrapped inside a copy of the *Guardian*. Then she walked slowly, casually glancing in shop windows as if this was precisely the way she'd planned to spend her morning. She came to two cafés almost next door to each other, but she eschewed the crowded one that indulged mums and toddlers with cappuccinos and crayons for the one that didn't. She wandered in as if the fancy had only just taken her. It was filled with the creak of pensioners but there was an empty table by the side window towards the back and it was perfect. Dumping all her stuff on the empty chair, she ordered poached eggs on toast – white please – and a pot of tea. And there she sat, watching the microcosm of Wells going about its business, as if the street in this small seaside town typified the world at large. Mothers with strollers, people with dogs, builders taking a break, pensioners taking their time, a couple of kids playing hooky, a traffic warden trying to be inconspicuous, a horse and rider, a lorry headed for the Londis – and just an off-duty author having a fulfilling breakfast of eggs and toast and tea.

Alice?

Alice?

You should see this place – why don't you come and sit with me awhile?

I don't like towns, Frankie.

It's hardly a big town.

I like fields.

But this is fun, it's different. No one knows you here, Alice. See – a lovely blank piece of paper. Hop onto it – it's what you know. I'll look after you.

He won't come you know – not here. He's too shy. You know that.

You went trick-or-treating together though? That was in a town – remember?

That was in Cloddington. You created Cloddington for me to live in. This place is not there.

But it's similar.

It's completely different Frankie. I don't want an adventure here. But if you eat your eggs and finish your cuppa, I'll race you home.

So Frankie ate her eggs and finished her tea and walked briskly to her car and raced Alice home. But Alice won. By the time Frankie made it back to her kitchen table, Alice had found one heck of a hiding place and wasn't going to give Frankie even the tiniest clue as to where she was.

* * *

'Frankie Darling.'

The voice of Michael, her editor, came through on the answering machine and Frankie closed the door to the kitchen as if he might spy the pages devoid of any creativity strewn over the kitchen table.

'My surname's Shaw,' Frankie muttered at the answering machine, 'not Darling.'

Actually, she quite liked the way her publishers always referred to her as Frankie Darling. Her agent simply called her Author. She liked that too.

'Frankie Darling – it's time to lure you to London. We want to run through the pre-publication plans. And of course I want to hear all about what Alice is up to. We'll put you up somewhere gorgeous for a couple of nights. Call me.'

Somewhere gorgeous. They were the very words Frankie had used to justify her relocation to everyone. *I'm going to move to somewhere gorgeous*. North Norfolk: the dictionary definition of precisely that – and everyone had agreed with her, everyone said they envied her.

Soon she was lightly telling everyone it didn't matter that she couldn't afford the Burnhams, she'd found instead a detached cottage in gently undulating fields two miles from the sea, decorated inside with soft chalky shades reminiscent of a handful of blanched pebbles scooped from the shore.

She was aware that the interior of the house had seduced her as much as the vast sky and endless quiet lanes. But there was something else: the very concept of being detached: the house, herself, her little family, it brought with it a sense of comfort and freedom, independence and excitement. Solitude would be novel and welcome after years in flats squashed between other flats like the patty in a burger, having to look down on other people's gardens and listening unintentionally to the thunks and arguments above, below, to either side. So last year Frankie spent all her money and borrowed heavily to purchase the traditional flint-and-brick cottage with a bedroom each for the children, a spare room rather than a sofa bed for guests, an en-suite for herself and a garden that wrapped itself protectively around the house in a fragrant and pastel-coloured embrace.

Frankie looked around her home today, nine months on. Weathering winter, it transpired that the tasteful paint scheme had just whitewashed a multitude of faults and problems. What began as annoying niggles soon became a major headache in the hands of a rogue builder no one thought to warn The New Lot about. And now, in late spring, the windows that leaked could open but not close and a peculiar patch of damp had appeared in the hallway that just didn't make sense. The plug socket in her bedroom sparked, some of the light switches became too hot and the tap in the kitchen often vomited out the water, soaking everything.

Being detached.

She saw it as a quality though it was often a criticism levelled at her by her mother, her sister. Even Miles. In fact, Peta said she was becoming increasingly introvert, even used the word *deluded*, but Frankie found it easy to hang up on her. Actually, Frankie found assurance in privacy and a certain relief that she could keep the devils out of the details of her life. For the time being anyway. Because apart from Miles's cheque, which would be swallowed by the bank in one gulp anyway, there was no more money until the next Alice book was in. Currently, Alice hadn't found her way to Norfolk and Frankie's sense of direction had never been her strong point.

Standing at the bottom of the stairs, she caught sight of a lone sock halfway up which she'd nagged Sam about since the weekend. Suddenly it struck her how easily she could spend the day just as she was, feeling in a fug, scuffing her feet in absent-minded arcs over the clay-tiled floor. Easy to let her editor's call go unanswered, the bills to stay unopened, the pages on which Alice and the Ditch Monster should be adventuring to remain tauntingly blank. She could go to the sea. There was something so energizing and validating about gazing at the constant swell while being buffeted by the wind, tasting the briny air while she said to herself see, *this* is why I moved here. For the fresh air and the good life; for the peace and quiet of feeling miles away.

Or she could take herself to task and do something about it all. She could pick up Sam's sock and kick-start her day. She could wash the floor and make the beds, she could phone her editor with her diary to hand. Then she could sit at the kitchen table and attempt to draw Alice back into existence.

With the children bickering over TV channels, moaning at her *not pasta again Mum*, the concept of a couple of nights in a swish hotel at her publishers' invitation was just then very attractive even if she'd have to lie about progress on her current book. However, Peta said she wasn't free to come and housesit because she was hosting her book club.

'But if you're organizing it, can't you rearrange?'

'Can't you phone Mum?'

'Can't you just change the date? It's important, it's my career.'

'Listen Frankie – I know you think I have all this spare time because I don't work, but every day I have to ferry my teenage boys in a car which stinks of rugby boots or rattles with cricket bats. My husband is never home before nine and all I ask is that once a month I can get lost in a book with a bunch of people even more frazzled than I. It's good for me – it *restores* me.'

The sisters paused in self-righteous stalemate.

'Isn't there *anyone* local you can ask?'

'No.'

'I keep telling you – you need to get out more. You're becoming too introverted – and don't call it self-sufficient.'

'I'm not.'

'How about a teaching assistant from Annabel's school? What about your new friend Mrs Alexandra Technician?'

'Ruth has two young children of her own.'

'Ask Mum.'

'Come on, Peta.'

'What about Steph?'

Quietly, Frankie considered how Steph hadn't crossed her mind for weeks. 'I thought she was working in a ski resort?'

'It's May, Frankie. The snow has gone.'

Frankie thought about her half-sister as she looked at the caller-id photo in her phone's contacts. Neither she nor Peta had taken much notice of Steph when she bounced into their lives; they'd been too busy pursuing their twenties, then raising their own families in their thirties. Frankie's children adored Steph, especially Annabel who thought Frankie hopelessly uncool. Just this morning she'd said, what's going on with your hair, Mummy?

'Steph?'

'Frankie?'

'How are you?'

'Oh my God! I'm good! And you? How's Suffolk?'

'Norfolk.'

'That's funny.'

Is it? Would Annabel laugh too?

'And the ski season was –'

'Oh just the *best*.'

'Are you working now?'

'No I'm in my flat.'

'I don't mean right now – I mean, at the moment.'

'Yes – I'm a barista.'

'What is that?'

'I specialize in coffee.'

'You work in Starbucks?'

'God no – an independent coffee emporium. I know everything about coffee.'

'Wow.'

Steph laughed. 'Actually, I work in a local café.'

It was Frankie's go. '*You're* funny,' she said warmly and she meant it. She thought, my half-sista the barista.

'How are Sammy and Annabel?'

'They're fine – they'd love to see you, though Sam insists on being Sam these days. Actually, I was just wondering if I could tempt you to visit next week? They'd love it and it would help me. I have to come to London to see my editor. I was wondering if you might come and stay? I could pay, so that you don't go short, being away from work?'

There was a pause. 'I'm family. You wouldn't need to pay me.' Steph sounded appalled. 'Normally I'd say yes – but I'm going away next week. With my new boyfriend.'

What Frankie really wanted to do was hang up and wonder what to do next.

'He's called Craig?' Steph seemed to be waiting for a response.

'Is he a keeper?' Frankie said.

'Are you on Facebook?'

'No.'

'Twitter? Instagram?'

'God no.'

'I've posted loads of pics of Châtel and Craig and my life. Everything.'

'I can barely use the Internet, Steph.'

'Frankie!' Steph all but chided her. 'You, with your work, your fans – you should be! Do you have WhatsApp or Snapchat, at the very least?'

'I don't think so,' said Frankie. 'Do I?' And Steph laughed and laughed and said oh Frankie, you're so funny.

Frankie looked at her phone and thought what's the point of calling Peta – she'll just say phone Mum.

'Hello Mum – it's me.'

'Yes?'

'It's Frankie.'

'I know.'

'How are you?'

'Oh – you know.'

'It's lovely here at the moment – we had rain but it's just made everything lush.'

'You said it never rains in Norfolk.'

Fill the pause. Just fill it.

'My publishers want me down in London next week. For a couple of days and I was wondering –'

There was silence.

'Might you be free? I'll have everything organized. If you'd rather take the train I could collect you from King's Lynn.'

'The train?'

'If you'd rather not drive.'

'Meaning?'

'I didn't mean – I just.'

I just always say the wrong thing or I intend to say the right thing and it always comes out wrong.

'I will come,' her mother said. 'Otherwise no doubt I won't see my grandchildren this side of Christmas.'

So that was that.

Sometimes, Frankie told herself, you have to be grateful for your third choice. Her mother could come to Norfolk and pick holes in Frankie's life while she'd be in London, in a triple-glazed hotel room. Glancing in the mirror, she conceded that Annabel was quite right – what *was* going on with her hair? It no longer bounced off her shoulders but seeped over them, like seaweed lanking over a boulder. She'd washed it yesterday and it was already lifeless. She couldn't turn up at her publishers looking like this. She looked at her hands, they were dry. Jeans, shapeless T-shirt and trainers. This is what my kids see every day. I have to have my hair cut before my mother sees me.

* * *

As Frankie parked her car at Creake Abbey, she could almost hear Peta saying ah! now *this* is more like it. It ticked all her sister's boxes. A short drive from Burnham Market, quietly set in rolling fields, old farm buildings in the grounds of a twelfth-century abbey had been tastefully renovated to house select lifestyle shops, a mouthwatering café and food hall, a monthly farmer's market and even a smokehouse. Hitherto, Frankie had only visited to walk to the Abbey itself, loving the brooding melancholy of the skeletal structure, the way what was left of the church seemed to grow from the land as much as being buried by it. She saw Alice having an adventure here, places to hide, secrets to discover, trees to climb and hedgerows to explore.

The ruins of the Augustinian priory, but so much more – that's what Peta would say and she'd head straight for the shops. She'd approve of Frankie's choice of hairdresser; hip salon, skilled stylists, Aveda products and bare stone walls. Well here was Frankie today sitting with her hair hanging like twisted wet yarn around her face, no time to stroll around the ruins hoping Alice might pop up. The stylist combed and cut and chatted. Was Frankie just visiting, on holiday? Where was she from, what she was she planning on doing here in North Norfolk? It crushed her a little, she thought she might be recognizably native by now.

'I'm a friend of Ruth?' she said. 'Ruth Ingram? She recommended you.'

'Oh – so you live here?'

'Nine months now – I live out Binham way,' Frankie said as if being half an hour away was reason enough for the stylist not to know she was local.

'Do you want your hair like Ruth's?'

Frankie thought of Ruth's immaculate ebony-glossed bob and she started to laugh. 'My hair would never do that.'

'Well, you don't have to have a Ruth,' the stylist said, her hands lightly on her shoulders. 'But you needn't look quite so mumsy.'

Sometimes, Frankie found it difficult to tell the difference between a compliment and an unintended insult.

Flipping through magazines, she found the lowbrow celebrity gossip and articles on improving her figure, her sex life, her family's diet soothing in their inanity. One magazine proposed the power of saying Yes. Another, the thrill of saying No. She marvelled that this stuff was even published. If Alice had no story for her, perhaps Frankie could just scribble off 10 Steps to Sizzling Sex. Or, rather, Regaining Your Virginity if You Haven't Had Sex in Three Years.

'So you moved here with your family?'

'Yes – last September.'

'Does your husband work locally or go to London?'

'I don't have a husband,' said Frankie. 'I'm on my own.'

'Oh I'm sorry.'

People often told Frankie they were sorry.

'I hope you haven't come to Norfolk looking for love!'

'No. Not at all. Just for the lifestyle. And the sea. And the solitude.'

'You know that expression *seek and ye shall find*? Well, in my experience, it's the times when you aren't looking that love finds you.'

Frankie thought about that, how people often hoped that love was on its way for her. 'I'm happy as I am,' she said. 'I'm used to it. I'm too busy anyway for extra headaches in my life.'

'But love isn't a headache. Not when it's what's been missing.'

'Nothing's missing,' she muttered. She glanced at her reflection and thought her fringe was way too short. She caught sight of the time. She'd have to forgo the blow-dry and rush away to school. No time to linger over the cheeses and meats, salads and delicacies in the food hall. It would have to be fish-finger sandwiches for supper. It didn't matter about her fringe, she'd be late to pick up Annabel and everyone else would have gone.

'What do you think, Buddy?' Scott stood at the window which spanned side to side, ceiling to floor, one entire end of the room. In the soft silence of his home, he looked across to Mount Currie where the spike and march of the myriad firs made easy work of the steep climbs. Under his hand, the feel of his dog's warm round head. It was his ritual before leaving – to fill his senses with the sights and sounds of home to tide himself over during his time away. 'A good day to fly?' Scott looked down and his brown dog looked up and they conversed silently for a moment or two. 'I thought so too,' Scott laughed.

'Is Aaron on his way? You sure you're not cutting it fine?' Jenna said.

'Stop worrying,' Scott told her. 'And anyway, I like to stand here awhile – I always do.' He returned his gaze out over the vast valley.

'I know – I've watched you over the years. Same spot, same view, different dog.' She linked her arm through his and he kissed her forehead. They could see Shelley's car snake up the steep serpentine drive to the house and noticed Aaron not far behind her.

'Our own personal cab service,' Scott said.

'I'd do anything to drive my own car and be the lift-giver.'

Jenna's light tone belied the deep emotion. There was not a lot Scott could say. He checked his watch. 'Listen, Saturday the kids are coming up to use the studio.'

Jenna nodded. Scott mentored young musicians, forming and coaching bands that combined young talent from the white and Líĺwat communities. 'How's it going with them?'

'They're good – but they think they're better than they are. They just want to jam instead of work at it, practise. They get a little dumb – but hey, they're kids.'

'As long as they're not smuggling in beer like the last lot.'

Scott had to laugh. 'And there was I thinking that mentoring high-school kids would be all about the music.'

'You love it really,' Jenna said, nudging him. Shelley was walking towards the house. 'See you next week – have a safe flight.'

With his hand back on his dog's head, Scott watched Jenna leave, chat awhile with Aaron and say something that made his friend tip his head back and laugh at the sky. Then she waved and blew a kiss before climbing into Shelley's car to head to work in Whistler.

Aaron loped up the steps and Buddy turned circles at the door, yowling with joy.

'Yep,' said Scott, 'you get to hang out with Aaron while I'm gone.'

'Beautiful day to fly,' Aaron said, letting himself into the house and heading straight for the kettle and ground coffee.

'Jenna says we're running late.'

Aaron laughed, not so much at Jenna's expense, just that he was always laughing. When Scott was a kid, a serious, reflective kid, Aaron's laughter would physically rub off on him and he'd feel lighter about life and better about himself. Forty years on and Aaron still had that effect on Scott. *That boy's laughter could lift the tarnish off silver*, Scott's mother used to say.

'We're all fuelled up and ready to go. Took her out yesterday and treated her real good.' Aaron licked his way seductively around the words as if his little Cessna was a woman.

'It's enough that you have my dog for me. I'm happy enough to drive to Vancouver. It's no big deal. I always tell you.'

'And deny Buddy here – the flying dog – his time up in the skies?' Aaron shook his head and whistled long and slow. 'You're a cruel man, Scott Emerson. I always say it.'

'You tool,' said Scott.

'*Splaont*,' said Aaron, in his native tongue.

'Don't you go using your tribal insults on me, *hoser*,' Scott laughed. 'Anyways, did you just call me a skunk? Are you going to try and tell me the skunk is a heroic symbol for the Líĺwat nation?'

Aaron just laughed. 'You remember when we were kids and I'd teach you Úcwalmícwts words and have you believe they were compliments?'

'Aaron, you made me tell your dad he was *slícil* – fish slime – and I thought I was telling him he was a mighty eagle.' Scott took the cup of coffee Aaron had made him, thick enough to stand a teaspoon upright, and drank it down quickly. 'Well, it's a beautiful day to fly, so thank you.'

'I'm not doing it for you, man – I'm doing it because I get to drive your truck and hang out with Buddy. Your truck cost more than my plane.'

In the air, with Buddy managing to fit on his lap, Scott looked down and around the landscape. Mount Currie, stately and benevolent today, like a wise old monarch surveying her kingdom. Pemberton and then Whistler – both glinting and self-contained, as if unaware that life also went on elsewhere. The ice fields and falls and meadows; the mercurial paths of the Lillooet, Elaho and Cheakamus rivers. All the blues and every green. Blue and green should never be seen, wasn't that what his grandma said? What a load of bull Gramma, Scott thought. He looked at Aaron, grinning away, delighted to be flying him to Vancouver, choosing a circuitous route for the sheer joy of it. Birds might fly economically, with purpose, from A to B. Not Aaron. That was not the point of flight. Scott would still make his international flight with time to spare – so for the time being, why not just fly for the hell of it. It's beautiful down there. Up here. Everywhere. Life doesn't get much better than this.

* * *

Margaret Shaw could not guarantee what time she'd arrive and certainly she was not prepared to arrive before lunch. Actually, she arrived at her daughter's at 11.00, which was a blessing and a curse. Frankie might make the earlier train but the house was still a mess and her mother greeted her with a sharp kiss and a raised eyebrow.

'I did have a cleaner,' Frankie said. 'But she was a bit useless. So I'm looking for another.'

'And you're not doing it yourself in the *interim*?' It seemed highly unlikely, to Margaret.

'Actually – I am. With the children. I think it's good for them to help. So we have our little timetable for an hour on Saturdays mornings.'

'*An hour?*'

Frankie thought of Oscar Wilde. *A handbag?* It gave her a comforting private giggle. Margaret Shaw and Lady Augusta Bracknell. What a fabulous comedy of manners that would make. Who would play her mother? What a role! Her children thought their grandma to be lifted straight from the pages of a Roald Dahl story. When she was very little, Annabel had pointed to a Quentin Blake illustration of Aunt Spiker and said look! it's Grandma!

'Let me take your bags to your room. The kettle's just boiled. I've written out everything – and been through it with the kids.'

'Children.'

'With the children.' Frankie paused. 'I've made supper for tonight and tomorrow night – that's the snack drawer there. I've put Annabel's fruit for school on the windowsill – there.'

'You have labelled an apple?'

'Well, the ki – children – put their fruit in a basket in the classroom. You see.'

'I see.'

'There's Rich Tea for you. And real butter. And full milk.' Frankie thought about what else what else what else. 'Palmolive soap,' she said quietly. 'Vosene shampoo.'

'Have you fixed that interminable draught in the bedroom?'

'Yes,' said Frankie. 'I hope so. I put the electric blanket on your bed too.'

'It's May.'

'It can get chilly in the evenings still. Here's a map to Annabel's school. And here's Sam's mobile-phone number.'

'He has a *mobile phone*?'

'For emergencies,' Frankie lied. Actually, Frankie had bought Sam his phone because he desperately wanted one because everyone has one these days, Mum, *everyone*. However much she hated technology and couldn't bear to see children obsessed by screens often at the expense of books, that her son could feel he was cool and that he belonged was something she yearned for him. Sam with his orthodontic braces and protruding ears and two left feet when it came to football.

'I'd better go, Mum,' she said. 'Just call me, or have the kids-children call me, for the slightest thing.' And she kissed her mother and gave her a squeeze if only to pre-empt Margaret from saying I raised two girls single-handedly, I'm sure I can cope with your offspring, Frankie.

*   *   *

Jenna needn't have worried; Scott was at Vancouver airport with time enough to do a little work. He could have gone through to the lounge – they were flying him over business class – but the place he always favoured was right in the middle of the International terminal, in an amphitheatre of sorts dominated by the immense sculpture of The Spirit of Haida Gwaii, a vast jade-coloured bronze canoe filled with symbolic figures of First Nations legend. He sat on a lower tier and set his laptop up on his knees. Somehow, amidst the thrum of people in transit he could concentrate far better than in an airport lounge clogged with the conversations of self-important businessmen. He hadn't checked his emails for a couple of days and ploughed through them, reading each carefully if only to answer them with his characteristic one or two spare sentences. His agent had emailed to say he needed to speak to him and it surprised Scott to see the missed calls on his phone from yesterday. Had he not checked it since then? He called him to apologize.

His relationship with his agent was a strong one stretching over almost two decades but the business side of his career bored Scott and he found himself listening to the sound of his agent's voice rather the content of his words. For Scott, even in spoken tones, there was music to the human voice and just now, his agent talking combined with the rhythm of rush in the terminal. To his left, seated a tier up and in a world of their own, young lovers clung to each other, forehead to forehead, eyes transmitting the depth of their goodbye. To his right, his guitar. In his head, suddenly, an idea.

'I have to go,' he told his agent. 'I need to work. I'll call you from London.'

For a few minutes more, Scott focused fully on the couple, disparate melodies flitting through his mind as the music formed. But the young woman whispered to her lover and they both glared at Scott before moving away, hand in hand, disconcerted. Scott felt simultaneously awkward yet amused. He looked around, surprised that no one else was sitting here. He made another call.

'Hey kiddo. It's Scott.'

'Hey man. I know it's you – your name comes up, right?'

Scott always enjoyed the fact that the kids saw him as both cool and yet pretty dorky. It made mentoring them touching and amusing, alongside the work and responsibility.

'I missed your call yesterday – I'm heading for the United Kingdom. But it's cool for you to use the studio on the weekend. You guys need to focus, eh? Three songs in as many months does not make a great band, Jonah. It's two and a half, really – you need to work on "She Moves". You need a killer middle eight – not a middle *bleugh*.'

'OK.'

It sounded to Scott as though Jonah was standing to attention. He didn't want to compromise the kid's confidence. 'If you can do that,' he continued, 'I think "She Moves" might be your best song.'

'Good enough for the Festival next year?'

'You never know.'

'Cool.'

'Good,' said Scott. 'And Jonah – no wine, no women, no weed.'

Jonah's protestations made Scott smile. The kids were fifteen, sixteen years old and touchingly serious about being the best band Pemberton had ever produced. They themselves decreed no distraction during band practice.

'I'll catch up with you next weekend,' Scott said. 'We'll see if you're ready to do a set at the Pony next month.'

Jonah's gratitude tumbled out unchecked.

'I have to go,' Scott interjected. 'They've called my flight.'

An airport terminal filled with all types ready to journey up to the skies and off into the world. Departures and arrivals, bound by time. Suitcases with condensed versions of home crammed inside. Stress and hurry, excitement, irritation, joy and sadness. For Scott, there was music in it all.

* * *

London changes quickly. Very quickly. Transient and restless, buildings and commerce and people are constantly in flux. In and out, up and down and out, at breakneck speed. When she lived there, Frankie saw this as a quality; that the city and its inhabitants were progressive and enterprising, pioneering even, and somehow more alive than in any other city. But that afternoon, the rush and pace seemed to blow through the streets malevolently, scuffing up the debris on the pavements, causing pedestrians to rustle against each other as if an ill wind was to blame. When she'd lived in London, Frankie had fed off the brittle energy. Now, back again, she felt bulldozed by it. Only nine months away from it all, suddenly she was the country mouse who didn't know the etiquette of pavement pacing or jaywalking or cramming oneself into the nooks of a crowded underground carriage. She was walking and walking and not seeming to get anywhere. She was the foreigner now, the stranger in town – returning to a city inhabited by a multinational cabal in a self-centred rush. If Alice ever gave her the chance, she had a series planned for older readers called *The Metromorph*. As she melded herself into a space amongst the throng in the underground, she scrabbled around in her head and focused on the ideas she'd stored rather than the smells permeating from all those bodies.

A passenger standing right by her spat on the floor. She thought of Annabel and Sam and Norfolk and felt a pang for what was now home. She thought of the sea, the briny mass that had in recent months benevolently pushed its energy right into her when she stood at its edge. She thought of the oversized sky that seemed to brag and boast its extravagant cloud formations by day and its effervescence of stars at night. It was a well-known joke, to say that Norfolk people had 'too much sky' as if it wasn't good for them. Just then, in the choke of human gridlock, Frankie couldn't disagree more. She didn't hate London, she'd been born and bred there. But for the first time she felt truly confident in her decision to leave.

And that's why, when Scott touched her arm and said excuse me – can you help – I guess I'm a little lost, Frankie turned to him and, with some pride, said sorry, I'm not from around here either.

The publishers had cake and compliments laid out and called her Frankie Darling all afternoon. She lied through mouthfuls of gateaux and brushed away the reality of her Writer's Block as though it was just cookie crumbs. Oh yes, the new book is coming on just fine – you're going to love it – I think it may even be my best yet.

'Alice,' Frankie told everyone, 'is on top form. She's having a blast.'

The Alice books had been the company's biggest children's seller in the age range last year and Frankie had been twice nominated for the *Guardian* Children's Fiction Prize. She was truly their golden girl but oh, the frustration of this particular author refusing to divulge the teeniest clue about the new book. Come on Frankie Darling – give us a snippet.

In between meetings, Frankie sat in her editor's office and the two of them swivelled rhythmic half-circles on the office chairs.

'You seem a little – out of sorts – darling. And you keep ignoring my calls.'

Frankie looked up sharply, off her guard and on the defensive. Though she was aware that she had a duty to reveal just how acute her Writer's Block was, suddenly she felt ill prepared and reluctant.

'I'm fine! Honestly!'

'I think I know what's wrong,' Michael told her. 'I think I know. We've known each other many years, Frankie. I can see you so clearly sitting at your kitchen table, or gazing out of windows for hours on end wondering what you're going to do, how to tell people, worrying about what everyone will say. I've guessed. I know.'

'She's lost,' Frankie mumbled. 'I haven't seen her – for weeks.'

There was a pause. 'Sorry?'

'I can't find her. It's like she's run away.'

'Run away? Who?' Michael was used to his authors darting off at tangents only to reappear halfway through internalized conversations. He'd found it was usually best to carry on regardless. 'Do you remember when I split up with Gerry and moved to Surrey? All my high hopes that Chobham was the centre of the universe and the answer to all my problems? Pretty quickly I hated it, yearned for London. And Frankie – Norfolk's far more remote.' He looked at her kindly. 'No one will think any less of you if you come back to town.'

It wasn't about Alice.

This wasn't about Alice at all.

And she thought, Alice – that's one lucky escape we've just had.

'And Frankie,' Michael said, 'about Alice – I really do want to see something soon. We don't even have a title.'

* * *

Michael's words reverberated in Frankie's ears as she elbowed her way into the underground, trying not to breathe in the swarm of the rush hour as the train lurched and rumbled on its way. Stop start stop start; more people oozing into a carriage now devoid of personal space. God this journey was far more stressful than belting to school late again. Mr Mawby loped slowly into Frankie's mind's eye and the image soothed her. Mr Mawby and his tractor; a man whose working day was long and constant but somehow conducted at a pace that was as dignified as it was productive. He didn't strike her as the type of worker who missed deadlines, unlike most of the stressheads in this carriage. He called her children Brocky and Emma Belle and he'd extended them his gruff welcome from the start, letting them sit in his tractor and swing on the creaky gate and climb the straw bales that surrounded his precious sugar-beet heaps in the autumn. She ought to make more of an effort, really; find the time to pass the time with a little chat now and then. She'd only ever seen Mrs Mawby from a distance, a rather lonely sight standing on the doorstep of their somewhat plain farmhouse surrounded by barns and outbuildings in harsh corrugated steel. What would Mr Mawby make of the rush hour? And Frankie thought he'd probably just laugh and denounce it as a load of old squit.

Thoughts of Norfolk provided a surprising and welcome steadiness to the rest of the journey and now here's the hotel, a stunning exposition of expensively understated design. They've upgraded her to a junior suite and all is suddenly very good with the world. She can have a bath free of soap-scum tidal marks and swathe herself in cloud-soft towels.

And in the foyer, reading his book over a coffee, Scott thought: that's the woman I saw earlier, who didn't know her way either. Well what do you know – this town isn't so big after all.

He watched as she left the front desk, her head tipped back to take in the soaring triple-height atrium, almost tripping over her feet in the process. He saw how she was grinning at everything. It made him smile and, just for a moment, Scott felt something intense and forgotten, a sensation that flipped his stomach and dried his mouth. He couldn't remember if the feeling was welcome or a warning. And then he thought, for Chrissake, just quit the contemplation and go walk up an appetite instead.

As lovely as her room was, there was only so much daydreaming Frankie could do out over gracious buildings to the Thames in its timeless flow beyond. She'd assessed all the dinky little miniatures bejewelling the interior of the minibar, eaten half a jar of caramelized nuts, put a selection of the toiletries into her bag for Annabel and flicked through all the TV channels finding nothing to watch. There wasn't anything on the room-service menu she fancied and, though she contemplated the snowy towelling robe and complimentary slippers, it wasn't even six o'clock and she couldn't possibly get ready for bed. It would be slightly pathetic. Maybe she'd go for a stroll and find somewhere for sushi. Maybe. And on her way, she'd go and have a cocktail, a grown-up drink at the bar downstairs, that's what she'd do.

But there was an art to sitting nonchalantly at a bar on one's own. She'd seen other women do it, admired and envied them, but whenever she tried it, she hated it. She'd simply felt awkward and conspicuous, sensing she was being stared at and then realizing no one was remotely interested at all. A clash of feeling exposed and feeling invisible, neither of which was good for the self-esteem. But the Cosmopolitan she'd hastily ordered arrived before she could cancel it so she drank it down as if it was Ribena and then walked over to the vast console table loaded with magazines and newspapers, for something to take up to her room. And coming back into the hotel having walked up an appetite, Scott thought, she's there *again* – that girl from before, and from before that. He thought to himself, once upon a long time ago, I knew how to do this because I used to do it a lot. I went up to women in hotels and bars. The antidote to boredom and aloneness. I knew all the steps of the mating dance; the perfunctory drink and small talk – the predictable prelude to sex and then dumb sleep.

Scott stopped. He looked at the bar area, noted a couple of women sitting alone exuding the telltale signs of confident expectation. Then he looked over to the lost girl from before, currently scratching the back of one leg with the foot of her other. That sensation accosted him again, like a zip being pulled sharply from inside. It was easy enough to walk past the bar with those slightly predatory sure-things because he just wasn't interested. But the girl who intrigued him still standing like a flamingo? There were hot coals underfoot if he wanted to go that distance. Why should it make him smile that she appeared to be rearranging the hotel's magazines? And now that he was so close, what actually was he going to do? He couldn't even figure out what he was thinking about, let alone what it was he wanted to happen.

'Excuse me,' he said to the back of her head, 'I think I'm a little lost.'

Frankie turned. She thought – I know you, don't I? Perhaps I don't.

'Hi,' he said.

'Hello?'

'The Underground Tube?' he prompted.

His clumsy terminology made her laugh and she *did* remember him, the man who'd momentarily infiltrated the protective bubble she'd put around herself earlier that day. The man she'd said she couldn't help. And here he was again. Well there's a thing! Somehow, they'd both made their way through a day and across the metropolis to arrive right here at the same time. Lost in the city and yet serendipity had given them a map to do with as they pleased.

'I'm sorry,' Frankie said with a glint, 'I'm not from round here.'

He liked her wry smile. It dimpled one cheek. There goes the zip again, catching his breath, tying his tongue.

His silence and his gaze disconcerted her a little. Perhaps he didn't realize she was only repeating her words from earlier. Perhaps he hadn't remembered them. Maybe she'd just said something that actually sounded idiotic.

'Are you really lost?' she asked him. 'Here? It's just I couldn't even find the lifts before – they're tucked away, over there, behind those massive urn-things. I couldn't even locate the slot in the door for my keycard.'

And there they stood, chuckling slightly awkwardly

while focusing excessively on the oversized furni-sculpture which had hidden the lifts and broken the ice – two huge hammered pitchers spewing bamboo poles of enormous lengths and staggering girths.

'I'm not lost,' Scott said.

'Oh good,' said Frankie. 'I'm pleased for you.' She cringed at her response and thought it best to turn her attention back to the magazines, to think about the bath and the towels and not this man with the nice smile and the this-way-that-way hair.

'So – I don't know a soul. But I saw you and I just got thinking –' He shrugged. 'You know?'

And all they could do next was stand there, side by side, looking intently at *The Times*, the *Guardian*, the *Washington Post*, *Bild* and *Le Figaro* as they wondered what to say next. *Harper's Bazaar*, *Vanity Fair*, *Country Life* and the copy of *Grazia* Frankie had had her eye on.

'I'm Scott,' he said eventually.

'I'm Frankie,' she said.

They looked up from the papers. She offered her hand and he shook it.

'Nice to meet you.'

Life had been uncomplicated over recent years, Scott had made a point of it. It's how he liked it; the gains being far greater than anything he'd had to forfeit to achieve it. What he had just done surprised him, what he was about to do surprised him more.

'I was going to have a drink,' he said. 'Read my book. Think about eating.' He paused. 'Care to join me?'

Frankie didn't do things like this – say yes to men she didn't know. She never had because the concept had never appealed. She'd never courted it, never experienced it and always bypassed any such situations. She wasn't even sure if this man called Scott's offer was as simple as it seemed. Was it in a code she didn't know? But actually, it seemed neither clichéd nor calculating. Was there any harm in saying yes? Would she regret saying no? And hadn't they met already, sort of, before? Why not take it at face value. Perhaps he'd asked because they had something in common; they were both from out of town in a city that was a little too big and busy for them. Face value; she looked at his. A gently awkward smile and dark eyes. Quite handsome, actually. But still, she said to herself, but still.

She glanced down at the magazines, as if the choice was between Scott and *Grazia*. Kate Moss was on the cover, staring straight at Frankie. Kate Moss appeared to be laughing at her: are you crazy? He's good-looking, polite and friendly so what are you waiting for? Go girl! Kate told her.

Annabel and Sam, safe at home, having supper around about now.

Alice nowhere to be seen.

All of them, some place other than here.

Here she was, side by side with a man called Scott who'd spoken to her earlier and made her laugh just now, who asked her a question and was shyly waiting for her answer.

'I could do with the company,' Scott said.

'Thank you very much,' said Frankie, 'I think I will.'

They sat together a little awkwardly, nodded and smiled, until Scott thought if I don't say something she'll change her mind and go.

'How's your drink?'

'Delicious.' She took a sip as if to make absolutely sure. 'Cheers.'

'Cheers – here's to invisible elevators.'

'My room was upgraded.'

'So was mine.'

'Do you come over from the States often then?'

'Never,' Scott laughed. 'But from Canada – yes, I come every so often.'

Frankie reddened. 'Sorry – cardinal error.'

'And you?'

'I live in Norfolk.'

'I do not know where that is.'

'It's east – by the sea. I used to live in London, though.'

'It's a great city – if cities are your thing.'

'That's why I moved. They're not.'

'I'll drink to that,' said Scott, thinking to himself there's a story there, Frankie.

'Do you live in a city?'

Scott shook his head and smiled. 'I live out in the mountains, in BC. In British Columbia.'

Spurts of conversation and steadying sips of their drinks, that's how they did it. That's how they relaxed in their chairs and into each other's company and yes, please – I'd love a bite to eat.

'I'm a creature of habit,' Scott told her. 'I always have steak and fries here. Every day.'

'That's not good for you,' said Frankie.

But Scott laughed. 'I can think of plenty of things that are far worse.'

'I'm usually pretty unadventurous. If I'm in a hotel, I mostly get room service.'

'And here you are having dinner with a stranger.'

She reddened again. He liked that, as if it spoke of honesty.

'Well, in that case, I'll go the whole hog and have *this*.' She pointed to a dish on the menu. 'It doesn't get more daring than ordering a dish I can't pronounce.'

Suddenly she wanted to text Peta or Ruth to say you'll never guess what! but her phone was up in the room and, when she thought about it, she liked it that no one had a clue what she was doing at this precise moment. It was liberating and novel. But was he actually chatting her up? Was she flirting back? She wasn't sure and it didn't matter. Her drink was delicious, she was hungry, he was handsome, he made her feel lively, effervescent even, and dinner was now served.

'So what do you do out by the sea that you're here in London on business?'

Frankie hated that question; it usually led to a barrage of questions she'd had to answer a million times before. And when it was known she was an author of some repute, people changed the way they spoke to her, even looked at her. She became a novelty. She'd never liked that.

'I'm an accountant,' she said.

Scott appeared to choke on his drink. 'Seriously?'

Frankie's face creased with awkwardness. 'No,' she said. 'I lied.'

'You *lied*?' He tipped his head back and really laughed. 'Who are you? A *spy*? Royalty?'

'I – work in publishing.'

'What kind of publishing?'

'Books.'

'What type of books?'

'Children's books.'

'OK.' It was the way Scott looked at her, steadily, interested, open. His eyes she'd thought were brown were actually a layered and dark slate-blue. 'Children's books,' he repeated.

'I write them.' There you go. That's me.

He tipped his head to one side. 'You're an author?'

'Yes,' she shrugged. 'That's what I do. What about you?'

Scott appeared to think about this, as if he wasn't entirely sure. 'I'm in music.'

'A musician?' That was much better than an accountant.

'Well – I guess.'

'Are you in a band?'

Scott laughed at the way her face had lit up. 'No. God no.'

Frankie thought he didn't really look like a rock star anyway; no piercings, no visible tattoos or rings in the shape of skulls, just a pair of dark jeans, a shirt loose, brown shoes or boots, she couldn't tell. On looks alone, she'd hazard a guess at university lecturer, or perhaps some outdoorsy career. Close up, there was something rugged and lived in about his face, soft stubble that might be consciously groomed or simply because he had chosen not to shave away from home. The eyes she knew now to be steel-navy; hair in carefree brush-strokes of brown. Well, perhaps once upon a time, he had been in a band. She placed him a little older than her.

'What do you play?'

'So – guitar, piano.' He appeared to be thinking whether he played anything else. 'Harmonica.'

As he cut into his steak, his reserve struck Frankie. Perhaps her questions were precisely those he tired of too. Perhaps he was wishing he'd told her he was an accountant. She turned to her food. It was just a pasta dish, despite the fancy name. And, on first forkful and to her dismay, speckled with olives.

'A children's author,' he said, chinking his glass against hers.

'A musician,' she said, raising her glass to him. 'What sort of music?'

'These days, I write for other people mostly.'

He smiled quizzically because she'd balked at that.

'But isn't songwriting akin to ghostwriting?' she asked. 'Producing work for someone else to claim as theirs and bask in unentitled glory?'

'Do you only write for the glory?'

And it was then that Frankie experienced an unexpected surge of pure attraction. His sudden bluntness, that he'd challenged her straight, his eyes steady, his smile wry. Actually, she liked it that he wrote music, she liked his face and his hands and that she was here, right now. She liked it that she'd gone ahead and said yes to a drink and to this plate of revolting pasta. She liked his even gaze, that he was focused on her, wanted to know her, wanted her in his evening.

'No,' she told him. 'I don't write for the glory. In fact, I often feel I'm little more than my characters' PA. I'm at their mercy, at their beck and call. I take dictation while they tell me their stories.'

He thought about that. 'I always assumed an author was – I don't know – like a Master Puppeteer.'

'Oh blimey no. My characters run rings around me, especially Alice,' she said darkly.

Scott didn't know who Alice was. He'd like to know. He'd ask later. It was just that she had a little sauce on her cheek and he was sitting there with an urge to take his finger and wipe it away, to feel how soft her skin was, to touch her. It all felt suddenly a little crazy. He told himself, just eat your steak and talk about books and music. He felt ravenously hungry and yet full.

'I *was* in a band,' he said, 'in my misspent youth. Nowadays, I hate performing but I love to write music, that's the sum of it. And you know what, I don't do so much songwriting these days anyway – I was finding it depressing. The lack of control. I'd put my soul into a song, create something I believed in, something – I don't know – *nourishing*. Then the producers change it, fuck with it, manufacture it and before you know it, the stuff the labels churn out is the musical equivalent of fast food. And the kids spend their money on it. It can get a little depressing.' Scott thought, if Aaron could see me now he wouldn't believe his eyes or his ears: Scott Emerson actively choosing to be sociable, talking away, engaging with a girl, seeking company and conversation. 'Mostly these days I write music for movies. That's why I'm here at the moment – the movie I'm working on has British funding so the music needs to be recorded here for tax breaks.'

Frankie just wanted to listen. 'You write soundtracks? Wow.'

But Scott just shrugged. 'And you write books. Double wow.'

'How many films do you do?'

'Well, depending on the budget, probably up to four a year.'

'Do they tell you what they want?'

'Well, I guess I'm lucky. Mostly I get to work with directors I know, who like my music anyways, who give me the freedom to read the script and interpret it my own way.'

'You're really a composer, then,' said Frankie.

Scott looked a little bashful. 'Sounds a little grand. I guess so – on paper. But you know there's a whole department that makes the music happen. The orchestrators, the editors, the producer, the engineers, the music supervisor, the copyist. You know, in a movie if there's a song you know playing quietly in the background of, say, a scene in a bar – that's no accident, that's been sourced very specifically. I'm talking too much.'

'No you're not,' said Frankie quietly.

'No?'

'Not at all,' she said. 'I spend most of my evenings with people who don't exist – my characters – so this is welcome. Can I ask you, how do you write, how do you compose?'

He sipped thoughtfully. Usually when he told people what he did they pretty quickly steered the conversation to wanting autographs, even phone numbers, of actors. No one had ever asked him how do you do it, how do you come up with the music, yet it was such an intrinsic part of his life.

'Well,' he said, 'I'll read the script and see what comes to me – like images or scenes come to you, so tunes come to me. Then, near the final cut, I'll have a spotting session with the director and producer and we'll discuss the various cues, then off I go. At that point, it's probably not dissimilar to you – though the process and the output are different. You probably go about your day with a head full of words and dialogue, eh? So – my head's full of disparate notes which tumble into melodies, feelings for rhythm, phrasing, which start to steady. Soon as I read a script – I hear it. It's weird sometimes. Like the music's already written, already exists out there in the ether, waiting for me to harness it. When I read dialogue something happens – I hear tone of voice in terms of musical tone, a conversation between characters carries melody, cacophony, harmony, dissonance. And I just take it from there, really. I play, I write, I'll record.' Surely he was talking too much, surely. But Frankie was alert, her face animated. 'But like I said, I only play guitar, keyboard – so then my music and my directions are passed on to an orchestrator or an arranger and finally the fixer organizes professional musicians to really spin the magic and give gravitas and meaning to my simple notes.'

'I never met one of you before,' Frankie said quietly, with a shy smile.

57

'Well, you're my first children's author,' said Scott.

Their eyes locked and silently, they marvelled. Of all the places. It's here. It's now.

'You don't like your food?' He noticed she'd hardly touched it.

'Olives,' she said darkly, giving an emphatic shudder. 'It's full of olives.'

'Here.' He loaded his fork with his own food and passed it to her, insisting she try it.

'You're right,' she said, 'that's the best steak and fries.'

'You have mine,' he said. 'Please.' And the creature of habit that's Scott let his favourite dish go, happy enough to have to eat around the olives himself, happier still to watch Frankie tuck in.

What *was* that feeling, that zip sensation? A heady chemical misfiring of excitement and unbalance, desire and calm. Chatting girls up in hotels was something he used to do so efficiently he could switch off part of himself in the process. It was a routine, motions, a set pattern that was self-centred and greedy. But the end product was never in doubt. He came, he went. Was that what he wanted tonight? In an hour, or two hours? No, strangely, no. Tonight wasn't about edging towards something; it was about being in the moment. This wasn't chatting up some girl, this was talking to a person he wanted to get to know. It was different and new and he wasn't sure if he was doing it right. What he did know was that he liked her.

'Norfolk?' he said, clearing his throat and downing a glass of water. 'But you once lived here, in the city?'

Frankie dabbed her mouth with the napkin. She'd

still missed the little smudge of sauce that Scott had been so taken with earlier. It felt natural, now, to take his napkin and wipe her cheek, smile at the way she was both grateful and a little embarrassed. She called herself a mucky pup.

'It was a fresh start,' she said. 'I wanted a house, not a flat. I wanted space and the sea. I wanted peace, quiet. For my writing. For my children and me. I have two children. Sam – my son – is thirteen. Annabel – my daughter – she's nine.' There. That's me. 'But actually, it wasn't just about geography and logistics. I wanted to be gone from what I knew.' She thought how she'd put into words for Scott something she'd never expressed to anyone else. 'I'd felt like I was stagnating, time tumbling on with me just rooted to a spot that wasn't letting me grow. It was like being planted in a barren place.'

Frankie saw him glance at her finger, note there was no ring.

'I'm a single mum,' she pre-empted.

'So that's a brave thing you did,' he said and his voice was gentle, 'finding a new place for you, your kids, on your own?'

She shrugged. 'Or mad – if you asked my sister Peta.'

'Frank and Peter?'

'Peta. Our mother wanted boys.' She rolled her eyes and Scott really laughed.

'They see their dad?'

Again, the bluntness, the straightforward question unembellished. It could have sounded impertinent but it didn't, it came across as thoughtful.

'Sporadically,' said Frankie. 'He's – unreliable. He's mostly abroad.'

Scott thought about this and looked steadily at Frankie. 'Hard on you, hey?'

She laughed that one off. 'I'm used to it. It's been a long time. I have a friend who summed up Miles as little more than an annoying fly on the windowpane of my life.'

Scott nodded. They both nodded quietly, then he looked up at her quizzically. 'She said what?'

Frankie giggled. 'My friend Kirsty talks a load of old bollocks sometimes.'

Their laughter ebbed away but it left its vestige, like the reprise of a melody remaining in the air long after the song has faded out. Frankie thought, how do we keep this evening going?

'Room for pudding?' she said.

'You betcha,' he said. 'Any idea where the washrooms are?'

'Probably hidden inside a huge column of bamboo.'

She watched him as he went, suddenly surprised by all the action in the busy foyer beyond; guests and their guests and bellboys and bags, the scents and the sounds and the comings and goings amplified by mood lighting and mirrors at strange angles. I am tingling, Frankie thought. It's all mad and wonderful. A sudden recall of Ruth's hairdresser randomly telling her it's the time when you're not looking that love finds you. Frankie hadn't looked for ages, years really, because she truly believed the landscape of her life lacked nothing. But tonight? It felt as though her blood was infused with colour and sound and an energy she couldn't believe was hers.

Just then, in between their plates, on top of a napkin, Scott's phone beamed into life and right there, between

60

her drink and his, Jenna arrived on the scene like an unwanted guest.

Who's Jenna?

Frankie deflated. The caller ID photo showed Scott and Jenna, cheek by cheek, cosy in woolly hats and snowy smiles, bathed in togetherness against a stunning winter landscape.

And Frankie thought you stupid idiot – why wouldn't there be a Jenna? Of course there's a Jenna.

An utter fool, that's what she felt. What had she been thinking, ordering a dish with olives when she'd've been perfectly happy having that bath with the glass of wine and the free copy of *Grazia*? Why had she listened to Kate bloody Moss?

'Hey.'

Scott was back and Frankie thought, why would he be available, someone like him? Of course he's going to be with a Jenna.

'Sticky Toffee Pudding,' he said, passing her the menu. 'I have it every day.'

'Your phone – you missed a call.'

Scott checked it. Checked his watch. 'Shit,' he said. 'I have to call home.'

'And I think I'm going to call it a night,' Frankie said, folding her napkin precisely. 'I'm tired.' She smiled in the vague direction of the lifts. She was standing up and it struck Scott that he really didn't want her to go. Not just yet.

'Wait.'

'Good night,' said Frankie, moving away, 'thanks so much for supper.' But he stood too and put his hand on her arm though she continued to turn.

'Frankie.' He caught her other arm. 'Wait?' He said

it quietly, now searching for what to say next. 'Look,' he scratched his head. 'OK – so here's a thing. I hate olives too.' His eyes were coursing her face. 'It's just – I wanted you to eat. And I'd *really* like you to stay.' He was rubbing the back of his neck now, agitated, frowning a little. 'Please,' he said, and he slipped his hand into hers for a moment, 'please don't go just yet. But I *need* to make this call. Please?'

Frankie watched him walk to a quiet corner to make the call back to the smiley Jenna in those picture-perfect Canadian mountains. If Jenna hadn't called, Frankie would have been none the wiser. She wasn't sure whether she should hate her or thank her for it. Bubble bath and a glass of wine. Divine hotel linen, a good night's sleep. That's what she needed most. Alice was required on parade for her agent tomorrow and it was getting late.

Oh but Scott and his eyes and his mussed hair that she wanted to touch. Scott who could be only one great big transatlantic fuck-up. Scott who she'd happily kiss. It had been so long. She turned and faced their table. Why didn't she just stop being Frankie and take advantage of one lone night with a man she desired who she'd never see again anyway? For once in her life, why not pack her personality at the bottom of her case and not bring it out until she was back home, nice and private, in Norfolk? Why didn't she just live a little, switch her mind off and give her body a treat?

But that's never been me.

No. She'd go to her room.

She turned again, to head to the lifts.

But here's Scott, back already, happy as you like.

'That was Jenna,' Scott said, standing close, eyes refusing to let her go. 'My daughter.'

* * *

'My daughter has epilepsy,' he said. 'She wasn't too well last week, she had a pretty big seizure and oftentimes they're not isolated. So when you told me she'd called –' He shook his head and Frankie watched him process a parent's what-ifs quietly to himself.

'How old is she?'

'She's just turned twenty years old. You look surprised,' he said. 'I'll take that as a compliment – I was twenty-five when she was born.'

So he's four years older than me.

'Your wife?'

Was there a wife?

'We split when Jenna was small,' he said. 'Really small.' He paused. 'She had – has – problems with alcohol. She – Lind – and I were in a band. You know, when there's music and alcohol and drugs and you're on the road, that's just how it is. It's about dangling yourself off the edge of life just for the heck of it. But those who know it's mainly bullshit and temporary – they end up like me. Those that don't – so, they end up like Lind. She wanted to seize the day, I wanted to live for tomorrow. So it's been just me and Jenna.' He paused again and regarded Frankie levelly. 'And it still is.' He raised his glass. 'Here's to single parenting.'

There's no such thing as soulmates and love at first sight, they both knew that from the experiences that had led to their acceptance that life not in a couple was OK. Really, after all this time, it was fine. Nothing lacking, nothing to be craved. Best for the kids. It is what it is.

But as their eyes locked again for another caught moment, they sensed a surging inevitability that outweighed any cliché of finding each other in a crowded station, any coincidence that had thrown them back together right here and which overruled any tastelessness that the anonymity of a hotel far from home insinuated.

How could a new face be known so well so quickly? It was all unfathomably liberating and dangerous and comforting and nonsensical. In this vast city, in which neither of them lived, they'd managed to meet and somehow they knew they'd now never not know each other.

Frankie scrolled through the photos on Scott's phone, his face close to hers as if guiding her to see exactly what he saw.

'So this is Jenna outside her apartment in Whistler which is around fifty minutes from me. You've heard of Whistler, right? She has a job there before starting university in Vancouver this fall.'

Frankie enlarged the picture, Jenna and a friend; their arms outstretched, roaring with laughter. She imagined them larking about while Scott had said hey, come on girls – just one picture. Come on – stop goofing. Just smile for your old Pa, will you?

'And this is my home. I live around twenty minutes from a village called Pemberton.'

Jenna, Scott and a dog. A majestic mountain, its ravines and peaks slashed with snow, fir trees scoring dark trails through its sides, like mascara tears. A broad

64

veranda wrapped around a home made of huge logs set in an extraordinary landscape whose vastness couldn't be compromised by a phone screen.

Frankie turned to face him. He was very close. Aftershave. A neat nose. Bristles dipping into the vertical laughter lines on his cheeks. Eyes the colour of the rock on that mountain outside his home. 'Wow.'

'Pretty much sums up my life, that picture,' he said.

'What's the dog's name?' She liked the look of the brown Labrador, he appeared to be grinning.

'Buddy. He's a Seizure Alert Dog – and his name fits. He's older now, a little arthritic. It's our turn to look after him. Actually, he's English – he came from this incredible center in Sheffield.'

'How does he help?'

'He can sense tiny changes in Jenna's manner, in her behaviour or mood – sometimes up to fifty minutes before a possible seizure. He's trained to let her or me know.'

'Where's Buddy now, though?'

'So he's with Aaron. Here,' Scott found a picture of Aaron with Buddy in the cockpit of the Cessna. 'Aaron's as close as I have to a brother. We grew up together, went to school together and we still live close by. He's a First Nations man – a native. Aaron's people are the Líĺwat – they've been living in the territory for over five thousand years.' He observed how intently Frankie was looking at the photo. 'He's a crazy, beautiful guy – he has his own plane and runs a skydiving business. He flies me to Vancouver when I have to go abroad.'

'Does Buddy fly too?' Frankie hoped he did – there could be a story in that. Buddy Flies to the Rescue, Buddy Takes to the Skies, Buddy and the Eagle's Nest.

'Oh sure,' said Scott, 'he loves it.'

'What about when Jenna goes to college – could she take Buddy?'

'She could – but she won't. She wants to be seen as normal. She doesn't like people to know, really. There are still a lot of misconceptions about epilepsy despite the fact that it's the most common brain disorder world-wide. Unfortunately, we're still on a bit of an expedition finding the right medication for Jenna. She's one of the twenty per cent who don't have much luck on that front.'

Frankie looked at Scott. 'When Sam was a toddler we were out in the park and a man started having a fit.' She paused. 'It frightened me. Somebody else went to his aid.'

'It is frightening. It still scares the shit out of me and I know how to deal with a seizure.'

Frankie thought of Sam. Taller than her now, his voice swinging from childlike to croaky; a boy-man in the making sometimes battling with himself to figure out if he was to become a rebel or remain a geek. She thought of Annabel with her button nose that was just the same as when she'd been a toddler; a contrary yet thoughtful child with a vulnerability she kept hidden behind liveliness. She thought of how they loved their bedrooms, their things, the chaos and clatter, the tempers and laughter. She'd never had to worry about their health. On those blessed occasions when all went quiet in their rooms, she always thought thank God for that, a moment's peace.

'I just can't begin to imagine,' she said quietly.

'Well, my theory is you have to live life to the full, whatever is thrown at you. It's like a ball game really, keep batting, keep playing, keep believing yours is the winning team.'

'I like your philosophy, Scott,' said Frankie. 'I ought to pin it up on my fridge. Don't laugh – I'm serious! Authors can be introverted and overemotional souls.'

Scott was grinning. 'I can't believe you told me you were an accountant.' Frankie reddened. He nudged her. She nudged him back. She thought, I've just smiled coyly, on purpose. She thought, he's not letting my eyes go.

But the hotel lobby was emptying. Sharp-suited businessmen, previously lairy, now just dull drunk, slumped around the bar like scrunches of rejected paper at the end of a brainstorm. In a corner, a couple engrossed in a hungry snog, only half-hidden by decorative bamboo. At a neighbouring table, an elderly lady sipping tea as though she'd quite lost sense of what time of day it was. And still Frankie and Scott sat side by side.

'How long are you staying?'

'Another night,' said Frankie. 'You?'

'I fly out Sunday afternoon. I'll have been here a week.'

'Are you working all that time?' Shall I say something? Shall I try? 'Are you working tomorrow?'

'Yes, I'm in the studio. You?'

'I have a couple of meetings. Dinner with my agent.' Try and make it happen. 'Where's your studio?'

'Abbey Road.'

'Well that's a good address for a studio,' said Frankie guilelessly. 'There's a world-famous one called just that. The Beatles – the zebra crossing.'

Scott laughed. 'There's only one Abbey Road, Frankie.'

'And you're *there*?'

'British session musicians are the best in the world

when it comes to sight-reading and playing to a "click". I think it's down to a lack of funding from your government – they have limited rehearsal opportunity. I love working with them.'

'Do you use the zebra crossing every day?'

'Oh I try to. Barefoot. Like McCartney. But the tourists get in the way. Reality is I'm inside all the time.'

'Recording your soundtrack?'

He nodded.

'Who's in your film?'

'Well it isn't my film – I've just written the music. But Jeff Bridges is the lead.'

'Oh I *love* him,' said Frankie, thinking Scott's modesty was beguiling. 'And anyway, music is often as much a lead character in a film – like setting can be in a book.'

'I'll drink to that,' said Scott but their glasses were empty and the bar was closed. Only the little old lady remained and she'd just asked for her bill. Scott was brought his though he hadn't requested it.

They were going to have to go, really.

Frankie wondered, how do we leave these seats, this table, our little corner in which my world expanded? How can we stay in our bubble?

And then, in her mind, she heard Ruth saying *go for it!* and Peta saying *don't be so stupid*.

'If you get some time tomorrow,' she said, 'and I do too – shall we try and meet? Perhaps I could come to *The* Abbey Road?' He was just looking at her, not speaking. 'Or if not there, somewhere?'

'Anywhere,' said Scott softly. 'Why don't we make it happen, Frankie. Crazy as it sounds.'

* * *

As slowly as they walked across the atrium, soon enough they were behind the huge urns and bamboo, back at the lifts. As they stood waiting, Scott looked down on her head and thought how Frankie would tuck just under his chin. And Frankie glanced sideways at his chest and imagined laying her cheek against it. He had his hands in his back pockets and she wanted to link her arm through his.

Into the elevator, just the two of them. Her mind reeling through a thousand movie scenes of impulsive kisses when the doors slide shut, of fumbling with keys and falling into an anonymous hotel room shedding clothes, broiling with desire.

But Frankie and Scott just stood side by side.

Fifth floor.

'This is me,' said Frankie.

'Tomorrow?' said Scott.

Frankie tapped her watch. 'Today.'

And she walked down the corridor on her own aware that, downstairs in the lobby, Kate Moss was still smiling on the magazine table.

Enormously tired. Stratospherically tired but high as a kite. Running that bath, eating chocolates left on the pillow, flicking on the television and zapping through the channels. One two three four five six seven scatter pillows pedantically rearranged at the foot of the bed. Four plump pillows and a waft of duvet enticingly folded back to reveal the downy comfort of a beautifully made bed. So long since she'd felt this wired, this alert, this sentient. So long since she'd had any of these feelings. Longing and kinship and warmth and attraction and wave after wave of desire. Something deep inside had stirred. Over the last few years, it was as if she'd switched off lights from necessity in those rooms within herself that she couldn't afford to use.

She eased herself down deep into the bath, bubbles up to her chin, the soothe of a thick warm flannel over her face. The plastic shower cap.

If anyone could see me now.

Tomorrow.
   Today.
   Earlier yesterday.
   Later today.
   Frankie, says Alice. Who was that? Who was that man, Frankie? Will you write him into your life like you did me?

'Can we get a rise on the string line?'

All of this was giving Scott a headache. There'd been too many interruptions and the music he'd written for a particular scene sounded all wrong today, with the full orchestra. Yet on first reading of the script three months ago, melodies had sailed through his mind like drifts of overheard conversation. His best work often germinated this way, subliminally almost. But today, though he'd watched the cut over and again all morning and asked the musicians to play it this way, play it that way, the music just didn't segue. He felt as clumsy and inept as a child furiously hammering at the wrong piece on a shape-sorting toy. The film's producers were in the studio today, along with the director, the music editor, the fixer and the technicians. Everyone making encouraging noises at Scott despite the stress clearly legible behind their eyes.

'You're a perfectionist – it's why people love working with you,' one of the producers said. What else could she think of to say? Sometimes she despaired at the amount of soothing flattery and ebullient bullshit her role necessitated when all she wanted to do was shake these creative types – these actors and musicians and directors – and say for fuck's sake, get over yourselves and do the fucking job we're paying you a fortune to do. But she'd worked with Scott before and had never known him so discontented. The director himself was concerned too. He'd worked with Scott many times. If previously Scott had struggled and vexed it had always been behind the scenes and out of earshot, before he brought a single sound to the table. He was always so quietly professional and capable, delivering excellent soundtracks on time with no drama whatsoever. Commissioning Scott to score a movie was as easy and satisfying as ordering a takeaway and having it delivered piping hot and utterly delicious exactly when you wanted it.

'It doesn't do what it's supposed to do,' Scott said quietly. 'It sounds shit.'

The producer looked at her watch and raised her eyebrow at the director, both of them quietly calculating the cost of the studio against the days they had Scott over here for.

'You know what? Take time out, Scott. Get out of here – go for a walk, go to London Zoo, go to Harrods or the Tate Gallery, go have a swim or a sleep. Clear your mind, then come back.'

He was watching the scene again.

'Go for a burger, go to a strip club,' she said, 'I don't know! Go and have a cuppa with the Queen at the bloody Ritz!'

It was three o'clock.

'You're fine,' she said. 'Go. Jimmy and the guys will have a play with what we've got so far. We just have piano this afternoon – you trust Lexi.'

'I'm sorry,' said Scott and everyone brushed his

apology away, relieved to see the back of him as he left the control room for Studio Two.

Midway over the legendary zebra crossing, his phone call to Frankie was finally answered.

'Hey.'

'Hello.'

'Fancy a "*cuppa*"?' he asked.

'You sound like Dick Van Dyke,' she said.

Scott walked straight past Maison Bertaux, reaching the end of Greek Street and having to ask at the minicab rank where it was. With all the previous talk of the Ritz and royalty, he'd been expecting somewhere grand to shout out to him, not a tiny little patisserie tucked behind a simple blue-and-white awning. However, once inside, the opulence of the pastries on display and the complex fragrances – fruit, vanilla, chocolate, baking – elevated the café beyond its modest setting.

Frankie had said on the phone that she'd find a table, now all he had to do was find her. Up the narrow crookedy stairs he went, wondering whether the café suddenly increased on the first floor, wondering if he'd have to negotiate white-clothed tables and velvet-backed chairs and little old ladies sipping their Darjeeling behind mountains of scones. But no. Just Formica tables and mismatched chairs jigsawed into a confined space. And there, in the corner, Frankie.

'Hey.'

'Hello.'

If he could have teleported himself to the studio right then, the whole movie could be note-perfect in the time it was taking Frankie to move her bag so that he could sit next to her. He marvelled at the madness of all of this. This place. Her smile. A cuppa. Little over twenty-four hours ago, he had no idea she existed. All these resurfacing feelings swirling and sweet as the cream and fondant on the trays of cakes downstairs.

'You can't work on an empty stomach,' she said. 'I've taken the liberty of ordering a selection of cakes.' He wasn't saying much. 'Did you want coffee? I ordered tea for us. Is this place OK for you?'

The rickety chair and narrow table, peculiar art-college paintings on the walls, his knee touching hers, their arms a hair's breadth apart. This place was perfect.

'Tea's just fine,' he said.

'Say – *a cuppa*.'

'A cuppa.'

'Sorry – I shouldn't laugh.'

'I like it that you do.'

A pot of tea, milk in a jug, cups and saucers and a plate of cakes in front of them. The two of them took it all in.

'How's your day been?' Scott asked, nodding for Frankie to pour.

She tilted her hand this way, that way. 'Arduous,' she said. In each of her meetings, she'd sensed Alice beside her, protesting. *You're fibbing, Frankie – you're a fibber – you haven't written me a story at all.*

'How so?'

Scott watched her redden a little as she fumbled in her bag. 'Here,' she said, 'I brought you this.'

'*Alice and the Ditch Monster*,' he read before flipping through the pages, lingering over the illustrations, charmed. He looked at Frankie's author portrait in the back when her hair had been longer and it had been winter, by the looks of her turtleneck sweater. He read the dedication in the front. *For Sam who's braver than brave*. Scott felt overwhelmingly proud of her. He turned to her. 'Wow.'

She shrugged. 'It's just what I do,' she said. 'I'm not very good at much else.' Adrenalin suddenly soured the tea.

'You OK?'

'I can't write.' She couldn't look up either.

'But by the looks of this – you can.' Scott dipped into the book again. 'Look at all these reviews. Prizes too.'

'I can't write just now,' she whispered. She looked ashamed and it upset him.

'How long?'

'Months.'

He thought about it. 'Anyone know?'

'The children. My sister.' She glanced up. 'You.'

He speared a glazed raspberry from the tart, scooped crème pâtissièrre over it and handed her the fork.

'I've been there, Frankie. I spent six months sitting *under* my piano, freaking out while everyone thought I was composing. A few years back – but the fear, the shame, is still vivid.'

She'd slumped a little. Gently, he nudged her. 'It passes. Talent like yours? It evades you from time to time, for sure – but you'll always have it.'

'How did you get through it?' Her eyes had gone glassy. He liked it that he knew exactly what she was feeling.

'I drank a lot of caffeine,' Scott laughed. 'Then I gave it up completely. I tried Valium at night and beta blockers during the day. I got angry. I got sad. I broke a guitar. Two, actually.'

'I just chew pencils and stare at nothing in particular.'

'Probably cheaper – but not healthier.'

'I am genuinely scared, not least because of the state of the industry. With all the discounting and cheap or free downloads, publishers are paying their authors less and less. A wonderful writer I know has had her advance cut by half. She feels decimated.'

'I can understand that. It's been the same in the music industry.'

'But what if I can't write at all, ever again? I'm the sole provider for my little family. What if that was it – my quota of books?'

It felt to Scott as if Frankie's eyes were clinging to his for reassurance. 'Has something happened?'

'Not that I can pinpoint.'

'But you've had all this upheaval – moving home. Don't be hard on yourself.'

'It feels utterly self-indulgent to give myself slack.'

'I know. I felt that too.'

And it struck Frankie that Scott wasn't saying any of this simply to cajole her into getting on with it, the way she anticipated her publishers might. It seemed he truly understood and more than that, he cared.

'Tell me about Alice,' he said, pouring more tea, reaching for the milk at the same time as Frankie, their fingers touching, their eyes connecting, time stopping.

'Alice?'

'Don't say it like that – like you blame her. Tell me about the Alice you know.'

Frankie thought about her and suddenly felt a little contrite, as if she'd been impatient with a child who was irritating simply by being a child, just a little kid.

'She's a monkey,' she smiled. 'She lives in the

countryside outside a village called Cloddington and, at the bottom of her garden where the hedge grows thatchety and the ditch is dank, He lives.'

Scott smiled. The colour was starting to come back to her cheeks and her eyes glinted. 'The ditch dude?'

Frankie nodded.

'Is he a euphemism? Did you consign your ex to a life in a quagmire?'

Frankie laughed, she really laughed. 'Miles? Oh God – I wouldn't dignify him with life in a ditch! I wouldn't enlarge his sizeable ego with a character based on him. Actually, Miles is just Miles, a law unto himself. For one so smooth he has a lot of rough edges but he's just Miles. Frustratingly, maddeningly Miles.'

'You been apart long?'

That direct bluntness again. 'Far longer than we were ever together.'

'So if the ditch guy isn't Miles, who is he?'

Frankie grinned. 'He's not anyone I know. He's lovely – in a slightly unnerving way – a contradiction between being inept and clumsy but sensitive and gentle. He's hideously ugly but really rather beautiful. He helps Alice and she helps him right back.'

'Is he an imaginary friend?'

Frankie shook her head earnestly. 'No. He isn't. He's real. But only Alice knows about him.' She thought about it. 'You could say they have a co-dependent relationship.'

'One of those, hey?' Scott said darkly but with a wry smile. 'And Alice herself?'

'Alice is Alice,' Frankie said.

'She's not Annabel?'

Frankie shook her head.

'Your artwork is gorgeous,' Scott said. Confident, quirky line drawings bloomed over with washes of watercolour. 'Is she always this age?'

Frankie nodded. 'Ten-ish.' She glanced at her drawing. She didn't see it as being from her hand. It was just Alice, clear to her as a photo.

'If Alice had a favourite song – what would it be?'

Frankie had never thought about it. 'I don't know.'

White chocolate striating the strawberries on crème pâtissière, atop a biscuit base. She loaded a fork and passed it to Scott. 'Her favourite song would be – oh God, if I'm honest, most likely something by One Bloody Dimension.'

'You know it's *Direction*, right?'

'I know – I like winding Annabel up. I reckon Alice is the same.'

'I don't know about that,' Scott said quietly, opening the book and reading. 'I reckon the guy in the ditch – he's been around. I reckon he's seen the Stones, Dylan, the Byrds. In fact, there were plenty of folk at Woodstock who looked pretty much like him. But I'd say he keeps Alice balanced – culturally. Those times when they're not solving mysteries or saving the day – when they're just at the end of the garden shooting the shit – I'll say they talk about music and he steers her straight, eh.'

'Are you saying there's stuff about Alice I don't know?'

Scott shrugged. 'Maybe. You're the secretary remember, not the puppeteer. Imagine what goes on behind your back. Imagine that.'

Frankie looked so shocked it made him smile. He split the gateau in two. 'Why don't you try to find out?

You *talk* about her like she's real – which I don't doubt. But seems to me perhaps when you're *writing* you lose sight of that.' He ate cake and read on, quietly. 'Seems like she's a really nice kid,' he said.

'She is,' Frankie said.

'And Annabel?' Scott said. 'And Sam?'

Out came Frankie's phone and a guided tour pictorially through her children's lives.

'How have they handled the move – to Norfolk?'

Frankie looked through the pictures of her children. 'Oh well, Annabel could run the country tomorrow,' she told Scott. 'But Sam – he's getting there. It's been harder for him – less of an adventure, more of a disruption. He left his pals, a school he liked, an area he knew. He's settling now – but there were a few hiccups to start with, a couple of occasions when he skipped school.'

'Where did he go?'

'He came home.'

'But he knew you'd be there, right?' Frankie nodded and Scott weighed it up. 'So he's happy at home?'

She looked at Scott. 'He's happiest at home. He likes to think of himself as the man of the house.'

A fresh pot of tea was ordered. The other tables emptied and refilled, not that Frankie or Scott noticed. They talked easily, eagerly and relaxed into the affable pauses in between. For all the sharing and conversation, it was privately and shyly that they revelled in each other's physical proximity. It confronted her how the man she'd given relatively short shrift to at the station yesterday, the same man in whose company she'd felt herself unfurl during an evening she wished was longer, who'd caused her heart to race in the lift and who'd whorled his way through her sleep, was today someone known to her and trusted. Since yesterday, he'd undoubtedly become the most handsome man she'd ever met but it was the fact that she knew him, that she was herself with him, which thrilled her most.

'Do you have to go back to the studio?'

'Yes.' He rubbed his eyes.

'Not a good session so far?'

He pushed the crumbs on his plate into an S. 'I have the music – but today, in the studio, with everyone there, it's not right.'

'Your music?' Frankie asked. 'Or the way it's being played?'

'If I say the latter, do I sound like a jerk?'

'No,' she said. 'It's personal – I get that.'

And Scott sensed that she did.

'Do you have to go back there soon?'

'Yes,' he said.

'More cake?'

'No – thank you.'

'More tea?'

'Sure.'

'Say cuppa.'

'*Cuppa.*'

The tea was now lukewarm but it didn't matter. They put their cups down at the same time, Scott's shirtsleeve just touching Frankie's arm, their hands so close. If he didn't do it now, he might never. So he did. He moved his little finger the short but loaded distance until it touched Frankie's. She linked hers around his, like those symbolic promises she used to make in the playground with her best friends. Scott and Frankie regarded their entwined fingers and looked at each other and gently placed their heads together and, while Frankie closed her eyes, Scott brushed his lips against her forehead. A kiss without being a kiss.

'Will I see you?' she asked.

'Of course,' he said.

'Not just later today – but will I see you? After? Again?'

'Without a doubt.'

'It's all a bit – mad – really.' She rested her head lightly against his shoulder.

'It's crazy, Frankie. It's insane.' He paused. 'But I like it.'

'I do too.'

Her agent appeared to know most of the other diners in the restaurant so Frankie had to smile a lot whilst fretting at the time this was adding to the evening. In the studio, Scott was utterly wrapped in his music; coasting on the vibrant energy from his afternoon with Frankie and all the Maison Bertaux calories. Why stop now? he said to the engineer – let's get this down. When he worked like this, hours polarized into mere moments. It was two in the morning when he arrived back at the hotel. The bar area was closed and, though he wondered whether Frankie might pop out from behind a giant urn, she didn't. He checked his phone. They'd spoken earlier – she'd ducked out of the restaurant telling him her agent was ordering a second bottle of wine but she should be back by eleven. At the time, Scott said he didn't think he'd be much longer either. And, until he looked at his watch on leaving the studio, he genuinely thought he hadn't been. Jubilance and frustration hand in hand. What a day.

So sorry – I'm only just back and I guess you're asleep. Scott x

Frankie read the message and wondered what to do. It was the early hours and she'd woken with a start, reaching blearily for her phone. In the vast bed, in a froth of Egyptian cotton, she thought and thought until she infuriated herself. She could text back. She could pad off along corridors in the complimentary slippers, holding up the voluminous towelling robe like a ballgown. And then what? Knock on his door, wake him? Stand there, the both of them, with expectation oozing from one to the other. What would he do? Pull her towards him, shut the door behind them, tug her belt loose so the robe fell open, slip his hands inside to find her body, find her lips and sink his mouth against hers. Then what? Fumble and fondle over to the bed and fall together in a writhe of lovemaking. This is what she wanted and she didn't doubt he wanted it too. But what would it be at this time of night? Sex for the sake of it because she was leaving tomorrow?

And it's stupid o'clock.

Frankie switched the light off and settled back into the darkness.

Not now, Scott.

But if not now – then when?

Scott woke early and he thought, she's going today. He thought, it's Thursday and that's that – Frankie's going home. Suddenly he wanted to be home too, not on his own here, negotiating the pace of London, working peculiar hours, living in a hotel, eating too much red meat and spending too much time indoors. He wanted to be sitting at his favourite spot on the Lillooet River, with Aaron and Buddy and a couple of beers. The rivers and creeks had recently turned a milky eau-de-nil colour, the glacial silt causing the change and heralding summer until the rain run-off turned the waters clear again in November. What's the sea like, near Frankie's place in Norfolk? What colour are the rivers there? Where can you fish? Who do you come across, whose landscape do you share? Eagles and otters, beavers, bears?

He left the bed and walked across to the window, looking down to the street five floors below, the besuited hurrying to work, their stress palpable. If this were a scene for a movie, he'd underscore it with a fidget of bickering strings and just the occasional soft melodious piano trying to establish a refrain for the pedestrian walking slowly, mindfully, against the commuting surge. He turned his back on the day and sat down on the sofa, switching the television on and a few moments later, off again. He checked his phone.

Morning!

She'd sent it an hour ago. He phoned Reception. Had she checked out? No Mr Emerson, she has not.

He left his room on the fifth floor and walked along the corridor to hers. Funny how he hadn't wanted her to know he was on the same floor, that first night. Yes, his heart had pounded in the elevator, the air between them thick and heady with attraction and desire. But something had told him to slow down, to give grace to what was growing so fast. He hadn't wanted the premature pressure of your room or mine; for the first time in a long time, his head was steady over his heart, his cock. That night had been too good, had had such a novel impact, he hadn't wanted to sully it with how things used to be. Standing there, outside her door, he thought back to how he'd let her leave then had to ride up before returning down to the fifth.

Quiet Please.

She'd hung the sign on the door. He could do quiet. It was a trait of his personality that most saw as a quality though it frustrated the hell out of all his exes. He knocked gently.

And Frankie thought, *Scott?*

The door opened and Scott thought Christ alive, the sun really does come out when that girl smiles. And Frankie simply thought it's him, he came.

'Good morning sir.'

'Morning.'

'Did you want to come in? It's a bit of a mess.'

No it wasn't. Her room was tidier than his. Funny how rooms which are identical can be so different. Same curtains, same furniture, same orchid, same grainy black-and-white artsy photographs, same background whir from the minibar. Yet Frankie's room was distinct; it was the same when Jenna was at home with him – a space personalized and warmed, made smaller yet fuller by a feminine energy. He glanced around. Perhaps it was the Converse trainers placed neatly just under the chair. Or the way her belongings were in a tidy pile on the coffee table. A drift of perfume, maybe. He didn't know, really, and it didn't matter anyway because as he sat on the sofa he felt this was as good as being in her living room in Norfolk.

'Coffee? Does your room have a Nespresso machine?'

He laughed. 'Think you're special?'

'Aren't I?'

'No – I mean yes. And yes – to coffee.'

'Have you had breakfast?'

'No.'

'You can have the rest of the jelly beans from the minibar.'

Scott laughed. 'Makes a change from granola.'

As Frankie made coffee, she thought about how Scott laughed so easily. She didn't think herself a particularly funny person, it wasn't any staggering wit on her part that made it happen. A gentle sound, deep and genuine, like an oversized soft chuckle. It struck her that Scott was a man who was alert for the happy in life and it was a quality that had its attractive physical manifestation in the laughter lines around his eyes.

'Here you are.'

'Thank you.'

'When are you leaving for work?' she asked.

'Well – soon, really.' He looked at her, sitting in the armchair just like the one in his room; hugging a scatter cushion, not drinking the coffee she'd made, her legs curled under, her hair loose with a bedhead kink to one side. 'And you? When do you check out?'

'In about an hour.'

They thought about that.

'That's too bad,' said Scott.

'I know,' she said quietly.

'I fly home Sunday.'

'I know.'

And she thought to herself, over the sea and far, far away. Insanity. She stood up and crossed over to the window, gazing down on the irritable heave of rush hour outside, mercifully silent five floors up.

'So glad I don't work in a job like that in a place like this.' He was behind her. Right behind her. His chin just perceptible against the top of her head, his body very nearly against hers.

'Me too,' said Frankie and she leant back just slightly until she felt him there. His arms encircled her, his lips pressed against her neck; she had only to turn just a little to kiss him.

'Is this just crazy?' she whispered.

'Crazy not to,' he whispered back and kissed her again, deeper and for longer.

On the train to King's Lynn, just pulling out of Liverpool Street station, her head against the window, Frankie's journey back to her life began. As the train moved, a completely new emotion swept through her; a swirl of euphoria and desolation. She was on her way home and soon, he would be too. To Canada. Would that she had never met him?

The train jolted and stopped. Started, slunk along, juddered, stopped again. Eventually, the tannoy crackled then went quiet, hissed again – then nothing. It was as if the driver had thought better of it. Now at a standstill in nondescript countryside, Frankie recalled how it was a journey like this when she'd first met Ruth. They'd been sitting opposite each other. Tall and elegant with her hair in the sleekest bobbed haircut, like varnished ebony. On looks alone, Frankie had the idea for a character, even more so when the woman called the train line bastards and buggers and for fuck's sake just bloody get a move on you sods.

'You speak my language,' Frankie had said and when it transpired Ruth had a son Annabel's age and a younger daughter and lived not too far from Frankie, the basis for friendship was formed

'What do you do? That you travel from London to Lynn?'

'I write,' said Frankie. 'And you?'

'I teach Alexander Technique.'

'Is that when you're meant to walk with a penny between your bum-cheeks and a pile of books on your head?'

How Ruth had laughed. 'No – but that's how our grandmas were taught to walk, nice and ladylike,' she'd said. Somehow, she'd detected that Frankie suffered headaches. 'Come to me for a few sessions,' she said. 'Mate's rates.'

Scott. What just happened? And what could happen next? Suddenly it struck Frankie that she wanted Ruth to know.

I met a man. Like no other.

Ruth phoned her immediately.

'There are only clichés to describe it. What he's like. I'm a bloody writer and I can't do better than *Love at first sight*.'

'But actually, you *can't* do better than Love at first sight,' Ruth laughed down the phone. 'What could beat that? I have to see you!'

Frankie gazed out of the window again. The landscape was now passing by fast in a blur. When did the train pick up speed? When did the points change? When did they get so far from London, so close to King's Lynn? Reality felt suddenly distorted. However present and alert, alive and sentient she'd felt in London, actually she was hurtling back to the real Frankie – Norfolk and children, the house that leaked and page after page of bare paper devoid of all trace of Alice.

'Don't let him leave before you've seen him again,' Ruth said. 'You can't let him go just because of clichés and complications.'

'Canada is a pretty big complication,' Frankie said.

'Rubbish,' said Ruth so passionately that it struck Frankie she ought to believe her.

'I have to go – the train is pulling in to Lynn.'

'I'll be phoning you later,' said Ruth.

Her mother had cleaned the fridge though Frankie had cleaned it the day before she left. Her mother had also reorganized its contents. It was a typical gesture that could be interpreted one way or the other and responded to graciously or defensively. Her mother had gone by the time Frankie arrived home yet she didn't know whether to be relieved or affronted.

Mum. Mother. Mother dear. Having a sparse relationship with your mother was as complex as having an overinvolved one. Would Annabel some day feel as distant from Frankie as Frankie felt from Margaret?

She left the kitchen and went to the children's rooms. The beds were made and it was a stark sight. The children never made their beds until, bizarrely, they were just about to get into them each evening. She cast an eye over the bathroom. Sam had obviously had a wee and forgotten to flush. Margaret was obviously making a point by leaving it for all to see – though she'd picked up towels, wiped the basin and hung a damp flannel over the tap. Frankie thought of Peta's boys and she wondered why her mother never passed comment on their bedroom walls festooned with semi-naked women, their floors obliterated with piles of dirty clothes. Neither Peta nor Frankie could work that one out at all.

She checked her phone. Nothing. She made a call.

'I'm home and it's very quiet.'

'I'm in the studio,' said Scott. 'Listen.'

'How was Grandma?' Frankie asked Annabel who'd run across the playground into her arms chanting Mummy Mummy Mummy – something she'd never do usually, though admittedly Frankie was usually late and her daughter was cross. This afternoon, she was bang on time. 'Was everything OK when I was gone?'

Annabel settled herself into the front seat, fastened her seat belt and leant forward to open the glove compartment. Mummy Mummy Mummy. Chocolates *and* crisps to choose from.

'She was all right,' Annabel said. 'She wouldn't let us watch *The Simpsons*. She wouldn't even let *Sam* watch *The Simpsons* and he'd done all his homework and everything.'

'You can watch double *Simpsons* this evening.'

'Her cooking is disgusting.'

'I don't like the word disgusting. Did she let you have ketchup?'

'Yes – but she blobbed it on because she said too much was bad for us. Stop checking your phone. You have to be hands-free to drive.'

That evening, during triple *The Simpsons*, Frankie's phone beamed through a text from Scott. He'd attached a photograph of the control room at the studio – his left arm just visible; a bank of switches and knobs and empty paper cups.

THE Abbey Road.

It wasn't how she'd imagined it.

Been thinking of you, Frankie. Scott x

She looked around the room. Could she really envisage him here? Was there room on the sofa? Yes, if they all squashed up a little. Did he like *The Simpsons*? Would he like everything she liked and would it matter if there were some things he didn't? She alighted on her CDs and LPs. Would he approve of her taste? Was Duran Duran a deal breaker? She glanced at Annabel and Sam. What on earth would her children make of a man in their home, a man in their mother's life?

If you ever get a boyfriend I will spill his dinner down him and make his life hell.

Annabel had come out with this, apropos of nothing, a few months ago. But the three of them had laughed because the sentiment was so random and the concept so far-fetched anyway.

'Mum – no double-screening, that's what you say to Sam.' Annabel tried to take Frankie's phone. 'It's "Grift of the Magi" – we love this episode!'

'I missed you,' Frankie said to her children, nudging them, trying to kiss them.

Sam grunted and Annabel said shh!

I miss you she texted to Scott.

Frankie looked up and away from the burning brightness of the empty paper in front of her, gazed out of the window to the sunlight dancing on dewy grass, the light from the unseen sea bathing the garden with clarity. But she wasn't focused on the garden. She was back in the hotel foyer with Kate Moss on the magazine and Scott saying care to join me? Over and over again she replayed the sensation of turning and seeing him and hearing his voice and thinking me? me? really?

She started to write, displaced words and short justifications, a technique she used to shape character and build a backstory.

Polite/thoughtful (hates olives/didn't say)
Strong/principled (raised daughter single-handed)
Talented/modest (shining career/doesn't court limelight)
Secure (happy to say he'd been thinking about me)
Handsome (but not the point)
Foreigner.

'A man who lives on a bloody mountain in sodding Canada.'

She took another page and quickly sketched Alice, enveloping her with chains. *Alice in Chains* she scrawled, leaving the table and going over to scan her CDs for the band of the same name. She played 'Check My Brain' very loudly, her forehead pressed against the wall.

What did her brain say? What was going on behind the scramble of thoughts? Was it ludicrous to feel that this could be life-changing and wholly good? Or was she just selfish and insane to pursue it? Her romanticizing tendencies had brought all sorts of trouble in the past.

'Be rational.'

She shook her head.

'Defy reason.'

She shook her head.

Returning to the table she pushed the page with the words onto the floor and stared at the furl of pencil sharpenings and tiny shards of lead.

She looked at the sketch of Alice and drew her again, quickly, with the chains now around her feet.

Thank you, said Alice.

It's a pleasure, said Frankie.

Can you write me a story where the Ditch Monster comes to my rescue? Instead of the two of us always unravelling everything together? Think about what Scott said.

What did Scott say?

When he told you – to actually ask me.

Frankie was transported back to Maison Bertaux and there she stayed awhile, conjuring the taste of the cakes, the warmth from Scott's knee next to hers, the lurch in her stomach, the soar of her heart, the buzz between her legs when his fingers had entwined with hers. All they had talked about. The timbre of his voice. The way he looked when he listened, the way his mouth moved when he talked, the way his eyes made her feel when they locked onto hers.

What's your favourite song, Alice?

Not that noisy one you just played about your brain, thank you. My favourite song is 'Mr Tambourine Man'.

I never knew that.

You do now.

It had been a jingle-jangle morning of sorts.

I'll be back in a mo' – don't go anywhere, Alice, I just need to make a phone call. Then I'll play you the Byrds' version. Which I like better than Bob Dylan's.

Frankie walked into the kitchen, to the window which looked out to the garden. It was her favourite place to muse. Her heartbeat competed with the silence. She phoned Scott.

'It's Frankie.'

'I know.'

Just two words and she could hear him smiling. She laid her head gently against the wall.

'How are you?' he asked. 'How's Norfolk?'

'Alice is back.'

'Well that's just great.'

'Are you at work? Can you talk?'

'I'm at work but I can talk. I'm playing some guitar.'

'Really?'

'Listen.' He really was. 'You liked it?'

'It's beautiful!'

Should she tell him about the Byrds? That's not why she'd phoned.

'It's Friday,' she rushed.

'Yes, it is.'

'Scott.'

'Yes.' He waited. 'Frankie?'

'If I – if I.' She caught sight of herself reflected back from the window, changed her focus to look out over the lawn to the hedge and the Mawbys' fields beyond. A beautiful day. 'If I could make it to London, tomorrow, could we have any time?'

'I would like nothing more. I need to cancel something, rearrange something else. Can I call you back?'

'Of course you can call me back.'

And, behind the silence, they could hear each other grinning.

Frankie arrived at Annabel's school later that afternoon a full half-hour before the bell went. She wasn't worried about being late, she just needed to know that she could sit in the car and have the time to phone her sister and not rush.

'Peta? It's me.'

'I know – it says so. How was London? Did the kids cope with The Mother?'

'Yes – they did. She cleaned the clean fridge and reorganized the contents.'

'You know she changes the sheets on my spare-room bed as soon as she arrives here – even though I lay them fresh for her?'

'I know.'

'And Alice?'

'I don't want to jinx it – but we had a little progress today.'

'Good for you, Frankie.'

'How was your book club?'

95

'It was – heated. I drank too much and told them I thought the choice was over-verbose, pretentious and essentially dull and that they were silly twats if they thought otherwise.'

'You rebel.'

'Anyway – I got to pick the next book.'

'What did you choose?'

'Maggie O'Farrell.'

'She's a genius. I'm phoning – I'm phoning, Peta.'

'I know you're phoning me!'

'I mean – I wanted to –' Frankie slapped the steering wheel. 'Peta I was just phoning, really, to tell you something. And actually to ask you something.' She took the phone off hands-free and pressed it to her ear. 'Something happened in London.' Her voice had changed, she liked the sound of it – no awkwardness, just delight. 'I met someone.'

Nothing from Peta.

'A man. Called Scott.'

It remained silent in Hampstead.

'Who?' Peta finally responded.

'He's called Scott.'

'I don't understand.'

'You know something, I felt exactly that way. Only now I *do* understand – I truly do.'

'Who is he?'

'He's – just amazing.'

'But who *is* he, Frankie?'

'He's called Scott Emerson. And he's a musician.'

'Oh for Christ's sake, Frankie. Not a musician. Oh dear God.'

'What's your problem?'

'*My* problem? I don't have a problem, Frankie. You

96

do. A musician? That's the problem. No more artsy-fartsy fuckwits.'

'He's not a fuckwit!'

'You may well say that now, while he's serenading you.'

'You have to trust me on this one.'

'No Frankie – *you* have to listen to *me*. You had musicians and actors and painters and that stupid bloody poet and they all systematically broke your heart and then trod the pieces down hard into piles of shit. Then came Miles. *Oh Peta*, you said, *wait till you meet him. He's a free soul* you said, *he's amazing*, you said. *He's someone who can make a difference. He's an ideas man –* you said. *He's so spiritual and real and I never felt this way before.*'

'I'm not the impressionable girl I was then, I'm forty-one,' Frankie said quietly. 'And Scott is nothing like Miles.'

'How so?'

'Well he's older, for a start.'

'Oh great. Frankie! Some waster still tinkling the ivories, or strumming his guitar or playing his fucking fiddle because he's never knuckled down?'

'Jesus Peta. He's a talented musician. He writes soundtracks for movies. He's won awards. He's in demand. He's *respected*.'

'I have a respectable man I've been trying to introduce you to for months – Chris!'

'Oh God – not him again.'

'You could at least meet him.'

'We have nothing in common – and anyway, you showed me that picture of him.'

'Christ you're shallow.'

Peta wanted to retract that. Her sister was not shallow. Her sister's problem was that she was unable to see trouble even when it was up so close and very personal. She pitied her, really, worried for her. 'Sorry,' she said, 'I didn't mean that. I just meant – it's been so long, and I have to be your sensible older sister and say please, please don't go for anyone flaky who's going to hurt you.'

'Why should being a musician make him flaky? Maybe he really likes me and has no intention of hurting me – have you thought of that?'

'You've known him for what – forty-eight hours? Please don't come out with *but I feel I've known him my whole life.*'

'But it honestly feels like I have.'

Oh Frankie. Peta calmed herself. Soundtracks for films? Well it was better than poems that made no sense and were never published, or that actor who was too arrogant to learn lines or attend auditions, or the artist who didn't know one end of the paintbrush from the other. Or Miles – bloody Miles with his charm and his bullshit and his gorgeous face and abject disregard for responsibility and total uselessness when it came to anything important, anything that could hurt or endanger those he professed to love.

Peta laughed gently. 'What do you call a guitarist with no girlfriend?'

'Is this an actual joke?' Frankie asked. Peta's skill lay in neutralizing atmospheres, however bizarre and untimely her tactic.

'Yes.'

'OK – what do you call a guitarist with no girlfriend?'

'Homeless!'

Frankie had to giggle.

'Is this Scott person homeless? Ask yourself that.'

'No he's not homeless, you silly cow.'

'Well,' Peta sighed, 'that's something, I suppose.'

Frankie took a deep breath. 'He has an amazing house, with land and everything.' She let that information settle. 'In Canada.'

Peta thought, I am actually going to close my eyes, dig my nails into the palms of my hands and count to ten. 'Canada,' she said, when she'd done so. It wasn't a question.

'Yes.'

'You truly think it's remotely feasible to fall in love with a musician who lives in Canada?'

'Yes!' Frankie sang it out. There was nothing wrong with any of it. It was brilliant – all of it.

'Frankie.' Peta knew to tread carefully but she wasn't entirely sure what to say next. 'How long is he here for before he returns home – *to Canada*?'

'He flies on Sunday.'

'Sunday as in the day after tomorrow?'

'I need to see him tomorrow. That's why I'm phoning – to tell you what happened and to ask if the kids and I can stay.'

'You mean the kids to stay – because you'll be elsewhere shagging Scott senseless.'

'Don't say it like that. I just need to see him again,' Frankie said thoughtfully. 'Before he goes.'

'Have you slept with him?'

'No.'

'Are you going to?'

'I don't know. I hope so. I don't know.'

Peta heard her sister, her voice level yet full of

thought, passion, need. And she thought to herself, you know what, even if Frankie and this Scott bloke have a night of passion and she never hears from him again – is there really anything so wrong in that? She's only known him two days so he can't actually break her heart. Perhaps a stupendous shag – or whatever she wants to call it – is no bad thing. Hopefully, it will get it out of her system. He lives in Canada. He'll be gone the day after tomorrow, a different continent, a different time zone, a different world. Perhaps it's a very good idea – scratch that phantom itch and then pave the way for something more realistic with someone like Chris.

'OK,' Peta said. 'Come. I'd love to see you – and the kids. Come. You're welcome.'

'Thank you so so much.'

'You're welcome.'

Annabel was excited; she'd been given a Claire's Accessories voucher last Christmas but had been bemused to find she lived nowhere near a branch. But London? There were as many Claire's Accessories as there were pigeons. Sam, however, was utterly resistant. He'd have to miss a cricket match, his first for the B team.

'I'll write a note,' Frankie told him.

'That's not the point,' he said. 'It's not about the note – it's about what I want to do.'

'Sometimes I have to make decisions for the family, though,' said Frankie.

'Moving out here was a decision for the family,' Sam retorted. 'And I had to leave my old school and my mates and everything. And you told me to try hard to join in – well that's what I've been doing. I'm crap at winter sports but I'm good at cricket. And now I can't play because I'm being dragged off to London because of your stupid work. I'm letting the team down, I'll never get chosen again. God!' He was picking up random items and banging them down again; an orange, Annabel's school book, his mother's hairbrush, all of which he'd rather throw at the windowpane while yelling fuck! whatever the consequences.

'I'm sorry,' said Frankie, meaning it.

'No you're not.'

'I am, sweetie. But I can't change things now. Peta's looking forward to seeing us. So are Josh and Stan.'

'Josh and Stan are thugs – you said so yourself. Not even in private. You said so yourself – to us – after our last visit.'

'That was then,' she told her children brightly. 'Teenagers go through phases – they're probably sweetness and light these days.' Quietly, they all doubted that.

'If I can find someone on the team and they say I can stay at theirs – then can I stay?' Sam's cheeks had reddened and his voice creaked.

Hitherto, Sam hadn't asked if any of his schoolmates could come over and though the school assured her he was much more settled, she worried that his friendships were conducted via Instagram rather than reality.

'Yes,' Frankie smiled. 'That'll work.'

Still slightly slouched, Sam went off with his phone.

Annabel fixed Frankie with her oversized hazel eyes. 'Why do you have a work thing on a Saturday – when offices are closed at weekends?'

Frankie didn't lie to her children. Ever. She just

101

manipulated language instead. 'It's someone I met when I was down in London working last week. They don't live here. They live in Canada and I need to see them before they go.'

'What's their name?'

Frankie paused. 'Scott,' she said. 'His name is Scott.'

'They're a man?'

'Half the world is men, Annabel.'

Annabel looked at her mother long and hard. 'What time will you be back?'

'I won't know till I'm there, really. But I'll let Auntie Peta know.'

'Or Sam.'

'Yes – or Sam.'

'If he comes,' said Annabel, 'if he can't magic himself some friends by then.'

'Dom says I can stay at his.' Sam bounced back in.

'I don't think I've heard you mention Dom,' said Frankie.

Sam shrugged. 'He's a brilliant bowler.'

'Is he nice?'

Sam balked at the question. 'He's in my maths set,' he said. 'He's cool.'

'I ought to speak to his mum,' said Frankie.

Sam shrugged. 'She said it was fine.'

'Still – I ought to speak to her.'

Sam sent a text at breakneck speed and a reply pinged back almost immediately. 'Here – this is her mobile number.'

'What's her name?'

'I don't know,' Sam said, as if it was preposterous.

'What's Dom's surname?'

'Massey.'

'I'll give Mrs Massey a ring, then.'

'Unless she's a single mum with a different surname,' said Annabel. 'Like you.'

But Mrs Massey told Frankie to call her Sarah and assured her it would be a pleasure for Sam to stay.

'Maybe Dom would like to come over to ours one day,' Frankie said to Sam.

'Cool,' said Sam, settling down on the couch. '*Simpsons*!' he called to his family and they gathered together next to him, and did what they did so well, with Frankie in the middle.

'I love this one.'

'Me too.'

'Marge! She's my role model you know.'

'She has better hair than you, Mum.'

I'm going!

Ruth was the first person Frankie wanted to tell.

FanTASTic! Ruth texted back.

You coming? Scott texted Frankie.

Yes. Frankie texted back.

'Mummy! Put your phone *down*.'

There had been a time, after university and once she'd landed her first job at a greetings-card company, when Frankie aspired to living in Hampstead. It seemed such a perfect place: slightly bohemian, still villagey, up high as if it had cleaner air than the rest of London. She'd gaze at the buildings and imagine herself ensconced in basement flats or up in attics – all bare floorboards and faded kilims, old tub chairs, iron bedsteads and little framed engravings of the same streets in Victorian times. But she'd never been able to afford to rent and, when a decade later a healthy advance on her Alice books could have supported a debilitating mortgage for somewhere tiny around Parliament Hill, Hampstead had changed anyway.

Around that time Peta married and moved there. Frankie had gently envied her until, before long, there was a general exodus of everything unique in the area. Quirky boutiques were seen off by upmarket clothing chains, little delis replaced by pricey generic ones, humble cafés and the occasional corner shop swallowed up by each and every coffee company. But still, above eye level, the windows and chimneys and brickwork and roofs of the beautiful buildings remained unaltered. And, Frankie had to admit, a visit to Whistles or Karen

Millen for first time in nine months was attractive. She could stock up on jeans and tops for the kids from Gap and then pop across to Waterstones to check stock levels of her books after which a frappuccino might be in order.

Peta's house had changed since Frankie had last visited.

'Grey,' Peta explained. 'Actually – *greige*. It's all about greige these days.'

'Where are the menfolk?'

'Philip's at bloody work – of course – and the boys are at athletics. They'll be home soon.' Peta smiled at Annabel. 'They're looking forward to seeing you.'

Annabel rolled her eyes at her mother and, for a moment, Frankie was sure she was going to say *bloody thugs*. But then again, Peta would probably concur.

'Take your stuff upstairs and freshen up – I've made us a light lunch.'

Frankie poked her head around the door to the smallest spare room to find Annabel staring at the bed.

'Auntie Peta always puts this doll and this teddy out for me,' she told her mum.

'That's because she's thoughtful,' said Frankie. 'She has a soft spot for you because you're a gorgeous girl and not a monstrous boy.'

'I think I'd probably rather have stayed at home though,' said Annabel. 'What with you going out and everything.'

Frankie thought about it. 'But Auntie Peta has planned popcorn and chocolate and a DVD just for the both of you. Also she has much better nail varnishes than me.'

'Listen!'

The house appeared to shake.

'It's only Stan and Josh,' Frankie said.

'Do you think they'll talk to me?'

'Think of it as a mercy if they don't,' Frankie laughed.

'Do you think Sam's OK?'

Frankie looked at her watch. 'The match'll be under way.'

'Don't you think it's odd – not being the three of us?'

Frankie nodded. 'It is odd. But it's also normal for there to be times when we have to do – our own things.'

'I don't have my own things to do,' said Annabel crossly. 'I just have to follow.'

'Your time'll come,' Frankie said, stroking her daughter's little face and putting her hand back there even after Annabel had pushed it away.

Later, Annabel watched Frankie get changed.

'What's wrong with the clothes you were wearing?'

'Nothing?' Frankie said.

'So why are you getting changed? It's only teatime.'

'I felt stuffy in what I was wearing – after the long car journey and everything. Anyway, I'm going out to dinner – and I don't often wear a frock these days.'

'A dress – it's called a dress,' said Annabel. 'What time will you be back?'

How many times today had her daughter already asked her this? 'I don't know. But lateish.' Frankie wished Annabel would just rummage around her make-up bag or try on her shoes and stop asking her these questions.

'The boys are so rude!' Annabel whispered. 'Did you

hear them? Did you hear what Josh said about Auntie Peta's food?'

'I did. Ghastly – but it's just a phase.'

'Well, if Sam goes through a phase, we will have to kill him.'

'He might, you know – but we'll find a way to deal with it that doesn't involve death.'

'They're so *rude*!' Annabel shook her head. 'When can I have a phone?'

'A phone?'

'So you can phone me.'

'When you're at secondary school – like Sam.'

'But you can't phone me tonight to tell me if you're going to be later than lateish.'

'I'll keep in touch with Peta.'

'You look – lovely,' Peta told Frankie sweetly, glancing over at Annabel who was seemingly engrossed in *Frozen*. 'Smile?'

Frankie raised her eyebrow at herself. 'I'm so nervous. It's crazy.' She scanned her sister's face for reassurance. 'Am I mad?'

Peta sighed. 'It *is* nuts – all of it. But if you were me, you wouldn't be doing it and if I was you – then hell yes, I would!' She paused. 'Go. Stop thinking. Don't worry about Annabel. Go and have fun – or there's absolutely no point.'

Gazing at her daughter, Frankie suddenly thought perhaps I shouldn't be doing this, perhaps my place is on a sofa, watching *Frozen*. She thought of Sam and the unknown Massey family. Did they win the cricket? Was he OK? Did he feel palmed off? It all felt a bit self-centred, slightly dishonest.

'Go!' said Peta with a friendly shove.

Frankie looked down at her shoes. Were her feet going to be sore in an hour? Did Scott really want to see her?

'Will you make it really lovely for Annabel?'

'I have the best night planned,' Peta said. 'Pink fake cocktails in sugar-crusted martini glasses, popcorn, mini-marshmallows and chocs and we're going to watch *Pitch Perfect*. I've only ever watched it once, secretly on the laptop with headphones on in the top room. My boys would smash the DVD otherwise.'

'Where will they be? Josh and Stan?'

'On their phones in their rooms with music on and stinky socks.'

'So Annabel will be fine?'

'Yes, Frankie – and so will you. Now – *go*.'

The further the cab took Frankie from Hampstead, the lighter her nerves became, metamorphosing from a leaden plug of guilt and anxiety in the pit of her stomach, to a feathering of butterflies swirling up against her diaphragm. She loved her dress and it really was a frock, whatever Annabel claimed to the contrary. Petrol blue, scooped neck and back, little cap sleeves – it had something of the 1950s about it. Changing her shoes to trusty ballet pumps at the last minute was a good idea, and she felt a femininity that months of slopping around at home in old jeans and shabby tops had compromised. She checked her phone. No messages at all. The taxi was travelling down Fitzjohn's Avenue and all the traffic seemed to be going the other way. The lights were green. Nothing, it seemed, was standing in her way.

In Abbey Road, Scott was working. He'd be back again in the morning, for a couple of hours before his flight, but was nearly done for now. The week had been a good one and he was happy with the results. He looked at his watch. Almost six o'clock – a curious in-between time, not quite evening, long since afternoon. He phoned his daughter.

'Hey Pops.'

'Hey Jenna.'

'How's it going?'

'Oh – good. How's you?'

'Fine – I promise! Dad – don't do the loaded pause. What time do you get in tomorrow – is Aaron picking you up?'

'I arrive around six. And yes – or I'll be hitching home.'

'I saw him driving your truck yesterday – it's like a totally different vehicle with him. Windows down – music loud.'

Scott laughed. Aaron posing as cooler than cool. 'What was he playing?'

'Springsteen or Bryan Adams.'

He laughed again. 'No daughter of mine can possibly confuse the two.'

'All I heard was some loud guitar as he flew past. Buddy was riding up front – with a bandana around his neck.'

Scott could envisage it so clearly it sent a pang that coursed right through him. An evening of promise stretched enticingly ahead of him and yet he thought, Godspeed tomorrow. 'Will I see you next week?'

'Sure! I have a day off on Thursday.'

'I'll come pick you up.'

'So what are you doing tonight? How's the work going?'

'It's going great.'

'Did you meet the Royal Queen of England yet?'

'Nope – she keeps leaving messages though. All the time. Crazy old girl.'

'How about an English Rose – did you meet one of those yet?'

Jenna thought the connection had gone.

'Dad?'

'Yes?'

'I thought you'd gone. So call me when you're home?'

'Sure.'

'And see you Thursday?'

'You bet.'

'Travel safe, Pops.'

'Night sweetheart.'

'Dad – it's the *day*.'

'So save it for later.'

His phone rang.

'You here?' he asked.

'I'm here,' Frankie said.

Stock-still he stood in the control room while outside, Frankie fidgeted from foot to foot. They thought: any moment now any moment now. Out into the gentle light of early evening, Scott realized how he must have missed a lovely day in London if the warmth and clear sky were anything to go by.

And there she is. There she is.

'You look disappointed.'

'I was anticipating something less high-tech, more bohemian – more sixties.'

'You wanted Paul and John sitting in a corner jamming.'

'Yes – Ringo and George too.'

'If you'd have come earlier in the week, I could've done you George Clooney – he's producing a movie and the music was recorded here in Studio One.'

'I didn't know you earlier in the week.'

Scott stopped. Really? 'Next time, I'll make sure it's more rock and roll for you.'

'There will be a next time?'

Thoughts of Jenna weaved through his mind but he halted them, as if he was saying to her hang on honey, I'm just busy here. He looked at Frankie intently for a moment before nodding. 'Oh I'll be back for sure,' he said.

'Not just for work?'

'No – not just for work.'

They were standing in a corridor crammed with trolleys heaped high with all manner of gear and gadgetry. People with mugs of coffee, preoccupied expressions and heads full of music had to negotiate Scott and Frankie standing in their way. On the walls, framed photographs looked down on them benevolently, from the Beatles to an Oasis of calm while music filtered out when thick doors opened and muffled away again when they closed, like reveals of other people's thoughts.

'Come,' said Scott, leading on to the control room of Studio Two. 'I have around twenty minutes of work left to do.'

The control room had a stillness with its soft lighting and dark red soundproofing in long padded runs along the walls. But there was a busyness too; the vast mixing desk, screens running a cut of the film, speakers so huge they reminded Frankie of props for *Star Wars*, compressors, distressors, amps and limiters, a coffee table with a scatter of cups and a platter of fruit, discarded headphones and sheaves of music marked up in luminous highlighter pen. And people – for some reason she hadn't expected anyone else to be there. From the leather sofa, a woman and a man turned and nodded; at a desk by the interior window looking down on the studio itself, another woman was leafing through pages of music; at a table next to her a young man was working at a computer.

'So this is Frankie,' Scott said introducing her to the director, the producer, the music editor, the music supervisor and a chap called Paul Broucek from Warner Bros. who was working in Studio One but knew Scott well. Jeff Bridges was as good as there too, dominating the three large monitors running scenes from the movie.

'Scott – we're ready for you.'

He touched her arm and told her ten, twenty minutes, then he walked to the door at the end of the room and through to the studio itself.

'Frankie,' said Paul, motioning her to the table and chair by the interior window that looked down on the studio. 'Come sit here.'

Below, she saw what looked more like a school gym, a little shabby in comparison with the control room. There were chairs and music stands for at least fifty, but there was only Scott down there, settling himself, putting on headphones, tuning his guitar. She'd only heard him play down the phone at her, just a couple of bars.

'You see that?' Paul was pointing to a nondescript upright piano. 'Circa 1905 Steinway Vertegrand piano,' he told her. 'Or – in layman's terms, the "Lady Madonna" piano that McCartney played.'

And Frankie thought, I really love this place.

'Ready for you, Scott,' someone was saying.

'Sure.' His voice came through on the speakers.

And then he started to play. Though Paul encouraged her to watch the screens, to see how the cue fitted the scene, her eyes were constantly drawn to Scott, a solitary figure down there in that historic room, playing the music he'd written. A world of his own.

'He plays so so beautifully,' Paul said to no one in particular.

'One of the great guitarists,' someone else responded.

'When he plays acoustic, it's just so complete,' said Paul. 'Like four or five voices simultaneously. Just beautiful.'

Watching Scott, hearing him play, something swept through Frankie just then. It wasn't that he had added another string to his bow in her eyes; it was more profound than that. Another layer, extra depth in a world which, though different from hers in many ways, was a world she understood. To be lost in one's craft, the need to create, whether with words or music, using a language for expression which was simultaneously intensely personal and yet generous and universal. Writing for yourself yet giving it to an audience. A kindred soul, for sure.

'Have you known each other long?' Paul interrupted her thoughts.

She thought about it. 'A while,' she said because it felt that way.

The cue was recorded quickly without incident. Once Scott was back in the control room and happy with it, they spent a little more time at the studios before emerging into the early evening.

'You're not going to make me take a photo of you on the crossing are you Frankie?'

'Of course I am!'

'Damn tourist,' Scott laughed. 'You know it's in a different position these days?'

She slapped him lightly. 'Don't tell me that, don't spoil it – I'm having my moment.'

A short while later, in a taxi, while Frankie scrolled through the photos he'd just taken of them goofing on the zebra crossing, Scott looked out the window at London doing its thing on a Saturday evening. Passing all these iconic sights – double-decker buses, black taxis, red letter boxes, Abbey Road, Baker Street and signs for places he knew he'd heard of though he'd never been there, Scott realized he felt glad to be here. For a long while, work trips were all about ricocheting from studio to hotel, the specific country being somehow irrelevant. He thought how, back home at this time, he'd be feeding Buddy and taking a beer onto the porch to wonder what he'd eat, what he'd watch on TV, whether he'd just work. Most evenings in his life were contented places to be in their simplicity and predictability. He worked hard to achieve his uncomplicated sense of balance. But a giggle from Frankie drew him back to where he was, right now. London, in this taxi with this girl who was sparkling.

It struck Scott that actually, it wasn't about London or Pemberton, or comparing and contrasting usual Saturdays with this one, it wasn't about thoughts of Buddy or beer. It wasn't about listening to what Frankie was saying about this photo or that one or look at me here, my frock looks like a bloody lampshade. The present was not so much about what was happening, as about what he absolutely wanted to make of it. So he leant across, wove his fingers through Frankie's hair and kissed her. Only the traffic lights changing and the judder of the taxi made him stop. Forehead against forehead so that their features blurred, he touched his nose against hers before settling back in his seat with a grin on his face. That's what it's all about, he thought. That beats a beer out back, he thought.

Frankie undid her seat belt and shufted along to sit close next to him. With his arm around her and her head on his shoulder, they spent the rest of the journey side by side, hands clasped in exhilarated silence.

They returned to the hotel so Scott could drop off his bag, his laptop and his guitar. For Frankie, it was odd being back; two days ago seemed so distant it could well have been last year. There were different staff on duty, new guests and a vast floral arrangement in mauve and black, but the sounds were the same – strange acoustics amplifying conversations yet distorting any specifics into a tinny whir. It was clever, really. Some architect or engineer probably charged a fortune for it – to ensure a lively vibe while preserving confidentiality. Come and stay here! it's the place to be – listen! no one can eaves-drop on a word you say.

On her own in the lobby, she wondered about following him up to his room. But the cliché of Scott opening the door in a bathrobe with a smouldering smile was so unlikely it made her laugh out loud. Yes of course she wanted to get naked with him, she was practically stuck to her underwear after all that kissing in the taxi. But he'd made a dinner reservation and she liked the thought of that; an evening unfolding with the chance to talk, to discover and connect, to find further similarities over and above a loathing of olives.

She walked over to the table with the complimentary newspapers and magazines. Kate Moss had gone. It was Miley Cyrus now and Frankie really had nothing to say to her apart from where's your dignity, dear – put some bloody clothes on.

'All set?'

She turned to Scott and nodded.

'I hope you like where we're going – I asked the concierge, he said it was a great place to go and we can walk there.'

He took her to Covent Garden and Joe Allen's, taking great pleasure in whispering that even though it wasn't on the menu, if she wanted a burger all she had to do was ask. She hadn't the heart to tell him that she'd ordered from the not-so-secret menu many times before. However, though the wine was poured and the burgers came in their delicious brioche buns, the patties duveted with gooey cheese and all the condiments they could ask for, neither Frankie nor Scott had an appetite. She was aware she'd skipped breakfast and had only picked at the salad Peta had prepared for lunch; by rights she should be starving. But, with her stomach in a knot and her heart in her mouth, food was of no consequence. She glanced at Scott's plate to see that it was as loaded as hers.

'I don't seem to have an appetite,' she said.

'I don't either.'

'I'm sorry.'

'Don't be.'

They looked from their plates to each other and back again.

'It's nuts,' Frankie said.

Scott caught her eye and kept it, slipped his hand

over hers on the table, licked his lips before he spoke as if the taste of the words were to be sublime.

'Will you come back with me?' he asked her. 'Can I take you to bed?'

Housekeeping had been in and turned down the sheets; they knew by now that there was only one person in the suite and only one chocolate necessary for all those pillows. They knew that the guest was not profligate with the bath towels, which he folded and hung up again. The shower gel always needed replenishing but the body lotion and hair conditioner remained untouched. The complimentary slippers would still be in their plastic packaging, the bathrobe still cinched a number of times around the waist by the belt like a boa constrictor. All that they had to do was pile up the scatter cushions, dim the lights, draw the curtains, put the one chocolate on the pillow and fold the loo paper into a neat triangle.

Frankie looked around the room, noted Scott's guitar case propped against a wall, his old satchel in worn leather burnished like rich wood, slung over the chair. Out of the corner of her eye, through the archway, the edge of the bed. She slipped off her shoes for the feel of fat carpet underfoot and walked over to the window, parting the curtains to look at the view. It was a far better view than she'd had. Obviously, there were upgrades and upgrades.

'Hey,' he said, behind her, his hands lightly on her waist, swaying her gently, his eyes closing as he inhaled the scent of her; something floral and soft, freshly washed hair and clean clothes and whatever perfume it was she wore. She leant back against him and he put his lips on her neck, just resting them there. She turned instinctively, raised her face to find his mouth, placed her arms around his neck and looked at him.

'You're shaking,' he said.

'I know,' she said.

'You OK?'

Frankie thought how best to answer. 'It's been a while.'

He kissed her forehead, her nose, her lips, tipped his head to one side and looked at her quizzically. 'You reckon you've forgotten what to do?'

She giggled. Then she looked at him straight and shrugged. 'It's just it's been – a long time.'

'It's like riding a bike,' he murmured, while he unzipped her dress.

'Hold on tight and hope you don't fall off?' she said, running her hands over his shirt, wanting to feel his skin.

'Something like that.'

She slipped her hands up his shirt, her touch light and tantalizingly slow up his back and down again. The feel of a man after so long, the thrill that touching another's body could make her own body thrum. Scott pushed her dress down from her shoulders and focused on her standing there. Lace bras with obvious scaffolding had never done it for him yet over the years he assumed they were worn by women the world over. He never realized how there could be something so much more tantalizing about the sight of a girl just in a simple white bra and panties. And here she was.

Frankie wondered if everything was OK. Scott was motionless, his eyes apparently fixed on her stomach.

'I've had two babies,' she said with some apology, folding her arms over her abdomen.

'You're gorgeous,' he whispered. 'You're just –

gorgeous.' He took her hands away and trailed his fingertips up and down her arms, across her collarbone, down to the soft white cups of her bra.

For Scott, sex in the last few years had nothing to do with lingering or marvelling at what there was to behold, it hadn't had anything to do with taking his time and being in the moment. It had solely and soullessly focused on getting the fuck out of his pants and getting the fuck out of his system. It was, quite literally, about coming and going. He'd thought about Frankie often these last few days, fantasized about how she'd feel, smell, taste. He hadn't been far wrong but right now, reality was blindingly better.

Frankie stepped in close, unbuttoning his shirt.

'You're still fully clothed, Scott,' she said, 'and that's not fair.'

The feel of him rhythmically sweeping his hands up and down her back, over her bottom and down to where her thighs met her buttocks threatened to push her heart right through her breastbone. He unhooked her bra and that was that. He pulled his shirt over his head, unbuckled his belt, unzipped his flies and stumbled out of his jeans. White trunks, the shape of his erection. He pulled her against him, now kissing her hungrily while his hands were everywhere and she could barely breathe. Over her breasts, up between her legs, at her knickers, under them. So long since she'd been touched or felt desired, it made her almost giddy.

Better than sex – a stupidly overused phrase describing chocolate or buying new shoes or some vodka cocktail or other self-indulgent triviality. Just then, though, being enclosed in his arms, against his chest that had both strength and softness, was hard to beat. His lips against hers again, maddeningly slowly. With fingers entwined, Scott led Frankie to bed.

Having writhed and fondled, tasted and sucked, when Scott finally pushed up into her, they both became very still and, eyes locked, bodies melding, they just gazed at each other. Where did I find you? And now that I have you, where will we go? With surges of long-dormant emotion increasing the intense pleasure of the physical, they knew that this was something new, this was lovemaking. They marvelled at the fact that – my God – it's taken till now to figure out that *this* is how it should feel.

'Will you stay?'

A rapid tumble of calculations and scenarios filled Frankie's mind. She could text Peta. She could get up really early. She could text Peta and say she'd phone Annabel first thing. She could phone Annabel first thing in the morning and say Mummy's on her way back. But what if Annabel woke in the night – and found her gone? But tomorrow – Scott would be gone. And oceans and time zones would barge in on the connection and closeness they'd found tonight.

But – Annabel.

Frankie raised her face from Scott's chest.

'I can't – my little girl.'

'It's OK.'

'But I want to.'

'I want you to.'

'It's just –'

'I understand.'

'But you go tomorrow.'

'I know.'

'You go in – *hours*.'

'I do.'

If she asked him to change his flight, what would he do, they both wondered.

'Did you tell your daughter about tonight?' Scott asked.

Frankie shook her head. 'I didn't. She was a bit out of sorts. It's odd – not having Sam with us.'

'You're a tight little unit, eh.'

'We are,' said Frankie, liking Scott's description.

'I get that. Believe me.'

'But it's early – I don't need to go just yet.'

'Good.' He stroked her hair but oh to fall asleep and wake to find her here.

Frankie propped herself up on her arm and gave Scott a lascivious smile. 'I remembered what to do.'

'You certainly did,' he laughed.

'I hung on tight, and I didn't fall off.'

'You want to go for another ride?'

'Right now? Blimey.'

'I love that – *blimey*.'

She woke with a start. It was almost three in the morning.

'Please stay.' His voice, steady in the darkness.

'I can't.'

'I know. I shouldn't have asked. You can't have it all – but if I could, I'd have you stay.'

'Change your flight,' she said. 'Please. Even by a day.'

A stream of variants poured into his head. 'I can't.' He reached for the bedside lamp and flicked it on. He looked lovely, mussed with sleep.

Frankie stroked his cheeks, his bristles soft against

the back of her hand. He cupped her face and kissed her.

'This,' she started. However wide open it left her, she couldn't leave without saying it. 'I know it defies reason.' Even if she made a fool of herself, even if it was beyond ludicrous, she had to know that she'd said it. 'I just wanted to say –' She tried to concentrate, picking over a jumble of disconnected words and phrases, all of which seemed woefully inadequate. She sank back into his arms. Ten past three. She had to go. But what if Annabel remained fast asleep until ten past nine? Later, even? What if she hadn't woken since going to bed?

But what if she had.

Frankie thought, why on earth didn't I just say to her that I'm staying with a friend and you're staying with Auntie Peta – because I'm your mum and I say so.

Scott could sense Frankie's thoughts in freefall.

'You want to say that this is crazy – you and me. That we live in different continents, that we have commitments to where we live and the people in our lives – so what the heck are we thinking?'

She nodded. 'That this is real life – not the movies. Logic would say it will be impossible, stupid.'

'Common sense is stacked against us.'

'Friends and family will beg us not to get involved. You've never been to Canada, they'll say – don't go there.' Frankie thought about it. 'They'll say it'll end in tears.'

'All of that and then some,' Scott said.

'But I don't care about that.' She was serious. Then she started laughing, she wasn't sure why. Never mind

Canada or Norfolk, *this* was the place and she wanted more time in the now, in the crook of his arm, enfolded and desired. She traced patterns across his chest with her fingertip while he pulled locks of her hair through his hand. She sat up and looked at him. 'What I want to say is – I can wait between times, I can live between time zones. This feels good and I think it can get even better. So actually, who cares what's reasonable and what people think? I'm happy to do this and I wonder if you might be too? If that makes any sense.'

Scott thought about the warning bells he'd heard over the last three days which he'd systematically turned a deaf ear to. He thought of all the negatives that made so much sense but which he'd rejected one by one. Of course it was doomed to fail, on paper – so the best thing to do was to tear the paper up, take a new sheet and write something different.

'Want to be my girl?' he asked, looking at her straight.

In his one question lay all the answers to hers. 'Yes please,' she said.

'Look!'

Frankie woke to find Annabel brandishing her fingernails in her face, clawing at the air like a ten-legged arachnid.

'That's very red,' Frankie said.

'Auntie Peta says it's her favourite shade – for times when a girl wants to be a Scarlet Woman.'

Peta. Christ.

'Did you sleep well?' Frankie asked.

'Yes. I went to bed at half-past ten and I just woke up.'

'Did you have a lovely evening?'

'It was brilliant. Come on, get up now. It's ten past nine.'

Annabel left the room, blowing on her fingernails as if the polish was still drying. Frankie mused that it was funny, really, how her children rarely asked, and how are you, Mummy? How was your day? Did you have a lovely evening? They weren't wilfully thoughtless because their worlds were places that she had ensured were all about them. Mum's just Mum, isn't she?

How was your evening Mummy?

Oh, I spent it in bed with a man I've fallen for.

Did you have fun? Do you love him?

Do you know something, kids, I think I do.

Downstairs, Frankie found Annabel playing with Peta's hair, lovingly picking through it like a young chimp. Stan and Josh were thumping each other, careening around the kitchen. Philip stretched out the *Sunday Times*, holding it up in front of him like a barrier. Frankie remembered him doing this when she'd visited Peta at university. She'd told her friends how Peta's boyfriend was a pompous twat. But today, with the decibel level louder than in his student digs, she felt a sympathy for him. The boys were now throwing toast and calling each other pussy. Peta and Frankie glanced at Annabel but she regarded her cousins only fleetingly; quite obviously thinking them savages not worth her attention.

Only once the boys had left the house for some place called 'Out Just Out' and Philip had taken the business section to his study and Annabel had been granted her dearest wish to watch *Pitch Perfect* again with a packet of Haribo, were Peta and Frankie finally alone. Peta knew her sister had come in during the small hours and, from Frankie's current glow despite so little sleep, she knew that her night had been a success. Peta cursed herself for finding Frankie's euphoria so compelling – it was hard to play devil's advocate when actually what she wanted was to relive vicariously being on the brink of throwing oneself headlong into the first flush of falling in love.

'Sex with passion *and* meaning?' Peta sighed nostalgically, pouring more tea and regarding her sister with wistful envy. 'Rather than being a perfunctory and self-centred means to an end.'

'It was out of this world,' Frankie told her. 'Really intense. In the past I've flinched away from eye contact. It's unnerved me – too instrusive, made me feel self-conscious. But last night, with Scott, we just gazed and gazed.' She shook her head and grinned. 'He's just so –'

'Did you take photos?'

Frankie balked.

'Not *those* sorts of photos, idiot – just a regular one, of him.'

Peta scrolled through Frankie's phone. She had to admit it, he was lovely looking. Nothing like she was expecting. Not at all like Miles. Or the poncey poet or any of the other ridiculous entanglements her sister had consorted with earlier in her life. Scott was handsome in an open way – as if his looks, worn in and comfortable, were a product of his lifestyle and described him well. Even on the screen of a phone, he exuded contentment, kindness, strength, as though he spent a lot of time outdoors.

'Stupid as it sounds,' Peta said, 'he sort of looks like a proper man.'

Frankie took back her phone and gazed at the screen. 'He is.'

'And back off to Canada today. You'll see him again – when?' Peta's question was reasonable but sharp.

'We *will* see each other again – but I don't know when.'

'So – in between times, what? You'll stand alone for months on end on the metaphorical shore with your eyes trained on the horizon? You'll put your life on hold while you wait, increasingly lovelorn, lonely and paranoid?'

'Why would I get paranoid?' Why can't my bloody sister just be happy for me?

'Because he's a handsome guy probably with a coterie of bunk-ups on speed-dial.'

'He says not.'

'And you believe him?'

'Yes I do.'

Peta could feel her sister closing off from her, a self-defence tactic at which she was adept. 'I just really don't want to see you hurt. Or even distracted. You've your career to focus on. And your new life in Norfolk. And the children.'

'When you meet him – *when* – all your fears will be allayed,' said Frankie. 'You'll see why it makes so much sense. Scott and me.'

Peta nodded. 'OK,' she said softly, 'I hope so.'

A text bleeped through from Ruth.

'Is that him?' Peta asked.

'No – Ruth,' Frankie said as she texted Ruth: It was out of this world! xx

Peta was pleased about Ruth. 'If you think about it Frankie, now's the time for you to commit to Norfolk, for consolidating new friendships like with this Ruth lady. In London, you never really had a circle, a close friend in particular.'

'I was the odd one out – a mum who worked and a single mum at that. I couldn't do lazy lunches during the week and I was rarely invited to dinner parties – or even over for an evening – during the weekends.'

'So I'm really pleased about Ruth.' Peta paused. 'Perhaps just consider whether it's a good time for you to be throwing yourself into something so far away from so much that's taking root around you here.'

'Peta – you're pissing me off,' said Frankie. 'I juggle, I multitask. I tell you something – Ruth'll be far more encouraging about Scott than you. She'll be happy for me.'

'Have you spoken to him yet this morning?' Peta asked, deciding not to parry her sister's riposte.

'Spoken to who?' Annabel asked, coming into the kitchen to twiddle her aunt's hair again. 'Sam?'

'Not yet,' said Frankie.

An hour later, Peta waved them off and Frankie regarded her sister standing at the top of the elegant swoop of steps leading to her front door. She noted how Peta had pulled a chunky cardigan tight around herself though it wasn't cold at all. It was as if the recent influx of female energy in her house had warmed her up and now, gone, there was a chill in there.

Off they drove, Frankie and Annabel, listening to *The Archers* together though they'd heard every episode already during the week. Her daughter dozed awhile, affording Frankie time to think about how good she felt; tired and high, replete with true memories of recent days and daydreaming about what was possible. Annabel woke at Swaffham when Frankie pulled in to Waitrose.

'I wasn't asleep, you know.'

'You were snoring.'

'Girls my age do not snore. Can I stay in the car?'

'OK – I won't be long.'

'Can you buy me something yum? Something with icing?'

'I just might.'

'Oh – it's Scott. You've just got a text message – from

Scott.' Annabel waved Frankie's phone at her. 'Shall I tell you what it says?'

'That's OK,' Frankie said, aiming for nonchalance while grabbing her phone. As she left the car, she thought, why do I feel like I've been caught smoking? She wondered when she might tell her children and how would she couch it? How would she know when that time was right? How would they react? Icing. Something yummy with icing. Here you are my darlings, have this. And this and this.

In the queue, she read Scott's message over and again.

This feels good. Scott x

See – he feels just like me.

Safe flight & speed the days. Frankie x

Back with her little family in their home. She regarded Sam, in a slump of gangly limbs watching TV because he told her he needed a break before doing homework. It wasn't worth arguing about or pointing out that he'd been homework-free since yesterday. Annabel, still admiring her nails, tracing around her hand with a pencil on a blank piece of paper and scrabbling around the felt-pen pot to do some colouring-in. Both children slightly sticky from the iced buns they'd wolfed down.

Frankie looked around her home. Though there were times, still, when she felt unsettled in the house, more and more she felt comfortable here. She'd created such a home in one of her early books, then she'd worked hard and, years later, she'd been able to write it into reality. Selling up in London, putting everything she had, all the money, all the hope, into realizing a dream. How many people get to do that? So what that she couldn't afford somewhere bigger, somewhere not so isolated, somewhere in one of the picturesque and hip locations not so far away? She loved the way her house facilitated family life: the downstairs had such flow – hallway to living room, kitchen to utility room, a back door into the garden – while upstairs it felt more intimate with the bedrooms in a hug around the landing. This house epitomized the dynamic of family – whether cuddled up together or carving a little space for oneself.

Standing there though, Frankie was aware of that odd smell again, which came out of nowhere like a chill gust on a perfectly warm day. Not really textbook damp – but certainly on the spectrum. But maybe it wasn't worth stressing about and maybe she could live with the old blinds for another year. Perhaps a roll of draught excluder would be a perfectly good and quite literal stopgap until she could afford new windows. The clay-pamment tiles which floored the hallway weren't to her taste but instead of letting them irk her, perhaps she'd just buy a rug. She trailed off into a daydream of Scott being here. Welcome to our home. This is where we eat, Scott, at this table I've had for ever – I sit here, Sam here and Annabel there. Oh, don't worry about that window – it's stuck like that. The loo is through there on the left – but careful with the doorknob. The damp smell? I don't know what's causing it but it doesn't get any worse – it just is what it is. Look at our garden – next year we're planning to grow veggies but this year we're excited just to see what pops up. And beyond the garden and out over the fields, isn't it amazing how you just know the sea is out there, though you can't quite see it from here.

It made her feel happy. She really could envisage

Scott here with them all, feeling at home. Comfortable over there on the sofa. Happy and content in the mundane. What's for supper? Kids – are your school bags ready for the morning? Hey Frankie – go have a bath, I'll tidy up. Scott, can you just –?

So easy to conjure.

But he's boarding the plane. He's doing so right now. He's on his way home; he's leaving.

Aaron glanced at Scott again. His friend was gazing out of the Cessna with a beatific smile on his face but Aaron sensed this wasn't purely for heading home. At Squamish, he circled high over the mammoth domed granite monolith of Siám' Smánit – Stawamus Chief – but despite the breathtaking views of the coastal mountains and Howe Sound, Scott just kept grinning to himself, seemingly oblivious to Aaron's detour.

'You had a good time?' Aaron had already asked him this, after their trademark bear hug at Arrivals.

Scott answered him as if it was a fresh question. 'Yep.'

Yep. The same answer as before. What the fuck kind of answer is yep anyways? Aaron smiled to himself. Old dog, he thought. You old dog, Scott Emerson. They were at 10,000 feet, high over Whistler, when he next spoke.

'So what's her name?'

'Frankie.'

They continued on in affable silence until, a few minutes later, they were preparing to land at Pemberton. From up high, Scott could see his truck, gleaming, the only vehicle at the airfield. Aaron always returned it spotless after he'd borrowed it. Scott almost waved at it before silently calling himself an ass. He looked at his watch. It was three in the morning in the UK. He hadn't slept on the plane, he hadn't been able to concentrate on any of the in-flight entertainment. Stupendously hungry, however, he had eaten anything and everything on offer. Throughout the flight, melodies and lyrics had lurched around his brain like sudden turbulence; hard to steady and contain. Now, standing on the grass by the runway with his luggage beside him, the drifts of music came flooding through again. He was home, back at the heart of all he knew and all that he was. Emotions collided and he took lungfuls of air to steady himself. Gazing at Gravel Peak to his left, its staggered peaks like the armoured spine of a slumbering dinosaur so familiar to him, Scott asked himself now that I am here, was I really ever there?

He climbed into his truck, started the engine and made to drive off.

'*Tay!*' Aaron shouted, hammering on the door. 'What the fuck, man!'

Scott had forgotten him.

Aaron jumped in beside him, muttering '*Xet*' under his breath.

'What did you just call me?' Scott asked.

'Skunk cabbage,' said Aaron.

Scott drove the 17 km home hardly noticing the route or that Aaron was talking about something or other that had happened. Out beyond the Líĺwat reservation at Mount Currie and on to the D'Arcy road all the way home. In Scott's driveway, Aaron's clapped-out truck, dusty and dented. At the living-room window, paws on the sill, Buddy.

'Thanks pal,' Scott said, unloading his bags. 'Thanks

for meeting me in – again. For taking care of Buddy. Cleaning the truck.'

'Are you kidding?' said Aaron. He was looking at Scott quizzically.

'Oh – you want to come in?'

'Are you kidding?' Aaron laughed heartily. 'Of course I'm coming in. I'm coming in, we're having a beer, you're talking about Frankie and I'm listening.'

While Scott took his bags upstairs and unpacked, shadowed in everything he did by a delighted Buddy, Aaron stepped out onto the back porch and called his wife. He knew he needn't have whispered – the immense cedar logs from which Scott's house was constructed gave ample soundproofing. Scott, Aaron realized, hadn't slept on the plane, he was jet-lagged – and quite obviously in the thrall of this freak and unexpected situation of some chick in his life making him gurn and grin like a baby with wind.

When Rose heard the words *couple of beers* she was ready to fume – like Aaron hadn't been gone most of the day already. But when her husband backed it up with *Scott's met a girl and he's smiling*, Rose's indignation was replaced with curiosity. Her barrage of questions, however, was met with *I don't know, I couldn't say, I'm not sure* from her husband.

'What *did* he say?'

'That her name is Frankie.'

'And that's it? Scott's got himself a sweetheart – *ńeńxwa7* – and all you know is she's called Frank?'

'Frankie,' said Aaron. 'And yes, so far – that's it.'

'So you better drink your beer and find out more. But just a couple Aaron – and then you're home.'

'You kiss Tara and Johnny for me.'

'You kiss them yourself when you're back.'

Rose hung up and she thought, Scott – well well well well well.

Everything familiar, as he left it and as it should be. All his senses had been given a welcome home. The scents inside the house usually unnoticed now vivid; old woodsmoke, leather sofa, overripe apples he'd forgotten to throw before he left. The whir of his fridge which generally he didn't hear now curiously audible. From every window, the view; startling even in the dusk; confrontational almost – as if to say, did you forget how immense and beautiful is the land in which you live? Buddy watched him, followed him, nudged his hand. Did you miss me, pal?

Scott changed into track pants and an old sweatshirt and came barefoot onto the porch, the sun-warmed boards under his feet while whispers of the coming night air trickled over the top of them. The sounds and smells of land and river and mountain, of cedar and fir, earth and grass, of the creatures that lived around and above.

'*Míxalh*,' Aaron said quietly. Scott followed his nod and located the black bear and they watched him lumbering peaceably just at the edge of his garden.

'He's a little guy.'

'He is.'

They observed the bear until he'd ambled out of sight, then they chinked bottles and sat in the two Adirondak chairs, absent-mindedly picking at the flaking paint. Dusk was coming in quickly now, drapes and furls of darkness running like a silent river over everything, making outlines blur and volume diminish.

'So her name is Frankie.' Aaron gave great gravitas to the information. In his mind's eye, he saw a woman tall as Scott, with yellow hair long and wavy, blue eyes and all dressed up nice. A handbag and high heels. When Scott passed his phone with photos to scroll through, Aaron was tickled by how wrong he'd been. Rose also would guess at a tall girl with the polite clothes and the long wavy yellow hair – that's what she'd want to hear, like she knew what was best for Scott. She's just a regular-looking girl, Aaron would have to tell Rose. She's not big or too little, she's not skinny or fat. She wears jeans. She wears dresses. She has brown hair and eyes to match and her face is happy.

'Yes,' said Scott. 'Her name is Frankie.'

'And what is Frankie like, then?'

'Well, she seems a little shy until she laughs.'

Aaron considered this. 'She made you laugh too?'

Scott nodded. 'A lot.'

'Did you sleep with her?'

Scott nodded again.

'What's there to love?'

Aaron's bluntness didn't offend Scott.

'I felt *something*,' Scott shrugged. 'Something new. Attraction – a deeper connection. I like how she looks, I like the history she's had and the life she's living now. I like who she is.'

Rose will really like to hear this, Aaron thought. And then he thought Scott needs this after all this time.

'You told your Jenna?'

'Not yet.' Just then Scott longed to see his daughter, his baby girl. He hadn't even phoned to say he was home. 'Jenna said she saw you – Buddy riding up front – windows down and music up,' he said while he texted his daughter. 'Only she couldn't tell whether it was Springsteen or Bryan Adams.'

Aaron laughed. 'It was Pearl Jam.'

Scott shook his head with fond exasperation at his daughter.

'Why do you have to find the girl over there? In England?' Aaron had his own exasperation and he whistled it at Scott, long and slow.

'I didn't go looking,' Scott shrugged.

'If you'd looked a little harder, you could have found a girl right here,' said Aaron. 'Years ago. So how did you find this one, then?'

'I was a little lost.'

'You're the least lost guy I know.'

As Aaron drove home, he thought about all Scott had told him, he considered his expressions and his tone of voice – the playfulness and the passion, the sense of calm and happiness. Aaron thought to himself that's that, Scott, that's that. He went through and kissed his sleeping children, then he sat with his wife out back.

'That's that, Rose,' he told her. 'It's Scott and Frankie – and that's that.'

Scott tolerated Whistler village the way he might a producer whose work he respected but whose personality he didn't much care for. These days, Scott just didn't like busy and whatever the season, Whistler was always busy. However, catching sight of his daughter, watching her attend to a table of diners while he stood just out of her view, settled him. If the place was good for her, then he was OK with it. Jenna's demeanour never changed – whether hanging just with her pa or a couple of friends, or at the beck and call of a crowd of fussy-eating strangers, she was the girl who blended calm with lively, always open and giving, smiling always smiling. That's why she made such good tips as a waitress. That's why her friends loved her. That's why she was Scott's best girl. And that's why she'd be so popular at UBC when she started university in Vancouver in the fall. That's why he loved her so, worried about her so – anyone hurts my little girl I'll fucking kill them.

Jenna caught sight of her father and waved for him to come in, insisted he sat down and had something to eat, bounded into the kitchen and told the short-order chef hey! my pop's here – can you do him something special? She knew when he was working he could forget to eat only to snack on stupid stuff at odd hours.

She planned to cook for them tonight, make extra and put it in the freezer for him.

'So how was England?'

Scott ate another few forkfuls of food, chewing thoughtfully. 'Oh,' he said. 'You know.'

'Does the score sound amazing?'

'It's sounding pretty good. Paul Broucek was there. He says hi.'

Suddenly, Scott remembered Jenna when she was little, coming down at night in her PJs to find him at the piano, how she'd clamber onto his lap, cosy between his arms while he worked. She'd fall asleep and he'd carry her up to bed. He'd work on into the small hours and she'd wake him in the morning. School – you have to take me to school, Dad! And she'd make him toast and feed the dog and get her bags ready, all the while humming, note for note, what he'd been working on the night before.

'Jenna,' he said. 'While I was away –'

She rolled her eyes. 'Dad – stop worrying – nothing happened. I was fine. I swear.'

He didn't mean that, he wasn't referring to her. For the first time in twenty years, another girl had snuck in front of Jenna.

On the way home, they stopped in Pemberton and took Buddy for a walk along the Ryan river then mooched back into the village for iced coffee, happy to chat to various people many of whom said Scott! where you *been*? Jenna! they said, your old pa's becoming a hermit these days. While Jenna shopped for food, Scott sat outside. Mount Currie sedate and awe-inspiring in front of him while next to him a hobo pushed a shopping cart half-filled with scavenged aluminum cans. He gave the guy five bucks and wished him well. The yin and yang of where he lived. Over the road, mountain bikers emerged from the Blackbird Bakery before taking to the hills and a couple of school kids assumed they were having an illicit cigarette unseen. A horse and rider clopped past, a delivery truck clanged to a standstill outside the pharmacy.

'Yoo hoo!' Valerie Megeney waved and came over. 'Hey stranger – how's it going with Jonah and the band?'

'They're pretty good, you know.'

'Will we hear them any time soon?'

'If they work on their songs, I've promised them a spot at the Pony perhaps next month.'

'And how's Jenna doing?'

'She's over there – in the store. She's doing OK – you know – but no change really. She has the usual tests in a couple of weeks – we have our meeting with her consultant.'

'I was reading about a new operation they can do – I have it at home. I'll send it to you.'

'Thank you.' He'd read the piece already, of course. It was unlikely to be appropriate for Jenna's type of epilepsy but he accepted the information graciously. There was a lot of love in the village for Jenna and a ready support network for him, should he choose to take it.

'Well, it's great to see you – say hi from me to Aaron and Rose when you see them.'

As they drove home, Jenna turned to her father and patted his face.

'You're going to turn into Grizzly Adams,' she laughed. 'And I don't mean *this*,' she emphasized, stroking his beard. 'You mustn't become too *self-sufficient* in your old age, Pa.'

Scott glanced at her. 'Can you let me worry about you – not the other way around, honey? That kind of role reversal – it's the first sign of old age.'

Jenna made soup for dinner. Just as they sat down, a picture message came through from Frankie; a blurred selfie of her holding up an ice cream that looked like shaving foam with what Scott assumed to be a chocolate stick tucked into one side. It made him laugh.

'What's so funny?'

Scott looked at his phone, looked hard at Frankie, looked over to Jenna and thought to himself do you want to meet my girl?

'What?' Jenna laughed. 'You OK, Dad?'

'Huh?'

'You're looking at me funny.'

'Oh.'

'You OK?'

'Sure – you OK?'

She frowned. 'Yes?'

'You fed Buddy?' he asked.

'Yes.'

'He's been out?'

'Yes! How's the soup – I put three more portions in the freezer for you.'

'When I was in England –'

And Jenna simply thought that some anecdote about British soup was coming. That it was served lukewarm like their beer. Or eaten in bowls carved from Stonehenge or something like that. But her father had stopped mid-sentence and, when she glanced over at him, he was looking at her unflinchingly.

'So, Jenna, when I was in England – I met someone.'

Jenna stared and stared at the photograph of Frankie with the ice cream.

'If you scroll through, there are some more,' Scott said, eyes fixed on his daughter's response as she scrolled very slowly backwards, forwards, backwards, forwards through the last week of his life. Scott picked up on an emotion that was curiosity mixed with disbelief.

Finally, she met his gaze. She blinked, a lot.

'Wow,' she said. 'Just *wow*, Dad.' She thought, this is *weird*. This is crazy! 'I don't know what to say.' She shook her head, laughed, frowned. She looked from Frankie on the phone, to her father sitting there opposite her.

What the hey – perhaps this is not so crazy!

'I'm so happy for you,' Jenna said. 'I'm just so happy for you.'

* * *

It felt to Frankie that she was now inhabiting three different worlds. Home. Alice. Scott. It was as if these three components that defined her were unanchored pontoons, sometimes floating close to each other, at other times precariously distant in the suddenly fast-flowing waters of her life. Sometimes she felt utterly grounded, sometimes thoroughly adrift. She wasn't getting much done.

They wrote to each other daily; lengthy emails sharing secrets and intimacy as well as just chatty prose outlining their day-to-day. They attached photographs detailing everything about their lives now and then – from their children growing up, to corners of their rooms, the views outside, current selfies and old pictures, anecdotes, memories and news, that filled in all the gaps of their histories and, somehow, enabled each to feel part of the other's past.

'Look what we're having for supper,' Frankie emailed one picture. 'Fish 'n' chips – the "a" and the "d" are always silent.'

'Why are you photographing our food?' Sam wanted to know.

'It's not like you cooked it yourself,' said Annabel.

'My friend wanted to see,' said Frankie.

'Your friend is weird,' Sam said under his breath.

Regardless of the time zones, despite Scott's unpredictable mobile signal and Frankie's ineptitude when it came to digital communication (forgetting to attach photos, thinking she was leaving voicemails when she wasn't, simply not pressing send on an email) their contact was regular and easy and defiant of the miles separating them.

But talking to Scott by phone when it was his morning, her evening, or his yesterday while she was already in tomorrow, suspended reality. It was like time travel in some ways, somewhere without borders where they could meet and privately pick up from where they'd left off. Their conversations were unstilted, whether searching and involved or lightweight and mundane. They chatted as easily as if they were sitting knee against knee in Maison Bertaux, tucking into the details as though they were gateaux. They exuded tenderness as intense as if they were lying in each other's arms replete from lovemaking. Their calls took them to the still point in their turning worlds whilst they spoke, but the echo of each other's voice afterwards was unsettling. FaceTime too alternately brought them within an inch of each other and yet amplified the distance between them. Frankie and Scott never quite knew whether it was to be praised or cursed. A moment ago we were together but now I'm alone.

Frankie's children noticed a change in their mother's mood – it was excellent most of the time, amusingly distracted some of the time and, just occasionally, downright bad. She appeared to moan less about Alice, or their homework, or time spent by Sam faffing on his phone or by Annabel not doing her recorder practice. They noted, with delight, how she seemed to have forgotten to question TV time – in fact, some evenings she actively encouraged it.

'Just going to make a phone call,' Frankie might say. 'Why don't you two chill out with some back-to-back *Futurama*?'

Frankie had promised the children toad-in-the-hole for supper. Which wasn't going to be easy with no eggs or sausages in the house so, with strict instructions not to even look at the remote control let alone turn the TV on until all homework was done, she left Sam and Annabel in the house and drove to Howell's in Binham.

'I don't have much homework,' Annabel told Sam. 'Just art. I have to draw a self-portrait but I do that all the time anyway so I'm just going to stick one of those in my book.'

'I have German revision – but anyway, we have the whole weekend to do homework. Mum seems to have forgotten it's Friday.'

'So therefore we don't have any homework to do – right now?'

'I guess not.'

'So therefore, we can watch TV?'

'I guess so,' said Sam, surfing channels. '*South Park*!'

'But Mummy says –'

'Only if Mummy finds out,' said Sam.

'Just phone her, though – and see how far away she is. So we have time to switch off and pretend.'

Sam dialled Frankie's number. And over on the kitchen table, her phone rang.

'She forgot to take her phone!' said Annabel.

'Duh!' said Sam. 'Don't worry, we'll just keep the volume down.' Out of all the programmes at their disposal, *South Park* and *Family Guy* were contraband.

Frankie's phone rang out again.

'Who's that?' said Annabel, imagining the TV Police somehow tracking them down.

'That's not a call, that's FaceTime,' said Sam, a little confused. He left the sofa and walked over to the kitchen table. He looked at the screen very intently until all was quiet.

'Who was it?' Annabel wanted to know.

A moment later the same FaceTime alert trilled through again.

'Annabel,' said Sam. 'Come here.'

'Who *is* it?' Annabel asked.

'I don't know,' he said, 'but I think it's why Mum's been acting – weird.'

Annabel came over and peered at her mother's phone. 'Who's *he*?'

She read out loud: *Scott would like to FaceTime*. 'Oh – I think he's the *work* man she had to see in London last week.'

'Only one way to find out,' said Sam, accepting the call.

It was midday and Scott had just returned from taking Jenna back to Whistler. She'd given him a long hug, told him perhaps they'd go to the farmer's market on Sunday, and then off she went, looking over her shoulder and waving, giving him a wink and a grin. Dad's got a girlfriend? No *way*! Crazy weird!

He'd heated up the soup she'd made and thought how right she was; lunch was a good idea and his daughter's soup was excellent. He thought, I'll share this soup with Frankie – it's around her dinner time over there.

'Zucchini and dill!' he said as soon as the call connected.

But two young faces came into view, staring at him so unflinchingly he wondered whether the connection had stalled.

No, they were live. All of them.

'Hi,' he said, putting down his soup bowl.

They didn't reply.

He took a spoonful of soup and peered in very close so that his face was huge, then sat back again and gave them a little wave. 'Hi,' he said again.

Still nothing.

Did Frankie know?

'Is your mom home?'

'She's at the shops,' said Annabel. 'She forgot her phone.'

Scott nodded. This was – odd. He showed them the soup. 'Zucchini and dill. I'm having a bowl of soup for my lunch,' he said.

'It's supper,' said Annabel.

'Not here it isn't,' he said.

'Where's here?' Sam asked suspiciously, taking the phone from Annabel.

'Well – I'm in Canada.'

Scott heard Annabel repeat Canada in the background and watched Frankie's home shake as she jostled her brother for the phone. There they were again, the two of them, watching him eat. Scott took another spoonful, buying time to think what to do next. So he ate and they watched and every now and then, he nodded at them while they glanced at each other.

'So,' he said. 'My name is Scott. I know there's a Sam and an Annabel – you want to tell me who's who?'

Annabel giggled but Scott could clearly see that Sam thought him a bit of a jerk.

'I'm Annabel.'

'Oh,' said Scott as if the penny had only then dropped. 'So your mom's gone to the stores?'

'She's gone out because she forgot eggs and we can't have toad-in-the-hole without eggs,' said Annabel.

Scott had no idea what that was. Did the kid just say *towed*? It can't be toad, surely? I mean, OK, the French with their frog's legs, but he'd never heard of the British with their toads eaten whole. He was about to tell them that he'd licked a toad once, when he was at college, but then they'd ask why and he'd have to say for the trip and they'd ask what kind of a trip and he really wasn't going to start explaining about the weirder hallucinogens in life. So they all just sat quietly, looking at each other. Scott thought how Sam looked more like Frankie than Annabel did – but that Annabel had her mother's mannerisms – tipping her head when she listened and talking with dancing eyes, which glinted and darkened.

'Is that *South Park* I can hear in the background?' Scott laughed.

The children looked at each other, alarmed; looked at Scott, guiltily.

'Did my mum come and see you in London?' Annabel suddenly spoke up. 'When I stayed with Auntie Peta and had my nails done and watched *Pitch Perfect*?'

Where was this going? 'Yes,' said Scott, 'she did.' Did the children know? Frankie hadn't mentioned anything. 'I had to fly home the next day.'

'Oh.'

Still, Sam was not saying anything.

'You were at a cricket match – right, Sam?' said Scott. He watched Sam give a reluctant nod and then whisper something to Annabel.

'Don't be stupid,' Annabel told her brother, giving him a shove. 'Don't say that.'

'Ask him,' Sam challenged his sister.

Ask me what, Scott wondered.

'Mum's coming back!' Annabel suddenly exclaimed. 'We have to go! Sam – switch him off!' And Annabel disappeared from view.

Sam and Scott looked at each other a moment longer.

'Well – it's nice to meet you Sam,' Scott said. 'You look after your sister. You look after your mom.'

'I do,' said Sam and he cancelled the call. 'Don't tell Mum,' he said to his sister. 'I mean it.'

They ate an entire tray of toad-in-the-hole between them and polished off a tub of chocolate ice cream for pudding. Later, when the children were showered and ready for bed, Frankie encouraged them to watch even more TV, justifying what she called 'any old dross just to rest your brains'. She wanted a little uninterrupted time with Scott. She took her phone upstairs

149

to her bedroom, sat on her old loom chair which was sandwiched between the wardrobe and the chest of drawers.

Scott was expecting her call. God knows what they'd said to her, the kids. Your soup-eating Canadian boyfriend has never eaten toad – can you believe that?

'Hey,' said Frankie.

'Hey,' said Scott. In an instant, he knew the children had said nothing and he knew it wasn't his place to say anything either.

'Hello,' she said and she laughed. 'Are you having a lovely day? We've just had supper. Toad-in-the-hole.'

'What the *fuck*?'

'It's sausages,' Frankie explained, 'plonked in a tray with a sort of batter that puffs up.' She paused. 'You don't look convinced.'

'Tell you what – if I try your toad, you can try our *poutine*.'

'What's that?'

'So – it's French fries.'

'I love chips –'

'And you slather them in gravy.' Scott laughed. 'And cover it all in cheese curds. We also eat beaver tails.'

'You *what*?'

'My favourite is spread with chocolate hazelnut and chopped banana.'

'That's barbaric!'

'It's a pastry, Frankie. Fried – you'd love it.'

'I would?'

'I know you would.'

'This time last week,' said Frankie, softly.

'Only a week ago?'

'And here we are.'
'Pretty cool, hey?'

The downside of a long phone call was the subsequent knot of emotions binding buoyancy with aloneness which took time to carefully untwine. Frankie looked around her room blankly. She remembered back to nine months ago, how hard she'd worked at making everything just so before the children spent their first night there. Pictures up, beds made, favourite possessions placed perfectly, clothes put away, wellies lined up by the back door, familiar furniture in place, the TV tuned, the Wii set up, candles lit, central heating on and supper all prepared. Home. Welcome home, kids, we're going to be so happy here.

Now, today, this man who'd flipped her heart was sitting down to an afternoon's work while she was having thoughts of a bath and then bed. She looked around her bedroom – at the painting on the wall, the scatter cushions and the reed diffuser, the photos of smiling Frankie and her beautiful offspring at various stages of their lives. She regarded the black hammered-iron light switch she'd spent a fortune on, the skirting boards Farrow & Ball-ed to perfection and she thought, I wish I wasn't here. She closed the curtains on a darkening sky which curved over the land like the ceiling of a planetarium.

n bed the next morning, Frankie thought of Alice to whom she'd given so little time these last few days and she knew it wasn't all down to the maddening impasse she'd suffered with her writing. Gazing out of windows had been devoted to Scott, not the new book, and emailing had been exclusively to Scott, not her editor. It struck her too that time she should have spent with her children, helping with homework or just hanging out together the way they'd usually do, had been given to sneaking off to phone or FaceTime Scott. She understood how Sam and Annabel would always have mixed feelings about Alice, but Scott? They couldn't fail to love him, and him them. Really, it was time to tell them about him but she wasn't quite sure how she'd do that.

'Brancaster or Holkham?' Frankie asked the children. The sky was cloudless.

'Why are you so obsessed with us having fresh air?' said Annabel.

'Because!' said Frankie. 'Now – Brancaster or Holkham?'

'Brancaster,' said Annabel.

'Holkham,' said Sam.

'That's helpful,' said Frankie.

She looked from Sam to Annabel. They were in a silent tug of war on opposite sides of the kitchen table and neither was going to let go.

'OK,' she said, 'the Jolly for lunch – or the Victoria?'

'The Jolly.'

'Victoria.'

What Frankie really wanted to do was say right! We're not going anywhere then! But she yearned for the beach and so she tried a different tack.

'Heads,' she said. 'Or tails.'

'Heads,' said Sam.

'Tails,' said Annabel.

This certainly made things a little easier.

'Tails it is,' Frankie said, uncovering the flipped coin from her hand. 'Brancaster, then.'

'We could go to the Victoria for lunch,' Annabel told her brother with a sweet diplomacy.

'It's fine,' said Sam, as if the world was against him.

'You like the pizza at the Jolly,' Annabel reminded him.

'It's *fine*!' said Sam. 'God!'

'Sam –' Frankie spoke in her warning tone.

'What,' he mumbled. '*God*.'

He stomped away and Annabel told her mother, don't worry, he's just being teenagerish. But I do worry, thought Frankie, I do.

Sam unwound as soon as they were out of the car and the salty air whipped over the dune and encircled him, luring him towards the sea with a smile on his face. Annabel scampered off to see just how far out the tide was and Sam walked alongside his mother.

'Sorry,' he mumbled. 'About before.'

153

'It's not a problem,' Frankie said, linking arms. 'I'm sorry if I was stroppy last night. I just have stuff on my mind.'

Sam shrugged it off and, while doing so, surreptitiously wriggled free from his mother. Frankie was used to it. Sometimes, Sam let her hold his hand until he suddenly realized what she was doing and how old he actually was and then dropped it as though it was a leper's. But he usually made amends without making a fuss. A hug in the privacy of the house, or taking her hand and placing it on his head for a hair-ruffle while they watched television, or his arms suddenly around her neck when he was sleepy in bed and she came in to kiss him goodnight. Just now, he extricated his arm from hers as if running to catch up with Annabel was the main reason. Frankie watched them scamper, heard them jabbering, grinned as they came running and skipping back to her. A fighter jet tore across the sky, long gone from view by the time its sound caught up. The jets had unnerved her when they'd first arrived in Norfolk; now she saw them as an exciting part of the sky, never knowing when they'd come, never quite knowing where to look to locate them as they went roaring past.

'Are they just practising?' Annabel asked, worried.

'Yes,' Frankie laughed.

Brancaster was not as breathtaking as Holkham in so much as the beach wasn't reached after a magical walk through pines and dunes, but the sand was just as soft, the light just as extraordinary, the sea just as far or near depending on the tide. Often, a little less crowded too.

'Can I take my socks off?' Annabel asked having

done so already, her feet scrunched into the sand as if she was toeless.

'Where are they? Where are your trainers?'

'There!' she pointed blithely at nowhere in particular.

'I'd better take mine off too, then,' said Sam, hopping about as he divested his feet of shoes and socks.

'Am I carrying these?' Frankie called after him.

'You're the mum,' he laughed over his shoulder as he belted for the shore. 'It's your job!'

She found Annabel's a little way along and sunk herself down onto the sand with only her children's shoes for company. I have a boyfriend, she told them, and his name is Scott. He's important to me and I think you'll really like each other. Jesus Christ I'm talking to shoes.

Sam and Annabel flopped down beside her a little while later, asking after snacks and towels and cans of Coke when it was quite obvious that their mother, in only a T-shirt and jeans, had none.

'Come on,' she told them, 'let's walk on to where the beach curves and then we'll have an early lunch at the Jolly. Or the Victoria. I don't mind – you choose.'

'I'm cool with the Jolly,' Sam said and started chanting *the jolly sailors the jolly sailors* tunelessly as he strolled ahead, kicking sand.

With her son's shoes in one hand, her daughter's in the other, Frankie listened contentedly to Sam singing and Annabel rabbiting on about something very involved about Harry and Hermione until she realized which Harry and which Hermione and then she joined in. Annabel loved it that her mother knew the Harry Potter books so well. And she loved that, although her brother had read them some time ago, it was a topic he was still happy to join in with.

'You would have thought you'd have met JK by now,' Annabel sighed. 'With you doing the same job.'

'Hardly the same job,' said Sam. 'Mum's not a gazillionaire.'

'I did meet Jay Kay once,' Frankie told them, 'but a different JK. He was the singer in a band called Jamiroquai who wore funky hats.'

This barely registered on her children's scale of cool.

'And – also – I know someone who writes the music for films. For the movies.'

Had they heard her?

She filled her lungs with salty air. Should she repeat it? Elaborate?

'Can we have a dog?' Annabel asked, looking wistfully at the motley assortment gambolling about on the beach.

Frankie looked around. Various breeds were bounding about but her attention was drawn to a brown Labrador having a good roll in the sand.

'My friend has a dog called Buddy,' she told her children. 'The same friend who writes music for films.'

'Dogs make walks feel – not so boring,' said Annabel. 'That's why we should get one. I'd *never* moan about going for a walk if there was *a dog*.'

'With or without a dog, this beach is an optical illusion,' said Sam. 'You think the end of the curve is so much nearer – then it all straightens out and there it is again, ages away.'

Frankie bopped his bum gently with his shoes. 'So, kids – I wanted to talk to you about something.'

She didn't see her children glancing at each other; she was looking intently at the beach as she walked, believing there to be as many words to choose from

as there were pips of shale and grains of sand underfoot. I've met . . . There's this chap . . . You know
how I've been on my own for a while . . . So, guess
what . . .

'Frankie? Frankie!'

Just ahead and walking towards her, waving and
calling, was Ruth with her two children, husband and
two black Labradors. Scott, Frankie realized with both
disappointment and relief, would have to remain out
of sight.

A day for new friends. It was a table for seven that
they nabbed at the Jolly Sailors a little later. Ruth's
children were in awe of Frankie's who appeared to
relish being regarded as supercool. Frankie was flattered
to find Peter knew so much about her from Ruth.

'Any news?' Ruth said quietly when the kids were
utterly focused on pizza.

'Lots,' Frankie told her. 'Twice, maybe three times a
day.'

She passed Ruth her phone so she could see the
photos.

'Miss him?'

'Desperately.'

'Happy?'

'Very. But fantastically frustrated.'

'You need to plan, Frankie. You need to plan The
Next Time.'

'How do I do that?'

'You look at your diary and he looks at his and you
make the effort.'

'It's not like midway between us is somewhere like
London or even bloody Baldock.' She looked at Ruth
and started giggling. 'Actually, I've already checked. It's

somewhere called Pangnirtung. And the bizarre thing is – it's in Canada.'

Ruth considered this. 'I guess you can hardly nip there and back in time for the school run. I had no idea Canada was so vast.'

'Huge,' said Frankie. 'British Columbia alone is four times the size of Great Britain. And he lives right over that side.' She gestured to her left and Ruth laughed and said what? in the Jolly's car park?

'We'll get you there,' Ruth said. 'Let's do wine one evening. See if there's a short cut?'

'I'd love that. I still don't know local babysitters though.'

'I do.'

'Am I seeing you on Tuesday morning? For an Alexander session?'

'Definitely,' said Ruth. 'And let's do Thursday evening when we don't have to watch what we say.' She motioned to the children, to her husband and she winked at Frankie.

I like you, thought Frankie. I really do.

Driving back home, Frankie's children agreed that Brancaster had been a good plan and that lunch had been so amazing they could have eaten it all over again.

'Isn't Ruth lovely?' Frankie enthused. 'We're going out one evening. Probably Thursday.'

'I heard,' said Annabel. 'For wine.'

'That's OK, though, isn't it?' said Frankie.

'Is Ruth the friend, then?' asked Annabel.

'She is my friend, yes.'

'*The* friend,' said Annabel.

'The *friend*,' said Sam.

Frankie glanced at them in the rear-view mirror.

'The one you were talking about on the beach in your Important Voice,' said Annabel and Frankie saw her daughter glance at Sam.

'The friend that writes music for movies,' said Sam, though he knew that Ruth taught something like Alexander's Yoga.

'With the dog – called Buddy,' Annabel chipped in, though she knew the Ingrams' dogs were Bessie and Alfie.

The lane ahead twisted as though it kept changing its mind which way to go and the hedges were banked so high to either side they threatened to converge overhead. One needed to concentrate on a road like this, which could narrow to a single lane as suddenly as it could turn sharply with no warning. It was one of the reasons Frankie's mother said she really didn't like Norfolk. *It's not like the Cotswolds*, she'd told Frankie. *It's not like the Cotswolds at all. It can be quite oppressive. You can't see where you're going.*

What was this obsession her mother had with the chuffing Cotswolds?

'Mummy?'

Frankie realized she was deviating her thoughts to buy time not to answer her children.

But not here, not now. This wasn't how she'd planned it. This wasn't the right place at all. She'd wanted to tell them while they walked on the beach; if it wasn't to be there, now she was envisaging the kitchen table, always a conducive location for their heart-to-hearts. She wanted to be able to look at them intently, to gauge their reaction, to sit and talk and tell them all about Scott and answer all their questions.

This road was not built for that; it could be potentially hazardous.

'No – that's not Ruth,' Frankie told them. 'She's the one who teaches Alexander.'

'Who's Alexander?' asked Annabel. 'She has the most amazing hair. Not even the wind or her sticky little girl could mess it up. It's called a bob. Let's call her Bob.'

'So if Ruth doesn't do the film music – who does?' Sam asked.

OK, thought Frankie. OK.

There was a lay-by approaching. Indicating – though no other car was anywhere to be seen – Frankie slowed right down and pulled in. By the time she realized how uncomfortable her seat belt was, with her twisting to face the children seated in the back of the car, it was too disruptive to unclip it.

'Well,' she said and then paused. 'Kids,' she said, looking from one to the other. 'I made a friend, you see.' She scrabbled around her mind for the next sentence the way she might rummage in her bag for her keys. She tried again. 'You know that I've been on my own for a while –'

'Single Mum,' said Annabel, knowingly.

'Yes, that's right,' said Frankie. 'Well, it's important that you know that it's not like I haven't been happy. I have – you two and me, we're a team and it's the best thing in my life. Only, without warning, without looking, I met someone – a man – who I felt.'

The children stared at her blankly. Frankie thought, I can't leave them with the fact that I felt a man.

'A man who I *feel* – a. Lot. For. For whom I feel a lot. And who feels the same way about me.'

The children regarded her unflinchingly, silently, expressions neutral.

'We met and really like each other – and we have things in common as well as unique qualities which just seem – to complement – each other.'

Still there was no response from the back row. Not even a widening of the eyes or a smirk.

'And he's been on his own for a while too. And sometimes, you have this situation where grown-ups who are strangers, who never knew the other person even existed, who never thought any of it was possible – well, as luck would have it, they meet. And they experience this really strong connection. And even though he lives in Canada and we don't – we live in Norfolk of course – and even though the world is a huge place – Canada is vast, massive – and he was happy enough and I was happy enough – still, somehow, we managed to meet and feel that special, unexpected – *connection*. So that's what I mean. That's who my friend is. That's why he's so special – as a person. And that, children, is what makes him so significant to me. And anyway his name,' said Frankie. 'Is Scott.'

Both children thought immediately that Scott was the reason they were watching so much TV these days and for that, they liked him enough already. They looked at their mother very intently. They thought, really for an author she doesn't half get her words in a jumble. There was a redness dashing up her throat in a mottled path, as if what she felt inside was being expressed on the outside. Her eyes were going this way and that, as if there was so much more to see when you had a special connection with someone significant who lived in Canada, and she kept licking her bottom lip and then her top lip in turn as if there was a fantastic taste to her words.

'So what you're trying to say is that Scott is your boyfriend,' said Annabel.

Frankie didn't know whether to laugh or cry, whether her children were waiting for an affirmative or negative. Just the truth, she told herself, nothing beats the truth.

'Yes,' she said, 'he is.'

They were in a snuggle that evening, the three of them, watching *Monsters, Inc.*, their go-to film when they couldn't agree on what to watch. When it was over and the popcorn was finished and even the non-popped kernels had been masticated and were stuck in their molars and down the side of the sofa, Frankie had an idea.

'Hang on,' she told her children and she disappeared.

'Hang on,' she told Scott when her FaceTime connected.

She was grinning at him as she made her way through her home and he tried to catch the details as she walked him by. Photographs on walls, stripped wooden doors, an old-fashioned dresser heaving with books and bowls and an assortment of pretty china, sudden skeins of evening light blanching her features.

Switch off the telly, he heard her say. *Kids – switch it off!*

Then there was a fuzzed darkness which Scott realized was her phone attempting to focus on her jeans and, when the images came into view again, there she was, sitting between her children.

'It's Scott,' he could see her saying quietly to them. 'This is Scott. I thought you'd like to see him. I think he wants to say hello.'

Everyone stared at the phone in front of them.

'Scott! May I present Annabel and Sam!'

The children looked at Scott and Scott looked at the children and, for a moment, they each wondered who'd say what next.

'Hey.' Scott spoke first.

'I'm Annabel,' said Annabel.

'I'm Sam,' said Sam.

'This is Buddy,' said Scott. 'Oh – so he's a little shy right now. See – there he goes.'

There was an awkward pause as everyone focused on the brown Lab in a slump doing absolutely nothing.

Don't say about before. Don't tell her about *South Park*.

Of course I won't, kids, of course I won't.

'So one day I hope to meet you guys,' Scott said.

Annabel looked at her mother eagerly.

Sam, however, stared at a point just over Scott's shoulder, skilfully avoiding eye contact without actually appearing rude.

'Hey Buddy.'

Scott took a moment before replying. It always amused him when he answered the phone and someone said Hey Buddy. He wanted to say, oh this isn't Buddy, it's Scott – but I can fetch him for you if you like.

Today, it was Dave, his agent.

'Good time to talk?'

'Sure.'

'You well? Jenna?

'I'm doing great. And Jenna – little blip, but she's good right now. How are you?'

'Good. So there's this movie – Reardon's just come on board after Morrison pulled out. It's – fuck – romance slash comedy slash family drama. Think *Steel Magnolias* meets *This is 40*, for fuck's sake. It's a mess right now but the money's there. And it's something a little different for you. They're over in Europe right now but I said no way would you go to Paris so we'll set up a conference call, Skype, fucking smoke signals, instead. They love your work.'

A tangle of thoughts wove through Scott's mind fast, twisting around themselves and sending out shoots like rampant brambles. On the one side, there was Jenna, on the other side Frankie and there, sitting resolutely on the fence, Scott himself. Jenna had said she felt queer last week and had taken a day off work. She was fine – he'd been to see her and they were seeing her specialist tomorrow. But still.

And Frankie last night – whispering to him that she was lying in her bed thinking of him, longing for him. Saying I wish you were here. I wish you weren't so far away.

He'd been back home almost three weeks.

'I can do Paris,' Scott told his agent.

'Listen, I'm pretty sure you have it in the bag. Don't stress about travelling.'

'It's OK – I can do it.'

'You don't have to sell yourself, you know? They've bought in already.'

'Sure I'm sure,' said Scott and he turned away from the framed photograph of Jenna with Buddy.

'Send over the script.'

He went for a long walk with Buddy that afternoon, filling his lungs as he tried to empty his head. Since he'd been back, whenever he'd seen Jenna, she'd asked after Frankie, asked about her. When is she coming here? Jenna wanted to know. When do I get to meet her, Pops? What's she like?

'Frankie out here,' Scott said quietly. He could so clearly envisage her right by his side, right this second, trying to talk and walk at his pace, marvelling a little breathlessly at the expansive views. She'd say, wow – it's beautiful. She'd say, we don't have mountains like this in the UK – we hardly have hills in Norfolk. She'd never have seen cottonwood, or an ice field, or the Lillooet or wild blue lupins. She won't have had a double double from Tim Horton's, a cinnamon bun from the Blackbird Bakery. He wanted her to see Joffre Lakes, perhaps even a bear or two. And Aaron. And Jenna. Valerie. The Sturdys.

He sat down at the base of a cedar, the scent of the tree familiar and comforting, the shade welcome. Summer, when it came, was going to be really hot. Buddy was panting – when Scott's mind was full, he walked fast. He put his hand on the dog's head and said sorry old pal, sorry to drag you out and into all of this.

All of what?

When had he ever not known which way to turn? There had never been a time when he'd felt caught between two women. Sure, there had been girls who'd said, don't you love me Scott? when he'd said no, I can't see you, I'm hanging with my daughter; other girls who'd said, make your mind up Scott, when he'd declined a holiday or an invite to a wedding of people he didn't know; some who'd said, I need to know where I stand, when he'd made an excuse not to meet parents or best friends. There had been one, Lisa, when Jenna was much younger – she'd come close but he hadn't let her come close enough. And since then? It was easy. A no-brainer. It wasn't about love, it was never about love – whatever gave them that idea? It was just about someone cute and a period of sex. Nice when you can get it but what the hey – life's not so bad without it. He never gave false hope.

He didn't really need anyone to make his life better than it already was. Then Frankie came along on a day when he didn't know where he was going.

'Buddy.'

The dog looked up.

'What's going on, hey?'

Up in the sky he could hear a small plane. Was it Aaron, taking someone up there for them to bale out with a parachute on their back, the crazy fuckers? He couldn't locate the plane for a while, then he saw it – a speck at 10,000 feet, too high to know who was flying. He glanced at his phone, no signal. He mused how he preferred his phone to be out of range than in but this last month, he'd never before checked it so regularly; hopeful of a text or a picture message, an email, a missed call, a FaceTime request.

'Frankie.'

The word tasted good. Such a beautiful day up here, way up a hill, a soft breeze that wouldn't reach his porch until much later. He thought about potentially seeing her next week. It excited him. There were commitments to rearrange – he didn't want to cancel the kids he was mentoring and he had a meeting in Vancouver as well as Jenna's appointment.

He rested his head against the tree and closed his eyes. Love was simple and life was complicated. Was that right? Was that how it should be?

His eyes snapped open.

Christ.

What the?

'As I thought of Frankie, so I thought of love.'

Driving home, Scott decided to call in on Aaron whose door was always open to him. Friends since childhood, nevertheless when Scott drove through the Lílwat reservation at Mount Currie, he was aware that he was a white man on First Nations land. Some people waved because they knew him, others who recognized his truck might nod, but still there were some who looked away. He respected that. Though he knew this road, this place well, it was still humbling to acknowledge the disparity of wealth and circumstances in the valley typified by the different people who lived within it. He felt a little awkward driving up Aaron's street in his shiny, expensive truck – even though he knew that when Aaron drove it, it was with pride and aplomb, kids and friends flocking to admire it.

The sight of Aaron's home always raised a smile. Compared to Scott's house, Aaron's was a glorified trailer. In fact it was a trailer, because that's what Aaron could afford ten years ago. However, it was soon rooted down, as stable and proud as a house costing a million dollars more. One summer, he'd helped Aaron clad it in cedar and a couple of years ago they'd built the porch out back too. Rose wanted a fancy porch – and a fancy porch was Aaron's pleasure to provide. He'd changed the colour last year, painting it a shade of rich honey with the windows and porch picked out in white.

Rose was watering her pot plants, little Johnny was taking handfuls of soil from one area and depositing them in another. Tara was sitting on the steps, brushing the hair of a doll with a queue of other dolls by her side. Johnny was at the side of the car before Scott had turned his engine off, stroking the door because he loved the truck and he loved Scott and he didn't stop to think about his muddy little hands. Scott noted that Rose glanced around before she welcomed him. It was another thing he acknowledged and took no offence at. Rose hadn't known him her whole life like

Aaron, only since she'd been married. She was Squamish who had married in to Líĺwat. But aside from her heritage, she was quite simply a little shy.

'Hey Rose.' Scott waved. Johnny had slipped his hand into Scott's and the small fingers moving rhythmically, and the grainy earth felt nice in the palm of his hand. 'Hey Little Miss Tara – your barber shop open for business?'

'It's for my dolls,' Tara said, glancing at her mother. 'It's for *dolls*,' Tara said again, as if Scott was thick.

'Aaron's out,' Rose said, still busy with her pots.

'I might have heard him,' said Scott, nodding to the sky. 'Up there. I took a long walk with Buddy just now.'

'Is Buddy here?' Johnny asked, tugging Scott's hand.

'He's in the truck. He's sleeping.'

'Can I see?'

Scott lifted Johnny up and Buddy opened his eyes. The dog liked small kids. They tasted salty, usually, and never pushed him away when he licked them.

'Can I get him some water?'

'I think he'd like that.'

Rose handed Johnny a tin tray and she poured in a little from her watering can. 'Don't spill it on Scott's fancy truck, now.'

Scott helped Johnny place it inside the back for Buddy to lap. The dog was thirsty and Scott felt bad.

'Aaron's not in,' Rose said again. 'I don't know when he'll be back. But you can catch him at the airfield, most likely.'

Scott nodded. When Aaron was around, Rose relaxed; those were the times when she'd rib Scott and tease him and make him coffee and always put sugar in it, laughing privately at how he'd grimace, how he was too polite to complain.

'Well – it's good to see you,' said Scott.

'You too Scott.'

'Can we come to your house?' Tara asked.

'Sure – any time.'

'In your truck?' asked Johnny.

'Sure.'

'Can I drive it?'

'Maybe when you're just a little bigger.'

'My dad let me drive it.'

And Scott thought back all those years to having Jenna on his lap with her sticky hands clamped to the steering wheel believing that she was taking them home. Now, there hadn't been a period of more than just a few months when she'd been safe to drive. She hated that halt on her independence more than anything. Thoughts of Paris raced across his mind like a darkening sky.

'You OK, Scott?'

He looked up at Rose. 'Yeah. I think so. I –'

'You in love?' She asked it deadpan but her shoulders gave the shake of a momentary giggle.

Scott hooked his thumbs through the belt loops on his jeans, kicked at the ground, looked at the sky.

'You *are*,' said Rose as if it was a fact as everyday as Scott having dark grey eyes, being forty-five years of age, having a dog called Buddy and owning one beast of a truck.

'I can go to Europe again – next week – if I choose to,' he said as if it were an expedition to the South Pole. She raised her eyebrow at him. 'But I need to think of Jenna.'

Rose looked at him archly. 'Not so good for a girl her age to be thought of all the time,' she told him.

'I'm all she's got,' Scott said defensively.

Rose whistled. 'Mister Important! King of the World! Jenna's got a life all her own. Don't push your shadow over her sunshine – however soft you do it.'

He looked at her levelly.

'Go to Europe, Scott,' Rose said as she tended to her plants, the sparkling arcs of water seeming never to dry up.

As he drove home, Scott thought how he always found Rose's spare way with words and the glimpses of wisdom refreshing. Had Aaron been home when he'd called by, there'd have been laughter and lively joshing. Are you kidding? Aaron would have said, giving him a punch, no doubt. Get on that plane – Jenna knows we're here. We'll keep an eye on her.

Jenna hated having the EEG, still finding it no less daunting over the years. There was a panic button for a reason; the noises from the machine, the aloneness, the anticipation of what the readings revealed. The procedure might only take half an hour but the effects lasted far longer; she hated having the pads pasted to her head, finding the stuff impossible to get out afterwards. Three, four, five shampoos, making her scalp sore and her temper frayed. She'd still be picking out little nibs of hardened glue all week. The first time Scott had heard her swear was when she was fifteen and, after spending all afternoon washing her hair she'd come down crying saying she looked like shit.

'Not a good look,' she said today, reluctantly brave, when she was wired up.

'I've seen worse,' said Scott. 'You've seen those pictures of me in my high-school band in the eighties.' But it didn't raise a smile.

Afterwards, the neurologist discussed her medication, his aim always to find alternatives to polytherapy. She was currently on four different drugs and he was concerned about her weight loss since he'd last seen her a few months back. However, having been on meds not so long ago that had increased her weight dramatically, Jenna was more worried about her drowsiness and that sometimes her gums felt so sore.

'There *is* a new drug,' he told them. 'Containing no carbamazepine – that's what you were allergic to when you were a kid. But it's being directed at sufferers a lot older than you. My problem with it is that it has idiosyncratic side effects – symptoms occurring in some but not all who take it.'

Jenna looked at her lap and her father took her hand.

'Last time she tried new meds, she wound up in hospital for a week.'

'I know, Scott, I know. Going on your past history, Jenna, and your intolerances, I wouldn't be happy putting you on it.'

'Can you lessen her doses?' Scott asked.

'Like I've said before, we risk the absence seizures becoming more frequent and possibly the tonic-clonic events lasting longer. Which we absolutely don't want. I feel we ought to stay as we are – and I'll see you in three months. Hopefully, you'll have been seizure free.'

'And the vagus nerve stimulator?' Scott pushed.

'Maybe next year.'

'Jenna?' Scott spoke to her softly.

The men looked at her, waiting for her to raise her head.

'I'd really like to work out at this new gym some of my friends have just joined,' she said, brushing away an angry tear. 'I don't care about alcohol – that doesn't matter to me – but when I go to UBC in the fall, I want to go to the parties, go see bands, stay up late putting the world to rights. I want to be able to drive a bunch of friends home for the weekend.' She paused, her voice creaked. 'You know what? What I'd really like is not to have to always make sure I'm in bed early to get enough sleep. It's so *lame*.' She sighed very deeply. 'I just don't want to have to tell people.'

Jenna, who so much of the time smiled her way through her affliction, whose brave face on it all was as beautiful as it was painful to see, felt that her consultant's room, with her dad at her side, was the one place she could truly vent. And they always let her.

'Last time – a month ago – the headache I had afterwards was unbelievable. I slept for almost an entire day after, didn't I, Dad?'

'She was wiped out,' Scott said.

'Have you tried introducing caffeine back into your diet, Jenna?' her consultant asked. 'We're now seeing that quite a few sufferers have found stimulants can actually help suppress seizures, as irrational as that sounds.'

But she hated coffee. She never drank pop. She didn't like the taste of rich dark chocolate.

'You know what I want most of all?' She was now truly fed up. 'I just wish I could be selective, I wish I could choose who I tell on a need-to-know basis – but the thing is, I have to tell *everyone* because it just doesn't seem there's ever going to be a time when the whole world around me won't need to know.'

Scott took Jenna out for lunch in Vancouver even though she said she'd be happy to go straight home. Over the years, he'd learned that it was important to provide a diversion from the inevitable frustration of her appointments. Well we're in Vancouver anyway, he'd say, so while we're here why don't we do something fun before we head home? When she was little, it was visits to toy stores, when she was a young teen it was shopping trips down Robson. Recently, he'd found lunches at lovely restaurants had managed to put distance to the disappointment and raise her spirits a little. Her favourite place was Bridges on Granville Island and there they sat on the warm, wide decking right on the waterfront, looking over to the glinting city and, beyond, the mountains. Scott knew she'd find that the sunshine-yellow parasols couldn't contradict her mood for too long. Sometimes it broke his heart that her default was to be so determinedly positive.

'You OK, kiddo?'

'Well apart from the fact that I have to wear a base-ball cap on such a lovely day because my hair is covered in glue – yes, I'm fine.'

'Pizza? Burger? Fuck it, Jenna – let's have the lobster.'

She always giggled when he swore.

'You know,' she said, 'you *have* to go to Paris next week Dad.' Over and above the movie her dad was thinking of taking, Jenna was intrigued by thoughts of Frankie. If her dad went over there, perhaps next time this Frankie would come over here. What was she like? What was her dad like with her?

'I'll think about it.'

Scott always felt an instinct to stay close to Jenna after she'd had her tests. The movie – maybe it wasn't something he wanted to be involved with. Frankie – how he longed to see her. But he hadn't told her about Paris. Not yet.

'If you don't go – it won't be because of the movie, it will be because of me,' Jenna said. 'I don't want that to be the case.'

'I said I'd think about it,' Scott laughed. 'They want me to write music for some chick flick.'

That really made Jenna laugh.

'Let's eat lobster,' Scott said, nodding at the waitress to come over.

Jenna didn't want to stay at home, she wanted to go back to her apartment in Whistler and work the evening shift and meet Shelley's new boyfriend properly. She hugged her dad and laughed at how slowly he drove away, knowing he was still looking for her in his rear-view mirror long after she'd stopped glancing over her shoulder to wave him away. Arriving home, Scott felt he could do with some company too, really, after a day like today. He could easily phone Aaron. Even the youngsters he was mentoring – but they'd have school-work and anyway, they'd had a session with him a couple of days ago. He could go down to the Pony – but he wasn't hungry. He picked up one of his guitars, played for a moment, put it down. He opened the fridge, closed the fridge. He flipped through unopened mail. He thought about going for a run but actually, he was really tired. And he thought about Frankie. Hers was the company he wanted right now.

He looked at Buddy.

'What would you have me do, pal?'

He phoned Jenna. She didn't pick up. He left a message and phoned again five minutes later.

'Dad – I'm at work?'

'I think I *will* go to Europe next week.'

'That's great – you go. I said you should go.'

'Are you sure though, honey?'

'Will you stop worrying? You're getting worse!'

'But I can stay home – it's no big deal.'

'Oh my God, Pops – I'm hanging up now. OK? I'm hanging up. See!'

It was too late to call Frankie. She'd be sound asleep. Just gone five in the morning over there. Buddy was ignoring him. Scott took a different guitar and strummed thoughtfully. Romance slash family drama slash comedy. That pretty much summed up his life these days. If he couldn't write for that, he'd better just hang up his guitars and sell the piano and do something else instead.

'Looks like I'll be going to Paris, then,' and he listened hard as his words and his music spun through the absolute silence in his home.

'It's coming,' Frankie tried to assure her agent. 'Honestly. A couple more weeks. Two – maybe three.'

'Author,' he said sternly, 'I do hope so.'

Damn you, Alice.

You're the one neglecting me, Frankie. You've hardly given me a passing thought recently.

* * *

Frankie walked over to her wardrobe and opened the door, staring at herself in the mirror, moaning that she looked like shit. She peered in close. Were those *jowls*? Starting from her chin, she ran her fingers firmly along her jawbone, recognizing the tighter face it revealed more than she did the softer version when she took her hands away. And why were there lines under her eyes if she wasn't smiling or grimacing but just keeping her face neutral? And why was she calling them lines when she should be more honest and just call the bloody things wrinkles? And why was she wasting time looking at herself when it only depressed her and when she should be sitting down and trying to work?

'I can't meet you in Paris,' she said quietly, repeating words she'd said on the phone only minutes ago. 'It's just too complicated,' she said again. 'Midweek, with the children, with work, with logistics, with finances.'

'Paris, France, right?' he had said to her. 'Not Paris, Texas?'

There'd been a long silence.

'We'll find a way,' he'd told her, but just then, alone in her room, this seemed a complex route with no map. She went over to the window and gazed out at the sky as if solutions were carried on clouds. She did love the fact that the view out over the land was now so familiar though the sky was never the same. There were no answers out there though, just the question of her children downstairs yelling up when's supper Mum, we're *starving*.

'Do you want a cup of tea?' Sam asked. Sam's tea was legendary in its awfulness but was always on offer.

'I'm all right – thanks darling,' Frankie said, though it was quite obvious to the children that she wasn't. She'd pushed her food around her plate and they'd had to say everything twice.

'Are you all right?' Annabel asked.

'Oh,' Frankie said breezily, 'yes and no. I almost got to see Scott again. Almost, but not quite. So I'm just a little – blue.'

'Why only almost?'

'Well, he'll be in Europe next week.'

'Whereabouts in Europe?'

'France – Paris.'

'But we're neighbours – with the French.' Annabel thought about this. 'So near – yet so far.'

'You know – we could *all* go to Paris,' Sam said.

'It's midweek,' Frankie told him.

'I know. But we could make it – educational – go to museums, speak French all the time.'

'Nice try,' Frankie said. 'Now come on you two – showers and then bed. It's a school night.'

Frankie woke with a start and scrabbled around for her clock. It read 3.47. Slightly sleep fuzzed, it took a few attempts to count backwards by eight and she had to use her fingers to do so. Whether she had it right or wrong specifically, she knew it was a decent hour in Canada. She tiptoed downstairs, avoiding the steps that groaned. Moonlight drizzled over the clay tiles in the hallway. They looked rather beautiful. If only they looked like that by day. She sat in a curl on the sofa, pulling the throw that lived across the back of it around her.

'Do you like trains? You know, it's only one stop on the train,' she told Scott as soon as he answered. 'Or two – I don't know. I think it may stop in Kent or somewhere like that.'

'So if I take a train, I get to see you?'

'I would have loved to come to Paris,' she said forlornly.

'I guess I'll just have to bring a little bit of Paris to you,' Scott said.

Ruth and Frankie strolled down Staithe Street in Wells, having dipped in and out of the shops for greetings cards and second-hand books, vegetables, bread and brightly coloured welly-socks that were on sale.

'Come on,' Ruth said. 'Let's buy a bag of chips and take the dogs onto the beach for an hour.'

With the wind in their hair and the tang of vinegary paper in their nostrils, they walked across the sands.

'I can't believe I've eaten all those chips,' Ruth said. 'I made a pact with myself that it's salad only for lunch during the week.'

'Am I a bad influence?' Frankie asked, gazing at the beach huts and wondering how much they went for.

Ruth laughed. 'It's me leading you astray – I suggested chips. *And* all that wine last week.'

'And you made me come here after my Alexander session this morning – when I should have gone home and tried to haul the bloody book out of me.'

'Oh yes, Frankie – you came kicking and screaming.'

Frankie gave Ruth a gentle shove then she looked around. 'God this is lovely. Is this where they filmed Gwynnie walking on the beach at the end of *Shakespeare in Love*?'

'A little further up, Holkham.'

On they walked, the two black Labradors playing grandmother's footsteps with the waves.

'So,' said Ruth, 'he's coming?'

'I can't quite believe it but yes, yes he is. I keep thinking, will he like it, what will the kids think, will they get along?'

'Are you nervous?'

'My sister asked me the same thing. Nervous – no, strange as that may seem. I know it sounds slightly unbelievable – but I know him, there's been an honesty between us, an openness right from the start. The things we talk about, the depth we talk to.'

'You sure you haven't made him a bit mythical in your eyes? Remember, the day-to-day stuff can cast a different light,' said Ruth.

'You sound like my sister,' said Frankie, comfortable enough to add a certain discontent to her voice.

'I'm just looking out for you,' Ruth said. 'I care about you.'

'I'm not a romantic you know,' Frankie told her. 'I think people think I must be, doing the job I do, living in a land of make-believe. I'll happily admit that when it came to men I was a *fantasist* in my twenties, my early thirties. Since then, since Miles, since the children – no. I've had a few mini-flings – that's all. And then I met Scott. And all I can say is, the fact that something so unexpected, so extraordinary, happened – it actually *happened* – means that actually, it has to be believed.'

Ruth put her hand to her heart, even though she was holding a chip between her finger and thumb. 'I love it!' she said. 'Honestly I do. It's a little bit thrilling to live vicariously through you. Will we meet him?'

'I hope so,' said Frankie, who'd already thought how much she wanted them to meet one another.

'You look – worried?'

'It's my book, Ruth – I really need it to come. I don't get paid till I hand it in.'

Ruth turned and faced the sea, today its surface like wafting silk. 'You know, sometimes, when you're with me and we're doing the Technique, I sense you holding back. So for what it's worth, I'd say it must be hard to be there in Alice world, if you're not quite here, in your own world. Does that make any sense?'

One of the dogs came bounding back with a stick twice its size. Frankie threw it as far as she could. Then she stopped and inhaled deeply, turning a slow 360 degrees.

Freya North

'You know, sometimes I still feel like a visitor, like the house can't possibly be mine, can't really be home. I *think* I'm happy, I *think* I feel at home here – but sometimes, I'm not quite sure.'

S cott yawned as he checked the departures board. The jet lag had been vicious this time around, not helped by the fact that one of the producers was insufferably boring, the director was notoriously neurotic, the script just seemed silly and from what he'd seen of the rushes it wasn't going to win awards. It all seemed a bit chaotic. He wasn't even getting to see much of Paris as the meetings were in nondescript offices away from the city centre. They'd put him up in an airport hotel because they thought that was the right thing to do. It transpired that rail to the UK wasn't viable. He liked the idea and it was comforting to think of Frankie just a train ride away, but in reality, door to door would have taken a long day. He couldn't change his flight home to leave from anywhere other than Paris but he could delay it by three days. Timetables, options, bookings websites, maps of East Anglia, train routes, airline information, car hire – that's how he'd passed the time when he was wide awake while all of France slept.

It was only when Frankie had his text and the details were there in black and white – a flight to Stansted arriving the following morning – that she told the children.

'Scott *is* coming to visit.'

Annabel's eyes lit up.

'Where is he going to stay?' Sam asked.

'With us,' said Frankie.

'*Where* with us?' Sam had muttered under his breath, slouching off to pack his bag for school.

'What did Sam say?' asked Annabel.

'Not quite sure,' said Frankie, glancing anxiously at the space he'd left. She'd heard him very well.

Frankie took Annabel to school early the next morning, arriving ten minutes before breakfast club even started. They sat in the car together, bonding over their tangible anticipation.

'I wonder what he's like,' Annabel said. 'In real life.'

'I hope you like him,' said Frankie.

'Does Daddy know?'

'Daddy?' She hadn't thought about Miles in weeks, nor had they heard a word from him.

'Yes?' said Annabel, wondering why her mother looked like that. 'Does he know – have you told him?'

'I haven't.'

'Well, won't he want to know?'

When has he ever wondered about anyone other than himself?

Annabel thought about her father while her mum played with her ponytail. 'We haven't spoken to him for ages or seen him in ages.'

'Well, that's because he's busy – and far away.'

'Is Canada as far away as where Daddy is?'

'Some parts of Canada are nearer, some are further – it's a huge country. Let's look at the atlas when we get home.'

'There are maps on your phone, silly,' said Annabel and Frankie watched her little fingers scurry over the screen until she'd brought up various maps of Canada. They pored over one together, finding Pemberton and having fun with names like Chilliwack and Garibaldi on the way.

'See you later, pumpkin,' Frankie said and Annabel waved and darted into school for a second breakfast.

Frankie took a moment in the car, the imminence of Scott's arrival shooting adrenalin like arrows through her blood. Was he really going to be in her house, filling the space that hitherto had been draped with daydreams of him? Would he feel at home here, with her and the children? She turned away from the niggling memory of Sam's displeasure and looked again at the map of Canada on her phone, which somehow her daughter had saved into her photo stream. She wondered if Scott had studied maps of the UK, whether he'd zoomed in on East Anglia, whether he'd found the triangle of Binham, Langham and Cockthorpe and tapped his finger somewhere in the middle wondering what it was like, wondering when he'd get there.

It was a good two hours' drive to Stansted. She wouldn't hear of Scott hiring a car. *After all*, she'd said, *when I come to Pemberton, you're hardly likely to make me find my own way there*.

She was early and his plane was on schedule but still she paced Arrivals, never more than a moment or two from glancing at the board, or a step or two from her chosen spot to greet him. Hurry up! She looked around her. How many people here were waiting on this particular flight? Some of those people in Costa Coffee appeared so relaxed and unaware of where they were, Frankie wondered if they were there solely for a drink and a cake. But none of her meanderings were making time pass faster.

Passengers arriving were filtering through all the time. Officious businessmen out first pulling their wheeled carry-ons as though they were annoying children. Families ambled through, nattering and bickering, trolleying a snaking path which held up the people behind.

Where are you?

Here I am.

Very real, very lovely and just feet away.

Hey you, he said over and over as she buried her face in his chest and clung to him. And there they stood. So what that people had to swerve a route around them? No one tutted, no one raised an eyebrow, no one minded at all. It was an iconic sight: a couple reunited. Scott and Frankie in each other's arms gladdened the hearts of all who had to detour around them.

Days like today I think I believe in God, thought Frankie the long-time agnostic. Scott was with her and nothing was impeding their journey home. There was no traffic, not even around Barton Mills, and the deeper they drove into Norfolk the more lovely the weather and the prettier the views. She felt proud of her county today. Scott watched her drive, taking the back of his hand lightly to her cheek. She glanced at him from time to time, liking the way he filled her car, that he'd had to shunt the seat back, that he'd found a way to make himself comfortable. He was in her space and he was a good fit.

'That's where I bought Sam's bike for Christmas. Are

you hungry? I thought we'd stop for lunch. Look! That's where I get my hair cut.' She wafted her hand at the sign for Creake Abbey as they drove past. Scott could have asked her to slow down so he could take it all in, but he liked her slightly hyper energy all the same.

At Burnham Market they parked.

'Wow,' said Scott, standing on the green marvelling at the historic buildings lined up on either side as if they were having a good look at him. 'It's what every tourist wants from an English village.'

'To be honest, this is the place that inspired my move,' Frankie said. 'I rented a cottage here two Easters in a row.' She motioned to a young woman walking towards them, wearing a dreamy smile and strolling along to the shops, a wicker basket over her arm. 'When I was on holiday here, that was me. When I was back in London, this was how I could so clearly envisage myself. Then I came to live here and realized that wicker baskets are too cumbersome and hard and not that feasible.' She giggled at herself, then she shrugged. 'Actually, for quite a while, I was disappointed.'

'Living the dream needs a certain amount of practical awareness,' Scott said. 'Even if it doesn't look that pretty.'

Frankie pointed out the Hoste Arms. 'That's where we're going for lunch. That's my sister Peta's favourite place in the world. It's the sole reason she was so supportive when I told her I was moving this way – and so disappointed that where I bought has a very different character to here. She'll tell you – if it isn't Burnham Market, it's the Back of Beyond.'

'Frankie, if money wasn't the issue, if you could have afforded a property here – is this where you would have bought? Would you have preferred it? Do you feel you're living a Plan B?'

She thought about that and then shook her head. 'I love doing this – what we're doing – dipping in and having a mooch before heading home. But they call it Chelsea on Sea for a reason, on account of so many Londoners having second homes here, so no – it's OK that it transpired everything was out of my reach.'

She was taking him a circuitous route to lunch, walking him over the road and in the opposite direction as if presenting the shops and boutiques to him like personal friends.

'I'm just going to buy a blob and then let's go and eat.'

Scott thought, I must remember to tell Jenna they call their bread a *blob*.

After lunch, she drove a looping route home, stopping at Holkham. Through the pines and over the boardwalk, hand in hand, to the golden sands stretching vast and relatively unpeopled to the sea and to either side. The last few days, Scott had felt hemmed in, in Paris, on planes, even in the dining room at the Hoste Arms. It felt good to be out in the very wide open. He filled his lungs with sea air and brought Frankie in close to kiss her.

'This is beautiful,' he said. The breeze had spun her hair into tangles around her face.

'Isn't it,' said Frankie.

'Nice beach too,' he said and she laughed.

'There's more,' she beamed, 'there's more.' She walked on, pulling him by the hand. 'Come and see the sea.'

Scott spoke readily to the people they passed, people

who might just slow down and remark on the weather, or the tide, or the daft antics of their dog or child. They picked up on his accent immediately.

'Do you live here?'

'No,' he'd say. 'I'm just visiting – but Frankie here, she does. She's local.'

And they'd give her a nod, as if they'd never have guessed.

As they walked back to the car, Scott glanced at her. 'You know, those times on the phone when you've said to me you feel you don't fit in, you feel you're still a visitor?'

'Not *all* the time,' she qualified. 'But some of the time, yes.'

'Seems to me you're a head-down-in-your-own-world type of girl,' he said, giving her hand a squeeze. 'That's very attractive to someone like me. But you know, sometimes, all you need to do is look up, greet the day and see who's around and happy to say hi.'

'I'm so glad you're here,' she told him. 'I like every-where so much more now that you're in it.'

'Stiffkey,' he said.

'Pronounced Stewkey,' she told him as they drove through, the road becoming a narrow passage between flint buildings and walls. Even in the car, Frankie always had the sensation her knuckles were just inches from being scraped. She told Scott this, she told him that when she had to squeeze her car through a tight gap, she tended to breathe in, believing it would help. He laughed and realized that it was these details he'd give Jenna to paint a picture of Frankie.

'Binham,' Scott said quietly when he saw the sign.

'Drop the "h" and soften the "a",' Frankie laughed.

He tried it again. 'Is it the same for Langham?'

Frankie nodded.

'I've seen this – all of this – on the map,' he said, looking out. He chuckled. 'And here I am.'

'Almost home,' said Frankie. 'Sorry about the hedges.'

'You're apologizing why?'

'I feel they crowd in on me sometimes.' They were on a straight stretch of road where the hedgerows were so high to either side it felt as though they might arch right over the car. 'You can't see the view.'

'But I know it's there,' he said. 'And anyway, what's lying directly ahead looks pretty good to me.'

This is our wall, she told him. 'We have a postbox in it – do you see? Sometimes, nosey parkers spend a long time putting in their mail while they try and look over the wall. Half-four every weekday. Half-ten on Saturdays.'

'Have you said hi, though?' Scott asked. 'Do they know you're here, even? So maybe they just wonder, who's that mysterious family who moved in all those months ago who don't come out to shoot the shit while we mail our letters.'

Who were the people who used this postbox, she wondered? She'd never stopped to ponder that one. 'I'm always too busy anyway,' she laughed. 'There's usually something bubbling over on the stove, or a war between the children to sort out. Anyway, that small field on the other side of the lane – that's ours too,' she said and then, in silence, they rumbled over the uneven drive and came to a stop, the sudden stillness of the car welcome. 'And this,' she said quietly, 'this is our home.'

Scott just sat and took in her house. He'd seen photos of course but now, here, the pretty little building made perfect sense. Of course she'd live here. He mused, if an architect could have designed a house to complement Frankie, this is what they would have drawn. It suited her. It was quite an unassuming cottage, really, but its components and proportions were lovely. It had a quietness about it, sitting steady on its plot, but a rose rambled up one side and, on the steps leading up to the front door, a squabble of pots puffed out the clashing colours of early summer. A hedge and a wall protected the house from the lane and orchard trees screened the other side from the metallic sprawl of the Mawbys' farm buildings. Just like Frankie herself, he thought, find ways to shield herself and her little family. He remembered that first evening in the hotel, asking her not to go when suddenly she'd stood to leave. He looked at her now, put his hand gently on the back of her neck and waited for her to set the pace.

'It *is* flint,' Frankie promised him. 'Only some time ago it was slathered in all that paint. It's number one on my to-do list, to have it blasted off.'

'It's lovely.'

'And the windows around the back were replaced with hideous aluminium at some point – so they're going to go too. Number two – funds permitting.'

'It's lovely.'

'You like it?'

He turned to her. 'I do. It's your home.'

'Would you like to come in, sir?'

Scott turned her chin with his thumb and kissed her. 'You bet.'

Frankie had taken Scott on juddering FaceTime tours of her home so he felt he'd already sat with her in the living room, at her kitchen table, on the back steps while she had a cup of tea. He'd lain down next to her on her bed many times. But stepping inside for the first time that afternoon, what struck him was how all the senses are needed to truly figure out someone's home, how they live. The feel of a door stripped of its old paint to reveal its worn wood, the bounce of her sofa and wobble of her dining chairs. The sound of the stillness and quiet which wasn't so still or quiet because he could hear an irritated fly, a groan from the water pipes, the creak of a floorboard underfoot. The scent of washing powder in the utility room and the lemon cake on a rack in the kitchen, the sight of Frankie bathed in afternoon sunshine which streamed through her bedroom window and touched the tips of her eyelashes with gold. When she placed her arms around his neck, when she raised her face and brought her lips against his cheek, he inhaled deeply. Now he could detect the fragrance of her shampoo and laundry powder mingling with the scent of her skin which had remained so vivid for him; providing both comfort and torture whilst he'd been back home.

Home.

The simple word was now such a crazy concept – that there could be two of these, parted by thousands of miles of land and ocean and yet connected.

She was kissing his neck lightly, the sound of her hastened breathing as seductive as the feel of her hands wandering over his back, his arms. He tilted her face and put his mouth against hers, his fingers in her hair, his body up close. They tumbled down onto her bed, shedding clothes and bringing skin against skin, hard against soft. He lay on his back, caressed by skeins of her hair on his face, his neck, his stomach as she worked her way down his body in a long line of feathery kisses. The intense sensation of Frankie lowering herself down onto him a millimetre at a time, the exquisite feeling of her body closing, hot and moist, around him while he pushed up deep inside her. Scott drank in all that was on view. She was flushed and smiling, her lips wet, her skin glistening, her hair in damp whorls and slicks against the curve of her neck. Frankie and Scott making love, in her bedroom with the curtains drawn back and the window wide open. Nobody can see in, no one can hear them, nothing to hide from, to cover up or to shut out. Outside, just the land, just nature. Not unlike his own bedroom actually.

It was decided that Frankie would collect Annabel on her own and that Scott would stay back. Frankie had told him of Sam's apparent circumspection so a little man-to-man bonding time was deemed to be a good idea.

'Is he here?' Annabel asked, slipping her hand into her mother's as they left the playground. 'Did he come?' Frankie squeezed her daughter's hand, noting how fast her little legs were taking them to the car. For the first time ever, Annabel didn't even look in the glove compartment hopeful for a chocolate bar to have magically appeared, nor did she ask her mother to go via Howell's in the village. She spent the car journey

chattering full speed about the minutiae of the day so
that she wouldn't have to waste time doing so once at
home.

'We're home!' Frankie called out.

'Hey.' Scott came through to the hallway. 'Well,' he
said, looking at Annabel with obvious amazement. 'The
famous Annabel – I'm really pleased to meet you.'

Frankie, who'd been half-expecting her daughter to
run into Scott's arms, sensed Annabel immediately
deflate and then bristle, as if steel rods had been inserted
into every vein.

'Hello,' she said and her voice was taut and small.

'So how was school?' Scott tried. 'Do you have a
bunch of homework? I'm pretty good at math you know.
I reckon your mom isn't, on account of her working
in words and all.'

'I have English and my project,' Annabel told her
mother.

'What's your project about?' Scott asked.

'Nothing,' Annabel mumbled at Frankie.

'It's on the Tudors,' Frankie told Scott, focusing on
Annabel. 'Isn't it?'

Suddenly, Annabel looked immensely tired. 'I'm just
going up to my room for a bit,' she told the floor. 'Then
I'll do my homework.'

And off she went.

Frankie watched her go, looked up at the ceiling,
following the clump clump clump of her daughter
trudging across to her room, the squeak and creak of
her bed being fallen upon. She looked over to Scott
who shook his head kindly in a don't-worry-about-it
way. She shrugged apologetically as she walked towards
the door to the kitchen, Scott catching her arm and

pulling her close, kissing her, brushing her hair from her face, kissing her again.

'Cuppa?'

'Sure.'

'Sam,' she called as she opened the door, 'do you want anything to drink?'

'Sam's not home yet,' said Scott.

'What?' He should have been home before Frankie. She checked the time. The bus had never been this late. 'That's odd.' She checked her phone and there was her son's text.

Getting the late bus.

'Oh!' Frankie said pushing lightness into her voice. 'He's getting the late bus,' she said as if she'd clean forgot though she knew well enough that Sam only stayed late on a Tuesday. It was Thursday.

Annabel reappeared half an hour later. 'What's for supper?'

'Toad-in-the-hole.'

'I've never eaten a toad,' Scott told Annabel. 'Does it taste good with ketchup?'

Annabel glanced at him before glaring at her mother. 'I *hate* toad-in-the-hole,' and she stomped off again.

'Excuse me a moment,' Frankie muttered to Scott and made her way up to her daughter's room.

'Young lady.' Frankie's whisper had a hiss to it. 'What on earth are you playing at? Why are you being so rude?' Annabel was lying on her bed, facing the wall, motionless, resenting her mother's indignance. 'What will Scott think?'

'I don't care what Scott thinks.'

'Well you should.'

'Why should I?' She turned briefly.

'Because –' Frankie paused. What she wanted to do was shout at her daughter: don't spoil this! This isn't about you – it's about me. For once – it's about bloody me. She swallowed hard on the urge. 'Because he's lovely and he wants to get to know you.'

'He's stupid.'

'Well you're just horrid,' said Frankie. As she left Annabel's room she caught sight of Sam hovering in the garden, glowering at the house.

Frankie thought, give me strength. She descended the stairs on one long inhale and exhaled measuredly before opening the front door. She grinned and waved in a slightly manic way and decided then and there not to mention the bloody bus.

'Hi darling! Hi! I'm just making hot buttered toast.' Sam scuffed his way up the path while she resolutely smiled and nodded. 'Scott's here,' she said, breezing off to the kitchen, busy busy busy with the butter and the toast and faking happy fucking families. Out of the corner of her eye she watched Sam slouching in, head-phones on, fixated by his phone.

Very slowly, Sam raised his eyes and eventually took out one earpiece. 'Oh,' he said to Scott, 'hi. I'm Sam.'

Scott offered a handshake which Sam wasn't expecting. He shook Scott's hand, popped his earpiece back in, increasing the volume despite knowing the tinny half-music would infuriate his mother. What had eaten her children, she wondered, and spewed them out as these alien reprobates? Frankie boiled the kettle again to drown it out. Bringing tea and toast through to the table, she saw that Sam was lost in music on the sofa.

'I'm sorry about my revolting offspring,' she said very quietly to Scott.

'It's cool,' he said. 'The Brady Bunch isn't going to happen overnight.' He had his guitar and was quietly picking out a tune she knew but couldn't quite place. 'Wait till you meet Jenna,' Scott said. 'She's already sticking pins in a voodoo doll.' Frankie looked so crest-fallen he had to reach and stroke her face as he laughed. 'I'm joking. But this –' he tipped his head to signify Sam sullen on the sofa and Annabel stomping around upstairs – 'it's perfectly natural.' He shrugged. 'They're younger, it's new to them – who the heck am I?' And there they sat, Frankie feeling so wretched that it took the taste from the tea and turned toast into cardboard. Scott, though, remained steady; sipping his drink, taking a bite of toast, picking out that tune again, adding chords, playing it a little louder.

And that's when Frankie was aware that Sam was hovering, wearing a completely changed expression. He was standing at the furthest end of the table, just staring at Scott's guitar. And then Frankie realized why she knew the tune. It was one that her son frequently played on a loop. It was the one that, right then, was coming out of his headphones in a compressed and tinny stream, Scott now playing along in perfect time. Sam took both earpieces out and then he did the unthinkable: he switched off his phone.

'Foo Fighters hey?' Scott said to him though he didn't look at him. 'That's a pretty cool choice for a kid your age. Who else do you like? Audioslave?'

'Yeah,' said Sam, and his tone of suspicion trailed away. 'And Kings of Leon.' And his supposed cool voice could have reduced Frankie to tears.

'You heard of Silverchair?'

Sam paused. 'Yeah.'

'You like them?'

Sam shrugged. 'They're OK – I really like, y'know, Soundgarden and Pearl Jam.' He glanced at his mother and then focused on Scott. 'My mum likes Alice in Chains.'

'So that means you can't like them?'

Sam smiled and reddened.

Scott laughed.

'Great band,' Scott said. He was playing Kings of Leon's 'Closer' and Sam was transfixed.

'Sometimes, my mum plays them really loud,' said Sam as if Frankie wasn't there. 'It's really annoying – it makes the cool uncool. She does this stupid dance.'

Scott laughed. He'd love to see that.

'Does she like Green Day too?' Scott decided to ask Sam, still standing a few feet away, not Frankie, sitting next to him.

'Yeah,' said Sam. 'She plays that one song over and over and over.'

'Let me guess,' said Scott and he segued into the gentle melody of 'Good Riddance'.

Sam and Frankie just listened, the familiar song beautiful enough as they knew it but somehow, sung very softly right there at their kitchen table, new and magical.

'I don't want toad-in-the-hole but I might want fish fingers,' said Annabel and the other three looked over wondering how long she'd been standing in the doorway.

'Well, it's toad-in-the-hole and that's that,' Frankie said levelly.

Scott tapped his guitar three times and launched into a new tune.

'Oh God.' Sam put his hands over his ears. 'Not One Dimension.' He looked at his sister who was biting her lip pretending she couldn't hear a thing but standing there all the same.

'It's One Direction!' she shouted. 'Shut *up*.' And she disappeared off again. Frankie gave Sam and Scott a stern look that they knew was mock and she left the room.

'Ignore your brother,' she said, sitting next to Annabel on the floor of her room.

'I'll ignore you all if I want to.'

'You can ignore me,' Frankie said. 'But not Scott – not yet. You don't know him well enough to ignore.' She nudged her daughter. 'Please let him see the lovely you.'

'I'll be the real me if I want,' Annabel said. 'But I am quite hungry and I suppose toad-in-the-hole will be fine.'

Frankie yawned. Scott was desperate to be tired too but was still lagged in West Coast hours as if walking in thick clay. It was gone ten o'clock; an hour had passed peacefully since the children had gone to bed, an hour spent on her sofa, occasionally chatting, mostly just happy to sit there close and enfolded.

'You think it's OK for me to be in your bed tonight?'

Frankie looked at him, puzzled.

'I can sleep right here – or in your spare room. It's OK.'

Frankie thought about it. She shook her head. 'I've been very honest with the kids. I don't want to deny who you are – what we are. That'll send a mixed message. Kids like clarity.'

'But for Annabel –'

Frankie thought about it. 'No,' she said but she didn't sound so sure.

'If she wakes in the night – if she needs you.'

'What do you think we should do?' She liked the way Scott looked when he was thinking hard. Little muscles in his cheeks flexed and his lips parted and then closed.

'I think we should make out right here,' he said, kissing her neck and sliding his hand up her top. 'Then I'll sleep in your spare room with a smile on my face.'

Frankie giggled. 'It's like some weird age swap – doing naughty things behind your kids' backs. Sometimes – very occasionally – I'll have a cheeky ciggy at the back door, terrified that Sam and Annabel will catch me. So I smoke it fast and get whacked with an almighty headrush.'

Scott laughed and kissed her.

'But the thing is – when I was a kid, I was at the bottom of the garden having a smoke terrified *my* mum would catch *me*.'

Scott raised his eyebrow. 'So the moral of the story is that smoking isn't just bad for your health, Frankie Shaw – it's hell on your nerves.' He took the tip of his index finger and traced a path down her forehead, her nose, over her lips, her chin, her neck, her arm before trailing his hand up to her breast and cupping it gently while he kissed her.

Making out on the sofa. Moving against each other fully clothed, ears peeled for the patter of small feet. Their bodies buzzing with desire while their souls soared. Their combined years of experience, the relationships they'd had that had failed, the trials and errors of the mating game, some good times and a fair few regrets all fused so that they understood how their pasts now had purpose and their future was simply in the singular. They felt ageless and weightless, supported by the swell of positive emotions. Frankie and Scott falling in love; the energy that it brought heightening every sense.

What a day. Now, with Frankie off to collect Annabel from school, Scott sat quietly in her garden. He liked it all. He'd liked lying in bed this morning listening to the household trip over each other downstairs, the scurry and cussing of being late, we're always bloody late, get your shoes on *now*, Sam – no Annabel I haven't seen your pencil case and your hair looks like a bird's nest. You have *not* brushed it, young lady. And every now and then shh! Scott's sleeping. Will you hurry bloody up, kids. Shh. Not funny – come *on*. I don't even have time to count to ten. Get. A. Move. On. Shh – Scott's sleeping.

The bang of the front door, voices fading down the garden path still snipping at each other; the angry start of the car engine, the crunch of tyres on gravel, the fading, the coming quiet. How to capture such sounds in music? The family drama of the everyday? He lay awhile and wondered. Then he got up, showered and stood in Frankie's house on his own, listening and watching, taking in the smells and the feel of the place. He liked it that the kitchen drawers were mostly well organized, all of them except the very bottom one which was a jumble of old cloths, odd keys, string, takeaway menus, a screwdriver and used candles. Everyone needs an outlet for chaos in one part of their life, he thought, and if this drawer signified Frankie's then that was OK with him.

He made toast and coffee – terrible coffee – instant and bitter. He discovered that thick-cut marmalade was ambrosial and made more toast in its honour. He scrolled through his phone. Nothing since Jenna had replied to the picture message he'd sent her capturing a corner of the rustic kitchen and the open cottage window.

Sooooo quaint!)xx

He thought about it. Quaint suggested old – and all of this to him sparkled newness.

Sitting in the garden now, at teatime, this morning seemed so long ago. They'd done so much in the handful of school hours, that returning here had offered a familiarity that was comforting. Just relax, Frankie had told him, make yourself at home. And that's precisely how he felt. He looked at his hands around one of her mugs. Hot drinks in other countries usually tasted so different to back home – something to do with the water, the milk, he was never sure what. He was drinking tea out of a mug that said *Supermum* and it tasted perfectly normal to him. He yawned, closed his eyes and lifted his face to the sun, hazy behind high cloud but still warm. His first visit to a new part of the world and, to be honest, as beautiful as the beaches were, as charming the villages, as delicious the lunch, what had made the day for him was just being with his woman; the laughter and the talking. Once or twice he'd thought to himself, if Aaron could see me now, he'd have something to say. When they'd been younger and wanting to chat up girls, it used to frustrate the hell out of Aaron, strong silent Scott letting

Aaron do all the talking. If Aaron could see me now. And then Scott thought how much he'd like Aaron to see him now.

He watched a snail make its determined journey over the paving slabs. The grass needed a cut. He thought, I could do that for her. He regarded the trampoline with its safety screen. He thought, sometimes you just need to leap, with hope in your heart outweighing the risk in your head. That's what he'd done. He'd be homeward bound tomorrow, via a four-hour stopover in Paris. He didn't mind but oh, he could have done with a few more days right here. Another week. A month. OK, so it wasn't possible this time – but maybe next time, maybe for longer.

But Jenna.

So, maybe next time Frankie could come to him. Looking at her garden, terracotta pots that needed weeding, paving stones that could do with a scrub, an old barbeque that ought to be chucked out, he thought what would Frankie make of his garden, his view, his stamping ground, his people? And then he thought, how exactly do I get her over to me?

'Hi Scott.' Sam was back from school.

'Hey.'

'I'm listening to Smashing Pumpkins.'

'A great way to welcome in the weekend.'

Sam slung his bag onto the patio and sat on a chair next to Scott.

'Mum getting Annabel?'

'Yes – she says we're going out for dinner.'

'Cool as!'

'Fish 'n' chips,' said Scott, congratulating himself on his inflection.

'Have you heard of a band called Wayward?' Sam asked him.

Scott frowned. 'No. Can't say I have.'

Sam grinned but reddened. 'If I ever get to be in a band, it would be called Wayward.'

'You were testing me?' Scott laughed.

'Yes?' Sam squinted at him, the sun in his eyes.

'So – I passed?'

They sat in affable silence.

'What's in there?' Scott nodded to the back of the garden. 'I'm thinking of cutting the grass.'

'Oh it's not a shed,' said Sam. 'It's my mum's office – or at least it's meant to be. We spent one entire weekend decorating it but she's never been in there. She just faffs around at the kitchen table these days, getting in a bad mood.'

'It's her office? It looks like a shed.'

'From this angle, yes – but come.'

Wooden and windowless on the elevation facing the house, the opposite side was one long window with views out over the fields. They were standing inside, Scott and Sam.

'It took us all weekend, the three of us. What a waste of time. We had to paint it white – some really expensive fancy white with a dumb name like Swan's Neck or Pillow Puff or something.'

'Looks like white to me,' said Scott, patting the wall. 'You did a good job, though.'

'I don't know why she doesn't like it.'

Scott looked around. An old frayed rug on the floor, a flimsy-looking table and a dull office chair. Boxes of books in a corner. He looked through those nearest the top. Alice, Alice and more Alice.

'Anyway, we'd better go,' said Sam. 'It's kind of off limits and see – no lawnmower.'

'Does she have one?'

'No – she had some blokes come a while ago but they weren't very good, they were a bit weird.'

'How so?'

Sam scuffed at the rug with his foot. He shrugged. 'I didn't like the way they were – the way they spoke to her. You could tell – they were being friendly but, I don't know, not sincere. They cost a lot of money. I heard her say to them – *you hacked my plants and scalped my lawn and now you want how much?*'

'But she paid?'

Sam shrugged. 'Yes.' He looked at Scott very straight. 'Sometimes I think my mum could run the country – but other times she seems quite small.'

Annabel regarded Scott warily.

'Hey,' he said and he walked past her placing his hand gently on her arm as he went. He kissed Frankie softly on the cheek.

'So – fish 'n' chips?' he asked Annabel. She shrugged. 'It's Fry Day,' he said but she pretended not to understand.

Off to Wells they went, Annabel looking defiantly out of the window as they drove while Sam fixated on the world in his phone; Frankie pointing out this view or that when the hedges thinned out or the road rolled and dipped to afford a vista. Sitting at a melamine table in their favourite fish shop in Wells, with plates heaped with food, Annabel pretended she wasn't actually starving, sprinkling vinegar and dolloping ketchup as if it was a tiresome task. She was sitting next to

Scott, trying to keep her body concaved away from him. She ached all over, really. And then Scott did what Annabel considered the unthinkable. It was so heinous all she could do was stare. Despite having food on his plate, he started helping himself to hers. Chip after chip after chip. She looked at him in horror, and looked at her mother and brother in horror because they weren't looking at her or Scott. They were too busy eating, shovelling it in. So she hooked her arm around her plate, as though it was work at school she didn't want her neighbour to copy. But Scott had long arms and he reached over her shoulder and took another chip. He actually broke off the end of the cod, where it's at its battery best, and ate it. He actually did that.

'I'm going home to Canada tomorrow,' he told her. 'I don't want to think of this plate of good food going in the trash – best fish 'n' chips I ever had.'

'Get off!' she hissed.

'Oh – you're hungry?'

'Yes!'

'Why didn't you say? What did you have for lunch at school?'

'Diarrhoea with worms.'

'Oh my. You mean spaghetti bolognese?'

'Yes. It's school diarrhoea.' She was finding it difficult to hiss while having to answer his questions. 'With worms.'

'That's child cruelty,' he colluded. 'You must be gut-foundered. Here. I apologize.' He pushed his plate over and nodded at Annabel who methodically took back the precise quota of chips and pried off some batter until she considered the score to have been evened.

Scott had a notion about Annabel. It had started to germinate when he caught the way she glanced at her mother while her mother was smiling at him yesterday. He saw it again when he took Frankie's hand while they stood in the car park at Wells and marvelled at the tiniest one-up-one-down house he'd ever seen. There was a glower to the little girl's face but behind it – something else. He recalled seeing it in Jenna a long time ago. He'd forgotten about it and now he remembered. It made him long for his daughter. He looked again at Annabel and then he thought, it might be that the kid just doesn't like me.

'Don't go tomorrow.'

Frankie loitered in the doorway of the spare room watching Scott sort his bag.

'A voice in my head has been saying the same,' he said.

'But you have to go tomorrow?'

'I have to go tomorrow.'

They were standing either end of the room. Downstairs, the children were watching a prequel or a sequel to some film that shouldn't have been made in the first place but gave Frankie and Scott the ideal opportunity to leave them to it.

Frankie leant heavily against the door frame.

'You can come in, you know.' Scott laughed quietly.

She sat on the edge of the bed and he sat alongside her. Out of the window they gazed. It was dusk outside, the clarity of details gone now, replaced instead with a strange non-light that infused all it touched with an ethereal weightlessness.

'I like having you here,' Frankie whispered.

He took her hand and held it in his lap, stroking his thumb rhythmically over her fingers.

'I – don't think I've ever.' She paused. It had been very easy previously to blurb out platitudes to men she only now realized she hadn't actually loved. She laid her head on Scott's shoulder. He kissed her, inhaling deeply.

'I made a note of what hair products you use,' he said. 'So I can buy them at the airport. So I can have them in my home.'

'For when I visit?'

'I didn't think of that so much – as knowing there'll be times when I just need to have you close. So I'll flip the lid and breathe you in.'

My God, he thought, that sounded lame.

Not to Frankie though. 'You'll sniff my shampoo and try and conjure me?'

'Something like that,' he laughed.

She thought about it. 'Will you leave me one of your tops? Maybe your grey shirt?'

'My all-time favourite grey shirt? That I've had for years? That's my second skin?'

'Yes,' said Frankie, 'that one.'

He thought of her here without him. He thought of bullish gardeners ripping her off, of the white office devoid of creative warmth. He thought of her kids driving her nuts in the mornings. He thought of her turning the house upside down looking for a screwdriver some day and forgetting there was one in the tangle of the bottom drawer of the kitchen. And then Scott thought of home. His kitchen. His garden, his gardeners. Hey Dan! Hey Richard! He thought of his daughter whom he drove crazy with his fretting and his nagging. His tools, neat and organized in the shed. His studio, all the tech, his haven.

'What?'

'Huh?'

'You seem miles away.'

'I was.'

'But come back – because tomorrow, you'll really be gone.'

'I know.'

'Scott.'

'Yes.'

'I don't know – I just like the sound of me saying your name.'

'Frankie –'

'I like the sound of that too!'

'No – I mean, Frankie – you think we can do this? Make it happen? With you – here. And me – there?'

She looked distraught. And there was his answer. 'Of course I do.'

'So, I do too,' he said. 'It's not going to be straightforward – you know that, right?'

She nodded. She stood and went over to the window. 'I love this time – when the day just dissolves. I never noticed it when I lived in the city.'

He stood behind her, wrapping her inside his arms. 'We have this time of day where I live, too.' He kissed her neck and brushed his cheek against hers. And she was just about to turn to him when a rustle brought their attention to the door. There stood Annabel, transfixed until she was seen, backing away and going downstairs, shutting the door to the living room, taking her place tight against her brother saying switch it up, Sam, switch it up a bit.

Scott watched Frankie staring at the space Annabel had left.

'Don't take it personally,' Frankie told him. 'It's not you – it's me. My daughter detests me.'

But Scott shook his head. 'You've got that wrong, Frankie.'

'Did you not see the way she looked at me? The way she's been?'

He nodded at the empty hallway, as if it held all that Annabel felt. 'She doesn't hate you, baby,' he said. 'It's not hate at all. It's fear. It's fear.' He thought back over the years. 'Jenna – it's the same look Jenna gave me when there was a woman I liked, who hung around for a while. It's fear – Frankie. She's had you all to herself all this time, she's never known you with a man, never seen you siphon off love for someone who's not her or her brother. When I was just a concept – sure, she thought that sounded cool. But when I turned up here, in her home – no. She didn't like that. She doesn't like seeing you and me together. She doesn't want change. She's worried the love you give me is from the reservoir you have for her. She's scared that you'll leave her – for me.' Scott paused. Frankie was very quiet.

'Perhaps.' He shrugged. 'Something like that. I'm not a shrink. I can't explain it better. But from one parent to another – that's what I saw.'

'But you put Jenna first,' Frankie said, her voice cracking. 'You told me – there hasn't been anyone, because you put your daughter first.'

'Only because no one came close, Frankie. Love wasn't there.' He turned her towards him. Deep shadows and silvery slicks to her face from the moonrise outside. 'But it's here now.'

'What do I do?'

'You look after your little girl,' he said. 'Show her there's nothing to fear. Show her love's a good thing, that it's expansive, limitless. Surely that must be the best example a parent can set.'

How Frankie hugged Scott just then, as if sensing she could absorb by osmosis some of his solid goodness the tighter she held him.

'You're a wise soul, Scott Emerson. And I love you.'

He caught Annabel on her own the next morning, drawing at the kitchen table. Sam was in the shower and Frankie was on the phone to Ruth.

'Can I ask you a favour?'

She looked up at him suspiciously, glancing around as if for backup or escape routes.

'If your mom is struggling with her work can you tell her one thing?'

'We're always moaning at her,' Annabel assured him while engrossed in creating a page of bubble writing.

'So try this – tell her *you can't take a break if you haven't been to work.* Does that make sense?'

Scott looked out over the top of Annabel's head, outside to the high hedge over the top of which a tractor was rumbling past. 'I thought maybe you'd like to take a holiday – out to where I live. There's bears you know. And my dog. I know you work hard at school – so you deserve a holiday. But your mom? I'm not so sure.'

'She has Writer's Block,' Annabel said, tapping her pens vehemently against the paper for spots.

'I know. Can you help shift it, do you think?'

'She tears up paper and stabs pencils into the table.'

'Do you think you can be clever and bribe her?'

'I can try,' Annabel mumbled.

'Would you like to visit Canada? Meet the bears, meet my dog?'

She shrugged, concentrating on her artwork.

'Meet my daughter, Jenna?'

Her shrug turned into a just perceptible nod.

'I'm asking you – not Sam, you know,' said Scott. 'Because when my daughter was your age she made sure I worked hard. She was clever – like you. She had this way that I'd feel guilty if I didn't work.'

'Is it true your daughter is poorly?'

Scott looked at Annabel. 'Not so much poorly in that she isn't sick all the time. But yes she has an illness that makes her sick some of the time.'

'Is she *sick* sick, do you mean?'

'Huh? You mean throwing up, *sick* sick?'

Annabel nodded.

'No – sorry, that's my language. So, she has epilepsy – have you heard of that?'

Annabel shook her head. She put down her pens and looked at him, ready to listen.

He wondered how best to explain it to a nine-year-old. Then he remembered how Jenna herself would describe it at that age. 'There's a part of her brain that sometimes has a meltdown where everything fires at once,' he said. 'It means she has a seizure – a fit. It's scary for her – and for us.' He flinched away from a vivid recall of a young Jenna convulsing. 'But she can't help it.'

Annabel had become very thoughtful. 'But will she get better?'

Scott shook his head.

'There isn't medicine? Or a pill? An operation or a cure?'

Scott shook his head. 'There are pills and operations – but they only help a little and they don't suit everyone. Like a Band-Aid might help with a wound but can't stop you getting that wound in the first place.' Annabel nodded. 'You know, forty *million* people worldwide have epilepsy – but thirty-two million of them have no access to any treatment because they live in poor countries.' Scott could see how mammoth the figures were to Annabel. 'So Jenna and I – we help raise money to send to those countries, for the children who have this disorder.'

'But how did Jenna get it?' Annabel was asking. 'And is it catching?'

'No – it's not a disease, you can't catch it. And we don't know why Jenna has it – she was born early, that may have something to do with it.'

'How do you know when it's about to happen though?'

'We don't,' said Scott. 'But Buddy is trained to try and warn her – he can pick up on the tiniest changes in her behaviour. Things we can't see.'

'Dogs are amazing. My mum says we can't have one. But what I want to know is, what happens when Jenna's brain fires up?'

'Well, seizures can look and sound very scary indeed. Sometimes she has a focal seizure – and she just stands staring, she can't hear you, she isn't aware of anything. Mostly, this leads to tonic-clonic seizures – that's when all her muscles go stiff and she falls down. Then her body jerks really badly.' He blinked away another memory. 'It can last a couple of minutes. It's very dangerous if it lasts longer. Sometimes she hurts herself when she falls, if something's in the way. Then, she goes all limp and she can be pretty confused and sleepy for a long while after.'

'Might she – *die*?' Annabel whispered.

'There's not a day I don't worry about that,' said Scott and Annabel detected his tired grown-up's voice.

She let him have a think while she thought hard as well. 'We raise money at school for charity,' she told him. 'We bring in cakes to sell. For about 10p.' She thought about it. 'I can ask if we can help epilepsy, if you like?'

For some reason, the thought of Annabel and her friends and their ten-pence pieces brought a knot to the base of Scott's throat.

'I think that would be excellent. You can be our UK ambassador,' he said, clearing his voice. 'You can tell the class about epilepsy. I can write down words like tonic-clonic. You see, many people who have epilepsy are very shy about it – because most strangers don't know enough about it so they don't understand it – and oftentimes, they don't know what to do to help. People often don't come forward to help because they find it scary.'

Annabel sat there, appalled. She looked hard at Scott. 'I'm very sorry to hear about all of this.' She intended for it to sound formal and grown up.

Scott knew that. He smiled at her and finally he sat down, a careful distance on the opposite side of the table. 'I'm sorry I ate your food last night.'

'It's all right,' said Annabel, resuming her colouring. 'They give you loads at that restaurant. They're much more generous here than in London. We're regulars now.'

215

'You like it here? Better than London?'

'Yes.'

'What are you drawing?'

'The names of the friends in my class. In bubble writing.' She turned the page so it faced him. 'Each friend has a different design. Do you see?'

Tiffany, Ella, Grace, Tilly. And then Scott spied his own name, very small and facing the side of the paper shyly. In careful bubble writing, filled with tiny blue dots.

Frankie and Ruth's texts had been like a frenetic game of ping-pong. But it was sorted. Frankie was to drop the children over to the Ingrams' to save traipsing them to Stansted and back. Sam was not impressed. He liked the Ingram kids well enough – but they were little kids. He rolled his eyes at Scott who raised the palms of his hands as if to say what can I do – I'm not the boss around here. Annabel didn't mind. But she told her mother that she didn't mind about coming to Stansted and proposed that it would give her company on the drive back to Norfolk again. Frankie glanced at Scott who gave her a very distinct *don't look at me* response. The truth was Frankie trusted Sam to be home without her – he was sensible enough to invigilate Annabel too – but it was likely that she'd be gone most of the day, really. And actually, what Frankie wanted was an opportunity for Scott and Ruth to meet – and then to have him to herself.

'Ruth said pack swimmies and Crocs,' Frankie said, burrowing into drawers and cupboards to find them.

Scott still sat at the kitchen table, where Annabel was now writing her friends' names in a curlicue script. Sam came and plonked himself down, earphones on,

Instagram at the ready. Scott reached to take a piece of paper. Then he remembered the fish and chips.

'May I have a page?'

Annabel pushed one over to him.

He wrote down his email address and gave it to Sam. 'Ever you want to share music stuff, write me. I'd be happy to send you some links to bands I like.'

'Are you not on Instagram or Twitter?'

'God no.'

'You're just like my mum,' said Annabel. 'Can I have your email too?'

'Sure,' said Scott, writing it again.

'You don't even have an email,' Sam said.

'I don't have an email,' Annabel told Scott.

'You will do some day,' Scott told her.

On their way out to the car, Scott noticed a woman mailing a letter into the box within Frankie's wall.

'Go say hi,' he nudged her.

Frankie glanced over. 'Oh that's just Mrs Mawby – she's the farmer's wife, next door. And we're in a rush – I said we'd be at Ruth's by now.'

Scott raised his hand to the woman who gave him a quick, awkward smile before she was on her way. 'I met Mr Mawby yesterday – Sam and I saw him when we were waiting for you to get back with Annabel. We walked down to visit the ruins of the priory and he passed by so Sam waved and he stopped. Amusing guy. His name is Keith.'

Frankie realized she hadn't known Mr Mawby's Christian name until now. She'd never thought to ask, really.

* * *

Scott and Frankie stood side by side, engrossed in the departures board. His flight was on time but perhaps if they kept staring at the information long enough they might jinx the flight and it would be delayed. And then he'd miss his connection and he'd have to stay. He could cut the lawn and help with the school run and become good pals with Ruth's husband Peter. He could teach guitar or play in pubs and bring home the bacon and fish 'n' chips on a Friday.

GO TO GATE.

He looked at Frankie. 'I guess that's me then.'

She nodded.

'Write your book,' he said. 'It's in you – write it out of your system.' He kissed her forehead, lifted her chin, kissed her lips and brushed his nose against hers.

'I'll try. Will you phone me from Paris? Will you let me know when you're home?'

They'd discussed many times when the next time would be, they'd sat at her table poring over the kitchen calendar, with a pen to hand. All those empty days apart, stretching beyond June and through July. The concept of a date with a big red marker on it making the time between now and then finite and manageable. But they couldn't find one. Possibilities, yes, with some major reorganization of their lives. I'll push forward here, you do that then and move this there and then and then just *maybe*.

GO TO GATE. It felt as though they'd done something wrong. GO TO GATE.

'I have to go.'

Even Paris seemed too far.

In the end, it wasn't Annabel, working covertly for Scott, who brought Alice and Frankie back together again. It wasn't Scott either. It wasn't down to the sharp email from her agent or the call from her editor she hadn't managed to avoid. In the end it was the final-demand gas bill arriving in the post with her credit-card statement on the same day she visited a class of eight-year-olds.

Frankie looked at the sea of hands, the expectant faces, enthusiasm mingling in the air with the stale classroom smells of pencil shavings, a hidden apple core and, faintly, bums. Frankie had been invited to Annabel's school, not as Annabel's mother but as a special guest during the school's Reading Week.

A real author? Frankie Shaw who writes the Alice books. *The* Alice books? And Frankie Shaw looks – like – *this*? I thought she was a *man*! I thought she was a little old lady! She's Annabel from Year 5's mum as well.

'Good morning children,' Frankie said. 'It's lovely to be here. Hands up if you don't like reading.'

One hand, defiant. She smiled at the child and spoke to her.

'Well, it's my job today to see if I can help you change your mind about that.'

As she started her talk, she remembered how much she loved this part of her job, interacting with the children who often turned out to be her liveliest critics and most honest fans. Her publicist would call it something like *reaching to the core readership* or *engaging the target market*.

They're kids! Frankie simply thought of it as hanging out with Alice's friends. So she did what she always did – read aloud from the very first Alice book. Two, three pages she read, before placing the book face down yet continuing the story verbatim. She moved through the class as she told the story off by heart, charmed and bolstered by small faces with eyes wide, transfixed.

'Frankie Shaw,' asked one who had her hand up but just couldn't wait for permission to speak. 'Do you know every single word in the whole book?'

In answer, Frankie just kept reciting, crouching at the desk of the little girl who didn't like reading but who hung on Frankie's every word.

'Frankie Shaw,' another asked, 'Are you writing a book now?'

And it struck Frankie that she had to. She just had to, if not to ease her financial headache, then at least for this child. Alice and her friends.

'I'm trying,' she told the class. 'You know in your lessons when you try your hardest and you still find it difficult and you don't know if anyone believes just how much effort you're putting in?' Thirty nods. 'That's what it can feel like for an author. Some days, I call and call for Alice and she doesn't come. Other times, it's like we're talking in different languages. Some days she's in a grump with me. Other days I'm in a bad mood with her.'

'Why don't you both just say you're sorry, Frankie Shaw – that's the best way to get on with things.'

'And why don't you put your hand up before you speak, Ryan Smith?' said the teacher.

'Sometimes I just sit immobilized by a day-long fog,' said Frankie, looking at the floor. 'Followed by restless nights when disjointed sentences come at me out of the dark like spears. Sound ideas that I can't capture which taunt me by remaining just beyond my grasp. The tiredness and the worry. No book, no money. To be honest, I feel catatonically inept. I sit there and sit there and wonder what on earth I can do for a living instead. How am I going to support my family? I sit there, not writing, day after day, weeping, severe stomach cramps and blinding headaches, thinking of my children and –'

The teacher cleared her throat and Frankie was suddenly aware of thirty brows furrowed with unease at a grown-up imparting distress. Frankie's head throbbed. She needed paracetamol, or a session with Ruth, but she pulled herself up tall, waved at the air as if there was a nasty smell and forced out a jolly laugh.

'But you don't want to hear about all that nonsense! You want to know about Alice don't you? Who has another question?'

'Miss,' asked a boy, who promptly forgot his question to much laughter. 'Oh yes!' He took a deep breath. 'When you were my age, what was your favourite book?'

'I liked a book called *The Six Bullerby Children*, by

Astrid Lindgren – who wrote *Pippi Longstocking*. This time last year I was living in London – but I started thinking about those books. Bullerby is in a country called Sweden – but I feel where I live now is a little like my own slice of Bullerby. Oh, and I also loved Roald Dahl too – but that goes without saying.'

He wasn't finished. 'And exactly how old were you when you wrote your first story?'

Frankie considered this. 'Well, I can't remember a time when I didn't write stories. If I found things difficult at school, or if I felt lonely or sad or angry or worried, I'd write a story. I liked disappearing away from the real world for a while – and I always felt better when I returned.'

'So how many have you written?'

'Scores – I have two boxes full of old green exercise books filled with my stories. If I used up all the pages, I'd continue on the covers, squidging my writing, tiny tiny, to cram in all those words that were spilling out. Would you like to see one? I brought one with me today. I wrote this when I was your age. It was called *The Mystery of Mangrove Manor*. See – can you recognize my artwork even then?' The child was still looking at her expectantly. 'But to answer your questions, I've had fourteen books published – including the six Alice stories.'

'Can you buy them online?' a child wanted to know.

'Yes,' said Frankie. 'Or better still, at an independent bookshop run by impassioned hard-working and knowledgeable people who love books.'

The teacher cleared her throat again and peered at Frankie over her glasses. 'Next question? Lucy?'

'Are you really rich?'

Frankie balked. 'No! These days books are sold too cheaply to make anyone in the industry much money.'

'Yes, but how much do they pay you for each book?'

'That's enough now. Charlie, pipe down, please,' said the teacher. 'Time for two more questions. Yes – Georgia?'

'Do you have any pets?'

Frankie was relieved at the left-field question. 'No – our cat died last year and my children are nagging me for a dog.'

Sympathy filled the room like feathers.

'Hush children – final question. Yes – Felix?'

'Well, it's not really a question like everyone else's,' the boy said. 'I was just going to ask you – please Frankie Shaw, can you just try and write a new book because I've read all your other books. It's like Alice exists.'

Frankie looked out of the French doors to her writing room at the end of the garden. Barefoot she stepped outside and crossed the lawn tentatively. She peered in through the window. Why wasn't it working for her in there? All that expensive paint, Swan Down or Eider Kiss or Duck Nuzzle or whatever it was called. Her study in Muswell Hill had been relatively stark – it was how she liked it, how she worked best. But out here there was a coldness, an isolation too. She turned and walked back to the house, stopping to gaze at a pair of honey buzzards wheeling high. She turned her focus to the garden chairs, the wood already warmed by the midday sun. She could sit there awhile, coax ideas to keep her company.

No.

Come on.

She turned her back on the day and went into the house.

Three hours. She had three uninterrupted hours if she wanted them. She made a cup of tea, filled a pint glass with water and took them to the kitchen table. She had a pad of lined paper to her right, and nine leaves of plain cartridge paper set out in a square to her left. Sharp pencils and a rubber. Watercolours in a tin, a set of coloured inks, six brushes and a water pot near enough so that she wouldn't have to stretch. Before she switched off her phone, she reread Scott's last text message.

Morning baby x

Funny how he called her baby when actually Scott made her feel truly grown up.

She propped the gas bill and the credit-card statement against the water pot and looked at them.

Alice?

Yes?

You have to help me here. Are you ready?

Yes.

It's your birthday, isn't it?

Yes.

But you sound glum. Why is that?

Because I'm having a party here – all the kids in my class are coming.

That's fantastic.

No – they'll want to go outside.

And you're worried they'll see Him?

Yes. And if they do – well, what might happen?

Shall we find out?

I don't know, Frankie.
Don't worry Alice – I'll look after you.

Over the day which followed, it felt like the time Frankie broke her leg and came out of her plaster cast; relief but also frustration that she still had to limp awhile though she wanted to run again, a sense of freedom despite feeling still weakened. The illustrations came more fluidly than the words at first and she'd dip her brush in the ink and sweep it into the outline of Alice in her one long, signature stroke until the ink ran dry and the girl was on the page. To that, Frankie added washes of watercolour like faint music in a background, building carefully into a tune she knew. The setting, the weather, a gloamy sky, the scratch-dense hedge where He lives. And then the fine details; the glance of the eyes, the up or down turn of Alice's mouth, her hair bouncy or flat to echo her mood. And Him. Gnarled and fantastically ugly but drawn with such care that his sweet shyness danced off the page.

The credit-card statement and gas bill were hidden from the children but then placed against the water pot to invigilate Frankie's day. It took willpower and tears and, little by little, surges of euphoria. The book started to dominate Frankie's life. When she drove, she wondered how on earth she just got from A to B because she certainly wasn't thinking of the road. She burnt the dinner and forgot to do the washing, the children's bedtime was whenever they wanted. She found her mobile phone in the cheese drawer in the fridge and walked past knickers and socks on her bedroom floor three days in a row. But there was a book in the making; however slow the progress, it was happening. The milk was off and life was good.

Ruth was there. She'd come to Frankie's and check her posture and make her laugh; sometimes the two were interlinked.

'Don't cross your legs. Always think of the flow up and out the top of your head. Imagine your spine ending right in the middle of your skull, somewhere behind and between your eyes.' Frankie had grown to love the feeling of putting her body in Ruth's hands. She remembered Ruth saying to her how she felt she held something back; not any more. 'People with sedentary jobs underestimate ergonomics,' Ruth said and tutted. 'We do it all wrong. It's not our faults – we just do.'

That she could make Frankie laugh, amidst the intensity and gravity of writing again, was crucially important.

'Imagine a pair of tiny shoes, one on each bum bone,' Ruth said.

'Jimmy Choos?'

'I was thinking Converse.' Ruth tapped Frankie affectionately. 'The point is, when you're sitting, your seat bones become your feet and the chair becomes the ground.'

And actually, Frankie found it worked. She didn't twist in her chair and therefore she didn't ache at the end of the day, despite how tired she felt.

It was time to contact Michael, her editor.

'I had a bit of a blip,' she confessed. 'I found it very hard. But we're going great guns now, Alice and I. Do you want me to send you the first couple of pages?'

To: scottmusic@me.com
From: samtheman888@gmail.com
Subject: hey!
Hey Scott
So my Mum is madly working on her book thank
God. You probably know that by now. Did you really
write the music to the Matt Damon film? Also, I got
this brilliant album called The Glorious Dead – it's
by The Heavy and it's epic sort of indie-soul-rock.
See ya!
Sam

To: samtheman888@gmail.com
From: scottmusic@me.com
Subject: re: hey!
Sam
Great to hear from you. Yes – your Mom told me
about the book – that's so good. I did write for that
movie – but with others too. I wrote the song 'What
Darkness Sees', it plays at the end and the melody
weaves through some of the scenes. Thanks for the
recommendation – I'll check out The Heavy. It's really
warm here in Pemby right now. The mountain bikers
are having a blast – do you ride? So, say hi to

*Annabel – and hug your Mom, not just from me, but
also from you!*
Scott

It was novel, really, having a kid email him. He liked
it. He liked the connection with Frankie but also the
feeling that Sam simply quite liked him, looked up to
him. Mostly, emails sent to Scott were business related,
curt and badly phrased, from people wanting stuff from
him. Then there were Frankie's emails, which weren't
like emails at all. They were like long intimate conversations which could make him laugh out loud or
become intensely thoughtful or overwhelmingly joyful,
even horny. Sam's emails, however, made him feel
alert, that he had a duty to read them carefully and
then read them again and detect what was between
the lines. They weren't long but they usually contained
something shyly said which Scott had to find and
consider. Like last week – when Sam mentioned that
a boy in his class was a jerk but said that it wasn't a
problem because his dad was a jerk too so he could
deal with it. Jerks, Scott told him, make us happy to
be who we are. Bullies, he wrote in conclusion, are
something else – don't stand for those, Sam.

Twice in one email Sam had written of his own relief
that his mum was writing *even if it means other stuff's
not getting done*. And it crossed Scott's mind that the
household on the lane behind the high hedge might
be in something of a churn. Frankie's calls were sometimes distracted, sometimes almost manic. He could
hear in her voice that she was both wired and exhausted
and he thought if I was there, I could help. If I was
there, I could make sure there was fresh milk and the

kids didn't miss the bus. But he wasn't there, in that undulating landscape that petered off to a great flat grey sea, he was where he loved, where he belonged, in the mountains. With a new movie to score that he was really looking forward to, and Jonah and the boys' debut at the Pony which would raise a little money for the epilepsy charity and which he wouldn't miss for the world.

PART TWO

JULY TO DECEMBER

'Hello you. I thought I'd phone to say Happy July. What are you doing? Is it a lovely day?'

'It's going to be hot – I was just about to take Buddy out.'

'I've just brought Annabel home from school. We're going to rehearse her lines for the school play.'

'She sounded pretty word perfect the other day – that was funny.'

'Won't you come? There are three performances. Please?'

'Frankie –'

'I miss you.'

Oh her voice.

'I miss you, Scott – it's hard. Feeling so much and not having you here.'

'Frankie – come. Book a flight and just come.'

'It just doesn't seem fair – finally feeling all of this and not spending time together precisely when we should be, really. Are you there?'

The line had gone quiet and when Scott replied, his voice was quiet, fractured.

'Book a flight and come – tomorrow, the next day. The weekend. Just do it.'

'The kids, Scott. I'm a three-headed being.'

'You're *all* welcome – you know that.'

'But it's school until the eighteenth.'

'So *you* come, then, just you. This week. Next week. My God, you've worked like a crazy person. You need to recharge. Frankie?'

'Yes?'

'You thinking?'

'Sometimes when I speak to you – and then we stop – I just feel so incredibly lonely. You seem impossibly far away.'

'For God's sake.' His voice creaked. 'Will you at least think about it? I need to see you too.'

'But I've never left the kids – gone that far.'

'Maybe you should. It's not going to damage them. Won't make you a bad parent – you need to do things for you. They need to see you make decisions. They need to see you embrace your life as an independent being.'

'I can't leave them on their own!'

'Crazy girl – I know that. I'm just saying – think about it. There'll be solutions – people you can ask. Doesn't have to be your ma.'

'There's no chance of you coming over here?'

'I have a lot of work on at the moment.'

'I know. But – in some ways it's easier for you. Like Paris.'

'Not right now, hey – I need to be here just now, for work, for Jenna. But Frankie – you know what? I'd like *you* to come *here*. I want you in *my* home, *my* bed. I want to show you my life. You know – you can do your job any place. I was thinking about that. So if you feel it's too – say – self-indulgent to take a vacation, just come out here and *work*.'

234

'You don't understand.'

'Excuse me?' Scott was taken aback by her defensiveness. 'Meaning?'

'Me – and the children. We're – tight.'

'And you think I don't understand?'

'I didn't mean—'

'It's been a month – since I came.'

'I'd have to come over for at least a week – just to make sense of the journey.'

'And that's a hardship?' He paused. 'A week with me?'

'Scott I didn't mean—' Frankie was wishing she could rewind the conversation, start again. Or just phone later and blether about something bland.

'Do you want this relationship to be based on me coming to you? Is that how you see it? On your timescale, in your home?'

She hadn't heard him like this. She'd offended him unwittingly, he was challenging her and it was unnerving her, pissing her off. 'It's not that – it's just *my* situation –'

'– isn't any harder than mine.'

'*Well* –' And immediately she knew she shouldn't have procrastinated, shouldn't have stressed the '*my*', shouldn't have infused her '*well* –' with such uncertainty. But why couldn't he just hop on a plane? It *was* easier for him.

'I'm sorry – are you implying that it is?'

'No – but I have two much younger children. Whereas Jenna's –'

'You know what? I'm going to go now, Frankie.'

'But –'

'We'll talk later.'

Fuck the sodding the phone. It made things so stilted. How could it bring such joy and togetherness one day,

such discord and distance another? And sod fucking
Canada where he was fresh with morning whereas she
was tired and crotchety because it was evening after a
long day with bolshy kids in bloody Norfolk.

What just happened?

They'd had day after day of gloriously mundane
emails and phone calls chatting about nothing and
loving whatever it was that the other said. They'd hung
on each other's words, relishing the affection, the every-
dayness, and always delayed hanging up. The things
that irked them had nothing to do with each other,
just general annoyances that made the other one laugh.
The longing they felt had always been shared – as if
they were helpless yet united in the undoubted
romantic tragedy of being flung so far apart.

But then what just happened? Scott asked Frankie
to come over to him because she told him how she
missed him. And it all deteriorated into heated silences
and stuttering sentences said badly and taken the wrong
way. Now he didn't want to speak to her and she didn't
know what to say.

He wasn't answering his phone. He was making a
sandwich, filling a water bottle, Buddy watching his
every move, the dog's brow lifting this way that way
trying to read his master's agitated silence, wondering
if it had anything to do with him.

'You stay here Buddy.'

Out Scott went, driving to the meadows road between
the Ryan and Lillooet rivers, turning off up the old
Hurley pass, driving his truck hard, finding a peculiar
comfort in the way his brain shook in his skull. Parking
along the old logging road, he hiked hard up the trail

to Tenquille Lake. It was a favourite hike, 12 km, but one he usually took his dog on, one he usually took his time over, chatting to fellow hikers. But not today. He wanted to be on his own and he wanted his lungs to burn so that he had an excuse not to speak or even think about what he was meant to think or do next. Jenna had left a chatty message about nothing, really, and Aaron had sent him a text about meeting for a beer. He hadn't responded to either. Sometimes he just really liked being out here on his own. It's what he knew best.

Frankie in turmoil turned straight to others to straighten her out, needing female energy to infuse and soothe, craving advice and the company of people she trusted to workshop what she was feeling and what she was going to do. It was always a calculated risk to phone her sister, on account of her searing honesty and outspoken manner, but in the first instance, it would always be Peta whom Frankie phoned.

'Do not say I told you so,' Frankie begged her.

Peta's sigh was exasperated. 'But you're miserable – and what's making you miserable is the fact that you've gone and fallen headlong for a man who lives on the other side of the world. Don't say I didn't warn you about that. Don't say you didn't have ample opportunity not to.' She paused. 'I know it sounds horrible of me – but I wish you'd never met him. I wish you'd listened.'

'I love him.'

'Really?'

'Yes.'

'Match dot com could have brought love within a

ten-mile radius of where you live, Frankie. Love's love – wherever you find it.'

'I don't agree with you.' Frankie wished Ruth would text back so she could hang up on her sister. 'It would have been wrong not to embrace it, to turn away from an opportunity, a gift, like that. Everything with Scott – it's been extraordinary.'

'And now it's not.' Peta paused, acutely aware that no one else in her sister's life would dare speak to her the way she could. 'I highly recommend you finish it now. It's only going to get worse. He'll never leave Canada and you're hardly likely to up sticks and move there – it was momentous enough for you to make the break with London and sometimes I still don't feel you're even sure about that. Did you join Ruth's book club?'

'No.'

'Have you got to know your neighbours better?'

'They're ancient farmers, remember.'

'Have you made an effort with the mums at Annabel's school?'

'I just don't get the feeling that they're my people. For God's sake Peta, this isn't about Norfolk, it's about Canada.'

'If you're going to be with Scott, then the two places are inextricably linked.'

'He just wants me to go out there – so we can be together again. So that he can bring me into his life.'

'I beg you not to. Jet lag on your already ragged state will make you ill. You're a single parent, the sole provider, you cannot afford to be ill. You've only just got your writing back on track, you can't afford to disrupt that – you *literally* can't afford it. Look –' Peta softened her voice – 'you've done so well – all this upheaval, the writer's block – and look how you've pulled through. It's just stupid, Frankie – potentially counterproductive in all areas of your life. Don't entertain thoughts of going out there. You'll drive yourself mad about the kids anyway and want to come home early. You'll have all this passionate sex and gaze at him in the moonlight – it's not based in reality. You cannot have a real relationship with this man.'

'Thanks for the support.'

Peta understood her sister's petulance. 'It *is* support – you'll see it, some day. You need to let him go. It's not like you'll have to deal with bumping into him the whole time. You can count on the fingers of one hand how many days you've actually spent with him.'

'And you can count on the fingers of one hand the number of meaningful conversations you've had with your husband your entire marriage.'

'That's below the belt.' Peta paused but decided to let it go. 'Please Frankie – use your head, not your heart. Love is just chemical imbalances playing havoc with your system. Get your head out of the clouds and ground yourself where you've set up home for your family.'

'So if I said I wanted to go – could I ask you to stay?'

Hadn't she listened to a bloody word Peta had said? 'I can't leave my family for a week, Frankie. I won't.'

'But the boys are old enough to look after themselves.'

'But I have my husband to think of.'

'Lucky fucking you,' said Frankie and she hung up.

Frankie was, quite literally, in Ruth's hands; standing barefoot in Ruth's studio, a vaulted room drenched by the sun and almost soporifically warm. Frankie was standing still, looking out onto Ruth's garden and Ruth was behind her, a hand gently at the base of Frankie's skull, another under her arm. Without Frankie having to do a thing, Ruth was standing her up, sitting her down, standing her up, sitting her down. Over and over until Frankie's mind left her body and floated around the room as if in zero gravity. Ruth's hands moved fractionally, a little vibration now and then; smoothing a shoulder blade, easing torsion, straightening a kink. Stand up sit down stand up sit down stand. Up. Down. This was Frankie's sixth Alexander session with Ruth and if the Technique was meant to free her body of habits and her mind of muddles, it was working.

'Come and lie semi-supine.'

Frankie settled herself on the treatment table, a pile of magazines supporting her head.

'I bet you haven't done this have you?' Ruth, unlike Peta, spoke sympathetically not accusingly. 'If you can find twenty minutes a day to lie like this, it's so good for you physically. You're all bunched up today. You'll give yourself a headache.' She slipped her hand between Frankie's back and the table, her other hand gently rolling her shoulder, repositioning her arm.

'Why does this feel so good?' Frankie asked her.

'Because you're letting go, allowing me to move you. You're feeling the emotional benefit of the physical release. That's what it's about.'

Frankie could never be sure what exactly it was that

Ruth was doing, in fact sometimes it was almost too subtle to detect. But what Frankie did know was that she could quite suddenly experience an overwhelming sense of openness and flow. None as powerful as just then.

'Frankie?' Ruth was suddenly aware of silent tears.

'My sister tells me to end it. Scott is angry with me.'

'You haven't ended it have you?'

'No.'

'Don't listen to your sister.'

'She's often right.'

'Why is Scott angry?'

'He wants me to go over. I've asked him to come here. I implied it's easier for him.'

'But perhaps it is.'

'But I didn't mean to belittle the things that keep him out there. And I know I did.'

'I'm sure he didn't –'

'But he did – I know he did.' Frankie put her hands to her face. 'I was stroppy, indignant. And he went cold.'

Ruth sat Frankie up in one fluid movement.

'I can't leave my children.' Frankie looked at Ruth flabbergasted. 'I'm all they have. I can't just up and leave and take a break in Beautiful British Columbia because I fancy a change of scene. I need to finish my book, I need to agree my publication schedule with my editor. My agent wants a synopsis of a new book so he can draft a new contract. My life is *here*. Scott needs to see that.'

Frankie could see Ruth thinking by the way her glossy bob moved, as if various theories were streaming out.

'But Scott's life is there – and you need to acknowledge that. You either need to pick one country – or find a way to straddle the two that you're both happy with.'

She put her arm gently around Frankie's shoulder.

'Well, I think you should go over – not just because I think he's lovely.' Ruth thought back to meeting him the day he'd left for Canada via Paris. He'd been everything she'd hoped he'd be. 'He's good for you. You should go.'

'How?'

'Book a flight, bite the bullet – just go.'

'I've never done anything like that.'

'How liberating, in that case. Think about it – you've met someone who makes you feel closer to yourself than ever you have, who's brought such pleasure into your life and a depth of connection you've never had before. Don't feel guilty about that.' Ruth laughed. 'Oh my God girl – this one's for keeps.'

'But the children –'

'What?' Ruth mimicked them. '*Mum – I can't believe you're leaving us here – in our home, being looked after by someone you trust while you visit the man you love who we really like too.*' She laughed again, made her voice higher still. '*Oh Mum – why are you going to Canada when we have to go to school every day?*' She looked at Frankie, tipped her head to one side. 'They're far more likely to say cool! bring us an amazing present when you're out there. You need to do this for *you*. Yes, being their mother defines you – but not exclusively. If your heart and soul are yearning to go – you must find a way or you're just denying a fundamental part of you that exists. That's not right. That's not healthy.'

'It's not possible in real life. Only in films.'

'Oh bollocks Frankie. Aren't you itching to see where he lives, how he lives? Don't you simply *need* to be with him again?'

'Of course.'

'Sex?'

'Oh God – yes.'

'It's a beautiful place, the world – and do you know what, it's not so very big. The distance between those destined for each other isn't impassable. Make it happen, Frankie. Get out there.'

Frankie looked at Ruth, a little awe-struck. She'd never before had a friend quite like her.

It was the adrenalin that woke Frankie, churning through her veins and compromising the gentle transition of reverie. No slow yawning, no leisurely stretching, no lying under a waft of sheets listening to the dawn and musing on the day ahead while warm feet purred against cool cotton. Instead, she lurched from fitfully asleep to wide awake and fretful.

She felt nauseous. Cross with herself, frustrated with fate for bringing Scott to her, for bringing love into her life but forcing them to live a ten-hour transatlantic flight and eight-hour time zone apart. She put her hand to her heart, convinced it was beating far faster than it actually was. She didn't have to get up for another hour and she tried to lie still, to focus on the tumble of thoughts, attempting to sift through the emotions that accompanied them. It was no good. She crept out of her bedroom in the oversized T-shirt she slept in, grabbing the throw from the back of the sofa in the living room, and took her phone out into the garden. There was dew on the grass and a mistiness out over the fields.

She'd never been awake, out here, at this time. It was beautiful. She thought about time, how this scene played out like this whatever the century, whether folk witnessed it or not. Mist and dew and daybreak. She could hear sounds of life from the Mawbys' farm: barn doors sliding open, machinery being coaxed awake. He's up at this time every day, Keith Mawby, thought Frankie. He knows when's best. I never knew dawn could be so useful.

She walked beyond her defunct writing room, aware of wet feet squeaking in flip-flops. A nettle flicked its sting-itch against her leg. Dawn here, not quite ten at night there, leaving Scott still in yesterday, enabling her to somehow turn back time.

'I wanted to phone you before you went to bed,' she said as soon as he answered.

'Hey.'

Was his voice soft because he was tired? Or not happy to hear from her? Please not neutral.

'I don't believe in going to sleep on an argument,' she said. 'But I had to do it last night here – and I had a dreadful night. I woke feeling quite sick . . . Scott?' Was he there? Did he hear?

'Yeah?'

'Say something?'

There was a long pause and a sigh and Frankie thought no, please no.

'So,' he said at length. 'I guess that was our first argument.'

'Yes,' she whispered. 'And I didn't like it. And I'm sorry. I didn't mean to hurt you. I didn't mean to insult you – or offend.'

'I know.'

The pauses between them, necessary but unnerving.

'I know you live there and I live here – and there's equal importance in what keeps us both bound . . . Scott?'

'Your kids are younger and you're still all settling in to a new place,' said Scott. 'I get that.'

'But whether she says so or not, Jenna needs you there.' Frankie pressed the phone against her cheek as if it was the flat of Scott's hand.

'And whether I tell her so or not, I feel I need to be here too, in the main. The thing about epilepsy is that you are constantly balancing the presence of the disorder with the need to live a life as normal as possible. There's still a stigma attached to epilepsy. I worry about my daughter every single day – teens, young adults, they like to think they're invincible. No amount of time of seeing your child have a seizure lessens the trauma of witnessing it and the feeling of utter helplessness. This is how it is, Frankie, for Jenna *and* for me.'

Frankie thought how she wanted now to go to him even more.

Scott cleared his voice and lightened his tone. 'Plus they don't call Vancouver "Hollywood North" for nothing – most of my work is out here.'

'I *want* to come out – I *want* to bring the kids at some point. If I could hop on a plane today, I would. I promise you. I long to spend time just me and you.'

'Can you make that happen – not just talk about it?'

Frankie nodded vehemently, until aware that Scott couldn't tell and had only her silence to go on. 'I am going to try,' she told him. 'I'm going to pull in favours and check out air fares.'

'It's a beautiful time of year to visit.'

'Scott – trust me when I say I believe you and I'm sold.'

'Frankie.'

'Yes?'

'And we're OK? You and me?'

That voice.

'Better than ever,' she whispered.

'Can we go the distance – in every sense of the word?'

'We can.'

'Where are you?'

'In my garden. The grass is wet and I'm in flip-flops. Slippery toes. Where are you?'

'Oh I'm just in the house. Watching the game on TV. Thinking of bed.'

'I have to go and get the children up. Sam's hollow legs are back and I need to shovel a ton of breakfast in him before he leaves for school.'

But Scott didn't want to slip into prosaic chat, though it was a novel side to a relationship he hadn't truly experienced with anyone but Frankie. What he wanted to do was focus on welcoming for the first time in his life the challenge of taking a risk, of seeking courage and honesty to keep him steady on the edge of his comfort zone.

'You know – I never got close enough to someone to fall out with them,' he said. 'But I never got close enough to someone to fall in love with them either. I never really wanted anyone hanging out here. I never really *missed* anyone, never craved company between times.' He looked around his home, silent and warm yet devoid of something crucial which he never realized was missing because there'd been no need to consider it in the plans.

'And then I came along?' The mist was lifting in Norfolk.

Over Frankie's sing-song laughter, Scott's words came through clear and steady.

'Yes. Yes you did.'

When there was a knock at the door just two days later while Frankie was having supper with her children, her heart vaulted to the other side of her chest and back again. The children looked at her and she looked at them. They scraped back their chairs and stared through beyond the hallway to the front door. There, through the frosted-glass panes, the silhouette of a man.

Another knock, spritely this time, like a triumphant drum roll.

Frankie wasn't one for praying but, as she joined the children in a scramble for the door, she sent hopes and requests heavenward. The children, in school socks skating over the tiles, reached the door before their barefooted mother. Sam let Annabel open it. Frankie stood a little way back, hands clasped and a great daft grin on her face. Scott you beautiful man.

Only it wasn't Scott.

'Kids!'

It was Miles.

'Kids! Say hello to your Old Man, then.'

It was Miles.

'Frankie – hi.'

It was Miles.

'Hi Frankie,' he said again. 'Hi. So – it's just I had to take a cab and I didn't have a chance to get any cash. Could you just . . .'

He looked so different. After all, it had been over a year since they'd seen him last. He looked flummoxed, irritated even, because Frankie, Sam and Annabel simply stood there and stared.

The children needed to compute that the person standing right there in front of them that very second was in actual fact their dad. The fabled man who was last heard of panning for gold on the equator or at the end of a rainbow, the man who was meant to be somewhere else doing whatever it was he did, was simply standing there in jeans with a rip at the knee, a T-shirt that looked a bit dirty and a pair of old boots. There again, his hair was now long and in a pony-tail tied back with a red band and that was pretty cool.

Frankie's task was harder. Over and above having to compute that her ex-husband, with the most ridiculous hairstyle for a man his age, had apparently teleported from Equador to her house, was the thunking great disappointment that Scott was still in Canada. It was Miles here right now. Here in England. Not Scott.

So much for the power of prayer.

'Hi,' Miles said as if they hadn't heard him the first time. Annabel scurried up to him and hugged him for all she was worth, her eyes closing as he put his arm around her. Sam stepped close enough for this father-man to give his shoulder a squeeze. 'Hi kids.' Frankie was stock-still. 'Hi Frankie,' he said.

He's standing there with his hands on my children. 'Miles – what are you—?'

'Surprised, right!' He said it as though Christmas had come early. He could see a maelstrom of thoughts racketing through her head so he decided the best thing to do was to barge on. 'My project – well, let's just say it's on hold. So I thought – I know what I'll do. I said to myself, I'll go and see my family!'

Frankie thought, how can he make it sound like it's a magnificent brainwave blessing us all? She thought, what's he even doing *here*? She thought, why would the universe send me Miles and not Scott? She was sure Equador was even further than Canada. And then she thought, how dare he use the word *family*.

He was nodding, grinning all the while, as if he was agreeing with everything that Frankie was saying to herself. 'So – any chance of a brew? Haven't had a proper cuppa for a long, long while. Desperate for a change from the old *canelazo*.'

They hadn't a clue what he was talking about.

'Sam makes tea,' Annabel said helpfully, forgetting how appallingly he did so.

And Frankie heard herself say, Sam – make your father a cup of tea.

Annabel pulled Miles further into the hallway and Frankie stepped aside as they passed through to the kitchen. He touched her arm as he went by and she wished he hadn't.

She didn't hate him; she never had. Any acrimony she'd felt had been transitional and so long ago. Now, whether by letter or phone call, impromptu visit or lengthy desertion, he exhausted her, exasperated her. He wasn't a bad person, he wasn't cruel – Miles was just feckless and a bit useless and not what dads are meant to be made of. And that's why she'd left him.

All these years on, she didn't really feel very much for him at all but she felt for her children. However, when he'd put his hand on her bare skin moments ago – that she felt. It was real. He really was here. She didn't know why and she didn't know how she was going to get rid of him.

Frankie watched from a distance as he spun his synthetic yarns around the children – tall tales of danger on the high seas, narrow escapes in the jungle, life-and-death situations in dormant volcanoes, fool's gold in secret mines. She saw how the children allowed themselves to be bound by the bullshit, as if tied to their chairs by ribbons of his rubbish. She was aware that he was throwing her way every type of smile in his vast repertoire. They were all familiar and, though she knew how to deflect them one by one, Miles in all his extraordinary lightweight glory was still a heavy presence in her home.

She glanced at the oven clock: 6.30 in the evening. Any minute now, she thought, any minute now.

He left the table, making a clicking sound with his tongue while pointing gun-fingers at the children as if they were part of his special gang. Frankie quickly busied herself, scraping the cold food from the plates because there was no room for appetites with Miles filling the kitchen.

He came over to her and put his hand tenderly between her shoulder blades.

'Sorry for turning up out of the blue,' he said quietly. 'There was a tsunami of events and suddenly I was here before I really knew it.'

God you speak a load of old toss, Miles.

251

Frankie bit her tongue, smiled briefly, continued with the dishes.

Please move your hand.

Not up and down – just remove it.

'Anyway,' he said, 'it's always lovely to see you. And the kids. They've grown!'

You don't say.

'They're so big, so beautiful – I think of them all the time. Everything I do – it's for them. Did you get the money the other month?'

She nodded.

'There'll be more,' he said hurriedly. 'In a month or two. In a few. When this tornado rights itself.'

His continued reference to natural disasters was ridiculous. Frankie couldn't actually comment. Dishes, don't let them drain – dry them. Keep busy, distracted.

She thought – here it comes, any minute now.

'So – I might be around for a while,' Miles said.

'Well that'll be nice for the children. Where will you be based?' The level stare she gave him was meant to say don't you dare – just don't even think about it. He was about to speak – it was coming, it was imminent. She had only moments to intercept. 'Would you like a lift back to King's Lynn?' she said brightly. 'Just give me five minutes.'

'Oh Mum,' said Annabel who was keeping watch over the chair her father had vacated, as if guarding it from anyone else. 'He's only just arrived!'

Sam was looking down at his phone, but his cheeks had reddened and when he looked at Frankie, she couldn't quite read his expression.

'Your dad's staying for a while,' Frankie tried to appease them.

'Staying here!' Annabel was ecstatic.

And before Frankie had a chance to say no darling, he needs to get back to wherever but I'm sure he'll come and visit lots – Miles had already staked his response.

'Would that be OK?' he said softly, his bloody hand on her bloody arm again. 'Just for a night – I can make a couple of calls tomorrow, tonight even, and sort myself out. I am so tired – you wouldn't believe the journey I've had.'

'Oh Mum *please*!'

'It's so good to see you all again,' he murmured. 'Oh God you don't know how good it is.' His voice cracked and husked and Frankie thought damn you, Miles. Damn you.

'He's made himself at home,' Frankie whispered into the phone though she was at the end of the garden and no one could hear her. The children were in the house, sitting either side of their father, the way they did their mother, watching *The Simpsons*. It's what we do every night – it's a family tradition.

'He's sitting there, on my sofa with my children like he does every evening, like it's normal. Like it's his sofa in his house.'

There was a long pause at the other end of the phone.

'Do you feel in any way threatened?' Scott said. 'Do you feel unsafe?'

Frankie smiled a little sadly. 'No. He's not dangerous. He's simply a prat. And I just feel really annoyed at the intrusion. And a bit bewildered. It's easier when he's in far-flung places doing his thing. It's disruptive

253

enough on my children when he sends a card or some weird gift.'

Scott thought about the words she chose. 'You know, Frankie – twice you've said "my children". But, whatever shit he put you through, whatever shit he's caught up in right now, however poor a person he is – your kids know him as their father.' He paused to let her think about that. 'He may be a crap dad – but he's *their* crap dad.'

There are too many nettles in this garden, thought Frankie.

'He is what he is,' said Scott.

'You know, I've often felt that whoever I'd become pregnant to, I was only ever going to have Sam and Annabel. Like they pre-existed out there in the ether, little souls waiting for me to be ready. I don't actually credit Miles with – anything.'

'That I understand,' said Scott. 'But it's not about you – it's about Sam and Annabel – their reaction to him. They'll know his failings – you can't kid a kid. But if they want to file it away in a soundproofed part of their soul for a while so they can just *feel* the fact that their dad's come to see them – you have to let them.'

And then it struck Frankie what was happening. Fate might have dumped Miles on her doorstep this evening, but Fate had also given her a wise man, a good man who was far more present in her life than that oaf sitting between her kids on her sofa in her new home in Norfolk.

Peta was apoplectic.

Ruth was fascinated.

Peta told Frankie to tell Miles at the earliest opportunity to get the fuck out of her house.

However, from where she stood, Ruth had a completely different viewpoint.

'You know,' she said to Frankie on the phone, 'if he has nowhere to stay – and the kids seem pleased to have him around . . .' She trailed off, lit a secret cigarette at her back door.

'Are you *smoking*?'

'I'm *thinking*,' Ruth laughed. 'If the likelihood is that he'll bugger off for God knows how long to God knows where in the not-too-distant future.' She stopped for a moment, not to smoke but to phrase it as best she could. 'If you don't like being in his presence,' she said to Frankie, 'there's the most blindingly obvious solution. To everything – to absolutely everything that's in a whirl in your life right now.'

'There is?'

'Yes.'

'You really don't want Miles staying at yours, Ruth.'

Ruth snorted. 'My door is *not* open to him,' she said. And she thought how open her arms were to Frankie. On paper, such a new friendship, but actually such a solid one already. 'You haven't thought of this because it's all a bit bonkers right now. And you haven't thought of this because you're the mother of all mother bears.'

And then Ruth started laughing. 'Frankie,' she said. 'Frankie – leave Miles in charge for a bit. And go to Canada.'

* * *

'Who's your mum on the phone to?' Miles asked his children. 'She's been out there for ages. Doesn't she like *The Simpsons*?'

'She loves *The Simpsons*,' said Annabel, slipping her arm through Miles's and squeezing up close, truly believing that the yellow tribe from Springfield united her family.

'You're sitting in her place,' Sam said under his breath. Miles let it pass.

Annabel leant forward and looked out of the French doors, seeing the back of her mother, watching her head nod and her hands move to emphasize whatever it was she was saying. 'She's probably on the phone to Scott.'

'Who's Scott?'

'Her boyfriend,' Sam said.

* * *

'Are you out of your tiny mind?' Peta gasped down the phone.

'No,' said Frankie. 'I'm not.'

* * *

'Your house smells really nice,' Miles told Frankie. He was giving a big stretch, a yawn. He was lounging on the sofa, his hands behind his head, a little glimpse of nut-brown stomach. He looks thin, Frankie thought. 'It smells lovely,' he reiterated. 'You obviously rustled up a feast for your supper.'

She smiled politely and minimized eye contact though she could feel his eyes burning into her. He's looking at my breasts. She turned quickly and straightened a picture that didn't need it.

'There wouldn't be any left would there?' he said.

'Any what?'

'Delicious-smelling dinner,' he said. 'I haven't eaten properly – for days, I don't think.'

Unbelievable! But this is Miles, remember, so not so unbelievable after all. And then Frankie reminded herself that a sure-fire way to a man's heart was through his stomach. She needed him and he didn't yet know it.

'I'll heat some up,' she said.

The children were in bed, Sam reading, Annabel already fast asleep. Having had no men in her life, now Annabel had two. She felt lucky and intrigued and ever so tired with all the excitement.

Downstairs, Frankie sat opposite Miles, sipping wine rhythmically and probably too fast. Watching him tuck in so ravenously, she wondered whether the food wouldn't have been better served to him in a trough.

'Are you OK?' she asked. 'You're not in any – trouble?'

He chewed energetically, pushing his wine glass towards her for a refill. He shook his head. 'Not really,' he said. 'Nothing I can't handle.'

And Frankie thought, that's Miles – saying one thing and meaning another.

'How long are you staying?'

'As long as you'll have me,' he said, contorting his mouth as he chewed.

'I didn't mean here,' she said, 'I meant how long are you staying away from wherever it is you've been living?'

He glugged the wine. 'I don't know,' he said and his voice was a little flat. 'A while. Storms are raging – got to take cover.'

She had no idea what he meant specifically, but

memory served her well enough not to ask for the facts behind the metaphors. His eyes were boring into her. What does he want now? More wine? More food? He already has a bed for the bloody night.

'So – the kids were telling me you have a boyfriend.'

'Yes – I do.'

'Scott.'

'That's right.'

'So – where is this Scott? Is he coming here tonight? Do you live together?'

'No.'

'Will I meet him?'

'I doubt it.'

'Come on Frankie – it's been years.'

'He lives in Canada.'

'*Canada?* Couldn't you find someone a bit closer to home?'

Frankie wasn't sure whether Miles was being sweet or tart.

'Miles don't matter,' she said and she thought, never a truer word spoken.

He nodded and chewed thoughtfully. Then he was still and gazed at her intently. 'I'm happy for you,' he said. 'I hope it works out. You and the Mountie.'

'He's a musician.'

'Nice. Is there any more?'

Dolloping the last of the casserole onto his plate, she felt her heart and conscience twist and tighten like a rope twining fast. Miles's presence in her home was like the ants in the kitchen when they'd first arrived. Horribly annoying and making her skin crawl, despite their insignificance. But God she needed Miles now more than at any other time she'd known him.

'Here you go,' she said, putting the food in front of him. 'There's ice cream for pud. Cornish vanilla.'

'You know how to treat a man,' he said. He looked at her quizzically. 'You're looking good, Frankie.' His voice suddenly softer, considered. 'You're looking – lovely.'

He reached over and very gently touched a lock of her hair. She thought she saw his eyes fill. 'I –' Miles paused. 'I'm proud of you. All of this – all you've done.' For a moment, there was stillness as he contemplated her home. Then he forked up the last of the food, scraped up the juices onto his knife and licked it clean. He looked at her again. 'You look – almost beautiful. I've never seen you look like that.'

Almost beautiful. Was that a compliment or an insult? Classic Miles. She let it bounce off her and roll away between the floorboards.

'Being in love suits you,' he said, with thoughtfulness again. 'I've never seen you like this. Not in all the time I've known you.'

Miles walked Sam to the bus stop the next morning. He joined Frankie and Annabel on the school run and walked his daughter to the playground while Frankie stayed in the car.

'Have you a driving licence?' she asked him when he was back. He was rifling through the glove compartment. She had no idea why.

'Yes,' he said.

'Current?' she said. 'Valid? Legal?'

He laughed. 'Yes, Frankie, yes.'

'Good,' she said.

They were still in the school car park.

'I wanted to ask you something.' She turned in her seat and looked at him straight. A face she knew well and yet strangely not at all.

'Shoot!'

'I'd like to go to Canada – to see Scott. I'd like to go soon – soon as I can.' *This is a good idea*, she chanted to herself as a reminder. 'I wanted to ask you if you'd stay – at my home – and look after the children?'

For Miles, it was so left field it took some time to reach him. When it did, it was like a ball he hadn't expected to be within a hope of catching. 'Really? Seriously? *Me?*'

'Yes,' said Frankie. 'You.'

'Frankie.' She thought he was going to cry. 'Thank you so much. Thank you.'

She nodded. She started the engine and drove off.

'Just for while I'm gone, you understand,' she said in the tone of voice she used with the children when she was serious about something. 'Once I'm back, I want you to fuck off somewhere else.'

She let it hang then she glanced at Miles. He was sitting there, gazing at her like a small boy.

I t was only when Miles drove her to King's Lynn that it truly struck Frankie what she was about to do.

'Go,' said Miles because her nerves were palpable and he'd never liked the extremes of other people's emotions, especially not Frankie's. 'It's only a week,' he said. 'The kids'll be fine. You go – and just enjoy yourself. With your – bloke.' It struck him as just slightly weird to be encouraging and facilitating his ex-wife's new relationship. Their lives had been so separate he hadn't really given hers much thought at all over recent years. These last few days, however, seeing her operate in her home, watching how she interacted with the children, hearing how she chatted to her friends and her lover, Miles felt a little in awe of her and, as much as it was possible in his case, reflective too.

'You sure?' she asked him.

He tapped her knee. 'Yes.'

'I mean – sure about *everything*?'

'Yes!'

But still she sat there.

'You don't want to miss the train, Frankie,' he cautioned.

'I know – that's why I told you it was half an hour earlier than it is.'

He nodded. 'You don't trust me do you?'

Frankie looked up to see him pull his beseeching expression over his face like a mask. 'Not really,' she said. He looked immediately crestfallen. 'Sorry,' she said. 'It's just – you know.'

'Let the past go – feel the now, embrace the future,' he said.

Frankie snorted and giggled.

'I know,' Miles acquiesced, 'I sound like a tosser. But I just want you to know that it's all going to be good – at home. Over there in Canada. So – off you go. Bring me back some maple syrup or something. And just call whenever you want. The world's no longer that big.'

There was an authoritative but gentle cadence to Miles's voice, which Frankie had never heard. Maybe he had grown up, maybe he did now think beyond just himself. She took a deep breath.

'OK,' she said. 'OK. But—'

'No need for buts,' said Miles and he leant across and kissed her cheek.

She phoned her sister from the train but hung up before Peta answered and phoned Ruth instead.

'On the train,' she told her as if she was walking the plank.

'Bloody well done so far. I wasn't sure you were going to make it.' All those texts, those panicked calls and emergency cups of tea and an extra Alexander session crammed into the last three days.

'Am I doing the right thing?'

'Frankie,' said Ruth with friendly chide.

'It just seems suddenly terribly indulgent – spending

all this money on a flight, leaving the kids – I'm genuinely stressing that I'm going to get walloped by something awful happening. Bad karma, or something.'

'Oh – of course! You mean like the plane crashing? Or your house burning down?'

'Yes.'

'Scott being a pig?'

'No – not that.'

'Being eaten by a bear?'

'Maybe.'

'Are you crying?'

'Almost.'

'You know you're being daft? The worst thing and the most likely calamity will be your dumbfuck ex forgetting to take the kids to school. But you've given Sam my number. And I'll pass by yours, accidentally-on-purpose, twice daily if you like.'

'It just doesn't feel as good as I thought it would, when the notion of going to see Scott seemed a dream away.'

'It will feel better – once you're up in the air. We're guilty as women, as mothers, of demoting our needs, belittling our dreams, turning away from our wishes. Frankie, when you're with your chappie – you need to just let go and truly be *there*.'

Peta phoned Frankie who had just arrived at Heathrow. She'd seen the missed call. They hadn't spoken since Frankie hung up on her and four days was a long time for them.

'Hi,' said Frankie.

'Hello,' said Peta. 'Where are you?'

'Heathrow,' came the small voice.

Peta composed herself quickly. She'd done it, her little sister had done it. Oddly, she no longer felt any annoyance at all, just immense pride. 'Have you checked in?'

'No.'

'Are you crying?'

'Almost.'

'Check in, Frankie. Check in and phone me when you've gone through passports.'

Peta looked at their mother who was over for lunch. 'You know Frankie is flying to Canada?'

'Frankie?' The notion to Margaret was preposterous.

'Today – right now. Did you not know?'

'I did not.'

'To see Scott.' Peta let it hang as she loaded her mother's plate with chicken salad. 'You knew about Scott, though?' She knew her mother did not.

'Scott?' Margaret said it as though the name itself was unfathomable.

'Frankie's – boyfriend.'

'You can't have a *boy*friend at Frankie's age. It sounds ridiculous.'

Peta paused. 'He's more than a boyfriend,' she said. 'He's the love of her life.'

Margaret chewed at her food, her jaw clicking infuriatingly. Peta thought if Frankie was here they could share exasperated glances. She was acutely aware of being her mother's favourite. Rather than bringing her any joy, the fact had always made her fiercely protective of her younger sister.

'You should be happy for her, you know,' Peta said.

'Happy that Frankie is *embroiled* with Canada?'

Peta had to laugh. Mum says you are embroiled with

Canada – as if the entire country is a seething mass of anarchy and disease with Scott at the helm.

'Scott,' Peta pushed on. 'He's a little older than her.' She thought about what else to tell her. 'He's a famous musician.' That had fallen flat. 'He comes over here sometimes.' A flicker of interest. 'The children have met him – and like him very much.'

'That's as maybe,' her mother said. 'But while Frankie is gadding about on some silly romance, who is looking after the children?'

Peta took a large sip of wine. 'Miles.'

Her mother almost choked. '*Miles?*'

Peta took another sip, nodded. 'He's over for – a bit. So Frankie thought it would be good for the children. Good for her.' She paused. 'Good for her,' she said again, quietly.

'*Miles?*' Her mother had fury emanating from every pore. 'Miles – good for the children? Good for nothing! I've heard it all now,' she blustered. 'I've heard it all now.'

In the departures lounge, glancing around at the people who'd be on her flight, Frankie stared at the planes outside. They looked alternately far too big to be up in the air and yet way too small to make transatlantic journeys. Why is Vancouver YVR? What does that mean? Why couldn't she work it out? She found a seat on an isolated row of five, tucked in a corner that needed a sweep. She phoned Peta again but it went through to her voicemail. She texted Ruth but knew she'd be with a client. It was five in the morning in Pemberton and if anyone knew how she must be feeling it would be Scott. Bleary with sleep, he was half-expecting the call anyway.

'Did you make it to the airport?' he asked before she'd said anything. 'Have you gone through security?' He took her silences to be affirmative. 'Are you coming over to see me, Frankie?'

That voice.

'Yes,' she said.

'I'm so pleased,' he said. 'You sure you don't want Aaron to fly us back here? He's keen – it's no trouble.'

'No,' she said, 'one flight is enough. And I don't do little planes.'

Scott looked at his watch. 'Hey baby,' he said and it made Frankie feel she was right next to him. 'I get to see you in twelve hours' time.'

She texted Peta from the plane, seat belt fastened and a prized spare seat next to her.

I'm on the plane – I don't know what I'm doing. Fx

She sent a text to Sam

Sammy see you soon – love you, Mummy xxx

She wished she'd granted Annabel her number one wish for a mobile phone.

She sent another text to Sam

Annabella see you soon – love you Mummy xxx

She sent a text to Scott

I really am on my way. Fx

She was just about to turn off the phone when Peta's reply came through.

You're doing the right thing, F. Safe journey – and just be open to all that awaits . . . Pxxx

Frankie loved her sister very much. And then the air hostess said Madam I really must ask you to switch off your phone now. As the plane taxied to the runway,

Frankie sobbed into her hands. What on earth was she doing, leaving home and all that she knew?

She half-watched movies. She skimmed her magazine and she studied the safety information. She picked at the food. She tried to doze but couldn't. She balanced her manuscript on the tray table and, for the umpteenth time, honed and tinkered what she had written thus far. Look at us, Alice, you and me, in the sky and over the sea. She was fastidious about leaving her seat and moving around the cabin, drinking lots of water, dabbing essential oils on her pulse points and applying moisturizer regularly. Thank God for *Grazia*. She made sure to do a few of the exercises Ruth had taught her. Thank you Ruth.

Greenland was out of the window and it was unlike anywhere Frankie had ever seen. She hadn't expected green but nor had she expected anything so lonely, so lunar. Was this really her world – planet earth? Resting her head against the window, fitting her body in a neat furl over the two seats, the thin blanket equally comforting in its warmth and annoying in its static, she closed her eyes.

And then they were waking her up and she couldn't believe she'd slept.

Mountains like she'd never seen, stretching way beyond her field of vision. A land of mountains, striated with meanderings of snow, dimpled with lakes and divided by rivers ribboning as far as the eye could see. It all looked unfathomably different out there from anywhere she'd ever been and all that she knew. She was further than she'd been before and just twenty minutes from touching down in Scott's homeland. Look at it out there! It's like heaven's tablecloth rucked up.

It was then that Frankie began to smile.

Alice, you have to see this place.

She'd presumed that Vancouver airport would be something like Heathrow; noise and queues and miles of walking under harsh lighting and scuffed floors. Instead, an unexpected but welcome calmness greeted her, blues and greens and lots of glass, carpet underfoot and extraordinary First Nations art wherever she looked. Two huge Musqueam figures carved into red cedar greeted her and soon after, with little queuing, a small bespectacled immigration officer officially welcomed her to Canada. It was as if she was expected. She didn't even have to wait long for her suitcase. It felt to her that the airport had been cleared so that nothing should impede her exit.

It's one in the morning. No it isn't, it's five in the afternoon.

Her phone was busy with incoming texts. Sam. Annabel on Sam's phone. Ruth. Miles. And Peta. But no Scott. She liked his silence. Why send a text when he was right here, just yards away, waiting in Arrivals?

Frankie pushed her trolley, followed the signs propelled by adrenalin. She didn't see Scott at first. From the relative emptiness of the arrivals hall, suddenly there were throngs of people in the main concourse, eddies of activity and much noise. Where are you?

I'm here, baby. I'm leaning on the railings by Joe David's huge yellow cedar *Welcome Figures*. Their arms are outstretched to greet you the Clayoquot way. Here,

over here Frankie. I'm the guy who can't stop grinning.
Yes, here – it's me. Look at you! You made it. Over
the oceans, the mountains and through time: here you
are. My arms, tight tight around you. Your cheek against
my chest, placing my face against your head, inhaling
the unmistakable fragrance of you – shampoo and
perfume and something like apples and toast. Kissing
you over and again. I don't know what I'm saying, I'm
just murmuring some crazy old nonsense. Let the world
go on around us. Amidst it all we are steady and still.

'You'll have to pinch me if you see me falling asleep,'
Frankie told Scott, looking up at him, reeling with
exhaustion, excitement, disbelief.

'And you have to pinch me to prove that I'm actually
awake,' he laughed.

F rankie wondered if it sounded too shallow, too repetitive to keep gazing at the landscape and saying she'd never seen anything like it. But it was true, she hadn't. After the relative flatness of Norfolk living, where even a rolling incline in the road felt fundamentally uphill, to now see mountains of such magnitude was simply breathtaking.

'Not in my dreams – not even in the photos you've shown me – did I ever think it would be this beautiful,' she told Scott, 'this vast.'

'Oh it gets better,' he said. 'We're now on the Sea to Sky Highway – our Route 99. It's going to take us all the way home – around two and a half hours from here. You just say if you want to stop.'

'I don't know what I want – slow down so I can drink it all in or speed up so we can get there.' Out of the window, Howe Sound reflecting the mountains that soared heavenward and serrated the sky.

'So soon you'll see the Stawamus Chief.'

'Is he expecting us? Do you know him?' Frankie looked around. 'Is he First Nations?'

'That,' Scott said a little while later, 'is the Stawamus Chief and there's all sorts of Squamish legends about a giant two-headed sea serpent.' She stared up at 700 towering metres of granite. 'The views from the top, Frankie – out over Howe Sound, the mountains of Garibaldi – one day, when you come back for longer, we'll do it. Aaron climbs the Chief in a pair of trainers. And fast.'

'He's Lílwat and his wife is Squamish and both are Salish First Nations.' She wanted to make sure she had it right. 'Their children are Tara and Johnny.'

'They're coming to check you out tomorrow,' Scott told her. 'And Jenna too. There's a whole bunch of people waiting to meet you.'

'Look!' Never had Frankie seen a road sign warning of bears. 'Might we see one?'

'I can almost guarantee it. I have one guy who comes down maybe two, three times a week.'

'What does Buddy do?'

'Stays inside,' Scott laughed.

On they drove, few cars on the road to impede their progress. The ski runs of Whistler, now green, resembling the swipe of a razor through mountainsides bearded with alder and Sitka spruce, Douglas fir and western red cedar. The early-evening light caressed the landscape. Every now and then, Scott's hand on her knee.

'Nineteen Mile Bridge,' Frankie said. She was reading every sign now. With 5 km to go to Pemberton, the road climbed and curved dramatically with a vista after Nairn Falls that took her breath away. Scott had become quiet. She touched his arm.

'You OK, Scott?'

He turned to her. 'I just really hope you like it here, Frankie.'

He drove off the main road to show her Pemberton

village, so she could finally put into three dimensions a street map she'd learned off by heart.

'And that, Miss Shaw, is Mount Currie,' Scott said.

'*Tśzil.*' Frankie turned to Scott. 'Did I say it right?' The mountain struck her as benevolent, regardless of how vast it was and how potentially hostile parts of it must be in any season.

'Right enough,' he said. 'It means "slides on the mountain". It's hard to see in this light and from here, but the rocks form a profile of John Sky – in his feather headdress. To the Líĺwat, he was the last great medicine man and when he died they believe his spirit went to the mountain. You can tell the weather from his face – if the clouds are below it means rain or snow.'

They continued on with the Lillooet River to their right, signs for the airfield and golf, a distillery on the left and, Scott told her, his friends' North Arm Farm on the right. They want to meet you too, Frankie.

On through the reservation of Mount Currie where Aaron lived, then following the Birkenhead River a little way along the old Portage road to D'Arcy before turning off and climbing again. The sky was wearing the colours of a glorious day just gone, one which Frankie had spent up in her plane, hours and hours in no man's sky – not England, not Canada, just a mind-twisting conduit between the two at 40,000 feet. Tomorrow, she thought, I will wake up to this.

'Here,' said Scott. 'We're here.'

His home, still a little way ahead at the end of a long snaking drive, sat snug and yet confident in the hillside, like an experienced climber who knew just where to rest. It was solid in its plot, as if making camp at the best viewpoint out over the valley to Mount

Currie. The windows, huge windows, gazing up and out to all that wilderness, unaware of the tiny people in the toy truck approaching. Scott drove the final stretch slowly, aware that Frankie was soaking up the details. His garden, plotted and pieced by a series of steps and low walls as if, without them, it might slither down the hillside. The house, whilst not big in size, was immense in its construction; huge logs of cedar banked horizontally and interlinking at the corners like a giant's clasped fingers. Scott stopped his truck and lifted her hair away from her face, tucked it behind her ear and said, we're home, Frankie, we're home.

Stepping out into the evening, dusk coming in wafts, Frankie couldn't tell whether her head was light or her legs were weak but Scott stood close behind her as she breathed in all that she saw, exhaling the protracted but epic journey that had brought her here.

'Hey,' he laughed softly, 'want to come in?'

She turned to him, held his head in her hands and nodded.

'Hello Buddy,' Frankie said as a wet nose butted against her and big doleful eyes tried to assess her, with glances over to Scott for reassurance if not an explanation. It's all as it should be, Frankie thought to herself, it's exactly as I imagined. What she hadn't accounted for was how comforting the pervasive scent of wood was after long hours of warm sunlight. Along with Scott's arm around her waist, Buddy resting his body against her leg, the rhythmic tock of a clock she couldn't see, Frankie thought how she could very well fall asleep standing exactly where she was.

'You like it?'

'It's – everything,' she told him.

She followed him up the stairs to his bedroom. It was a large space dominated by a bed in dark walnut. Over the floorboards a faded and worn tapestry rug. On the walls, paintings in thick slabs of colour signifying mountains and streams, lakes and skies. An old chest of drawers, a crowd of framed photos: his dog and his daughter, perhaps those were his parents, that's Aaron with his kids, here are Scott and Jenna in all seasons in landscapes that would be known soon enough to her.

'I made space in the cupboards and in the middle drawer there,' he told her. 'The bathroom is through that door.' He thought it was pretty much time to put on the lights now but looking at her, she was all shadows and highlights and looked lovely. She also looked exhausted. 'I made a little food – you need to eat before you sleep. You need to fit into my time now you're here.'

Frankie, right here in his room, all the way over here in this new land of hers which had always been his home. She'd made it. 'You unpack – I'll go heat up the food.' He made his way downstairs, still amazed at the concept of having invited someone to unpack in his room. So much for baggage, he thought to himself and it made him chuckle.

The first thing Frankie did was take off her trainers and socks and settle her hot, tired feet against the floorboards, sensing their dry warmth travelling up her legs. Then she stood on the rug, moving her toes over its surface soft in some places almost threadbare in others. She made her silent introduction to the host of people in the framed photos and she peered into Scott's bathroom, wondering how he'd felt when putting out two towels. Had her flight already departed when he got the house ready for her arrival? Was all of that only today? Finally she sat on the edge of Scott's bed. And the next thing she knew he was cuddling her and laughing, tickling and pinching her saying no Frankie no! You mustn't sleep yet.

'Oh God I must've zonked out.' Her head was spinning and she felt a little sick.

'I only went downstairs a quarter-hour ago,' he laughed. 'Come on. Up! Up!'

'Just ten more minutes? I'm not hungry.'

'No!' he jabbed at her waist and flicked his finger lightly at her cheek. He took her hand and led her downstairs.

She woke with a start, convinced it was gone lunchtime. The clock, however, proclaimed a befuddling 3 a.m. She knew exactly where she was. Next to her, Scott slept, breathing slow and soft. The sheet was draped over his waist, his back towards her, moonlight slicking a few hazed tones over his skin. She lay on her side and just looked at him, tracing with her eyes the way his neck curved into his shoulders, the irregular pattern of a few moles in a spatter, his head cleaving into the pillow, the dip and run of his strong arm. As soundlessly as she could, she moved closer to him. On her fingers she counted forwards by eight. What would her children be doing now, at eleven in the morning? Even at home, during the day, she'd often wonder. She'd never slept this late in the UK, though frequently, she'd woken at an hour as ungodly as this. Over the last few years, there'd rarely been a period of time during which nothing was on her mind. A good night's sleep was really only one when she might wake just the once, check the time and drift off again after pushing a barrage of thoughts to the other side of the bed where no one had slept for a long time. She gazed at Scott's back and moved closer until her skin just touched his.

Nothing much woke Scott. But the warmth of a body in his bed in his home was the exception. He could easily count the number of times he'd brought someone back here, more usually favouring hotels, motels, their homes. He kept still, his eyes now open, just revelling in the notion of Frankie being here, right now. Her breath against his back. She was awake, he could tell; he could feel her think. He knew all about jet lag, how her mind would be jumping about as if her legs were straddling the Atlantic while she tried to catch reverberating thoughts and kid her body that it was not eight hours later. She moved a little closer still, her breathing trampolining lightly on the skin right between his shoulder blades. He willed her closer still. And here were her lips, kissing him just twice, as gently as she could manage. How easy it would be to turn to her, enfold her in his arms, make love again. But he knew she didn't want to wake him, she was kissing him just because she wanted to, in a private time that was uniquely hers. It was at that moment that Scott felt truly loved. And the emotions which swept through him were expressed by a single and unexpected tear.

He woke at seven and the other side of the bed was empty. He could hear her downstairs chatting to herself or Buddy, or maybe even the UK on the phone, he couldn't be sure. She was obviously trying to be quiet and failing – an occasional hiss at herself accompanying an inadvertent clatter. He turned and assessed the space in the bed. He rolled over onto it, found the pillow to carry the scent of her but the sheets to be cool. He closed his eyes and thought back to making love last night when he'd finally let her go to bed. He'd worried she'd be too tired but his dinner had revived her and built an appetite for him. She'd chosen to be on top most of the time, smiling at him, bending to kiss him, to trace her tongue tip along his lips, to whisper in his ear both words of love as well as screamingly rude requests. He could see her now, upright and moving, his hands travelling where his eyes were scanning; the vivid recall of how she crumpled down gasping, telling him to wait! wait! not yet Scott – I don't want to come yet. And then they'd fucked, fast and urgent, a month's pent-up longing driving their desire.

Lying there, knowing she was downstairs, he thought how he could do it all over again. He was hard and ready. But she'd just said shit, twice, and something had broken. Scott smiled. Just a regular day at the ranch, he said to himself. The notion that mundanity could be so extraordinary, so enveloping, struck him as profound. There was no need for drama or complexity, for high romance or a constant soundtrack. Some force out there had his dreams in a cradle because downstairs, right at this very minute, they were being played out.

'I'm so sorry!'

She was wearing his T-shirt and holding a broken mug in one hand, its handle in the other. Darth Vader was glaring out at Scott from across her chest but his legs were Frankie's legs and it looked comic.

'I broke it,' she said. 'Why do you keep your mugs so high up?'

'I guess it completely slipped my mind to design the kitchen around a clumsy small Englishwoman,' he said.

'I think I found your breakfast stuff – cereals, butter, jam. I laid the table,' she said, motioning to it. 'I couldn't find food for Buddy so I made him a scrambled egg.'

Scott looked from his dog to his girl.

'I hope that's OK?'

Buddy was siding with Frankie on this one and padded over to where she stood.

'I was going to make you pancakes,' he said. 'You know it's only seven, right?'

'I've been up since just gone half-five,' she said. 'I didn't want to wake you. I didn't – did I?'

Scott brandished a whisk at her. 'Pancakes?'

'I found the maple syrup.'

'Did you taste it?'

He knew she had. He could tell when he kissed her.

Frankie was at Scott's and everyone knew it. Aaron had broadcast the news at Mount Currie and Jenna had spoken of little else at Whistler; the information had converged at Pemberton and seeped through the village itself. It was spoken of as the cinnamon buns were iced at the Blackbird Bakery and the beans were roasted at the Mount Currie Coffee Company, it was discussed when the deliveries arrived at Frontier Street Pharmacy, it filled the tanks at Esso and Husky, and it went into the ingredients being prepared for lunch at Solfeggio. From North Arm Farm to the Pony, from teeing off at Big Sky to queuing at Scotiabank, from the medical

centre to the visitor centre – everyone knew that Scott's
girl had arrived from the UK.

Scott had told Aaron that it would be OK to call in
later in the morning. Though Rose chided him and
whacked him with a tea towel, her husband would not
step away from his reasoning that as he'd been up for
hours, therefore it was now later in his morning.

'Poor girl's probably still asleep,' Rose said, 'or in bed
being happy.'

'Well, I'll just go see,' Aaron said.

'You should phone first,' said Rose.

'When ever did I need to phone Scott?'

Scott was in the shower and Frankie was still in the
Darth Vader T-shirt rummaging in kitchen cupboards
to acquaint herself with what Scott kept where, when
Aaron let himself in.

'Ho,' he said.

She jumped out of her skin but he just grinned and
mooched over to feel the coffee pot. Warm but
it could do with freshening. 'I'm Aaron,' he said with
a broad smile.

'I'm –'

'Padmé?' he said. 'Princess Leia?'

'I'm – not dressed,' she squirmed and darted up the
stairs.

Aaron helped himself to blueberries and coffee and
sat down, listening with a grin to the scurrying and chatter
upstairs.

'Hey Buddy,' he whispered with a conspiratorial wink.
'What the fuck, man – *what the fuck!* Scott and Frankie.'

They laughed about their initial meeting later, as they
walked along Owl Creek, Aaron having invited himself

Freya North

along. He stared at Frankie a lot. He needed to – he'd previously cloaked her with all he'd gleaned from Scott but now she was here, he had to readjust some of that. She was shorter than he'd expected – pretty but just plainer and more natural in contrast to Scott's past predilections. Aaron liked the real Frankie a whole lot better. Once the Darth Vader incident had been laughed off, Aaron found her to be far from shy. He liked it that she already rolled her eyes at his lousy jokes and he liked the way she teased Scott, accompanied with little pushes and punches. There was a whole lot of handholding going on, he'd be telling Rose later.

Frankie also asked many questions but Aaron liked that. He was naturally gregarious and proud of his heritage but living here so long, known well by so many people, Aaron was just Aaron. He'd known Scott since he could remember, they'd been through school together and now he ran his little business from the airfield, shopped locally and got involved in most things. But Frankie wanted to know about what it meant to be First Nations, she wanted to know about his people and it made Aaron contemplate how he rarely had the opportunity to explain it.

'So the Lílwat Nation are an Interior Salish people – part of the Stát'yemc group,' he told her as they walked.

'I know,' she said. 'I read up on it before I came. Your ancestors have lived these parts for over five thousand years. They used to live in subterranean pit houses during the winter, called *ístkens*.'

'You know Úcwalmícwts?'

'Who are they?'

Aaron laughed. 'It's our language.'

280

'Well I do know that *skwímtscen* means rainbow and that it's your nickname for Jenna.'

'Do you know what my nickname for Scott is? It's *splaont.*'

'What does that mean?' asked Frankie.

'It means Smart Man with the Heart of Bear,' said Scott.

'Nice try,' said Aaron. 'It means skunk – and he knows it.'

'Remind me not to ask you for a nickname,' laughed Frankie as they walked on.

'Our territory is almost eight hundred thousand hectares – goes south to Rubble Creek, north to Gates Lake, east to the Upper Stein Valley and west to the coastal inlets,' Aaron told her. 'Our land is enclosed between two mountain ranges – we have beautiful names for all of them and legends for each. We're hunters and fishermen, we're the greatest basket weavers in the world. We're champion bronc riders and bull riders and barrel racers. We're front and centre on Canada's First Nations Snowboard Team. And boy, can we drum.'

'Christ, Aaron – you could take tours at the cultural centre,' Scott laughed.

'I'm too busy flying you to Vancouver and back,' Aaron retorted. 'Anyways, Frankie – you white guys came along and took our land in the 1800s, called us wild beasts and corralled us into reserves. We signed the Lillooet Declaration in 1911, for our right to our traditional lands. In 1975 we led a protest to protect our fishing rights. I was a little kid then – but I remember the talk. We also stopped clear-cut logging and the destruction of our sacred sites.'

'I don't know what to say.'

Scott and Aaron regarded Frankie who looked genuinely apologetic.

'Hey, I've been making Scott feel guilty for years.' Aaron nudged her and smiled. 'You know, the Líĺwat are over two thousand strong these days. Two-thirds of us live at Mount Currie while the others live off reservation. You know, when I was a kid and my mum sent me to Aaron's school, some of our people ostracized her awhile. You have to remember that in my grandparents' and parents' generation, the federal government sent many First Nations children to residential schools where they were forbidden to use their language, their songs and dances. But most of us are happy to get along with white folk – like most of you guys are happy to get along with us. There's respect now, that we campaigned hard for.' They stopped, all of them with hands on their hips, taking in the surroundings. 'But this is what matters – it's beautiful, right?' He turned to Frankie. 'If you're Native, if you're white – you share a love for this place.'

She tried to take it all in, her senses overloaded; the softest breeze delicate through the rising heat, the scent of freshness, the sounds of water, birds and branches, the sight of lake and land and sky. And mountains, always the mountains. Mount Currie – Tśzil. Owl Mountain – Skalúa7. Mount Meager – Múmleq.

'I've never been anywhere like this.'

'You'll take a little of it with you wherever you go now,' Aaron said to her. '*Pelpala7wít i ucwalmícwa múta7 ti tmícwa* – the land and the people are one.'

As they walked, Scott and Aaron told Frankie tales of their childhood, anecdotes to be laughed at and reflected upon. Aaron talked of fish as if they were lovers: sockeye, coho, Chinook, pink and chum salmon, steelhead, bullhead, suckers and whitefish. Scott pointed out cottonwood trees, western hemlock and red cedar, Douglas fir and Engelmann spruce. They showed her a cedar where long sections of the fibrous bark had been pared off to be used by the Líĺwat for mats, hats, blankets, baskets, fishing nets, rope.

'We live by two concepts when it comes to nature,' Aaron told her. 'Kúĺantsut and kúĺtsam – we take only food and materials that we need.'

'Unless it's my beer,' Scott said.

'Unless it's Scott's beer,' Aaron agreed.

'And I'll meet Rose later?'

'Oh yes,' said Aaron. 'You'll see a lot of us while you're here.'

'Not too much,' Scott said.

'*A lot* of us – all of us, Rose, me, Tara and Johnny. I'll take you up in my plane.'

'I don't like flying,' she told him.

'But the world comes to you when you're up there,' Aaron said.

They stood at the lake. They were the only people there.

'But everything I want in the world is right here,' Frankie said, wrapping her arms around Scott and grinning at the sky.

Once Aaron's family had gone home after visiting in the afternoon, Scott left Buddy looking after Frankie and drove to Whistler to collect Jenna after her shift. Alone in his home as Frankie waited, toying with the idea of doing some work on her book, she remembered how she'd felt on telling her children about Scott, able to smile now at their unexpectedly revolting response when they first met him. She thought about Jenna. If I were twenty, she wondered, how would I feel about meeting my father's new girl-friend? What would I think of Me?

She sank into the sofa, looking in turn at each of the guitars hanging from supports on the wall. They looked beautiful in their own right, wood carved into those sensual shapes, exuding silent music. Buddy came over, his tongue lolling as if he was mid-conversation. Frankie patted his head.

'You know something,' she told him, 'I was twenty-one when my father remarried and had my half-sister.' Frankie thought of Stephanie. How did I feel? She laughed out loud. 'I rolled my eyes at the concept and talked to Peta for hours on end about how to handle Mum when she found out.' She thought again of Steph. She hadn't spoken to her since she'd phoned to see if she could look after the children when she'd first met Scott. 'I must phone her more often,' Frankie told Buddy. 'She's a bit on her own now – despite always being so larky and so bloody bouncy.' She thought about her late father. He could play the banjo. There were few other defining features she really recalled about him. 'I didn't see him much – he left my mum, he left Steph's mum, he left the one after that and then he died.' The dog yawned. 'Why am I telling you all of this anyway?' she said. 'You're a *dog*.' At that, Buddy left and went to the open front door and out onto the porch. It was five in the afternoon. Frankie had been on Canadian soil for just twenty-four hours.

Frankie followed Buddy and sat on the swing seat, rocked it gently, her feet meeting the dog's back rhythmically with light strokes over his chocolate-brown coat. She gazed out over the valley to Mount Currie. Trees in a verdant blur appeared uniform until seen on the ridges where each stood uniquely delineated against the sky, some solitary, others in family groups, like a motley queue waiting to get to the top. She looked for John Sky's face but couldn't see it.

Scott's truck, still a way off, but approaching. A surge of nerves took her quite off guard. Was she to shake hands or kiss Jenna? What was the etiquette? Where's the handbook for finding love at this stage in one's life?

'I'm Jenna.'

'I know,' said Frankie naturally matching and mirroring Jenna's expansive grin and searching gaze. 'I'm so pleased to finally meet you.'

'Oh my God me too – like you wouldn't believe.'

They weren't quite sure what to do but they smiled and hugged warmly then turned and looked at Scott. He was standing in the doorway scratching his head at a scene he'd never even thought to imagine.

Frankie woke Scott at three in the morning.

'I can't sleep.'

He mumbled something soothing.

'Your daughter is just lovely,' she told him.

'Shh – you'll wake her up.'

'I'm whispering!'

'Sounds loud.'

'Wake up Scott.' She nudged him. 'Wake up! I'll be gone in a few days and you'll regret not waking up right now.'

He chuckled and sighed, turned to lie on his back, opening his arm for Frankie to snuggle into the crook. He smelt warm and sleepy, his body felt soft as well as strong and, while he pulled her hair gently through his fingers and she tuned in to his heartbeat, Frankie felt she might be able to drift off.

'All these years it's been just me and Jenna,' he said. 'And now you're here and it's all OK.'

'Were you worried?'

'A little.'

'Was she?'

'No.'

'What were you worried about?'

'You want the people you love most in the world to get along, right?'

'And we do.'

'I know – I hardly got a word in.'

'You disappeared off to your studio!'

'Shh – you'll wake her. I only went because you were talking about boys and stuff. You were talking about me. It was – weird.'

Frankie giggled and Scott again said shh! She travelled her hand down his body and found his cock.

'Stop,' he whispered, 'I mean it.' He half-heartedly tried to take her hand away but it felt too good. 'Not with Jenna in the house.'

'Don't be so daft,' Frankie whispered into his ear, giving the lobe a tantalizing suck. 'I can be ever so quiet.'

'*You* made me sleep in your spare room,' Scott objected.

'You offered,' Frankie said, kissing his neck while her hands swept along his body. 'But I'm wide awake – and, by the feel of things, you are too.' She kissed a path down his stomach. 'Be such a shame to let *this* go to waste.'

Scott grabbed her arms and pulled her up to him, flipped her onto her back and slid up into her, pushing in deep and then staying motionless. It made Frankie gasp and he placed the palm of his hand over her mouth.

'Shh,' he told her. 'Don't you make a sound.' He took his hand away and put his lips against hers.

Jenna could hear the bed creak in her dad's room. She could hear whispers and occasional soft laughter. In her old bedroom, Jenna put her pillow over her head and giggled, wondering when it would be safe to emerge.

Because oh my God – that's pretty gross.

* * *

Each day of Frankie's trip, Scott found some excuse to go into Pemberton, and the village that had seen so little of him was now treated to the regular sight of him mooching hand in hand with his girl. They ate at Mile One and the Pony, they bought food from the deli and browsed the aisles of both the small supermarkets. He proudly showed her just how stocked the pharmacy on Frontier Street was. Speaker cable, toys, T-shirts, electrical items, enough stationery to stock a school. He took her to the crammed and quirky General Store where they happily rooted around for half an hour. He had an amp in there still for sale three years on but he hadn't the heart to take it to the store in Kamloops.

Everywhere they went, people said well hey Scott, how you doing? He'd proudly introduce Frankie and they'd all chat awhile. Later, they'd say to each other, you know I saw Scott today with his girl and I could not stop him talking. Oh you saw him too?

'It's been a long time coming.' Aaron was discussing Scott behind his back. 'But it's no more than he deserves. Rose always says there's love enough in the world for all folk to find.'

'You think he'll stay?' Jordan mused. 'You think he'll move to the United Kingdom?'

Aaron looked a little startled. 'Scott? Leave?'

Jordan shrugged. 'So – maybe she'll move here? She has a family, right?'

Aaron stared into the neck of his beer bottle. He hadn't wondered about any of it. Logistics seemed a cumbersome concept where love was involved. 'I don't know,' he said thoughtfully.

'But it's serious – you can tell.'

Aaron nodded. 'It's the real deal.'

* * *

Frankie was washing up when Scott came up behind her, his arms around her. Giving her bottom a smack he looked at the clock.

'I need to do a little work,' he told her.

'I might try and work too.'

'You're on vacation,' he laughed.

'But I want to try – just to see.'

'I'll be in the studio – I'll surface around lunch-time.'

She did try but it was as if Alice had missed the flight and was therefore still in UK time and asleep. Instead, Frankie sketched Buddy. She thought back to the ideas she'd had when she'd first heard about the dog who liked to fly. Maybe she'd talk it through with her agent when she was back. Or email him from out here. I have a job I can do from anywhere, she thought. Although not, it seemed, from Scott's kitchen table.

He'd done a good morning's work and in the after-noon they walked.

'What I love about it out here,' Frankie said, walking the boardwalk out over the water at One Mile Lake, 'is that there's everything. Lakes and mountains and forests. And cinnamon buns and friendly people. It's such a thriving community. Everyone seems to actively embrace where it is they live. They really appreciate it. It's quite different to Norfolk. And you have *bears*,' she marvelled, 'though I've yet to see one.'

'You will,' said Scott. 'If not this time – then next time. BC has more races of black bear than any other part of Canada.'

'And you have two schools,' she said quietly when she stopped to take in the vista. Families were playing and picnicking back on the shore. Ahead of her, the forest. They walked on towards the trees. 'It's a good life out here, isn't it?'

'It is, for sure. But you know, we also live with the real threat of landslides and floods and forest fires – there's nothing like seeing fire candle up a tree. They say that fire doesn't travel downhill, well it does if burning trees fall,' Scott said. He pointed to a fire-ravaged area of hillside where the trees looked like ghost-trees, soft and thin like stained, tattered gossamer amongst all the strong and sturdy green. 'And winter can be a bitch.' He looked at Frankie. 'It is what you make of it, Frankie. But that's the same for any place.'

'But they clear your roads twice a day when it snows,' Frankie said. 'You want to try living in Norfolk,' she said darkly. 'There are razor blades on the wind in winter.'

'But if you ask folk around here, they'd say there's a lack of recreational facilities and it's a long winter. Skiing is expensive – you're looking at almost two thousand bucks for a season pass. We have no indoor pool, no arena, no gym. We could do with better trails networks. A bus that goes further than Whistler. That's why I feel my mentoring the kids is important – not just for the music, but to give them some impetus, something to do.' He thought about it. 'You have to commit to a place like Pemby. Like you have to make a commitment to your little cottage with the postbox in the wall.'

'But I don't have history there,' Frankie said. 'I don't have ties. I have a job I can do from anywhere.'

Scott knew what she was trying to say, but he knew too that his country was beguiling on a first visit in July. Stop and think, that's what he wanted to tell her.

Scott took her hand. 'Wherever we are, we're together.'

She thought about that.

The scent of spruce and fir was phenomenal.

'But not even Holkham smells this good.'

She closed her eyes and breathed deeply as if inhaling it straight into a vial she could use once she was back in the UK.

'Sometimes metaphors and symbolism aren't enough.' She turned to Scott. 'When we reach the turning points in life, we mustn't back off, we must stride out.'

* * *

'Do you have to go?' Tara asked Frankie. Scott was helping Johnny collect bugs, Rose was in the kitchen and Aaron was up at 10,000 feet tipping skydivers out of his plane. Tara had her dolls in a semicircle; she was reading to them the picture book Frankie had given her which Tara just couldn't quite believe she'd also written.

'I have to go the day after tomorrow,' Frankie told the child. 'I have my own babies waiting for me.'

'But Scott calls you baby – what about him?'

'You'll have to make sure he's OK for me, until I can come back.'

Tara went through the names of all her babies and then asked Frankie how old hers were.

'They're nine and thirteen.'

'They're not babies,' Tara said cautiously as if Frankie might not have realized. 'They're not babies any more Frankie.'

Frankie knocked gently at the frame of the screen

door. 'Rose?' she called. 'It's me – Frankie – come to say goodbye in case we don't see you tomorrow.'

'Please,' came the voice, 'come in.'

Inside, it was meticulously spic and something smelt good in the kitchen.

'It's been lovely to meet you,' Frankie said, not quite sure how best to express it. She put out her hand but instead of taking it, Rose placed something in it.

'Here,' she said bluntly.

Frankie looked at it. A small box, woven. She lifted the lid away. The underside of the weaving was as perfect and beautiful as the proud side.

'I made it.' Rose shifted a little.

'You *made* it?'

'Yup.' She came closer. 'Cedar root,' she said. 'Then the red of the design is wild cherry bark, the pale is canary grass, the dark is black cherry. The patterns – they're the landscape. I know you like the mountains.'

'It's exquisite – thank you very much.' Frankie looked closely. 'It's so – detailed, so precise.'

'You know when I was a girl and I started my monthly, my grandma made me sit and pick all the needles of a cedar branch. A big old branch it was too. Had to prove I had what's required to be a weaver and a woman – patience and skill. My grandmother could weave with pine needles.'

'I can't even sew a button on straight or mend a hole in a sock,' said Frankie. 'Things just fall apart if I try and fix them.'

Then Rose put her head back and really laughed, guttural and hearty, quite taking Frankie by surprise.

'Not Scott though,' Rose said. 'Your stitching's made

that man good and strong. I'll see you again. Bring your kids next time.'

Early in the morning, the day before she left, Scott took her on his favourite hike and at Joffre Lakes, Frankie wept.

'I had no idea that places like this existed.'

'It's the glacial silt particles,' Scott explained as if it was no big deal. 'Suspended in the water, illuminated by the sun, reflecting the sky.'

The first lake, through the trees and just a stone's throw from where they'd parked, had stunned her into silence; the most unimaginable dense turquoise without a ripple on the surface to say it was actually water.

'I thought I was fit,' she panted as they hiked steeply to the middle lake.

'It's different out here to where you are,' said Scott. 'We do this a lot.'

On they went, alongside tumbling creeks and dense woodland.

'Wait a bit,' Frankie said, breathing hard, hands on hips, gazing down the mountain as if that was the only reason she'd stopped. Her chest felt tight and sore and she was boiling. 'I must look a right state.'

He looked at her hair; licked by sweat into little kiss curls around her neck, her cheeks hot red, her nose shiny, damp patches darkening her T-shirt around the armpits, socks rucked and dirt on her legs. 'It suits you,' he grinned. 'Come on.' He held out his hand and pulled her along with her mock-moaning for the next few minutes.

At the middle lake, the colour was even more vibrant; the water enclosed by trees and rock; a glassy stillness and otherworldly quiet. It was so spectacular all she could do was giggle and say oh my God over and again.

'You want to go back?'

'There's *more*?'

To the uppermost and largest lake they climbed and clambered, the terrain rugged and in parts relentless, as challenging as it was exhilarating. Frankie's lungs screamed, her legs complained and her arms itched but when they made it, that's when she wept. The lake was her prize. The vivid cerulean blue, its surface glossy as polished enamel, held in the cupped hands of the mountain. The slashes and slides of grey-cold rock still striped with snow reached right down to the water and, most breathtaking of all, the vastness of the glacier. The midday sun seemed brighter up here. Where was this place? It seemed too heavenly to exist in the self-centred plastic rush of the twenty-first century.

'Don't cry,' Scott laughed gently.

'I'm so knackered,' she sobbed, rivulets of clean skin streaking down her grimy face. 'I thought I was fit – it's depressing. But I'm so happy.' She blew her nose on her T-shirt. 'This,' she said, gazing out over the lake, back to the glacier. Had it moved? Of course not. 'This,' she said again, waving at it all. 'I have no words – and I'm meant to be a bloody writer.'

She sat between Scott's legs, his arms loosely around her. Sweaty and gritty they rested awhile, drank water and ate their lunch.

'This is what you do,' Frankie said, as if she'd been quietly working it out. 'On a weekend – or a morning off – this is where you come. You jump in your truck and you drive twenty minutes and you hike to God's own country.'

'Pretty much,' Scott said. He thought of all the other places they'd been over the last few days – and all those he still wanted to take her. They'd run out of time and a wave of sadness swept over the still water. Next time he came to Joffre, he'd be on his own. She would be gone.

'I don't want to go home,' Frankie said, leaning back on his chest not knowing whether to close her eyes and just feel or keep them wide open and absorb all the details to bank for later. They stayed like that, in the moment that turned into a while. 'It's heaven on earth and I want to live here.'

Scott smiled to himself. He could recall in finest detail the patterns in the bark and the twist and reach of the limb-like branches of Corsican pine at Holkham. He could conjure that marshland road to the shingle beach at Salthouse, the mercurial hue of the sea there. He carried in his nose the mouth-watering tang of vinegary paper holding hot chips, the taste of crab dressed that day, of synthetic ice cream in a whorl stabbed through with a stick of flaked chocolate. He could still see in crisp detail the village of Glandford, considerably prettier than Pemby. At night, he'd recall the softness of her bed compared to his. The aroma of her tea which was nothing like his. The scent of her linen, her hair. The sound of the water in the pipes in her house as it argued its way to the taps. All of it contributing essential details to the portrait of Frankie he kept in his heart.

'Owl Mountain, Mount Meager, Mount Currie, the Camel's Back, Seven O'Clock Mountain. The Lillooet, the Ryan, the Birkenhead rivers – Twenty Mile Jim Creek, Gingerbread Creek, Miller Creek. One Duck

Lake, Tenquille, Joffre.' Her list sounded like a poem. Scott closed his eyes and drank in the sound of Frankie giving voice to his world. She interrupted his thoughts, turned to him, put her lips to his. 'But what I've loved most of all is just – this,' she said. 'Just hanging out with my –' She stopped. 'I don't know how to refer to you.' She giggled and her eyes danced above the smudges of mascara mingling with perspiration. 'Us being together, chatting and cooking, lolling about and popping into town. Cleaning our teeth side by side, feeding the dog and saying oh, hi Valerie, hi Richard – yes we have time for coffee.'

Frankie turned and faced the lake again.

'Against the most beautiful backdrop the world has to offer, the glorious prose of a normal day-to-day can be played out.'

'I had no idea,' Scott said, drawing her back against his chest and within his arms.

'And nor did I,' said Frankie.

Annabel's eyes were itchy and hot, tiredness and frustration mixed with a little fear. But she wasn't going to say so and she certainly wasn't going to cry. She wasn't going to fall asleep – not here on the sofa, not upstairs in her bed. She would force herself to stay awake until everything was fine. She glanced at her brother. Sam was double-screening; the volume low on the TV, the tinny sounds of Clash of Clans emanating from his mobile phone, his eyes flicking from one screen to the other.

'Who's he? Does Graham Norton actually know him?' she asked her brother. 'He's quite rude to him.'

'He's an American actor – you wouldn't have heard of him. He's only in 15s and 18s,' said Sam.

'Is Graham Norton American?'

'He's Irish, stupid.'

'I'm not stupid – he sounds a bit American and anyway, lots of Irish emigrated there, especially to New York and Chicago.'

Sam gave her a look that said he thought anything she had to say was insignificant.

'We were taught it in school,' she said grumpily. 'What's the time anyway?'

Sam sighed. 'Five bloody minutes after you last asked me.'

'I'm going to tell Mum you swore.'

'She's not here.'

Annabel paused. 'I'm going to tell Dad, then.'

'He's not bloody fucking shitting here either.'

'Where do you think he is?'

'I don't know.'

'Is his phone still off? Just try him one more time?'

'It's off. And he doesn't have voicemail.'

'What do you think we should do, Sam?'

'We'll give it until the end of *The Graham Norton Show* – then we'll decide.'

'Ok. But I don't like it. I'm not happy and I want Mummy.'

It seemed to Sam that they had too many choices once Graham Norton had gone. He went through them methodically with Annabel. They could try Miles's phone again. Which they did and still it was off. They could phone the police – but they couldn't recall actually seeing a police station since they'd lived in Norfolk so maybe there weren't any out here and if they had to send for a force from another county, it would take too long. And what could the police do anyway? They didn't want their dad to go to prison. They didn't want to be taken into care because they'd been left Home Alone. So – they could phone their mother, but she was over the sea and far away, and she'd go ballistic. And they didn't want their dad to get into trouble – they'd only just got him back. Or they could phone no one, just try and go to sleep – with Sam on the roll-out mattress in Annabel's room with his cricket bat to hand and a chair jammed against the front door. But the children knew sleep would not be possible. Should they go to the Mawbys'? But old people went to sleep early, didn't they – and they didn't know them well enough to ask for help. They wouldn't want to stay the night in their house, it looked too grey and cold. Sam could email Scott – but what if he didn't check his inbox until his evening, which would already be their tomorrow by which time no doubt their dad would be back and the can of worms would have been opened for nothing.

'I *am* thirteen,' Sam said, a little hesitant.

'I know,' said Annabel.

'So I have to take responsibility,' he said. He reached for his phone and scrolled to his mother's messages. She'd sent numerous texts each day of her trip, with updates about the weather and a zillion samey photos of this mountain or that stream. She was usually rubbish at selfies but the goofy one of her and Scott was classic. Sam couldn't bear to look at it just then. He scrolled back and back through the last six days to the last text his Mum had sent on British soil. He clicked on the number contained within it and cleared his voice.

Ruth and Peter were happily loafing on the sofa, in their traditional Friday-night post-curry inertia, the debris of which was still on the coffee table in front of them, like the spoils of war.

'Who on earth is phoning at this hour?' She didn't recognize the number and let it go through to voice-mail. She scooped up a little paneer shashlick with the nan bread and it was halfway to her mouth when she listened to the message.

'Oh shit,' she said. 'Shit.'

Peter collected Annabel and Sam while Ruth closed the curtains in the spare room, folded back the linen and made it all look welcoming. The children tucked down gratefully, sleepy almost immediately; their relief palpable at being safe in bed in a house with their mum's friends. Ruth sat next to Annabel who had cocooned herself tightly.

'Don't worry,' she said and both children thought to themselves that Ruth was someone they could trust. Her voice was soothing but authoritative; it was like their mum's. 'You did the right thing and I'm really proud of you. Jack and Penny will think it's Christmas morning when they wake up and find you here.'

All night Ruth's sleep was perforated with colliding thoughts on what to do about all of this. In the early hours, she slipped out of bed to lie semi-supine on the floor, her head resting on a pile of magazines. Even after two decades spent practising and preaching the Alexander Technique, she still marvelled at how soothing, proactive and empowering it was to lie like this. To be in the now and to have no physical tension opened mental pathways, while breathing deep and wide facilitated the unravelling of the tangle of thoughts. In some ways, she felt at her most upright when lying down.

'What are you doing?' Annabel, wakeful, had come across Ruth.

'Having a think,' said Ruth. 'Why don't you lie beside me and have a think too?' She made a lower pile of magazines for Annabel's head and gently positioned the child's body.

'Let's think,' said Annabel, letting out a long, contemplative hum.

'OK,' said Ruth lightly. 'I'm thinking that your mum flies back today so there's no point worrying her with what's happened because it's not like she can get back here any quicker.'

'Good point,' said Annabel.

'Thank you,' said Ruth. 'I'm thinking that we'll go back to your house after breakfast and leave a note for your dad to call us when he returns.'

'You *do* think he *is* going to come back though, don't you?' Annabel asked, audibly attempting to hide the concern in her voice.

Ruth's heart creaked. 'I'm sure there's an explanation.'

'Do you think he's gone back to the equator?'

'Not in your mum's car, no,' said Ruth.

* * *

'Don't go,' said Scott to Frankie.

'Come with me,' said Frankie to Scott.

They stood on the doorstep, her suitcase and bags already in the truck. Buddy in the back seat looking up reproachfully at the figures on the porch.

Frankie and Scott gazed out at the view: Mount Currie, tinged with salmon pink and eel grey, the trees emanating a purple-green light, clouds flicking at the sky here and there.

'Ready?' asked Scott.

'No,' said Frankie.

* * *

They drove via the airfield. Buddy tumbled out of the truck and loped over to Aaron, hopeful of a flight.

'Now you sure you don't want me to fly you to Vangroovy?' Aaron asked Frankie.

'No offence – but yes, I'm sure,' said Frankie.

'All right, all right!' Aaron shrugged. 'Crazy Englishwoman,' he said under his breath while he held out his hand, which she took. He placed his other hand over hers, shaking it warmly. 'You be sure to come back soon eh?' he said. 'You bring your kids next time, *liisáos.*'

It meant angel. She didn't want him to let go of her hand.

'You sure you wouldn't rather go in my girl here?' Aaron said, nodding over to his little plane. 'You sure you want to make your man drive near enough eight hours round trip? He's not getting any younger, you know.'

Frankie laughed. 'I'm sure.' My man. That's who Scott is. That's how I'll refer to him. Dropping to her knees, Frankie hugged Buddy who pushed his wide skull up under her chin. 'Look after Scott,' she whispered.

'I'll pick him up later,' Scott told Aaron. 'Thanks for having him.'

'Hey Buddy,' Aaron said, walking away from Scott and Frankie. 'We got the plane to ourselves, we got the whole sky to ourselves. What do you say to that?'

The dog trotted off with Aaron towards the Cessna without so much as a backward glance.

In Whistler, Jenna was busy in her shift but snuck out to say goodbye to Frankie.

'It's been so nice getting to know you,' she said.

'Oh goodness,' said Frankie, 'it's been a pleasure.'

'Come back soon – or have my dad come visit you.'

'Actually,' Frankie said, having given it no prior thought though it struck her just then as one of the best ideas she'd had in a long time, 'you must come over to the UK too.' She looked from Jenna to Scott, their little tight family of two. 'Will you come to me for Christmas?'

Back at Vancouver airport.

Was it only a week ago? Was she not somehow justified in feeling just a little bit Canadian now that she'd forever take her coffee double-double, that these days she was awake when England slept, that she felt more spiritually connected with the land here than at home, and that she'd entrusted a Canadian man with her heart. Frankie and Scott loitered in Departures, looking at the boards and all those planes separating and uniting countries and people. The flight was on time and her suitcase had trundled off. Without warning, the thought of England just over ten hours away brought a pang of longing for her children so acute that it could have doubled her up, had Scott's arms not been around her already. Guilt too – how could it be that she had not missed them more, that she'd relished this time on her own, without them? An image of her kitchen bolted across her mind, followed by a vivid recall of the patch of sunlight that pooled in the hallway which Annabel had termed supernatural. Her heart felt cleaved into two and it hurt.

'This is rubbish,' she said.

'It is a bit,' said Scott.

'In my forties and finally I find a love that makes total sense, that brings me so much complete happiness, that enhances my life but—'

'It sucks,' said Scott, 'but you know, we have what we have and for that I am grateful.'

'But shouldn't we be actively pursuing more? It's not greed – it's good.'

'Love has come into our separate lives,' Scott said.

She thought about that. Separate lives. It didn't have to be that way, surely? 'I have to go.'

'I know.'

'I'll see you soon?'

'I'll see you soon.'

'I love you.'

'I love you too, baby.'

304

Up the garden path to her home. Everything prettier than she remembered or perhaps just grown more so since she'd left. The patio plants and climbing roses blousy and fragrant, a tangle of sweetness echoed blissfully by the greeting her children gave her. Annabel's limbs vined around Frankie's while Sam – was he an inch taller? – hugged her and hummed. She didn't notice that Miles wasn't there but she was too euphoric and exhausted to wonder why Ruth was in the kitchen clearing away dinner.

'Did you see a bear?' Annabel asked.

'No,' Frankie rued.

'Do they all say "oat and aboat" over there?' Sam asked.

'No,' Frankie laughed. She gazed at her children. 'Scott says hi.' They were like puppies on best behaviour sensing their treat was imminent. 'He's sent you a couple of little gifts. And I may have picked up one or two things for you.'

Soon the sofa was piled with Frankie and her children, Canucks toques and home jerseys, hoodies from Roots, T-shirts emblazoned with traditional First Nations symbols, candies and cookies made with maple syrup.

'Ice hockey is so cool,' Sam said, pulling on the jersey. 'I wonder if there's a rink near here?'

Annabel's mouth was too full for her to comment.

'You look like you need a cup of tea,' said Ruth, bringing one through, thinking to herself *even if you don't feel like it now, you'll certainly need it shortly.*

Frankie looked around her living room; the clutter of family life strewn here and there because not enough hours in the day allowed for the Dumping Basket to be sifted through, or the DVDs to be put back properly, or old magazines to make it to the recycling pile, or the T-shirt slumped over the back of the sofa to be taken promptly to the washing basket. The bump and scuffle of children, dinting the paintwork and leaving their marks on the walls, a faint footprint on the floor, a ghostlike slump in the cushions. She loved it. Sipping tea, her thoughts drifted to Scott's living room, the walls constructed from long cedar logs, the lofty ceiling, the faded rugs and leather suite, guitars on the walls, the peaceful quiet of everything in its place, the vast picture windows affording those views out to the mountains, the wilderness.

'Yin and yang,' said Frankie.

Ruth and the children looked at her, startled.

'Sorry – just miles away.' And then she stopped. Miles away. Where *was* Miles? For a split second, she thought perhaps he was here and she simply hadn't clocked him, so low down was he on her radar of all that mattered most. And then Frankie thought, why is Ruth here? And then she thought, why is Miles not here? Ruth was regarding her levelly, telepathically saying from one mother to another, *not in front of the kids, Frankie*. Suddenly, the milk in Frankie's tea soured.

'Kids – can you clear this stuff up? Put it away in your rooms? That would be amazing.'

Once she'd heard them clunking about upstairs, Frankie turned to Ruth. She didn't need to ask.

'He's not here,' Ruth said bluntly.

'When?'

'He didn't come back last night. The children waited – and then Sam did exactly as he should and gave us a call.'

As much as Frankie blinked, she couldn't stop tears. 'Were they OK?'

'They were very OK – they watched Graham Norton here which was a treat, I believe. And then they gave us a call.'

However much lightness Ruth was laying over the events – and Frankie was aware that she was – Frankie was grateful. She realized just then that Ruth had taken on her mantle when she wasn't here.

'I want to call him a cunt.'

'Go ahead,' said Ruth. 'I've called him that already. Not in front of the children – obviously.'

'I feel horribly implicated by his behaviour,' Frankie said quietly.

'Don't you go feeling guilty about where you've been,' Ruth said, 'nor why you went. And it wasn't your fault that what happened, happened.'

'My mother and sister will have a field day with this one.'

'It's nothing to do with them. They needn't know.'

She hadn't thought of it that way. 'You've tried calling him?' Silly question. 'Is my car here?' Oh Christ alive.

307

'The children were really fine, Frankie. Sam sees himself as Man of the House.'

'I can't believe last week I felt *grateful* that Miles was here. I actually felt excited for the children. I justified my trip by saying it would give them quality time.' She paused. God, she was suddenly stratospherically tired. 'Now I just feel like a prize idiot.' She wiped away a tear. 'I should have known.'

'But I like it that you have a soul that wants to believe that people are inherently good,' said Ruth.

Miles did come back, much later.

Frankie and the children heard the car crunch up the gravel. The children didn't leap up and scramble to the front door this time. They just glanced at each other.

'It's OK, kids,' Frankie told them. 'I know what happened – and I think you did brilliantly.'

A jolly rhythm was knocked out on the front door. Frankie wouldn't put it past Miles to call out Honey! I'm home! Annabel walked cautiously to open the front door. Fretful with jet lag, Frankie couldn't remember what it was she was going to say. Just the word cunt.

She fixed a smile on her face for Annabel's sake who was high in her father's arms, regarding her mother anxiously.

'Samuel!' Miles bellowed jovially. Sam glanced at Frankie. No one called him Samuel, ever. It wasn't even on his birth certificate. Sam pulled his new hat down a little lower and mooched out to the hallway.

'How was your trip?' Miles asked Frankie, calm as you like, sauntering through to the kitchen, picking at leftovers whilst making himself a round of toast.

'Out of this world.'

'How's your – boyfriend? How's the Scott from Canada?'

'He's – beautiful,' she said. 'Kids – why not go upstairs and bring down the presents to show your dad. *Before he goes.*' She didn't take her eyes off Miles. 'But I've put it all away – like you asked,' said Annabel.

Sam got it. 'Come on Annabel – I think I got more than you.'

'You did not,' Annabel protested, chasing after him. 'Mummy would never do that.'

'So – Canada!' he said. 'Really great kids, by the way. You've done an incredible job, Frankie – just wonderful. Humbling, actually. The fact that Sam's so mature that I could leave him in charge while I saw to some business – just amazing. A credit to you.'

How Frankie wanted to hiss at Miles, scratch him, insult and rage at him. Not just for what he'd done, but that he dared to underplay any wrongdoing.

'Miles,' she said. How much toast does the man eat? He looked at her steadily but this time she wasn't going to let it unnerve her. 'You're going to say goodbye to the children and you're going to go. Away.'

'Well – actually, I thought the kids and I might—'

'No,' said Frankie and her voice sliced out through tightly clenched teeth. 'You're not fit to be a father. You never were. So fuck off to wherever it is that you're fucking up your life – again. And by all means, send your stupid, sporadic cards when you remember. Scott's been more of a father to them in the short time I've known him than you ever have.'

Frankie pointed her finger at him; silent momentarily

while she tried not to spit her rage out across the table and considered what to say next. He was looking at her blankly, staggered, as if finding it hard to reconcile her rage with his own self-regard.

'These days, I don't actually care that you don't man up and support your children financially,' she said. 'It's of no interest to me that you have so little self-respect, that your moral fibre is so frayed beyond repair, that you don't see how bankrupt you are on so many levels. But know this – if you ever plunder my children's emotional welfare again, if you ever squander their trust, or rob them of their hope, I will hunt you down, Miles. I will hunt you down.'

He reddened like a scolded child. However taken aback he was at Frankie's justified vitriol, there was a part of him in awe of her composure and passion. She was a lioness and he ought to cower. Just desserts and humble pie – both hard for a man like Miles to swallow.

Then Frankie did something she'd never done and she wasn't aware, until that very moment, that she would do it. Later, she'd doubt whether it had been right or wise, though it would garner fond praise from those who loved her.

Under the table, she kicked Miles hard, twice, right across his shin.

Oh good. He's choking on the toast. Finally.

'Where the hell did you have to go, that you left the children all on their own overnight?'

Miles cleared his throat and tongued food away from his gums. Frankie was tempted to kick him again, on the other leg.

'Actually,' he said, 'I was in London. About a job – which I'm going to take. About a flat to rent – which

I've now put the deposit on. I'm moving back in a couple of months, Frankie. I want to see more of the kids. I know I've been a total fuck-up, but for what it's worth, I want to try, now, to be a better dad. It's time for me to stop messing about. I really love them, Frankie.'

July rolled its way through Norfolk and British Columbia with long days, blue skies and a heat like no one could remember. Scott's house stayed cool and there was always the porch, but Frankie's was like a kiln; the flint baking the interior relentlessly though windows were kept open all the time. When she thought back to how cold the house had been during the winter months, how draughty, she pondered why no breeze now came in through wide-open windows. And why didn't the stone cool down in the summer or at least store some of this heat for the winter?

Annabel asked about air conditioning and Sam begged for a swimming pool.

'I hose my children down,' Frankie told Scott. 'I stand them in the garden and turn the hose on them, like they're mucky dogs.'

However enervating the heat was on the children in their final days at school, it cooked Frankie's writing well, enabling the ingredients of the story to prove and rise and bake to a wholesome finish like the perfect loaf of bread. She was proud to have finally pulled the book out of herself and she was pleased with the story. But though she sent if off to her agent and editor, still she thought about Alice. Now, in addition to the fondness she felt for her character, came a burgeoning sense of doing the right thing by her – and by the readers too, though Frankie anticipated they'd hate her for it. It was a risk to take. She was nervous about telling her agent and editor. She lost sleep over it.

'It's like I've clipped Alice's wings,' Frankie told Scott over the phone. 'I've prevented her from growing up because I don't want to lose her.'

'Well, she's a big part of your life,' Scott said.

'But niggling at the back of my mind is the feeling that in the next book, I ought to let her go.'

Frankie sat at the bottom of the stairs with her chin in her hand and her neck crooked against the phone. Ruth would have her work cut out in their next Alexander session.

'Do you think I'd be mad to take such a step?' she asked Scott.

'Only you can truly work that one out,' he said.

Scott had written a melody for Alice. It was simple and pure, suited a kid her age and was complete enough just on piano. But he could hear her tune in a larger work, carried on the crests of harmonies, finding its way through themes and variations. He thought of it in terms of maturing the melody, giving it gravity, bringing it to fruition, bestowing longevity. He'd read the Alice books now – Frankie had sent a package to him to give to Aaron's children. Jenna had read them too.

'I've never read anything like them,' Jenna told her father.

'You weren't short of books though.'

'I know – but I wish I'd had these when I was young.

I'd like to have had an imaginary friend – or whoever he is – like Alice's.'

'You had your dogs.'

Jenna gazed at Buddy.

'You OK, kid?'

'Everyone needs an adventure, Pop,' Jenna said. 'Everyone needs to sense that out there, something is saying that everything will be OK.'

'Don't let fiction twist away fact. Too much adventure is tedious,' Scott said. 'Believe me.'

Jenna rolled her eyes. 'I'm going to join all the clubs when I'm at college, Dad,' she said. 'And I'm going to go to all the parties. University is one adventure I want to experience first-hand. I don't want to watch it from the sidelines. I'm not going to let my epilepsy spoil it.'

Frankie told the children first. They were shocked initially and then greeted the news with a shrug and a change of subject.

She told Scott very late one night when she was lying on top of the sheets too hot to sleep. 'I've made up my mind,' she said. 'I need to let her go. The next book will be the last one in the Alice series.'

'You know, Alice may come back in another guise,' he said. 'It doesn't follow that you'll leave each other for good. You're not killing her off. You're just giving her freedom to leave – and I bet you she'll come back at some point.'

'I'll tell that to my agent,' Frankie said. 'He says I should stick with her.'

'He wants his commission,' Scott laughed.

'I'm going to start the book tomorrow. But I need a

title,' Frankie said. 'Give me a title that will give her the send-off she deserves – Alice as we know her now.'

Scott thought about it. It was late afternoon yet still he could feel his skin prickle with the sear of the sun. He moved into the shade of the porch. Buddy looked up at him. I should hose you down, Scott thought, like Frankie does her kids.

'*Alice and the Ditch Monster Say Goodbye,*' said Scott.

In an instant, Frankie sensed the story as if it was out there already, floating around waiting for an author to collect the ideas delicately, like a bee with pollen. It would be down to her to spin words into a story, to build colours into imagery, to weave the two into a detailed tapestry to be treasured on bookshelves and stick fast in memories.

'I can do that,' she told Scott. 'It's what I do.'

'Is it August with you?'

Frankie looked at her watch. 'Yes – it turned August around twenty minutes ago.'

Frankie told the children as they walked back to the car after a long, lazy day on the beach.

'I really feel like a proper local now there are so many tourists,' Annabel said.

'It's us and them,' Sam laughed. 'Look at all the stuff they have to heave and hoick down here every day. We're all about just a towel and flip-flops.'

'And when they go crabbing at Blakeney, they actually *buy* kits,' said Annabel.

'That's just because Mum's tight,' Sam said. 'Making us those pouches from the washing-tablets nets.'

'We catch bigger crabs than the tourists anyway,' Annabel said. 'That's my point about us being – *from here*. The visitors always look in my bucket and then they look at me. Like they're thinking she's a local girl, the big crabs know her.'

'You're so lame,' said Sam.

'Mum! Tell Sam off. Didn't you hear him? He called me lame.'

'Mum?'

'Hmm? The day after tomorrow, we're off to Canada.'

Frankie could hear Peta rolling her eyes. It wasn't something that she sensed; she could actually hear it, over the phone. It started with loaded silence followed by a just perceptible sharp intake of breath and then a frustrated exhale. Why was her sister always so disapproving? Was Frankie's happiness of so little importance to her?

'Have you told Mum?'

'Jesus Peta. I'm taking the children on the trip of a lifetime – and your only response is, have I told Mum? Like I have to confess to something I shouldn't be doing, like I have to justify what I've decided to do?'

She's bloody rolling her eyes again – I can hear it!

'What I meant was – you were due to visit her next weekend, weren't you? Now you won't be.'

Frankie's ensuing silence was downcast rather than contrite. 'I forgot.'

'I can tell.'

'I can't cancel our trip. Why have you gone silent Peta? You can't honestly expect me to cancel?'

'No – I didn't say that. Christ Frankie.'

There was a lengthy stalemate, which Peta finally broke. 'Look – I know she's awkward, but I know too that in some ways your visit was going to define the week leading up to it, the week after it, for her.'

'I'll phone her – right now.'

'OK – but don't expect her to express understanding or encouragement – whatever.'

'She rarely does, when it comes to me.'

'What I'm trying to say is – if she doesn't, it might just be because she's upset or disappointed, for herself, not at you.'

'I wish you could be happier for me, Peta.'

'I know you do. And do you know what? I wish that too. But I'm just worried, really – how fast this is happening. The Canada thing. Holidays are just time out, Frankie – a dreamy getaway from reality. It's not a genuine way to conduct a relationship – long melancholy periods apart and then intensive times together outside of the day-to-day.'

'You don't have any authority to make claims like that.' Frankie was on the verge of hanging up.

'But what if something happens? What if he breaks your heart?'

'He wouldn't do that,' Frankie said. 'You don't know him – so you can't judge. But when you've met him, then you'll know. Then you'll see how I mean as much to him as he does to me.'

August. Hot skin and sticky hair. Ice cream and lukewarm showers twice daily. Sand between the toes and somehow, always in the bed sheets too. Bugs and buzzing and bottles of sun lotion. The garden needed a drink each evening and birds vied for the vast arc of the Norfolk sky just as the tourists did for its beaches. Frankie looked out at her garden where the children were bouncing on the trampoline in their swimming costumes then leaping off to run through the garden sprinkler which was valiantly trying to infuse a little green back into the parched lawn. They'd never had a garden before. Potentially, she could give them a whole mountain range.

'Peta,' Frankie said, 'Scott's part of me now. You'll see. Christmas is at mine this year, not yours – and all of you are coming. Mum. Even Steph.' She waved at Annabel who was dancing across the lawn with such abandon that Frankie wanted to join her. 'And Scott. And his daughter. Family,' she told Peta. 'All the family will be here.'

* * *

What Sam loved most about Canada was arriving at Scott's after an insanely long journey, for Scott to show him to his room. They were all watching Annabel settle herself in, unpacking her carry-on and placing all manner of ornaments brought from home all around the room. She'd only been to France on holidays and stayed in hotels. This was home from home so she had to make it so.

Scott turned to Sam. 'So there's the room next door to this one,' he said. 'But I reckon you might prefer to stay in the studio.'

It was a separate building to the side of the house reached by steps. A self-contained annexe, with a tiny kitchenette, compact shower room and sofa bed. But it was the monitors, mixers, mics, instruments, amps, speakers, headphones, foam sound-dampening, gadgets and gear Sam loved at first sight.

'Cool,' he said under his breath.

'Welcome,' Scott said, giving the boy's shoulder a quick squeeze. 'I hear you did great at school, eh?'

Sam shrugged.

'You should be proud. Can't have been easy, starting all over.'

'I've settled in now. I have mates. I didn't at first – when we moved. But there's a couple of teachers who, you know, *get* me.' Sam wanted to say: *like you do*. He really did.

'I'm so pleased for you,' Scott said and Sam was startled by the sound of so much emotion. 'So! I'll let you settle in – should be everything you need. And make your way over whenever you want. Oh and Sam – don't lie down and don't shut your eyes. You have to beat the jet lag.'

'One thing,' Sam said as Scott was about to leave. 'Is this a bear-free den?'

Scott laughed. 'Bears don't like noise.'

'But there are bears?'

Scott nodded.

'Will we see one?'

'Jesus Murphy I hope we do,' Scott said. 'For your mom's sake.'

Sam had better things to do than succumb to his inordinate tiredness. Soon enough, his Instagram was awash with views from every possible angle. Of the interior alone. Yeah, huge mountains and stuff outside or whatever – but get THIS! Ultimate Man Cave yo!

Most mornings, so that Frankie could work on her book, Scott took the children into the village for cinnamon buns, or a swim at One Mile Lake, a visit to Nairn Falls, a walk along Owl Creek or the Ryan, calling in on the Sturdys at North Arm Farm or springing a visit on Jenna mid-shift.

Again, Frankie was finding it cripplingly hard to write and yet this time, the words were there, the pictures too; the sentences had slowly started to flow and the illustrations had her hallmark fluidity. But emotionally it was more draining than any book she'd written, because always at the back of her mind was the portentous fact that this was it. Time for goodbyes.

I'm going to miss you Alice, but you're moving house and it's for the best.

But what about Him, Frankie, what about *Him*? He's the truest friend I've ever had. Can't he come with? Can't you find a way that he could? Write him a journey where he treks over land and sea, over rivers and through forests, to find me?

But Alice, as much as you love him, you don't need him any more.

Oh but I do I do I do!

No Alice, it's time for you to go. It's time for him to be there for another child – like a slimy, freaky, clunkingly ugly, wart-worn version of Mary Poppins. The ditch and April Cottage are what's special, Alice. There'll always be a time when a new family needs to live there and so it passes on and on. The pretty house that draws grown-ups to it. Parents who'll say oh my little darlings! just look at the lovely garden! The children who'll find the ditch which the adults will think is just a straggle of weeds. Brambles, they'll say. Watch you don't get scratched and dirty, the grown-ups will say.

And He'll be there. Because he knows when he's needed. When a child feels lonely or worried, sad or angry, when a child feels misunderstood like there's no one in the world they can talk to – He'll be there.

He'll make their world an all-right place. Like he did for you.

But I don't want to go, Frankie. What will I do without you? Who will write it all out?

Alice my darling, you'll write your own story now. I'm going to miss you but your parents are emigrating to Canada and you'll thank them for it. I promise you.

Aaron took the children fishing a few times, enabling Frankie and Scott to have some time alone.

'You know it takes five hours for the water to come from Múmleq – from Mount Meager – to here?' Aaron told them. 'One time the hydro company tried to redirect the water but the river fought back and reclaimed its favoured path. You see all these logs? They just appear. Look at them all. Log jams are something else – and when they shift, the noise wow! Like a massive gun-crack.'

'Scott told me when the rivers flood, the very last thing to go are the beaver dams,' said Sam, toying with his fishing rod; loving the peace and the anticipation, waiting for the slightest feel at the end of the line, waiting for the water to spume silver with activity.

'*Twit*,' Aaron said to him. 'That's you.'

Sam frowned but Aaron just laughed. 'Not your stupid white word,' he explained. '*Twit* is Líĺwat for "young man who has finished his training", for a hunter with special powers.'

Annabel was delighted. 'You're a twit, Sam – you're a twit! But Aaron,' she said, 'if Sam's a twit, what am I?'

He threaded bait onto her line and cast for her. '*Liisáos*,' he said. 'An angel – like your mother.'

Scott and Frankie took the children hiking to Joffre. They made it to the middle lake where Annabel flopped down saying, yes it's blue and beautiful but now I'm on strike. Frankie was happy to join her daughter's picket line and just sit alongside her and contemplate the surroundings, stroking Annabel's hair while her daughter rested in her lap. Frankie loved it that Sam had said come on, Scott – I want to keep going. Yes she was excited for her son to see the upper lake, but the warmest thrill came from observing Sam and Scott's growing affection. Peta's husband Philip always ruffled Sam's hair and talked about sport but Scott gave Sam time to talk about himself and Scott seemed to know what he'd like.

But then she thought about Miles moving back to England next month because he loved the children too and wanted to be more present in their lives. Frankie shuddered and Annabel looked up, alarmed.

'What's wrong? How can you be cold?'

'I'm not darling – I'm fine. It's nothing.'

But it was everything. Frankie wanted Joffre to be on her doorstep. Miles wanted the children to be on his. Sam and Annabel shouldn't have to leap an ocean between two homes. There had to be a solution, there had to be.

Jenna came to stay the weekends they were there and Annabel experienced her first girl crush, while Jenna and Scott embraced the feeling of a larger family, a noisier household. There was a lot of loafing around, those weekends. Enjoying the house, hanging out in the shade on the porch, lying on the grass in the sun and gathering around the table for raucous mealtimes.

'My mum is absolute rubbish at plaiting hair,' Annabel

322

told Jenna who was combing it through. 'Rubbish rubbish rubbish.'

'We call it braiding,' Jenna told her. 'And your mom can't be brilliant at everything.'

'She's not very good at keeping the snack drawer full either,' Annabel said darkly.

Jenna giggled. What a cute kid. It was like having a little sister.

They were all in the living room. Frankie sitting quietly in the armchair, tweaking her manuscript in progress. Sam with a guitar and Scott next to him with another, teaching him a few chords. Buddy was outside, whining to get in but he'd licked the roast chicken that was resting on the table and Scott was cross with him. Jenna was dividing Annabel's hair. She looked over to the cabinet on which the television and hi-fi were kept. It was a lovely old piece of furniture, with lots of drawers and compartments. When she was at school, she'd kept all her bands and ribbons for her hair in one of the drawers. Were they still there? Buddy scrabbling at the door. She'd go and check.

Scott suddenly leapt up.

Frankie looked over. Jenna was by the cabinet, standing very still. It didn't look like Jenna, she looked like a waxwork.

'Scott?'

The children looked up quickly at the tone of their mother's voice.

'Jenna,' Scott was saying, low but insistent. 'Jenna, come. Jenna – come.'

Jenna wasn't moving, just standing there, trance-like.

And Annabel, Sam and Frankie all wondered, is this epilepsy? Is this a focal seizure?

And then a terrible sound, a disembodied scream they never imagined could come from the girl with the soft and sing-song voice. Suddenly, she was down on the floor, her body in spasms. Annabel burst into tears and Sam just said Mum! Mum! as if there had to be something Frankie could do. Jenna was facing them, Scott crouching near, his hands gently on her arm, her waist, talking to her all the time. Her lips were blueish, her face a flat white, her eyes half-closed, her hands in rigid claws while her arms and legs flailed and her breath came in staccato gasps and grunts.

'What can we do?' Frankie's voice on the verge of tears. That poor child. Jesus Christ, that poor girl. Her children were clinging to her. 'What can we do?'

But Scott didn't answer her, he was just talking at Jenna, using his voice to help him breathe too. Frankie and the children came a little closer. Annabel hid her face in her mother's clasp and Sam stared at the floor just in front of Jenna.

Two minutes and seven seconds.

And then the room filled with Jenna's long sigh and everything was still.

'It's OK, baby, it's OK. You're back, you're with us. Jenna. Jenna baby. You're here. You're OK. We're here.'

Little moans, as though she was six years old.

'Why did you scream, though?' Annabel, tear-streaked, was on her knees while Jenna recovered on the floor. 'Why did you scream like that?'

Jenna, too tired to speak. She'd never heard herself, anyway.

'She's not screaming – like you'd scream if you were scared,' Scott told Annabel. 'It's when her muscles tighten

– it forces all the air out. And when she sighs afterwards, that's because the muscles have relaxed again.'

'Why isn't she talking though? If she's relaxed now?' Annabel had started to cry again. Frankie sat down beside her. Sam joined her. They were all sitting around Jenna, close as they could.

'Because when she has a seizure, her body is beat up with the effort. Like it's run a marathon,' Scott said. 'In a while we'll help her up – she'll be groggy and she'll sleep a long time.'

Annabel put her hand tentatively out and touched Jenna's hair lightly. Jenna blinked slowly. Annabel started to stroke her.

Scott looked around at the family. Frankie brushing a tear away. Sam ashen. Annabel focused, frightened, but brave enough to stroke his daughter.

'See how I've put her in the recovery position? Can you see that? Sam?' Scott said quietly. 'That was a tonic-clonic seizure. I know it's so scary to see but you guys need to know what to do. So you can help – if you see someone having a seizure. Not just Jenna. Someone in Norfolk. Someone in London. Someone in the airport, at the bus stop, in a store. You must try to help. Because I'm telling you this, it happens. And a lot of people get kind of frozen with fear.'

Sam cleared his throat. 'What's the first thing we should do?'

'Make sure that nothing is in their way that they could injure themselves on.'

'OK – and then?'

'Don't try and hold their arms or legs – but try, if you can, if it's safe for you to do so, to ease them onto their side.'

'Like you did?'

'Yes.'

'And keep talking and talking, like you did?'

'Yes.'

'I can do that,' said Sam.

'If a seizure lasts more than three minutes, call an ambulance.'

'OK. I'll remember,' said Sam, knowing he'd never, ever forget.

Scott looked at their faces striated with worry. 'Please don't treat Jenna any differently later,' he said. 'It's just this Thing that happens to her. She's going to be tired, then she's going to be fine. You did brilliantly guys, thank you.'

Sam, Annabel and Frankie all wished they could have done more.

Frankie looked from Scott to Jenna and from Sam to Annabel and she thought to herself, if that was my child I wouldn't ever want to be too far away.

*   *   *

They did see a bear.

Every day, Annabel and Sam checked their watches in the late afternoon, Scott's casual comment becoming their mantra.

The forest starts moving around half-four.

Eight days in a row, 4.30 had come and gone with no bear in sight and when he finally came, it was closer to 7.00. The children were sitting out on the porch because their mother was cooking and had told them to chill out to the view – which just sounded so wrong. Grown-ups shouldn't say chill out for a start, and they shouldn't expect kids to be enthralled by views. But as supper was going to take ages on account of all the chatting and cuddling Frankie and Scott did, the children knew they could sit out there *not* gazing at the dusk-drenched mountain but at Sam's phone instead.

But something made them both look up, a movement that was silent, self-contained and yet filled the garden. And there he was, simply mooching about, black and glossy and round. He was littler than they'd imagined and amusingly pootling about almost for the hell of it, as if forgetting that he was in man's back yard. Then it was as though he suddenly remembered and that's when he stopped and looked over at the house, looked straight at the children. The bear looked at them and they looked at the bear and none of them was quite sure how long this lasted. Sam held his breath while Annabel felt she could not breathe if she tried. Then, as if with a shrug, the bear ambled off, heading out through the domestic boundary and back into the wild.

Suddenly, it no longer mattered what was going on in Instagram or who was tweeting what banality. In fact, Sam wouldn't realize until the next morning that he had left his phone on the swing seat out on the porch. The children rushed into the house.

'We just saw him!'

Scott and Frankie peeled away from each other and acted busy stirring pans and checking in the oven.

'Saw who?'

'We just saw the bear.' Annabel's voice was hoarse.

Frankie rushed outside. 'Why didn't you tell me!'

Sam looked at Scott, his face flushed and open. 'We

couldn't,' he tried to explain. 'We couldn't move, we couldn't speak.'

* * *

Eighteen days. The best holiday *ever*, the children said. Can't we stay longer? We don't start school for another week. Their final evening and Annabel was busy with Buddy for whom she'd made a loom-band embellishment for his collar. Sam was gazing over to the studio, his magical lair. In the palm of his hand his phone stuffed full of new music including a little something he'd recorded with Scott.

Frankie looked out to Mount Currie, sending her thanks and hope that she'd be back soon. Her daughter came and stood next to her. At the other end of the porch, her son and Scott. Scott with his hands loosely resting on his hips, Sam mirroring his pose. Everyone in the moment of wanting to stay but having to go. Frankie gave Annabel's hand a little squeeze and drew her close for a hug.

'You never saw the bear, Mummy.'

'No,' Frankie sighed. 'Maybe next time.'

Jenna looked around. She had everything she needed. Her dad was outside rearranging the back of the truck for the umpteenth time. Though really she'd left home last year when she'd moved to Whistler, it was only now that she realized how it had never quite felt like it. Living in Whistler had been like a halfway house, like a protracted sleepover at a close friend's less than an hour away. She'd been home most weeks anyway, never really been away long enough, or far away enough, to notice its quintessential scents and sounds. It had remained just the same to her, as if time sped up when she was away but for the house, for Buddy and her dad, it padded along just the same. Now though, she felt a growing sense that this was goodbye, she was to take leave of her childhood home for good, and her childhood too, really. She'd finished the charming year between school and university during which she'd earned money, laughed till she cried, had a one-night stand and two lousy boyfriends whom she could keep secret from her dad but dissect with her girlfriends. She'd stood on her own two feet perfectly happily and, on those occasions when she'd fallen, she'd found she could pick herself up again and cope. But what was it going to be like now?

She looked around once more.

She knew her dad was out there, packing the truck, wondering what lay ahead for Jenna, if she'd be OK. But inside the house, Jenna was confronting the same questions on her father's behalf. Then she caught sight of the picture she'd taken of him and Frankie last month. Annabel's shoe just visible, Sam a blur as he darted through the background. She remembered that day so well. And she thought yes, my pops'll be OK. Just then, Jenna felt truly grateful for Frankie. How great that her dad had found someone, what luck that it was someone she actually really liked. She plumped up a cushion and thought back to a couple of women who'd lingered when she'd been a kid, how they'd alternately avoid her and yet toady up to her too – as if the way to her dad's heart was through some pretence of acceptance and affection towards the girl who was his everything. She'd always be the girl who was his everything, but now he'd tidied up to make space for another. Jenna felt only gratitude, relief too. It freed her up, validated her growing need for independence.

'Feels like I'm holding the door open,' she said to Buddy. 'Like I'm holding the door open to let Frankie in on my way out.'

Vancouver beckoned. She was checking into her student accommodation today and registering tomorrow which was why her dad was packing up the truck to drive her there. She fingered her bracelet; it was actually a medical ID but unlike when she was little, these days they were much prettier. The old style made her feel branded like a cow, but now it was a piece of jewellery to enjoy, a conversation starter. She smiled, remembering Annabel trying it on, Jenna explaining its purpose. It speaks for me if I can't.

If her meds worked and she could be seizure free for another six months, she'd be able to drive herself. She'd be able to offer her new friends a ride for a change; she'd be able to say hey! let's go visit my home this weekend – and turn up on her dad's doorstep with a carload of lively people whom she'd be eager for him to meet, whom she'd be proud to show where she'd grown up.

'Perhaps it's all going to be just fine,' she said to Buddy. However negative and down she could become immediately following a seizure, her natural positivity always triumphed.

'Honey?'

'Coming, Pops – I'm coming.'

She took a last long look and sent her grin floating around the sitting room. Here we go, she thought, off I go.

Jenna didn't know that her father had booked into a hotel in Vancouver, in Yale Town, for the night. When she spoke to him on the phone that evening, she assumed he was back home. But Scott couldn't leave her, he had to stay close, to be her nightwatchman one final time. In the clean and positive light of tomorrow, it would be OK to go home. But not now, not on a day as monumental as today. He looked around the room, decorated in that modern and tasteful way that was a little too sterile for his liking. Buddy was curled quietly under the desk, not quite sure what to make of this. Where exactly was this non-stop place they'd taken Jenna? What was all that pavement under his paws? Who were all those people speaking in all those tongues? Such strong smells. Why did youngsters stand in that long snaking line by a Coca-Cola marquee? Why had they left Jenna standing right there? It was confusing for a dog like him who liked the simpler things in life.

'Hey,' said Scott. He loved the way the dog could raise his eyebrows so expressively. God he wanted to speak to Frankie. He felt in desperate need of comfort and he wasn't afraid, at last, to express it. But it was two in the morning over there. He lay back on the bed and closed his eyes, bringing to mind how Frankie looked when she slept, playing across the blank screen of his shut eyelids some of his favourite memories of their times together. He didn't want to think of Jenna because when he did, it wasn't the young woman he'd left in Grey Point today, it was the flaxen-haired baby with the saucer-size eyes toddling over to him, it was the child with the beatific smile who'd been patient with him night after night as he taught himself how to braid hair neat and pretty for school, it was the leggy kid who always waved at him from the school gates, it was the teenager who grinned through pink-dipped bangs when he came to watch her in some clangorous band or other. His beautiful girl who dealt with so much and called him Pops and had always told him not to worry.

Not worry? He was a parent, it was his job to worry! He remembered so well being Jenna's age, feeling invincible and immune, seeking thrills and extremes to prove how vibrant and alive he was. But Jenna had something he didn't, something many of the people she'd be meeting would never have encountered. Some would have preconceptions and others, fear. Would Jenna be able to say to her roommate, *I don't lock the washroom door – just in case?* He knew what three critical minutes of seizure felt like without having to look at his watch – would Jenna please befriend someone at college with that skill?

The girl he left today. Standing in line wearing a disproportionate grin just because she was going to get the name *Jenna* printed onto a Coke bottle. That couldn't have been his baby girl. Not so soon. Not gone so soon. No – he wouldn't think of her. And he wouldn't think of the little daughter he once had because where did she go? Where's she gone? What happened to the years one to twenty that had blinked by? Nope. He'd keep his eyes closed to meld into thoughts of Frankie, allow the warmth to seep over him like a coverlet.

'Hey Buddy – you can come up on the bed, if you like.'

Frankie wasn't answering her phone. Scott looked at the calendar on which he'd written up the dates she'd sent him. They did that for one another, so that daily lives separated by so many miles still made sense.

Manchester, that's where she was; back from Glasgow yesterday and off to Birmingham and Bristol tomorrow, then London. These were the names of the places keeping her in the UK, not just now but every time she brought out a book. Scott thought, maybe the cell-phone signal isn't so great in Manchester. He tried again and left another message. His house was quiet now, having pulsated with liveliness all weekend when Jenna came back for her first visit after a month in Vancouver, with four friends in tow. He'd slept in the studio. Though he'd always enjoyed having Jenna's friends over and liked to cook big pans of chilli for them, this time around he also wanted to be Cool Dad, so it would filter through campus hey! you gotta go stay at Jenna's place in Pemby. He noted that sometimes her friends called her Jenn. That was new and she seemed to like it; in fact, she seemed not to notice it at all. She looked well. She had a new haircut.

Frankie was phoning him back.

'So sorry – just finished back-to-back visits to three schools and now I'm off to Waterstones to sign stock.'

'Shall I call later?'

'But then I'll be asleep.'

'Where are you now?'

'In a cab – we can talk. How was the weekend? How was Jenna?'

Book tours were so hectic. She was exhausted. She needed some alone time with Scott. Thank God for such bad traffic in Didsbury.

'Is it going well?'

'We just missed the Top Ten,' she said. 'Maybe next week, if sales are good.'

'Want me to order a thousand copies? How are Sam and Annabel?'

'Miles is at home,' Frankie said a little darkly.

'It'll be OK – you know that,' Scott said. 'Seems to me he's a babysitter who'd gladly pay *you* for the honour.'

'Only he doesn't have any money,' Frankie muttered.

'It's a good thing, Frankie. Miles being around actually frees you up. You can come and go more easily.'

Frankie fell quiet. 'Can't you see, him being back ties me here more than ever?'

Scott thought about that. Her dream to move to Canada. 'For Annabel and Sam,' he qualified.

'As long as he doesn't let them down,' Frankie said. She thought to herself, how can I be so awful as to wish Miles would do just that – disappear off to another jungle so that, in some ways, I can get more of my life back into my control? She didn't want to go into it with Scott. He was always so level about it, so pragmatic, and sometimes she'd grow impatient which was not a good thing for a phone call.

'How's the score coming along?'

Scott looked around his studio, the script in a fan on the table. 'Good,' he said. 'It's a nice little movie. There's a character in it who reminds me of myself.'

'An all-action hero who's incredibly well hung?'

'Yes, Frankie, same six-pack as me.'

'I *love* you.'

'I love *you*.'

'When you're in Prague next month, might we snatch any time?'

'I'll be working eighteen-, twenty-hour days,' Scott said. 'And you, Miss Shaw, have your book to write.'

She thought about that. 'You know, I could probably write it faster, but I'm choosing to slow it all right down.'

'Because you don't want to say goodbye to Alice?' Scott said gently.

'No, I really don't.'

'You still on track to finish it next month?'

'Yes,' said Frankie. 'Unfortunately.'

'And how's home? The house, the land?'

'A bit dull,' she said. 'And all the sugar beet's in now – the farmers store it in their fields and farmyards in huge mountains ringed by walls of straw bales. Like castles.'

'Must look quirky,' Scott said. She hadn't thought of it that way.

'I've been there a year and a month now,' she said. There was a flatness to her voice.

'You know, Frankie, sometimes I think you heap the place with too much significance, too much responsibility – like it owes you, like it's down to Norfolk to make you feel happy and at home.' He thought for a moment. 'You need to greet it too, really. You need to forge a stronger friendship with where you live.'

Frankie shrugged. He could hear it. He looked at his view. Miles. And Miles. How he'd love her to live here. In theory.

A nnabel stood with her hands on her hips.
'I don't know where you think you're going to fit all those people, Mummy.'

On the landing upstairs, Annabel was looking at her mother the way a client might an architect who'd got it all wrong.

'I can stay at Luke's,' Sam said helpfully.

'Over Christmas? Don't be daft!' said Frankie.

'Let's go over this one more time,' Annabel sighed.

'Right – Auntie Peta and Uncle Philip are staying at the Hoste Arms in Burnham Market. Grandma will be in the spare room. Annabel – thank you so much – we'll make you nice and cosy in the boxroom so that Jenna and Steph can have your room.'

'Is Steph OK?' asked Annabel.

'Yes,' said Frankie. 'She now refers to her ex-boyfriend as *a complete and utter turnip* – and that's a very good sign.'

'There's no way I'm having Josh or Stan in my room,' said Sam.

'We shouldn't really have them in the house full stop,' Annabel said gravely. 'Even Auntie Peta calls them feral and they're her sons!'

'But Sam,' Frankie said. 'I can make downstairs really lovely for you – and you can see Santa arrive!'

'Mum, Santa doesn't exist. I don't mind sleeping downstairs but I don't want Josh and Stan in my room. It's *my* room. They'll trash it.'

Frankie had to admit, it was highly likely.

'Why don't we put them outside – in your office?'

Annabel and Frankie regarded Sam.

'Genius,' said Frankie. She thought about it. 'But it's freezing in there – the heaters don't do much.'

'They'll probably light a fire anyway,' said Sam.

'They're pyromaniacs as well as feral,' said Annabel. 'What exactly is feral and what time's Scott and Jenna arriving?'

'They'll be here around supper time tomorrow.'

'I'm really glad that we get to have them to ourselves for a few days before everyone else comes and stares at them,' said Annabel.

Ruth had Frankie on all fours and was supporting her head lightly. The Alexander Technique had become an essential part of her week. Sometimes, she thought it was like a sort of yoga but with massage. Her headaches had all but gone and she found she could sit longer at her work and finish a long day feeling less stiff. Ruth's house smelt lovely: gingery and of mulled wine and pine needles.

'Mine doesn't smell anything like this.'

'Pardon?'

Frankie giggled. 'Your sessions always do this to me – everything inside just flows out. My house, I meant. It smells of salty mud and low-level damp at this time of year. Yours smells of Christmas Past – it smells of calmness and luxury.'

'Did you phone my builder?'

'Almost.'

'Frankie,' Ruth chided.

'Just been – too busy.'

'Too busy building fantasy homes in Canada instead of maintaining yours right here.'

'Stop it – you sound like my sister.'

'Sorry. You know what I'm going to say now though, don't you?'

'Yes,' Frankie sighed. 'I have to embrace the present.'

'You do,' said Ruth. 'The "now" is at the core of everything and one day you'll see so. You've seemed on a real downer about Norfolk – really since you got back from Canada.'

'I'd much rather live there.'

'Have you thought about it seriously?'

'Yes.'

Ruth quite wanted to take her hands off Frankie and stand there with them on her hips.

'After all you've been through just to get your little family here in the first place?'

'It's quite difficult talking to you in this position,' Frankie mumbled.

Ruth guided her body up again. 'Please don't go – I'll miss you. We all will.'

'I have to think about what's best for me.'

Ruth gave her a stern look. 'Obviously you'll be giving it considerable thought.'

'Obviously,' said Frankie while thinking to herself how she'd move there tomorrow if she could.

Enjoying tea after the session, Frankie gazed at the Ingrams' Christmas tree with marvel and light envy. It was huge and even, decorated opulently with an authoritative and tasteful scheme. The tree she'd bought had looked fine when she'd seen it at the roadside stall. However, when it was up in the living room, its lopsidedness could not be corrected by any amount of repositioning and no matter how many times she relocated the baubles, it still looked as though the decorations had been thrown at it in a fit of decidedly unfestive pique.

'Hey,' she said, 'I signed a new contract yesterday – for the first book in hopefully a new series. They're going to be called the *Just My Luck* stories – if I can pull the first one off.'

Ruth chinked her mug against Frankie's. 'That's just great. And Alice's swansong is still due for the spring?'

'Yes. Which'll mean another tour.'

And Frankie thought, how am I meant to get to Canada any time soon?

'And Scott arrives tomorrow,' said Ruth. 'Do you want me to have the children so you can be alone?'

Ruth was moving Frankie's arm in what felt like a never-ending spiral. She drifted back to when she last saw Scott in mid-October just for two days on his way back from Prague. 'You know what I love most about my relationship? We just pick up from where we left off. It's the most normal thing in the world whenever I see him.'

'And yet your mother and sister have yet to meet him?'

Frankie buried her face in her hands. 'I think I over-ordered on the house-guests front. It's going to be – a squash.'

'God I'd love to be a fly on the wall at yours this Christmas,' Ruth said. 'Can't you secretly record the goings-on?'

* * *

The lanes were quiet, the hedgerows now a knitted wall of prickled bare branches, just occasionally enlivened with a little holly or a lone faded leaf still clinging on since autumn. It was dry and crisp, the sky a washed-out Wedgwood blue ceilinged by high clouds tinged bright by a sun that could not be seen. Norfolk really did have a unique beauty. As Frankie drove back home, she realized she hadn't given much thought to the possibility of all-out drama when her family gathered for Christmas. Practicalities of where to put them all – and just the anticipation of Scott's arrival – were what had preoccupied her most. Now, though, she thought back to when she'd last seen Scott, on his way home from Prague. After two weeks of twenty-hour days, all he wanted to do was lie on a bed with Frankie in his arms and not have to think. Much to her mother's disapproval – which was wordlessly delivered by an arched eyebrow and a slow exhale – Frankie had gone to him at Heathrow where they'd holed up in an airport hotel room for forty-eight hours. She remembered her mother's words on her return. For the first time Frankie had actually wanted to talk to her mother about Scott, to paint a picture of him and describe how she felt. It mattered that her mother should see her so happy; she hoped a little of her joy might rub off. But her mother also wanted to speak of Scott.

It's no way to conduct a relationship. There isn't an ounce of reality to it, you do see that – don't you?

Frankie pulled into her driveway. She remembered how her mother had left her tea half-drunk that day, as if the bitterness of her words had seeped into the cup. She switched off the engine and looked at her house. While she'd been at Ruth's, Annabel had been busy stringing paper chains in roller-coaster undulations across all the windows.

You'll see, Mother. You'll see.

Jenna looked tired. She looked different too, she looked wonderful. She'd gained a little weight back and her hair, which Frankie had last seen in soft-looking wholesome layers, was now shortened to a choppy bob. Frankie realized she'd only ever seen Jenna in warm weather, in cut-offs and T-shirts or her cute little uniform at the restaurant. Here she was in black jeans and chunky boots and an oversized thick woollen sweater in a deep maroon.

'That's some journey,' Jenna said. And it was true. Even an airport nearer to where either of them lived couldn't lessen the depleting impact of that long haul between their countries. Jenna hugged Annabel and Sam talked at Scott, eighteen to the dozen, brandishing his phone from which a track wheezed its way out. And then Jenna stopped and looked around. She really was here, in a picture-perfect English country cottage and a little colour came back to her cheeks.

'You sure you don't mind sharing a room? Not for all of your trip – just for while Steph's here?'

'I don't mind at all – I've gotten used to having a roomie.'

Annabel had curled herself next to Jenna. 'What's she like?'

'She's from Japan and her name's Natsuko.' Jenna started laughing. 'You know why my dad loves her? Because she's really studious and shy and geeky and he thinks there's no wild partying going on.'

Scott pretended not to hear.

Annabel was fiddling absent-mindedly with Jenna's bracelet, silver with a couple of charms, and her medic alert tag. 'Will you have a seizure while you're here, do you think? Don't worry if you do – I've moved a lot of sharp things, hard things, out of the way in my room, just in case.'

Jenna looked at Scott and Frankie looked at Jenna and they all looked at Annabel and smiled. 'I hope not to,' said Jenna, 'but that's very thoughtful. Thank you.'

'We had an epileptic cake sale at school,' Annabel said. 'We raised thirty-seven pounds.'

'Fantastic!' said Jenna, giving her a squeeze.

'You mustn't get too tired,' Annabel told her. 'Or stressed.'

'I'll have an early night,' Jenna assured her. 'And now I'm here, I feel very relaxed. It's just beautiful, your home.'

And then Sam appeared with a tray of his famous but disastrous tea. He'd given each person one and a half sugars, he'd used Frankie's vintage teacups and saucers and, by the time he was handing them around, there was more yellowish liquid in the saucers than in the cups. But there were mince pies too and the fire was lit, the tree lights twinkled and Christmas was coming.

In a bedroom illuminated by slivers of moonlight eking in through nearly-closed curtains, Scott and Frankie lay on their sides and looked at each other. He tucked hair that didn't need it, behind her ears over and over while she ran her fingertips in little races along his shoulder and down his arm. He caressed her face tenderly and she kissed his lips, his eyebrows, his nose, his chin.

'Here we are again.'

'I kinda love it that we whisper,' he said. 'Makes it all private and a little covert.'

'We'll have to resort to sign language when my mother arrives – for an old bat her ears are super-tuned.'

'You look beautiful in this light.'

'You do too.'

'You're turning me on.'

'I know. I can feel.'

'You want to?' Scott started kissing Frankie, urgent and insistent, his hands everywhere, his body achingly expectant of what had been restricted to fantasy these last weeks. Frankie giggled through her nose. She straddled him and dipped her face down to his. He loved the sensation of her hair falling on his skin. There was something exquisitely intense about keeping their love-making quiet, keeping it slow, keeping it secret. But what he most wanted to do was to flip her over and push way up into her, thrash about the bed with her, just be unbridled and simply let go regardless of how noisy it got.

'Why did you tell Santa you wanted something that's pretty and sparkles?' he said as quietly as he could. 'Why didn't you tell him you wanted a new bed that doesn't creak and a door that shuts properly?'

When Steph arrived, she and Jenna needed but a split second to assess each other, make their greeting and decide that this was going to be a fabulous new friendship. Annabel looked momentarily crestfallen until they invited her back up to her bedroom where she sat cross-legged, watching and listening in awe.

Peta arrived the day after that with the two boys and an ashen-looking Philip looking as though he needed a drink.

'Where is he?' Peta hissed, craning her neck.

'He's here,' said Scott, coming into the hallway with a tea towel over his shoulder, his shirtsleeves rolled up. 'He's been washing up.'

Seeing her sister's jaw drop and watching Scott warmly shake Philip's hand and then force the boys to shake his hand too, Frankie retreated into the kitchen and punched the air victoriously.

'I'm Peta,' she heard her sister say.

'Good to meet you Peta – Frankie talks about you so much. Guys, hey – Stan and Josh – shoes off in the house, OK?'

And Frankie heard Peta's sons mumble and scuff as they did as Scott had asked.

In came Peta who took a long look around. 'It looks lovely Frankie – it really does.' She hugged her sister and whispered, oh my God – why didn't you say? He's beyond gorgeous!

Sam took the boys out to Frankie's office where Scott had spent the morning fixing the gaping window and one of the heaters.

'Come back into the house when you're ready,' he told his cousins.

'What for?'

'Er – to eat? To drink? To be merry?' Sam rolled his eyes at them and left them to it.

Stan and Josh looked at each other. They wondered, when had Sam grown up, never mind the hair gel? They slouched around the room for a while, unzipped their holdalls, couldn't be bothered to unpack or fight over who'd have which futon so they shuffled back over to the house. Frankie gave them something to eat and drink – and once Jenna and Steph appeared, both boys realized there was actually quite a lot to feel merry about.

On Christmas Eve, Frankie asked Scott to take the children out for fresh air that morning as though they were dogs. Sam and Annabel obliged by barking their way down the path, dragging Scott and Jenna with them. When they came back, the mince pies were out of the oven.

'Here,' said Scott, fanning his mouth. 'For you.' He passed her an envelope. It was a Christmas card from the Mawbys. 'We saw Keith on our walk. Stopped for a chat – he was very interested in Pemberton being known as Spud Valley on account of our seed-potato production.'

'Keith gave us the card because he said we could save him the journey,' Annabel laughed. 'Hilarious! He only lives next door.'

'He was joking,' said Sam. 'He has a funny sense of humour. You know that.'

Frankie read the card.

> *To Frankie, Sam and Annabel,*
> *With warmest wishes for Christmas and the New Year,*
> *Keith and Peg Mawby*

'Did we send Keith and Peg a Christmas card, Mum?' Annabel asked. Frankie could feel Scott's eyes on her. It hadn't crossed her mind to. Over a year here and only now did she know her neighbour's name was Peg.

'These are out of this world,' Scott said, reaching for

his third mince pie. But Frankie tapped his hand and
took the plate away.

'Kids – can you take these over to the Mawbys and
say Merry Christmas from us?'

Sam and Annabel moaned. 'We've already had our
fresh air.'

And Scott said you do it, Frankie. You go. We'll clear
the table. You go.

Margaret arrived that afternoon. Frankie was out; she'd
taken Jenna, Steph and Annabel last-minute shopping
in Holt because the market town looked so magical in
its Christmas livery and there were bargains to be had.
She felt quite proud, really, to show off the town to
such an appreciative audience. Peta and Philip had
collected the boys and were making them run on
Holkham beach, timing them on the stopwatches on
their smartphones. They made them race again and
again, keen to tire them out for everyone's sake.

Sam and Scott were moving the furniture around
because Frankie had a brainwave about repositioning
the sofa so that they could turn the table and fit the
old desk at the end so that mealtimes wouldn't be such
a squeeze.

The doorbell rang.

'That'll be my grandmamma,' said Sam, gravely in
a mock French accent.

'You don't seriously call her that do you?'

'Behind her back we call her all sorts,' Sam said.

'You going to open the door or shall I?' Scott looked
at Sam. 'I guess I'm going to, right?'

Was he nervous? he wondered as he walked through.
No, not nervous so much as warily intrigued about this

woman with whom Frankie had such a fraught relationship. He opened the front door and the first thing he thought was how did Frankie come to have a mother so tall and regal looking.

'Margaret – I'm Scott. Merry Christmas. Here let me take your bags. Come on in, it's cold out there.'

And Margaret was so taken aback by his easy warmth and authority she couldn't very well be affronted by his first-name-term familiarity.

'Hey Grandma,' said Sam. 'Merry Christmas.'

'Merry Christmas.' She looked around. Frankie's home smelt of oranges and cloves, something buttery, something warm and delicately spiced. She'd never known the house to have such a pleasant fragrance. It made it immediately homely.

'Let me take your bags up to your room,' Scott said. 'Can I help you with your coat?'

'It's OK Scott,' said Sam, stepping forward. 'I can do that.'

Frankie had often tried to reason with the children what true Christmas spirit was. It's not about the presents – it's about being together. But that year, actually the gifts were fundamental; it *was* about the little bowl Rose had sent over with Scott for Annabel, woven out of cedar root and cherry and grasses. It *was* about the traditional drum Aaron had sent over for Sam. And, for Frankie, it *was* about the pair of earrings Scott had bought for her, sparkling and pretty. Next year she'd ask Santa for a bed that didn't creak and a door that shut properly. This year, she was just going to enjoy being pampered and feeling treasured.

And of course it was about being together. Though

Peta and Philip relished the peace and luxury of staying at the Hoste, they still arrived at Frankie's when the morning tea was still hot in the pot and long before their boys had even surfaced. The whole party went to Brancaster, meandering the beach for almost two hours without actually walking that far. Margaret took Scott's arm, initially to steady herself – she found gum boots such a chore at her age – and it seemed it was just easier to leave it there.

'And are there beaches where you are – or just mountains?' She wasn't actually after a reply. 'I've never liked mountains. I've always found them so oppressive – all that monstrous inhospitable mass closing off the sky. Suffocating!'

'Mother you don't much like Norfolk either because you say it's too flat,' said Peta.

'I like a more intimate landscape,' Margaret started.

And suddenly Brancaster beach rang out with Frankie and Peta shouting *I like the Cotswolds*.

The sisters glanced at each other triumphantly – they'd both seen their mother clamp down on a smile, but nevertheless they'd seen it.

Stan and Josh spilt stuff, broke two glasses and a plate and burped at the table but were coshed by their father and Scott – whoever was closest. Frankie overcooked the sprouts and everyone moaned at her in unison while she could see quite clearly the good cheer behind the party hats they were wearing. Annabel ate too much and felt sick so Steph took her upstairs and sat stroking her hair, which meant it only took five minutes for her to feel completely better. Peta watched Scott like a hawk until her mother, out of Frankie's earshot,

told her not to. Just let him be, she told her daughter.
You'll find out all you need if you just let him be. Peta
wasn't quite sure at that stage whether her mother
was hoping he'd fail or triumph. She did notice that
her mother had rather nimbly made her way to the
table to ensure that she sat by him. Stan and Josh fired
all manner of musical questions at him, mainly whether
he'd heard of this band or that, how many guitars he
had and who famous had he played with. Scott was
proud that Sam helped him out with the answers.
Philip talked a lot about Eric Clapton to anyone who'd
even pretend to listen.

Scott knew he was being assessed but he didn't mind.
He was having Christmas in England with both his girls
and for that he was grateful. When the table was at
its most raucous, Frankie chinked her glass against his
and said Merry Christmas my darling and Scott thought
to himself were we really not together this time last
year? the year before? or the year before? He thought,
has she really been in my life only seven months?
The notion was preposterous and marvellous at the
same time. He put his hand gently to her cheek, it didn't
matter to him who saw. He knew that happiness
didn't get much purer than this.

Peta's family left the day after Boxing Day, taking
Margaret with them back to London. Even the boys
had had a good enough time to be able to thank Frankie
without being asked. They thanked Scott too. Everyone
did. It had seemed to all of them that they had been
Frankie and Scott's guests.

'A pleasure,' said Margaret offering her hand.

'Pleasure was mine.'

He'd put her case in Peta's car and the two of
them stood watching Philip cramming the rest of the
bags in.

'And when are you returning?' Margaret asked.

'January third,' Scott said.

'I meant – when are you returning here?'

'Ah. February – I have around ten days' work in
London.'

'Perhaps you might visit.'

'Oh – I intend to commute in from here.'

'Me,' Margaret qualified, 'perhaps you might visit me.'

Over the last three days, Scott had thought of ways
to subtly sing Frankie's praises to her mother and
there'd been times when he could have said to
Frankie you know she's not that bad, your mother,
she really isn't. But he'd also seen the stern looks
that Margaret cast Frankie's way, he'd heard the
occasional sharpness that passed between the two of
them, he knew that sometimes Frankie's discontent
was an overreaction. This trip, though, he decided he'd
say nothing. For the time being, Margaret's invitation
was enough. Her hand extended to him had been to
Frankie also.

'Thank you,' he said. 'I'd like that.'

Annabel was grumpy, snuggled up against Frankie
plucking at a loose thread on her sweater. Scott
regarded Frankie enquiringly.

'Steph's invited Jenna back to London with her for
New Year's Eve.'

'And Annabel has to hang out here with the old
folk?' Scott sat on the coffee table, his hands loosely
clasped. 'That sucks.' Annabel looked up and nodded.

'Do you like fireworks?' He asked Annabel shrugged. 'Let's go and buy fireworks. Let's have ourselves a party.'

Frankie thought how actually she didn't want to move. For the first time all Christmas she felt completely relaxed and as if her home was her own again.

'Do you mind if I don't come? Do you mind if I just – zonk out here for a while?'

Scott looked at Annabel. 'Did you hear me invite your mom firework shopping? I don't think I did. See how she thought she was coming too?'

Frankie was grateful. 'Might you pick up Sam from his friend Luke's on your way back? It's not hard to find. I can draw a map if you like.'

'Don't let Mummy draw a map,' Annabel told Scott. 'She takes hours over it. Hours and hours. She puts all these details in – trees, windows in houses, people walking along.'

'You reckon we can track down Sam then, just the two of us?'

Annabel nodded. Scott put his hand lightly on her head, winked at Frankie and off they went. There was something about Scott and Annabel, or Scott and Sam, going off together, whether it was to do something nice, or just running an errand, off together in the everyday. There was something about Scott being insured to drive her car too; his name linked with hers on the forms and contracts that daily life demands. We need more milk. Don't worry – I was going to pop out to the shops. Can you fill the car up, while you're at it. What's mine is yours.

Jenna and Steph. Over Christmas, everyone started referring to them as 'the girls'. She could hear them right now, muffled voices chatting and laughing, the floorboards creaking as they moved around upstairs. Frankie noticed that Scott had been momentarily surprised that he wasn't the first to know of his daughter's New Year plans. But she'd seen him correct his reaction, nod at the news and turn his attention to Annabel who was feeling far sorer about the whole thing.

She looked around the living room. Those bloody pine needles of the supposedly non-drop tree. A small scrunch of wrapping paper hiding under the coffee table. Clementine peel in the fireplace. A pile of presents Sam still hadn't taken to his room. The tree twinkling yet somehow sedate, as if it had grown up these last few days, as if it had been a job well done. Annabel's paper chains at the windows, a couple of them broken. A candle scented with clove and orange flickering perhaps its last half-hour. She touched her earlobes, twisted her new earrings this way and that. Something pretty and sparkling. Christmas had been just that.

Steph and Jenna appeared.

'Can we make eggs and hash browns?'

Frankie nodded.

'Would you like some, Frankie?'

Frankie made to leave the sofa.

'Don't get up,' said Steph. 'I know where everything is.'

It struck Frankie that she felt more compelled to mother Steph now than at any other time. She'd been too self-obsessed in her twenties to think about her much, and she'd been just too busy since she'd had the children.

'I'm really glad you're here Steph,' she said. 'You know you're welcome any time.'

'Oh it's been brill,' said Steph. 'It's been so lovely being with the family – even though your mother still shoots me The Look.'

'Oh just ignore her,' Frankie said.

'I do!'

'I thought your mom was sweet,' said Jenna.

'Sweet?'

'She was very kind to me. Asked me about my epilepsy, asked me what it was like growing up in the mountains like I'm Heidi.'

'How have you been?'

'You mean – have I had a seizure?'

'Have you?'

'Not for six weeks. How about that!'

'That'll be the power of love!' said Steph and Frankie caught the glance that Jenna sent her. Then Jenna reddened and looked at Frankie.

'I'm seeing this guy,' she shrugged. 'He's on my course.' She paused, broke into a grin. 'I really like him.'

He was called Kyle and he was from Calgary. The photos Jenna shared showed a brawny boy with great teeth and an arm protectively and proudly around her shoulder. They looked, thought Frankie, blissfully happy.

'Your dad didn't say,' Frankie mused.

'I haven't told him,' Jenna said a little shyly. Frankie looked up. 'Would you mind not telling him either, Frankie?'

'Of course,' she said. 'But why?'

'He's my *dad*?' Jenna laughed.

'Isn't he the coolest dad in the world?' Frankie asked.

'Your dad is supercool, Jenna,' Steph concurred before

sharing with Frankie a momentary look that said *compared to ours who was crabby and remote.*

'He'll just want to meet him and give him the third degree – and I'm not ready yet. I like it being just the two of us, just Kyle and me.'

'Is he kind?' Frankie asked. 'As well as being profoundly handsome?'

'Yes,' Jenna nodded. 'He's thoughtful and we have a lot of fun. He makes me feel –' She drifted off and grinned.

And Frankie thought will this be Annabel? In ten years' time, will Annabel phone Steph and say I'm seeing this gorgeous bloke but don't tell Mum – she'll just interfere and embarrass me.

'It's a wonderful thing,' she told the girls, 'to have family.'

That's what she was to Jenna. That's what Steph was to Annabel. It made the world seem smaller and more manageable and that had to be good.

* * *

Scott lay awake long after last year turned into this. What would the year hold? He turned and gazed at Frankie, sleeping peacefully with both hands tucked under her chin like a squirrel. Where would they be, he wondered, in twelve months' time? Would they have New Year's Eve in Canada perhaps? Would she be fast asleep in his bed having gotten a little mashed on champagne? Would the year treat them well?

He liked it that now he could say that they'd been together since last year. He had the work coming up in London in February, she had the final Alice book to launch soon after and her new *Just My Luck* story to tackle. He was taking on another band to mentor and still helping Jonah and his gang with their music. What about after that? This time next year; 365 days' time. Didn't sound so long when he thought about how much could be crammed into it.

Jenna. She'd be over a year into her studies. Maybe she'd even have her driver's licence. The next appointment with the neurologist was early March. Would she still be with the guy he'd heard her talking to on the phone when Peta's voice had worn him down a little and he'd managed to slink up to Frankie's room for some peace? At what point during the year would Jenna say Pops, there's someone I want you to meet? He chuckled quietly to himself; he'd need Frankie's help with that one. Was he worrying for Jenna that the guy might not be good enough – or worrying for himself, sensing his reluctance to trust or welcome any boy or let go of a little more of his daughter? And what if Jenna's heart was broken? He knew the pain would crease him more. He pulled the covers over Frankie's shoulder. Was he a little sad that, at the moment, Jenna had said nothing to him? But that was normal, right? Lying there, he sent out deep hope for her soul, and profound hope for her health. A level of hope that turns a wish into prayer.

Scott moved a little closer to Frankie so that his shoulder touched her arm. He thought about the year just gone and the year that now lay ahead. He visualized it as a buffet stretching out in front of him – already all laid out to sustain and delight him over the coming months. The point of the year was to make his way over and sense where to start, decide what to take and what to leave, what would taste good and what might not, what to have now and what to leave for later. Sometimes the things that looked the most opulent and tasty were the driest and most bland. He knew that from the movie business. And from the music business he knew if you gorged on everything on offer, you'd get sick and tired. He thought of Lind, his ex-wife, Jenna's mom. He didn't think of her often, but he thought of her just then and hoped she'd have an OK year.

Would Frankie move to Canada? She talked about it so dreamily. He reflected on the subtle hints Frankie dropped to her children about moving. He'd seen the children perplex and contemplate, a little torn because how can we really really like Scott but actually not want to live where he lives? We don't want to leave our friends a second time and our dad has only just come back.

This was their home – right there where he was waiting for sleep. This place with the curved sky and slab-grey sea. He understood this more than Frankie. He knew it had taken the children a little while, but he could see that they believed in it now. They'd trusted their mother and it had been true – she'd done the best by them. They were settling into their grooves, making friends and doing well at school. If he were their parent, he'd think it wasn't such a good time to uproot them.

So much keeping him there, so much keeping her here. Scott liked to think that when Frankie said her dream was to move to Canada, what she was really telling him was that she loved him enough to want to be with him always. A vivid picture of his home shot across his mind, standing empty right now, all locked up until he and Buddy returned in a couple of days. There was a lot of snow, so Aaron said. Frankie needed to see it, Scott decided, it was just as beautiful when the little details were obliterated but the snowlight and softness of sound brought a different beauty to the land.

Sometimes, the clearest thoughts came to Scott when he was on the cusp of sleep. It was the same with music; a quick surge of notes, snippets of songs, snatches of melody. It was as if these moments were when he was at his most open, most receptive to ideas that the whirl of the day had kept reined in. On New Year's Day, as Scott fell asleep, he thought how he'd really like to marry Frankie. And how a married life split between Norfolk and British Columbia, though not conventional, could be a very good one. He'd remember this when he woke. And there on the buffet of the year ahead it would be placed, waiting for the right moment when it would taste its sweetest.

PART THREE

APRIL

To: scottmusic@me.com
From: samtheman888@gmail.com
Subject: yo!
Hi Scott
How's it going? Guess what – Captain George
Vancouver, who led the expedition to explore
British Columbia and stuff nearby was actually
born right here in King's Lynn! School's pretty
good at the moment but I'm still looking forward
to the Easter holidays (vacations). I never grow sick
of Easter Eggs. Last year my Mum fessed up that
when my sister and me were little she'd eat our
chocolate.
Well – cya!
Sam

To: samtheman888@gmail.com
From: scottmusic@me.com
Subject: re: yo!
Hey Sam
Great to hear from you. I'm glad you told me about
the child cruelty when you guys were small. I'll make
sure she buys you double for that. Seems a long time
since I was over – that was a lot of fun. I was

thinking about your Mom's office the other day –
want to help me surprise her?
Say hi to Annabel.
Scott

To: scottmusic@me.com
From: samtheman888@gmail.com
Subject: re: yo!
Hi Scott
What sort of surprise?
Cya!
Sam

To: samtheman888@gmail.com
From: scottmusic@me.com
Subject: re: yo!
Hey Sam
So it seems she's struggling again with this new book
she has to do – this Just My Luck story. I thought we
could make her office a place she wants to go to. It'll
take a bit of work – are you in?
Scott

To: scottmusic@me.com
From: samtheman888@gmail.com
Subject: re: yo!
Do you mean am I in right now I'm not I'm on
the bus doing emails on my phone but we could try
and FaceTime later or something I have to go
Sam

To: samtheman888@gmail.com
From: scottmusic@me.com
Subject: re: yo!
Hey Sam
I meant are you 'in' for helping me plan the room for your Mom. Sure – we can FaceTime later if you like. When I was over in February, I snuck a bunch of stuff into the small shed. I went to the stores when she didn't know. There's some wood and shelving and a desk that we have to put together. I was going to buy paint but I thought Annabel might want to choose colors. When I'm next over, we'll go get some drapes (curtains). That's the plan! What do you think?
Scott

To: scottmusic@me.com
From: samtheman888@gmail.com
Subject: re: yo!
Definitely 'in'! I'd better not tell Annabel just yet as she can't keep a secret. She'll just get too excited and let the cat out of the bag (the secret).
I have an unhuman amount of homework tonight. Sometimes I think it's the school's fault – they don't teach us properly during the day so they make us finish it off at night while the staff put their feet up. So I won't be facetiming tonight. Soz.
Sam

* * *

'C'est moi.'

'Hey baby.'

'I had a shit day. I'm making excuses to my editor

365

again. Feeling out of sorts – that nausea and adrenalin. That fear of the blank paper.'

'You know silence for a musician is the same as the bare page for the author. You have to see a kind of brightness to it, Frankie, not emptiness. It's there for you alone to fill.'

'It's so weird, writing about a ten-year-old boy – I'm not even sure if I like him much. I *still* think of Alice.'

'Poor Tom! Or did you change his name back to Ben?'

'No, I kept it as Tom.'

'You tried writing in your office?'

'Kitchen table.'

'How's that working for you?'

'It isn't.'

'You thought about having Alice be his friend? Ben, Tom whatever? Just have her come in every now and then? Frankie?'

'Sorry – I didn't mean to go quiet. Scott?'

'Still here.'

'Exactly. You're still *there*.'

'Frankie?'

'– it's just the missing you has felt exceptionally hard this time.'

'Yes. Yes it has.'

'February was just so lovely. But it seems so much more than six weeks since we were together. There's always a period when we're too far away, too long apart. It's this yawning ache.'

'Frankie if the world was small enough a place for us to find each other, it's sure as hell a small enough place to keep us together.'

'Why are you so content with things the way they are, Scott? Don't you want more? When I was a teen I read Richard Bach and he said we're not given a dream without the power to fulfil it.'

'Frankie, when I was a teen, I went through a period of listening to the Doors on a loop. And Jim Morrison told me it was The End.'

'What are you getting at? You're pissing me off – because I'm serious.'

'So am I, baby, so am I. Look around you, Frankie. Look right outside your window and way beyond it. Your world is a pretty good place to be in at the moment. Embrace what you have instead of tiring yourself out, hoping for more.'

'Is it so wrong to want more?'

'Is telling you how much I love you enough to keep you going?'

* * *

To: samtheman888@gmail.com
From: scottmusic@me.com
Subject: secret mission
Hey Sam
I hope you're good. I met up with Dave Grohl last week – we may be working on a project together later in the year. I thought you'd like to know!
So I've been thinking – next week I have a quiet week. I'm going to look into flights and come surprise your Mom. That way I can make sure she doesn't eat your Easter Eggs.
S

To: scottmusic@me.com
From: samtheman888@gmail.com
Subject: re: secret mission
Hi Scott
Omg she'll love that. I can make sure she's in – I can
fake flu or spill something just as we're going out. There's
loads I can do. I won't tell Annabel because she won't
keep her mouth shut (she's that age plus she's a girl).
Epic!
Sam

To: samtheman888@gmail.com
From: scottmusic@me.com
Subject: mission accomplished
OK Sam so I've booked a flight that'll get me in on
Thursday. I hope to be with you by the evening. I'll
let you know if there are any changes.
Take care big guy
Scott

* * *

April in Pemberton and the grass was green again; kids out playing soccer, families riding bikes and hiking. The black bears waking from hibernation, ready to regain the weight they've lost over winter. In the skies, finches, sparrows and collared doves, on the water trumpeter swans and buffleheads, in the rivers steelhead trout and in the woods Rufous hummingbirds lured by the wild red flowering currant bushes in bloom. All around, a feeling of renewed energy, a sense of welcoming true spring. And Scott wondered, what's Norfolk like this time of year? How cold the sea? How full the sky? Who's coming in and who's heading out?

'Buddy – if Johnny and little Tara offer you chocolate, you say no, OK? It's not good for you.'

Buddy and Scott, all packed and ready to spend Easter apart. The house on the verge of emptiness and silence for a few days. Aaron making his way up the drive with a honk of the horn and a sputter from the exhaust.

'Hey Buddy. Hey Scott – so there's no coffee?'

'We have time?'

'Did you ever miss a flight with Aaron Air?'

'You jerk. I guess not.'

Scott and Aaron shooting the shit over a cup of coffee.

'All set?'

'All set. Can we go via yours? I have Easter eggs for Tara and Johnny.'

'Sure – we'll drop Buddy off there too. He doesn't look like he wants to fly today. He looks like he doesn't want to leave his bed.'

'He's looking a little tired, right? I thought so too.'

'We'll keep an eye on him, Scott. So – you going to arrive on her doorstep dressed as the Easter Bunny?'

'You tool.'

'And she doesn't know a thing?'

'For all Frankie knows, I'm right here at home missing her as much as she's missing me.'

Safety checks. Scott had flown with Aaron more times than he could count but he never tired of seeing and hearing Aaron get ready to fly. Here was a man with flight in his blood, fiercely proud of his lineage, his granddaddy who flew and told him Líl̓wat legends of eagles and thunderbirds; his daddy who flew for his country. Aaron, a man whose passion for flight had propelled him from the joker in the class at school to running a successful little business and the owner of a plane he loved as much as his wife.

And all I do is play a little guitar, Scott thought as he looked out of the window. He was ready to get going. Frankie was still over half a day away. He smiled at the thought of her being blissfully unaware of him about to take to the skies, to make his way over to her with a bag full of Easter chocolate and, in a small velvet box, one plain gold wedding band.

'All set!'

The men grinned at each other and Aaron whooped as the Cessna made her way down the runway and up, up, up.

This time of year, with the tropic air coming over the cooler ocean, there was a lot of stratus cloud settling over the Pemberton Valley, forming a thick duvet from which rain or even a little snow was still likely to fall. Aaron called it *aboveground fog*. There'd been one time when he was flying home that he couldn't see around it, couldn't see through it. With the airfield being VFR, visual flight rules only, all he could do was just keep flying. A sea of white stretching in all directions above which he had felt utterly alone until a tiny hole beckoned him down and he found himself beyond Lake Lillooet and some way from Pemberton. He'd flown low back to the airport. He never told anyone about that day. The spirits were with him and it was they who landed the plane, not him.

Beyond Whistler now, and over the provincial park of Garibaldi they flew.

'Black Tusk,' said Scott. The volcano inky and jagged, clawing into the sky up above the cloud.

'Qelqámtensa ti Skenknápa,' Aaron said.

Scott laughed. 'Yeah – or Black Tusk for short.'

'Landing Place of the Thunderbird,' said Aaron, 'that's what it means. That's how it was formed – that's why it looks this way. From the Thunderbird's lightning. You know on the north side of the north summit there's a place that no man's ever climbed? You want to take a look?'

'We have time?'

'Oh sure, we have time.'

Aaron turned the plane and descended.

The remoteness, the darkness, spoke of power beyond the natural to Scott. He felt they shouldn't be there, up in the sky, masquerading as a bird.

'Let's keep going,' he said to Aaron.

'Whoa – it's bumpy!'

The plane shook and lurched down and up.

'We're good?'

'Sure, it's just a little drainage wind – the high-density air rushing down the slope.' Aaron started changing course, still low and continuing a little east off his intended route. Scott looked down over Garibaldi Lake icy cold, and beyond to Mount Garibaldi soaring above the Table. This God-given land in which he lived. He grinned at Aaron and held up his palm for a high five. Aaron clapped at his pal's hand and then clasped it for a moment. He needed to head west again, and he needed to climb. There were cumulonimbus clouds in the vicinity, a no-go area for pilots. Thunderbird, he thought, I could do with you now. He didn't like the look of the cloud in a spiral at the mountain. He really needed to climb.

'Hold onto your hat – we're going to get bumpy,' he told Scott. He knew from the rotor cloud that there was mountain wave; the wind heading up the mountain encountering a stable air barrier at the top redirecting it down in a rush. There could be downdraughts of 5,000 feet per minute, a turbulent vortex, strong vertical currents and, in this land of mountains, this could go on for miles.

'Fuck, man.'

It felt as though the plane was being sucked towards the mountain and yo-yoed. Aaron pushed the throttle forward into the bulkhead although he knew he was at full power and there was no more to come.

'We're good, Scott, we're good.'

A little Cessna 172. Built in 1967. Seating for the pilot and three passengers. And hey – Aaron's father and grandfather are there now, guiding him. You're going to stall, boy. Don't turn even though you're going to want to. Just keep it together. They don't call this the Coffin Corner for nothing. Just keep flying. Never stop flying. There is no turning point. You're going to stall around about – now.

'Aaron?'

'It's OK – we just stalled.'

'Aaron?'

'We've stalled.'

Rose and Tara and Johnny.

'Mayday.'

Jenna. Frankie.

'Mayday.'

The terror. The sheer terror. The utterly inconceivable becoming the indisputable truth. But love was a stronger emotion and love swept through Scott keeping fear at bay, keeping his heart aloft as everything else spun downwards. Love. For himself. For Aaron. For his parents. His dog. Mount Currie and Joffre and the black bear. His music, his guitars, his home. His densest, primal love for Jenna; his beautiful beautiful brave girl. And the most sublime and life-enhancing love he felt for Frankie. A bag of chocolate eggs and a plain gold wedding band.

Terror: when? when?

Sadness: so much to give. So much left to do.

Regret: he desperately wanted to live.

Love: how lucky he'd been to have had so much love in his life.

* * *

It took a day to locate the plane. Another day before Jenna and Rose knew for sure. Why didn't she have Frankie's mobile-phone number? Why didn't she have her email address? Why had she had no need of them before? Messages from Frankie to Jenna were passed on via Scott. Why couldn't she find any note of them at home? Why had her dad put a password on his laptop?

Why wasn't Frankie on Twitter or Facebook? Why had she no private contact details on Google? If you can find Brad Pitt's number on Google, surely an English author's details are there somewhere too? Jenna tried phoning Frankie's publishers but it was Easter Sunday and the offices were shut.

Pops. Oh Pops.

What am I meant to do?

To: scottmusic@me.com
From: samtheman888@gmail.com
Subject: hi
Hi Scott. I've tried facetiming you but your phone
is off so you must be on your way. Can you
let me know when you're arriving? You can
text me or email me or FaceTime. I thought you
said yesterday. I've worked out the time difference
– and I'm sure it meant our yesterday, not
yours.
Cya!
Sam

To: scottmusic@me.com
From: samtheman888@gmail.com
Subject: from Sam
Hi Scott. I just want to know if you are coming or if
you're delayed. But if you are still coming. Don't
worry – I haven't told my Mum. Please can you let
me know what's happening with the flight and
e.t.a.
Thanks. Hope to hear from you soon.
Sam

To: scottmusic@me.com
From: samtheman888@gmail.com
Subject: Please call
Why haven't you been in touch Scott? My Mum is
really upset – she says your phone is off all the time
and you're not bothering to return her emails or
anything. If you don't love her any more can you deal
with that because she's really worried and it's not
fair.
I thought you were coming?
I don't understand why you wouldn't.
Please call my Mum a.s.a.p.
Sam

A knock at the door.
Finally, thought Sam.

Mum! Mum – there's someone at the door.

Can you open it please, I'm cooking.

No Mum – *you*.

Sam – for goodness' sake, open the door. You're just sitting there on your bloody gadget, phone, whatever – instagramming. Get up and answer it.

It's not Scott.

And Sam thought, it's never going to be Scott again.

He really hated him just then.

'Steph!'

Frankie looked up from the stove.

'Wow! Now there's a surprise. Are you OK? What is it? Steph – what's wrong? It's not the Complete and Utter Turnip again, is it?'

Steph's head dropped. It struck her she hadn't visited Frankie since Christmas despite her best intentions. It suddenly seemed so long ago, all of them here together, all that noise and laughter and food and warmth and family and new friends. Now spring

beckoned and Frankie had her kitchen window ajar,
as if to coax it in.

'Stephy – what is it?'

'It's Scott,' said Steph.

PART FOUR

AFTER AND EVERMORE

My father has died and my world has withered. Some tutor I don't even know was waiting for me in my room after my classes, standing there by the window. Natsuko my room-mate was sitting on her bed hugging her knees. Not in a million years would I have guessed why they were there. It was unbelievable. What they told me – I just cannot believe. I knew he was going to the UK to surprise Frankie, but I never thought he wouldn't be coming back. It didn't cross my mind. The last thing I said to him was one word – a single-word text replying to his telling me he was going to England. All I said was cool xx.

Oh my God, what'll I do without my pa? How am I going to cope? How can I not have him there, steady and strong and always at home? How will I fix on my own the stuff that breaks or unravel the stuff that gets tied in a knot – the physical, the emotional? My pa has always been there to help me, in all aspects of my life, my whole life long. My bank stuff. My application forms. Somewhere to live in Vancouver. Driving me to friends, to work, to university. He bought Buddy for me. He booked my appointments with Dr Schultz and took me there. Fixed my pink bike when I was ten. Mopped up my puke the first and only time I got drunk.

Sat for hours with me first time I was dumped. So often there for me during a seizure, there with his kindness and gentle authority when I came to. He took me to task when I was lazy at school, or rude, or when I strung Billy Sayers along because I didn't know how to dump him. He was there those times my mom let me down, when I had to phone him to come get me and bring me back home. He was there even when I wanted to be on my own. When I flunked math. When Ty Jennings was an ass to me at our school prom. When they took my driver's licence away. In life as I've known it, my dad made everything seem OK. Not having him here – ever again – terrifies me right now. I need to hear him tell me to believe in myself in order for me to be able to do so.

Oh my God my dad is dead.

I hate it that sometimes I rolled my eyes at him and said Pops! give it a break already! Like he got on my nerves – which I guess he did. But shouldn't all parents care too much? That's no failing. And he had to find double the amount of care because he had to be Mom *and* Dad. He devoted a lot of his life to me and now he's gone so what does that mean? If he's not looking out for me, who will be – and will I be OK? My dad never judged me but he always guided me.

I just need more time with him.

Please. Just not yet. Not now.

Scott – my dad – would never consider that he made sacrifices for me but if you think about it, he did. He quit touring and performing so he could be a stay-at-home dad because my mom was, you know, not really capable of doing the job. Apart from one or two that didn't really play a huge part anyway, he didn't have girlfriends either. He said I was his girl and he didn't need another. He was my home, he was my morning and my night, he was the food on my plate and the warmth in the house. I have a dream-catcher by my bed that Aaron gave me years ago, but my dad was my nightwatchman. He was always there for me – sometimes maybe a little too much. Making sure I never locked the bathroom door. Making sure I had my meds, took my meds, got enough sleep – all of that. Often, those were the times I'd back away or just get a bit mad with him, tell *him* to back off, especially when I was, like, fourteen, fifteen, sixteen. I wanted to act like all my friends, even though looking back I can see how that's precisely what it is to be a teenager, a bit of an act. I wanted the freedom *not* to be looked after the whole time. But the truth is, I always felt safe and really secure because my dad was always going to be there for me.

I feel really scared right now. There's so much I trusted him with, so much that I'd say to myself oh it'll be OK, precisely because I had my dad so close in my life. We don't know why I have seizures, we don't know if I'll ever be free of them. We don't know what causes them but we do know that stress and tiredness can sometimes bring one on. I had one the day after I found out, which was the day after he died. Kyle was with me but it was my third or fourth since we've been together and he knows what to do, it doesn't freak him out, his dad is a doctor and I know he's watched a bunch of stuff on YouTube. He said I was going for a full three minutes. I really lacerated the inside of my cheek from biting it while I was seizing. It's still so sore right now. I slept for eighteen hours straight after that. When I woke up, I had to relive the reality of my dad being dead all over again. For the rest of my life, I guess every day, when I wake up, I'll have to know that my dad has died.

Very privately, I know we both thought I'd go first. SUDEP – Sudden Unexplained Death from Epilepsy – affects sufferers aged twenty to forty in the main. It's not common, but nor is it rare. It's just there. But as my dad has always said – and he kind of made it my mantra – I have epilepsy, epilepsy doesn't have me.

My dad isn't the sort of guy who dies young. He's too vital. Too many people need him. What'll the young bands do in Pemberton without their mentor, without someone helping them be the best that they can be? It's more than rock 'n' roll to those kids – he'd talk to them about sex and drugs and steer them right. How about the epilepsy charity he fund-raises for? What about all those movies yet to be made whose soundtracks will now be mediocre because my dad hasn't written the scores? What makes me so mad is that it was his time to live – with me pretty much leaving home and now away at college, why shouldn't he have had years and years of happiness with Frankie?

I'm looking out of the window passing by the sign for Brandywine Falls. I'm on my way home with Kyle driving me. Going back home which can't be home without my dad being there. He *was* my home. Now it feels to me that the walls that held me steady are crumbling, the windows out onto life are all misted up and there's no view anyway, there's just no view to look at.

People have been so kind. But none of that helps. I have to bury my pa. A little bit of me is going with him, you know?

found it very scary, seeing my mum like that – all crumpled and torn like the paper we find under the kitchen table when she hasn't been happy with her work. Sam tried to pull me away, take me to my room, I suppose. But I wanted to stay there in the kitchen, watching Steph hold up my mum. Steph literally held her up. I stood by because I couldn't leave. It frightened me seeing her like that. But it also took my mind off what had happened to Scott.

He died.

Well that didn't make sense.

And Sam said something about him being on his way to us. And that didn't make sense either. Sam was white as a sheet and still as a statue. We just watched as our mum went down. There was nothing we could do. We are just small kids. We needed someone strong to help her. The person we really needed was Scott. Recently, when things were going wrong in the house – like when the curtain pole came crashing down, or the second bigger leak when the pipe actually burst – Sam and me and Mummy all muttered *Wish Scott was here*. But when we found out, when I had to watch my mum disappearing and hear her sobbing, in some ways it was his fault that she was like that. Oh it was very confusing those first minutes.

It helped when Auntie Peta arrived. She was on the doorstep a little while after Steph. She hugged me and kept saying it would be OK. So I believed her. And that's when I started to cry. She kept saying I know, I know – well of course she didn't know. She didn't know what had happened other than that Scott had died and she didn't know all the little reasons I was crying. I was crying for *my* bit of Scott – because I really believed that he gave me a part of him that was just for me. Like when I made him sit on my bed and I heaped all the toys on his lap and painted his finger-nails. He sat very calmly. I can never get my mum to do that. She'll sit for a moment then get up because she always has something to do. But Scott sat on my bed having his manicure, which he called a Man Cure, and that's the only thing he had planned for that after-noon. That wasn't so long ago. That was in February when he was last here. The last time any of us saw him. He said he'd keep the nail varnish on till it all chipped away. He wore it when he was recording his music in London and he was still wearing it when he left for the airport. I wonder how long it lasted? Strange how I never thought to tell Sam to email him and ask him about it.

You wouldn't actually call Scott a chatterbox person – because he was someone who didn't waste time talking about all the this-and-thats that chatterboxes do. But when you were with him he seemed to really like to listen and then speak. I liked what we talked about. I loved those mornings in Canada when my mum was working and Sam and me had Scott to ourselves.

I miss him very much. I wanted to know him for ever. I liked him in our house. I liked seeing him bumble about with my mum. I liked it when he took me to school. Lauren's mum told her that he was a bit gorgeous. Lauren's mum phoned my mum and invited her out with the other mums to hear the whole story. Scott was very good at lifting things and opening things too which meant my mum had little reason to lose her temper and bang about when Scott stayed at ours.

When my mum's crying slowed down, I went over to her. She was sitting on the sofa with her sisters either side. I have never seen her look like that. She looked really terrible and it worried me until she held open her arms and I went onto her lap and cuddled into her neck. She made this tiny sad sound like a kitten. I just hugged her and hugged her and it felt OK to let my tears out too. Mummy, I said, what are we going to do? *I don't know I don't know I don't know. No. No. No. No.*

She went away the next day, to Canada to be with Jenna and for the funeral. She told me she didn't know how long she'd be gone for. I begged her to let me come. I didn't want to be apart. I wanted to stay with her. I didn't want to go to a funeral and see a coffin but I wanted to be back at Scott's house. But she said she had to go by herself this time. I don't know why. Me, Sam and my mum usually do everything together. We're a tight little unit – that's how Scott describes us. Described.

I gave her some things to give to Jenna, like the tiny teddy that Scott won for me at the arcade in Hunstanton. I made a card with a picture of all of us and the bear, and inside I wrote her a letter. It's private. I put a photo of me and Sam for Mummy in her suitcase. I thought about little Tara and Johnny and I wasn't sure at all what to do about them.

While my mum was away, Stephy stayed awhile and then Auntie Peta came back and then Stephy again. Our dad isn't around at the minute; he's had to go somewhere foreign again, for a little while he says, for business. We were back at school after our Easter break. I couldn't concentrate and no one told me off. I shoved Maddie hard in netball because she bumped into me and no one told me off. I pushed my plateful of dinner on the floor, I don't know why. Mrs Sharp came and took me into the medical room and there I howled like my mum had. It was shocking. I really missed my mum. I felt very sad and extremely worried about Scott dying. I mean what exactly happened? What happens when you die? Where do you go? Did it hurt? Was he scared? Did he know? Did he die quickly? Will he hear me if I talk to him? But I wouldn't want him to come back as a ghost to see me.

All that crap about when someone dies a part of you dies too? No. I was left painfully, vividly alive and acutely aware that we were parted now, Scott and I. Not by the mountains and the oceans. But parted for good. Flung asunder, one of us in heaven wherever that is – I just can't work that one out – and one of us on earth. It was done. We were gone. He was absolutely dead. Weeks and weeks of longing to be back with him in Canada. And when I boarded that plane, it was a journey that filled me with a dread so black it was like thick tar cloying up my heart. My poor children. My poor babies. I shudder when I realize what they saw, what they heard. Their mother the banshee, thrashing about in her grief. Their mother the brain-dead, sitting numbskull-still on the sofa; a human tap of tears drip drip drip, saying nothing, just staring. I hate myself for being so absent, in such self-centred turmoil in front of the children, but I was helpless to be anything other. I hate myself for not listening to a word they said to me in those hours – and they cuddled me and spoke constantly – but it was just sound that seeped into one ear then got lost. Thoughts and feelings came at me in bilious waves that never stopped to settle, so I don't know what I thought and I don't really know how I felt. And the next day I was gone. The long hard haul over countries and the ocean and through time zones to return to that beautiful place I'd fallen in love with, to bury the man I'd entrusted my heart to.

* * *

I am exhausted. I didn't sleep on the plane at all. I wanted it to fly slower; I didn't want to cross time divides. It seemed an extraordinary cruelty to have me going back in time because still he wouldn't be there. Why can't going back in time turn back the clock? I cried as we flew over Greenland. I looked down on that melancholy expanse of empty white and I imagined heaven. I thought of Scott out there somewhere, cold and not knowing.

How can the *Welcome Figures* do that to me? How could they take one of their own? Why didn't they protect Aaron? Why did the mountains that his people revere, that he and Scott loved so much, do that to him? They asked me at Immigration why I was here.

'I've come to see –' I started, and I wanted to say my love, my man. I wanted to say Scott Emerson. But the officer seemed happy enough to hear that I'd come to their country just to see.

No Scott waiting for me.

It's early evening and I'm in a cab heading for a hotel in Vancouver. It's too late to drive all the way home. I don't even know my way. When I've done the journey before, I've been Scott's passenger, daydreaming out of the window. I'm picking up a car tomorrow to drive to Scott's. Tomorrow, I'll be back in Pemberton.

Tomorrow, I'll see Jenna. What the hell am I going to say to her? Her dad left home to come and see me and on the way, he and his childhood friend were killed. Jenna couldn't find me. That poor girl. In the end, she sent a Facebook message to Steph to call her urgently. Jenna said to her, please tell Frankie yourself – I don't want her to be on her own when she hears, it can't be over the phone, someone needs to be there for her and for the children. Scott, you did well with that baby girl of yours.

Usually I love a fancy hotel. That's where Scott and I got to know each other after all. He'd planned that we'd have a long weekend in Vancouver this summer – told me that despite all his travels, it's still the most beautiful city he knows. We never will. We will never stroll through Gastown hand in hand. I'll never haul him up and down Robson looking at the shops. We won't have lunch at the market on Granville Island. He won't buy me Lululemon for my birthday. We can't grab that coffee from Caffè Artigiano and sit on the steps of the Art Gallery planning what we're going to do for the rest of the day.

The hotel room – I hardly notice it. I need Scott pinching me, tickling me, saying *stay awake, baby – got to beat the jet lag*. I can't. So I place two pillows in a line down the bed and I press the back of my body lightly against them, imagining it's Scott spooning up to me. Let's go to sleep.

The Sea to Sky Highway. Route 99. I just want to get there but the views, oh the views. Howe Sound and those coastal mountains. From Squamish to Whistler, everything to the right is Garibaldi Provincial Park, all 200,000 hectares of it. Mountains shouldering glacial lakes like Lovely Water and Garibaldi. Rolling glaciers like Misty. Douglas fir, western hemlock, western red cedar in the lower reaches; then higher up the alpine fir, white bark pine, mountain hemlock and yellow cedar. Those volcanic peaks, the stuff of legend for the Líĺwat and Squamish. Black Tusk – glowering and towering. I don't want to look.

It's very strange, but I'm driving and the sun is out and there's no traffic. It's as if the way has been soothed and kept clear just for me. However, there's a point along the route where quite suddenly something akin to freezing fog ripples through my body and I have to pull over sharp. I put my head on the steering wheel and I cry.

Was it here?

Am I close?

Then I'm passing Whistler.

I've passed the roadside warnings for bears. Are they sleeping this time of year? I can't remember what the proper word for that is. If I had Sammy and Annabel in the back, they'd know, they'd laugh at me. The road climbs and curves dramatically and here's the breathtaking vista after Nairn Falls. I remember Scott going pensive the first time we reached this point, how he looked at the road ahead and said I hope you like it.

I'm a little cross with Pemberton village as I drive by, a little surprised and shocked. I've slowed right down and all I see is that everything is as it was last time I was here. Why are they all going about their day? Why hasn't the entire village ground to a halt? Scott and Aaron have *died*.

And I'm passing by the road that goes to the golf club and the airfield and I just can't bear it.

The community at Mount Currie.
Aaron.

On to the D'Arcy road.
Scott.
I don't think I can do this.

I can see the house now. Home. I park up just after the turning and decide to walk the long drive up to Scott's. There are wild blue lupins everywhere. He told me about them, he said to come in spring to see them. The steps up towards the house. It feels like my chest is caving in. The porch with the chairs and the swing seat. He's put the cushions away for winter, or because he was leaving to come and see me. I don't know where he keeps them. Over there, the studio – my little Sam's first taste of a man cave.

I know he isn't home.

Opening the door. The warmth, the scent; homely and familiar. Jenna looking up, standing up, staggering over. Neither of us can speak, we just crumple against each other, not in an embrace, simply entwining to stop each other withering to the floor. I don't know how long we're standing there, bodies heaving with stinging tears, voices hollow, hoarse and not human.

And then she says, did you walk, Frankie – did you walk?

These past two days I have believed anything and nothing. It's the same for Jenna. In her mind, it's quite possible that I have walked here from England because everything else is far stranger at the moment.

The house is full of flowers. What would Scott say?

I have a peculiar urge to knock before I enter the bedroom. I don't but I push the door open very slowly, very gently. I tiptoe in and close the curtains. He made the bed before he left. The pillows are slightly skew. I bet he was humming one of his melodies as he whoomped the duvet. I bet he didn't turn and check before he left. He probably changed his hum to whistling as he made his way downstairs.

I lie on the bed, in the crevasse between the two sets of pillows, in between where he sleeps and where I do.

Don't go to sleep Frankie. Don't pinch me Scott. I'm not jet-lagged. I just want to close my eyes and breathe you in.

Kyle's on his way back. Jenna and I talk and sit and cry. I stroke her cheek, which is slightly swollen from where she bit the inside during her recent seizure. Stress and tiredness – a danger zone for those with epilepsy. How on earth is this girl meant to avoid such a place at the moment? Scott would be so worried about her right now. I'm so sorry Jenna, I wish he hadn't been coming to see me. I wish it with all my heart. Much as I was desperate to see him, I could have waited.

She tells me what she knows but it's hard for anyone to know exactly what happened. I don't know what an ELT is but she says that's how they eventually found Scott and Aaron. We're not allowed to see them. That distresses me, and the reason why I can't horrifies me. Images – get them out of my head.

We get very organized with lists and arrangements but this is interspersed with periods when we just

394

slump; inane and incapable. We push food around our plates, not knowing who made what dish. The fridge is full of food in other people's dishes and containers. Kind little notes saying heat at this temperature, eat before Friday, gluten-free, Scott's favourite. Jenna lights a fire. We are both very cold.

'Kyle will be here any minute,' she says.

'Your dad was so funny about him.'

Jenna smiles, hopeful and uncertain. 'What did he say? Can you remember? Can you remember everything?'

I can.

'I told him off because he said that some dufus from the mountains was going out with his daughter. I said Scott Emerson, if anyone's a dufus from the mountains it's you. He asked me if I knew – but I remembered you said not to tell him. So I just said I guessed. He grumbled and grouched, he said – *I have to go meet this kid*. I said, Kyle's not a kid – he's twenty-two.' I'm laughing. 'I'm sorry Jenna. I didn't think. *How do you know his name is Kyle?* your dad said. *How do you know his name when I only called him Dufus?*'

Jenna laughs and her eyes sparkle. I want to keep her laughing.

'I was mean to my dad, giving him all these rules about how he was to behave and what he wasn't to say,' she says.

'You were reasonable, Jenna. But you know – he was chuffed that you and I talk. I told your dad, don't you dare behave like a prick. He said, *if I don't think he's good enough, I'm going to let him know it*. Oh my God, I said, tell me you haven't composed a questionnaire. He thought that was funny. I told him to trust you.

Kyle makes Jenna happy, I said, and that should be enough.'

'I had to nudge him a couple of times when they first met,' Jenna says. 'Like when he asked Kyle what music he likes and then Dad just sat there and stared at him like all his answers were wrong.' Jenna pauses and her eyes fill at a memory. 'Afterwards, he just stood so still in the car park, watching Kyle drive away with me. I watched him from the rear-view mirror.'

'He really liked him,' I tell her. 'He told me so. He phoned me later and said, *there goes my baby girl, there she goes.*'

I remember how frustrated I was that we were in separate countries at the time. I wished I could have put my arms around him and I wish that now.

'Kyle called him sir and my dad didn't tell him not to – even though he hates that kind of thing. Hated.'

We consider how we keep having to change from present to past.

We go quiet.

Jenna and I aren't enough in this house.

I sigh. I think of my children. I'm so tired I can't remember whether to go forward eight hours or back.

'It seems so strange,' I say, looking around. 'So strange without Buddy here. I really notice him not being here.' He's stayed with Rose since the day the men left.

Then Jenna looks at me and I look at Jenna.

'*Buddy?*' she says.

And Jenna looks at me and I look at Jenna.

It was such an idiotic thing for me to say. It's strange being here *without Buddy*? Buddy – *the dog*? This house is strange on account of *the dog* not being here?

Scott tips his head back and laughs for all he's worth. Crinkles around the eyes and his bristles dip into his dimples.

Jenna and I start to giggle. Then we laugh. Then we roar and roll about, doubled up. We bang our fists on the table with mirth. We can't catch our breath. We honk and snort as we laugh and we laugh. We can't stop. It's all unutterably stupid.

And Scott thinks, will you look at my two beautiful girls.

* * *

There were so many people in so much pain sharing so much love and sorrow.

Jenna read e e cummings.

Jordan Sturdy spoke. I listened to everything that was said. My name was mentioned. I can't remember a word.

There was a plain box. A coffin. Scott Emerson was in that coffin, apparently. And then the coffin went into the furnace and soon Scott Emerson will be in a little urn.

Imagine that.

I can't.

* * *

That evening, back home, Kyle, Jenna and I sit next to each other staring at the flames licking up in the fireplace. Tiredness doesn't begin to describe it. We're aware of lights coming up the driveway – a procession of cars – and Jenna and I look at each other as if to say oh please no more people, not tonight.

So we don't go to the door. We sit where we are and stare at the fire.

Then we hear it, the sound of drumming. Emphatic and strong and rhythmic as blood through veins or a stream over boulders.

Kyle goes to the door.

'You need to come,' he says.

When the Líl̓wat drum it is as the heartbeat of their nation, the pulse of their landscape. Made by hand but never for themselves, always as gifts, their hand drums are from elk and deer rawhide, soaked and stretched over cedar and laced into wind-catcher patterns with beads at the back, the front painted with their symbology. The Líl̓wat drum when they lose their loved ones. They drum at nine o'clock, then at three and again at seven. Sometimes, up to 100 drums.

It's just coming up to seven in the evening. Immediately, I see Rose. Then I recognize others I may have seen when Scott held up a hand in passing, or when Aaron proudly took me and the kids around the Úl̓us community centre. There are also many, many people I don't know.

They stand on Scott's porch and on the steps leading up, they stand on the paving and on the grass. I don't know how many. A lot. There they stand and they drum for Scott, the white man who had a brother in Aaron.

* * *

I hike to Joffre Lakes by myself. I've never done anything like that in my life – being out in true wilderness on my own. There were hikers way in front of me but they were fitter than me, more nimble, and soon it's just me and the mountainside, the trees and the rocks and the Joffre Creek – swollen and frenetic, a thousand drops of glacial water racing over boulders. The noise is deafening and I find it immensely soothing.

Then I wonder if I'll see a bear and I feel a little frightened, somewhat exposed and vulnerable. I said to Scott so many times, *I wonder if I'll see a bear*. The first time he took me here to Joffre, he told me a lot about humans and bears. I'm at the middle lake now. I find a slab of rock right near the shore of the turquoise water and there I sit, hugging my knees, remembering how we chatted, Scott and I.

'First bear I saw up close was when I was camping up at Birken. I was with Aaron and my dad. I guess I was maybe seven or eight years old. It was a real big bear and he was very near. About as close as that tree right there.'

What did you do Scott, oh my goodness what did you do?

'We made a lot of noise, Frankie. That's what you have to do. They're shy, really, and they don't like noise. So we banged our pots and pans over our heads.'

I remember now how I stared and stared at him. I couldn't compute what I was hearing. You banged your pots and pans – over your heads? Good God, I said.

Scott shrugged in that easy-going way of his when he shied away from praise. 'It's what you do – when you're camping and there's a big hairy fucker wanting to get close.'

But you banged a pan – *over your head*?

And he looked at me, puzzled. 'Sure.'

That's insane, I laughed and I walked on.

'Wait,' he said.

And he caught my arm, wearing a grin that glinted in his eyes. 'Frankie – you thought we banged our pots over – *on* – our heads?'

Yes, I said. That's what you said. Insane!

'So – you thought that the bear took one look at us and thought whoa! those crazy fuckers are so hard they hit their heads with their pots and pans. And the bear thinks man, I'm outta here?'

I nodded. Confused at why he was clinging onto me, laughing.

'*Over* our heads,' he said. He dropped my arms, smoothed hair from my face, kissed me gently and looked at me quizzically, as if marvelling at this daft idiot he was in love with.

'*Over* our heads, Frankie.'

And he clapped his hands. High above his head.

* * *

I spend the afternoon with Rose. I fall to my knees when Buddy comes over, wagging his tail, butting his nose at me to say it's you, it's you – say, have you seen Scott?

Rose is wearing leather straps over her wrists and ankles and around her middle – to signify to all that she's in mourning. She tells me she must sleep on cedar boughs for seven days. Johnny and Tara are being Johnny and Tara. Do they know? Do they understand?

'Children have old souls,' she says. 'They're doing OK. They are open and accepting. More than me.'

I'm not having a good day today. I feel unwell. I can't remember what was the last thing I ate or when that was. The hike to Joffre was hard – my legs felt weak, my head throbbed and my lungs burnt. I didn't make it to the top lake and I felt shit about that. The turquoise didn't stun me, it didn't gladden my heart. It wasn't magical or soothing – it was just there. Now I feel tired and out of sorts. I miss my children desperately – I have this horrible sense of not knowing how to get back home to them.

I look at Rose and I feel swept through with guilt. I bow my head. 'Rose – I am so sorry.'

She sits very still, looking beyond me. It's like she's not breathing. I want her to hit me, shout at me, curse and swear at me. Then she slumps a little and our eyes meet.

'It's OK,' she says. 'Not your fault.'

'But Scott was coming to see me,' I whisper. 'That's why they were – up there.'

'Please forgive Aaron,' is what she says. 'If he was here – he'd be sad. He'd think he was to blame.' I can see she's thinking about her man. 'I married an eagle.' She sounds so proud.

'Will you stay here, with the Líĺwat? Will you go back to your Squamish?'

'This is my home,' she says. 'This is my children's home. But will *you* come back Frankie? You didn't just give a little of your heart to Scott – this place has a bit of it too, right?'

I think about that. Of course it's true. This part of British Columbia has become my spiritual homeland like no place before it.

'Frankie,' says Rose, 'we mustn't forsake *nkweĺánk* – the sunny side of the mountain. It's always there.'

* * *

Tomorrow I leave here. Today Jenna, Kyle and I are pottering around the house, looking in drawers and cupboards and sorting papers and mail. It feels rude and intrusive to be doing this. I don't like it and I'm not pulling my weight but Jenna seems OK with that. She knows who Scott's accountant is and their attorney is a family friend – people I don't know, names I've never heard. I feel awkward – there was so much of Scott's life that preceded me. A lot has nothing to do with me. We were together a short while in all, a small percentage of his lifetime, but it felt so total and I'm struggling.

'My mom is going to visit,' Jenna says, coming off the phone.

'Your mum? Here?'

She nods. Her mother didn't come to the funeral. It hurt Jenna even though she told me she hadn't actually expected her to turn up.

'Shall I make myself scarce?'

'Are you kidding?' says Jenna.

And so I meet Lind. Scott's ex-wife and the mother of his child. She doesn't look like an alcoholic to me, if I was expecting a lurching stagger of an unkempt woman. Very blonde hair, dark blue jeans, shiny high-heeled boots, a smart jacket and a capacious handbag. She's quite bony, she looks brittle and forlorn. Scott didn't talk about Lind much; it was so long ago for him, a lifetime away. He tolerated her and he made sure she was OK financially and he never spoke unkindly about her to Jenna. Jenna told me that one. When Lind arrives she starts to cry, holding out her arms to Jenna who seems a little reluctant to go into them. I realize that, even for Lind, Scott retained a distinct place in her life. However little they had to do with one another, still he signified steadiness and reason in her routine chaos. Take that away from Lind and life must seem quite scary and unbridled.

I keep back.

She's all over Kyle, touching his cheek as though he's a boy. Jenna sends a private roll of her eyes over to me. Kyle is wonderful with Lind. Scott – you have nothing to worry about, Jenna is onto a good thing there. Then Lind sees me and she tilts her head and stares.

'Mom, this is Frankie.'

'I'm Lind.'

'Hello.'

We shake hands. Her fingers feel like a loose bundle of pencils.

'You're the one,' she says.

I don't know what she means and I can't work out her tone. Is she accusing me?

She can see my confusion. Her eyes go gentle and her voice drops soft as she shakes her head, smiles sadly, and says it again.

'You – you're The One.'

* * *

I'm gut-curdlingly homesick now. In fact I threw up this evening and I never throw up. I want to be back in my kitchen with Annabel doing her homework yabbering, and Sam coming in from the late bus moody, all scruffy and untucked. I want to be cooking something they'll moan at me for and I'll say fine, don't eat it but that's all there is. All the scuffles for time on the computer with each child deeming their homework the more important. Sam saying, I don't need a shower Mum and me saying, Sam – I can smell you from here, get in the shower or I'll bath you myself. Annabel yelling at me when I brush her hair, proclaiming she likes knots. The day-to-day, something I know how to do because I've done it a million times. I can do Mummy without thinking. But I have no idea how to mourn for my man, how to grieve. I don't really know who I am in all of this. I'm not even a widow.

Lying on Scott's side in Scott's bed.

I can no longer smell him on his pillow. Nor in the clothes of his that I've packed in my case. A sweater. A plaid shirt. A layered T-shirt I'd forgotten about but cried when I saw. The faded design of a man fishing, a bear on the shore. Blanched pistachio green and washed-out damson with the lettering in vanilla. I told Scott he looked like ice cream in it.

So where exactly are you, Scott?

I'm so fucking angry with you right now. I'm going back to my side of the bed, turning away and facing the wall. How dare you just leave me?

* * *

I want to take Jenna with me and I don't think she wants to let me go. To each other, we each embody a little of Scott. It takes me a long time to leave and our farewell embrace is protracted. We know, once we let go, we'll be doing precisely that; letting go. Once I'm off the porch and in the car, it will signify the end of this hazed in-between time; it will mean an unequivocal return to real life, to getting on with things, inching forward in time without him, creating a blunt and increasing distance from the day Scott no longer lived. But I have to go and she has to let me. She goes back inside and shuts the door before I've reversed and I drive away not able to look back at the house.

Airport Road seems an awfully grand name for the little runway that licks along the grass, the couple of small buildings where operations are run from. Skydiving, helicopter tours. Aaron's little business. I need to make this detour. I have to stand where Scott last stood. What I'm not expecting to see is his truck parked there. For a crazy second, which I want to last for hours, I think oh! See – he's here after all!

They will, at some point, find the spare keys at the house and they'll drive Scott's truck back home for Jenna to decide what to do with it.

Today, though, it's here. There's no one else around. I park the car and step outside and walk towards the truck. There's still deluded hope in my heart but the tears catching in my throat are in combat with that. I do something really crazy. I walk past the truck and out to the airfield and actually look for Aaron's little plane. Scott was in a box and apparently he's now in an urn. The plane is, I know, a tatter and scorch of torn, charred and pulverized steel on a lonely mountainside. But, just now, I'm ignoring all of what's known and I'm going to have a little look.

I can't see Aaron's plane.

I go over to his office and peer through the window. It hasn't changed a bit since I was last here though of course everything has changed beyond comprehension. I stand on the decking for a few moments. It's so peaceful. The sun is out today and the sky is that diluted blue that's as strong as it gets so early in the spring. Scott's truck shines and glints and I leave Aaron's office and go over to it. I try the handle of the passenger door and it's unlocked. Why would it be locked? This is the tiny airfield in Pemby – no one needs to lock their truck. Aaron was only going to be gone a couple of hours. He'd've popped Scott's keys in his pocket. I stand awhile with my hand on the open door, then I clamber up and sit in my seat, shutting the door and putting my seat belt on. I just look straight ahead because I don't want to see the driver's seat empty.

Where are you taking me today, Scott?

Oh – I don't know – where would you like to go?

Surprise me.

How about we go to Lillooet and buy some tomatoes?

I sit there and remember how Scott thought nothing of a three-hour round trip just to buy tomatoes. Seed potatoes flourish in Pemberton, but not tomatoes. Drive for 100 km and the landscape changes dramatically, becoming semi-arid, and there the tomatoes thrive.

'Let's go and buy tomatoes,' I say and I hear my disembodied voice, paper thin and desperate.

The truck is so quiet, so still. Continuing to look ahead, I reach my left hand over to the steering wheel and I just hold onto it, as if I'm stopping him from driving off, preventing him making any journey. Let's just sit here, you and me, in nothing time while tears spill out of my eyes. I look around the truck. A plastic water bottle half full. I unscrew the cap and put my lips against the neck, not that I'm thirsty, just my deluded and desperate attempt to feel as though my lips are against his. In the footwell of the driver's seat, a little gravel from some hike or other. I open the glove compartment. CDs – Tom Petty, Beethoven, Mogwai, Bob Dylan, Aretha Franklin. The truck's handbook. A pack of opened gum, twisted off at the top, a piece of paper, a torch. On the piece of paper, I spy Scott's loping handwriting, even and confident, just like his walk. I pore over his words.

Milk carrots/onions COFFEE

Shwrgel

I wonder if *shwrgel* is a Líĺwat word, then I laugh out loud. Shower gel, silly.

I think he was trying out lyrics too. There are three separate phrases.

A love like this

All that I am

Mountain & Ocean & Us

You have a way with words, Scott, you can condense so much into such powerful brevity. I wonder about the song that's perhaps half-written as I turn the piece of paper over.

Melody & Midsomer. Fine Jewelers. Est. 1982

It's a receipt.

It is written here:

> *Wedding band. 18ct rose gold. Engraved. $300.*
> *PAID IN FULL.*

I hear my breath catch on my sob and my heart stutters.

For me?

Is that why he was coming to see me on the day he died? With an 18-carat wedding band, paid for and engraved?

Are these not song lyrics? Was one of the phrases for the ring?

I think of my Scott, so ready, so sure, coming to be with me. And I don't think of myself, left here now, I don't think of what I've lost and what I've got to plod on ahead without. I think of him, up there in that plane ten days ago. How I hope with every fibre of my being that he knew how much he was loved, that his heart was full and that he had that ring with him, when he died.

I do, Scott, I do.

'm not really sure about this but my form tutor made the appointment and he's a dude, I trust him. I didn't even know this particular office existed. They wouldn't have had a place like this in my old school in London, I don't think. I'm sitting on a chair with my headphones on. I'm listening to Deerhunter because Scott recommended them. I've pressed repeat on *Desire Lines*. I don't want anyone disturbing me till the song has come to an end. I don't even know what this person's name is. Just that she's the Counsellor and she's here every Tuesday.

'Sam?'

The song hasn't finished. I'll pretend I haven't heard. The outro is awesome – that's all I should be focusing on.

A hand on my shoulder. She's halfway between my mum and Steph in age, I'd say. The dicks in my class would call her a MILF, I bet. I don't actually call them dicks now, though. I call them hosers because it's a word Scott taught me.

'Sam?' She's nodding towards the room behind the door and guiding me through.

This is a room in a school? It looks like someone's living room. I turn my music off and stand and look around.

409

'Sit wherever you like,' she's saying. She's not sitting, though. She's boiling a kettle. 'Would you like a drink? Hot chocolate? Coke?'

Coke?

'Um – I'll have a Coke please.' And I sit on a massive leather beanbag, sinking in and held steady. We need one of these at home though my mum would probably say it's not Cath Kidston enough.

This is awkward. She's sitting in the armchair sipping thoughtfully like she's waiting for me to say something. But I haven't anything to say.

'How's your mum?'

I shrug. If you roll the leather of the beanbag between your fingers you can feel the little polystyrene beads, one by one. It's really satisfying.

'How's your sister – Annabel?'

Like I have another one! I shrug. 'Annoying, sometimes.'

'And you, Sam, how's you?'

I look out of the window. I can hear break time. Still, I'd rather be here, sipping Coke and fiddling with polystyrene balls. Everything's seemed too fast and noisy recently.

'How's you?'

'Oh, you know.' I want her to hear that it has a full stop after it.

'Do you think about Scott?'

'I try not to.'

'Why is that?'

'Because there's no point.'

'Why do you feel there's no point?'

'I don't *feel* there's no point – I *know* there's no point.'

I've seen people like this on TV shows – nit-picking your words and trying to coax out the deep and meaningful. You want to smack them in the mouth.

'Can you put that into words?'

'I just did.'

'The feelings behind it.'

The Coke catches in my throat. 'Scott is dead. So remembering him is useless. It's not going to bring him back.'

'No – but it can be helpful and it can be comforting.'

I look at the clock. I've been in here ten minutes. If I say the right things will she let me out? I'm not entirely sure what she's waiting to hear.

'I never met him,' she said. 'I've never met your mother. As you know, what you say in here is completely confidential.' She puts down her cup. She unscrews a little jar and dabs whatever's in there onto her lips. This is all just really weird.

'What was he like – Scott?'

She just wants to know what he was like. And suddenly, he's so clear in my mind's eye. And I can see my room – not here in Norfolk but in Pemberton, his studio. I'd give anything to be there right now.

She's smiling because I'm smiling.

'He was a really, really nice guy. He was this amazing musician. He really liked talking to me. I mean, I know him and my mum had this thing – you know, in love – but I know that I had a friendship with him that wasn't just because I'm her son.'

I can't stop.

'He stands like this,' I say and I get up to show her. Leaning a little against a wall, arms loosely folded, head slightly to one side. 'He's always relaxed, never ruffled.

That's why he's good with my mum – she can get heated and he's just there letting stuff flow over him.'

I'm back in the beanbag.

'I was really rude when he first appeared. My dad – Sorry, I've forgotten what I was going to say. When Scott first came I felt really – suspicious. And I know this will sound stupid but it was just weird him being in our cottage. Because I don't remember there ever being a man in our space – the space my mum makes for her, me and Annabel my sister. So suddenly there's this big actual bloke and I thought I haven't had a say in this and I don't think I want him here, filling the space, getting in the way. Sitting – there. Or opening the fridge. Or being in the loo. Or touching my mum's hair. So I was just rude – I just ignored him and got on with listening to my music or instagramming or whatever. Annabel took it out on my mum but I just blanked the lot of them.'

She seems really interested.

'And then he started playing his guitar – the song I was listening to at precisely that moment on my headphones. And I mean *precisely*.' I will remember that for the rest of my life. 'It was so unbelievably real. I'd never heard an actual guitar so close. It was something about the way he played and the sound he made. It had nothing to do with my mum. He wasn't trying to win me over or anything. He was playing just because he could – because that's what he liked to do. He loved music and so do I. Anyway, we bonded after that.'

'Bonded?'

'Yep. He was *my* friend. Definitely. He liked me for me. He wanted to know – about school, music I like, stuff like that. He liked to hang out with me – not because I'm my mum's son. If we'd met, say, somewhere totally random and he never knew my mum, he'd still like me; we'd still be mates. Some would call him a father figure.'

'Would you?'

'Dads are just dads in my book. You have no say in who you get. But father figures – are more. In some ways, I think they choose you and you choose them.'

Scott is dead.

'When we went to Canada he actually wanted me to stay in his studio – not in the bedroom in the house. He really thought about me.'

My father is a shithead.

'When my mum was over there visiting Scott, my father reappeared out of nowhere and was meant to be looking after us – me and my sister Annabel – but he was useless. He never asked me a single personal question, he doesn't care about who I am. He'd just ask where stuff was. Where does Mum keep the wine? Where's the loo roll kept? He asked me if I had any money. I gave him twenty quid and Annabel gave him four.'

My father is a total cunthead.

'And he fucked off and didn't come back and me and my sister didn't know what the fucking fuck to do. He's still fucking off even though he says he lives in London now. Anyway, I didn't think of my mum so much as Scott. I had this – thought – that Scott could punch my dad. Because I couldn't. Not because of my size and that I'm a kid – but because he wasn't fucking cunting *there* for me to twat.'

And Scott is dead.

'And Scott is dead.'

'It's OK, Sam.'

'No it isn't. How can you say that? How can it ever be OK again? We had this little – taster of a really good life. And it was ripped away. It was ripped away. I felt it rip. Hurts so much sometimes I can't breathe. Up in my room. Scared. When I can hear my mum sobbing or going deathly silent.'

'Sam – it's going to take a long while but –'

'But I want those emails back. I didn't know. I don't know if he read them. I have no way of knowing. I was hard and cold. The last feelings I had towards Scott were hate. I don't want him to have read them. Or felt that. I'm sorry. Oh God. Oh shit. Oh shit shit shit. Say he did? Say he thought I hated him? I don't want him to – not just before he died. I really need to know if he read them. I hate it that I hated him. It wasn't so much that he was worrying my mum by not arriving – though I told him it was. But the truth is that I was angry and confused and I decided to hate him because I feared he'd left us. That he didn't care. How could I think that of him? How could I? I know now I was wrong – but I want to say sorry. Scott – sorry. Scott – I'm sorry. I just want you to know that. That – I love you.'

I'm crying so much I'll never stop. I've spilled the Coke and it's all over my trousers. I haven't cried since I was a little kid, I don't think. Why did this heap of shit happen to us? Why couldn't we have Scott for longer and for ever? We deserved him and he had a place with us. What's the point of making a family whole – our tight little unit, making it even tighter – if it's then going to be shredded? Don't tell me stuff like what doesn't kill you makes you stronger. Scott was strong and he was killed and me and Annabel and my mum are weak.

'I don't know what we're going to do.'

'I'm here every Tuesday, Sam.'

For Frankie, grief's first flush came to be as changeable as the weather but to her, the process of mourning seemed to stretch ahead like the longest winter. So it was odd to return to Norfolk and find it so warm and sunny. In the garden, things were starting to grow: plants and flowers, cobwebs and cuckoo spittle, signs of life all around. Steph was there when she arrived back from Canada and stayed until Peta came for the weekend; Ruth visited every day. They became like pillows, her sisters and her friend; she'd push her face into them muffling tears, or she'd rest her head against them in the fog of exhaustion. Sometimes, when the fury came, she'd pummel them. But as wrapped in their love as Frankie felt, she wanted to be rid of them too, as though they were a thick, tight sweater and she was overheating. Extremes; her life had become one of extremes, from numbness to sorrow, from quiet to rage and the all-enveloping tiredness everything created.

In those early days, Frankie slept a lot, especially when Sam and Annabel were at school. She justified it as jet lag but to be in bed with the covers over her head helped her hide from the real world. The safest place was the most private place, between the sheets in an embryonic curl where the tears were free to come and she could heave out her rage at it all. Sometimes, she almost envied her children their opportunity to go to school, to leave the house and have to think about something else. Do maths. Kick a ball. Sit up straight and concentrate on what was going on. Chat about *The Hunger Games* and eat food slopped onto plates. Having to think about other things and not having to think at all. When the children were at home, Frankie focused on them though it was through a blear of numbing tiredness. She'd sit between them with her eyes trained on the TV, not watching Marge dart around the screen, not listening to a word that Homer said.

The children were gentle on her if supper was a bit crap and they had to wear the same school shirt three days in a row. Yet still they skirted around the truth about homework, and Sam still snuck time on Instagram and Annabel still fibbed about recorder practice. Frankie thought, they'd be doing that if Scott was still alive. They're kids.

But because they're kids, their mother's grief was a worrying thing. So Frankie learned to hide it without denying it. Early on she could sense when it was welling up, a little like being sick – knowing when it was imminent, when she couldn't stop it. She'd take herself to the downstairs loo, the furthest room on the ground floor. She'd shut the door, close the lid, sit down, grab the hand towel and hold it against her face, heaving out her pain silently.

Then she'd look in the mirror and give herself a gentle smile when she was done.

If Scott could see me like this, what would he say?

He'd say, kids – time to get ready for bed, I'll come

see you in a while. And he'd cuddle me against him and say shh, baby, I'm here. You're OK. I'm here.

When Frankie went to Howell's to pick up some milk, the lady serving, with whom she'd shared little more than a cordial smile over the months, put her head on one side and her hand on Frankie's arm and said, terrible thing, my lovely, what a terrible thing. And Frankie found herself recounting the facts as though it was a speech in the school play that she knew by heart.

'You let me know if there's anything I can do.'

Frankie looked at the woman, tempted to say can you raise the dead? can you bring him back? can you turn back time and change the future?

'If you want shopping bringing. Anything, really. Eggs or milk. Bread.'

'Oh. Thank you,' said Frankie. 'I'm OK, really – just very tired.'

'How are the children?'

And it struck Frankie then that, for all her attempts to live a little reclusively, actually she *was* known, she and Annabel and Sam.

'They're wonderful. My son – Sam – was very close to my, to my. And Annabel adored Scott.' She paused, fixating on the rack of chewing gum by the till. She couldn't move her eyes and waves of adrenalin made her feel as if she was swaying though her feet appeared to be stuck in clay.

'Do you want a cup of tea? I can make you a cup of tea.'

The lady was stroking her arm. Frankie thought, I might want a cup of tea. A sit-down. I'd like to talk about Scott today, just tell someone else of the amazing times, show the photos on my phone. But then she thought about how tired she was, how stratospherically tired, and that all she wanted to do was go to bed and sleep.

'It's very kind,' said Frankie. 'But I ought to be getting back – things to do before the children get home.' The lady's hand was still on her arm and Frankie gave it a pat. 'Thank you though – you're very kind.'

It was only when she arrived home, put the milk in the fridge and spent ages carefully arranging the eggs in the china holder, that Frankie realized she hadn't paid. All this time moaning that she wasn't local enough to have a tab at the shop – and then Scott dies and she's in the bosom of kindness and charity all around.

There was a green felt pen on top of the bread-bin. She picked it up and doodled a face onto one of the eggs. Which local farm did these eggs come from? Was the hen white or red? When had it been laid, this little egg, destined for Annabel's supper?

How she was looking forward to a sleep. She looked at the clock. She could zone out for a good three hours. But someone was knocking at the door. And Frankie thought, they've come for the money for the shopping. She thought, perhaps it's the police.

But there stood Mrs Mawby.

Mrs Mawby from next door whom Frankie really only ever saw at a distance, usually on her doorstep beating a rug or shooing out a dog or just standing there wondering when her husband would appear from over the fields with a trailer full of sugar beet. Peg. Peg Mawby. She'd last seen her at Christmas when she'd taken over the mince pies. The day she'd smacked Scott's hand and denied him his third.

'Mrs Mawby,' said Frankie.

There Peg stood, not moving, not even regarding Frankie. She looked as though she was seeing a ghost over Frankie's shoulder, in the hallway of the house.

'Mrs Mawby?'

'Well, dear,' she said and she started to wring her hands.

'Is everything OK?'

'Well, dear – I.' She looked up. She had eyes like those of a rag doll, glistening and black and sewn deep into her soft, doughy face. 'I'm ever so sorry for your loss.'

I have to ask her in, don't I? I have to invite her in.

'Would you like a cup of tea?'

Mrs Mawby came into the house, treading carefully, as if Frankie's pamment flooring was completely unlike her own, as if Frankie's home was on a whole different planet rather than bang next door. But once in the kitchen, Peg took charge.

'I'll make the tea, dear. You sit down.'

So Frankie sat. The tiredness had lifted but in its place that numbness, as though she was stuffed with cotton wool. When Peta and Steph had been staying here, cooking and cleaning and organizing the children and just letting Frankie be, it had been the same sensation. Nothing inside her but soundproofing.

She sipped. The tea was very sweet, very hot, not too milky. It tasted like nectar. 'Gosh that's good.'

'Tea is always good.'

Frankie looked over at Mrs Mawby sitting on her kitchen chair so politely, as if she was at church. 'I mean – you make a very very good cup of tea. Thank you.'

'So sorry, dear, to hear. Keith and I – so sorry.'

Frankie nodded.

'We lost our eldest. Our Bri. When he was twenty. Many years ago now. But just as – present.'

Frankie's eyes filled. She had no idea. What a totally corrupt place the world was, taking good people when they were loved and needed.

'Don't go upsetting yourself now,' said Peg.

So there they sat, quietly, until Frankie couldn't stop yawning and Peg Mawby remembered that, she remembered the engulfing tiredness and she said to Frankie, I'll be on my way now dear, but you know where I am. Just next door. If ever you feel like it.

Ruth truly became something of a beacon to Frankie. It was overwhelming to put her body in someone else's hands, someone she trusted.

'Grief is not different to physical pain,' she told Frankie, holding her head while she lay on the treatment table. 'We have to accept it and understand that it comes in waves. You have to allow yourself to let it come and let it go. You will learn to let it walk alongside you, Frankie. You will absorb it as part of you.'

'Mum? Mum! There's someone at the door. *Mum!*'

'Mum! Sam says there's someone at the door.'

'Jesus you two – I'm in the bloody shower. Why didn't you answer it?' Frankie had felt utterly fractious the last couple of days. This wasn't helping.

'You told me never to answer the door.'

'Annabel – you know I meant –'

'– you always change your mind about what you say. I hate you!'

'Annabel!'

'I'll answer the door.'

'Thanks Sam.'

'Mum?'

Christ – can they not let me get dressed in peace?

'Yes Sam.'

'It's Grandma.'

At first, Frankie thought Sam meant she'd died.

Like when Steph came into the kitchen three weeks ago and said it's Scott.

But Sam's brow furrowed and he motioned with his

thumb over his shoulder.

'Seriously Mum – she's downstairs. *With a suitcase.*'

* * *

'I thought I would come. I thought I might be needed.'

Margaret looked around and, with dismay, Frankie suddenly saw her home through her mother's eyes. The tumble of shoes and the scrunch of clothes, the scatter of mail and the pile of plates, the decaying fruit and flowers long past their best. There was a muddy footprint right in the middle of the floor. There was a sock on the kitchen table. Margaret's expression said, *not a moment too soon*.

'Mum – honestly –'

Frankie did not want her mother there. Her mother had this ability to make her feel small and ridiculous and, consequently, helpless not to behave like a petulant teenager. She was out of sorts enough as it was, she didn't need her mother exacerbating her mood.

'I was just in the middle of tidying up, actually,' Frankie mumbled, scooping up the heap of god-knows-what on one of the kitchen chairs.

'I think you ought to dry your hair first,' her mother said.

'It's fine – I let it air dry.'

'You have the type of hair that needs the shine to be blow-dried into it.'

And so it would be.

After taking Annabel to school the next morning, Frankie wanted to pop in on Ruth but she was with a client so she dawdled her way home, stopping in Stiffkey at the stores, for a coffee she just held and didn't drink. What she craved was to lie on her sofa in a numb, tired-out stupor. That's what she'd been doing whilst the children were at school and it was working very well for her.

But when she arrived home, the radio was tuned to *Classic fM* and Margaret was trilling to it, setting Frankie's ears on edge. There were three piles ascending the staircase, one for Sam, one for Annabel, one for her. To Frankie, it was as if their bodies had vaporized and that's what was left. Socks, tops, a pair of boxers, a toy, a book, a pair of headphones.

La-la-ing along to Elgar.

Frankie stood in the hallway and thought if she tiptoed upstairs, her mother might not know she was back. She could creep into Annabel's room and sneak into her bed for a sleep.

'Frankie? Is that you?'

Reluctantly, Frankie went through to the kitchen.

The table was devoid of all clutter and had been scrubbed and oiled. Margaret was on her hands and knees. The sight of her supremely irritated Frankie. She thought, it makes me feel like shit.

'For God's sake, Mum. Please – can you just get up.'

Margaret looked surprised. She looked as though she was saying *charming!* under her breath.

'Please,' said Frankie. It was ridiculous. Her mother was seventy-two. But obviously, she wasn't going to listen to her daughter with the kitchen that needed such a scrub with so much elbow grease, so Frankie went through to the living room and slumped on the sofa, vexed.

'Cup of tea?' Margaret called.

'No!' But Frankie suddenly thought of Mrs Mawby's tea and how medicinal it could be.

Margaret made tea anyway and brought it through. Frankie couldn't focus on the taste, only on the sound of the tea hitting the back of her mother's throat as she swallowed it down. It made her feel nothing short of murderous.

'I need to work,' she muttered. She left the house and went to the outside office, sitting there remembering the day after Boxing Day when Scott said, come on kids, let's go fumigate the office. It took them a long morning to rid it of Peta's boys. Frankie looked around her. It was a cold, sterile place. She thought, it was the sort of place where she could probably do her accounts, or banish one child or other for time out, but despite the views and the privacy, it was not a place for creative endeavours. She thought about her work, the first *Just My Luck* book she needed to be working on now. Her publishers had been amazing, telling her to take as much time off as she needed. Somewhere, deep down, Frankie knew that what would do her good was to write. But on the surface, she also said, maybe when I'm less tired. Maybe next week.

Then she thought, I'm going to stay out here until the children are back from school. She thought, I can zone out here for a few hours. She thought, then it will come to me that Scott's dead. And I'll hit the floor.

She had a terrible night's sleep. The dreams. She didn't want to talk about the dreams, not even to Ruth. The type of dreams you don't want to wake up from but, once you do, they're the dreams you don't want to remember. She was late taking Annabel to school and she was snapping at everyone. Margaret made porridge.

'When have I ever eaten porridge?' Frankie said. She saw her mother bristle and then she watched the colour rise in Annabel's cheeks as her daughter tried to shrink down into the collar of her school shirt. Sam was all of a clatter and slammed the door on his way out. All Frankie could think was, more ammunition for my mother, no doubt. Rude children, she'll say. She'll say, my daughter lives in squalor and her children are terribly rude.

Back from the morning school run after another circuitous and dawdling route home. Frankie thought how her house looked so pretty from the outside with the tulips and the daffs and the climbers in bud. But inside, it didn't look like hers any more. It's gone all minimal with my mother's obsessive tidying. She always wears an apron as if the dirt is everywhere.

'See –' Margaret was showing Frankie a drawer in the dresser – 'a place for everything. Welcome to your official Bits-and-Bobs drawer. I combined it with the contents of that chaos in the bottom drawer of the kitchen. You won't need to go hunting in hundreds of different places ever again – whenever you need a bit or a bob, you'll find it in here.'

Frankie thought the best thing she could do was to leave the room. She'd nod politely and go upstairs. That's what she should do. That's what she intended to do but when she reached the door, she stopped.

'Do you do this to Peta?' she said, casting it over her shoulder as though it was spilt salt.

Her mother didn't respond.

'Do you do this to Peta?'

'No.'

'No – oh! Silly me. Peta runs such a spic household – I quite forgot.'

'Frankie – I'm just trying to help you. I'm just trying to be useful.'

'You're not. You're making me feel shit about myself – like you always do.'

'I beg your –'

Frankie knew she was ranting but, in that moment, if felt cathartic so rant she would. 'You *do*. You disapprove of everything to do with me. I don't need another bits-and-bloody-bobs drawer. My little household functions on my children and me tearing around saying where oh where oh where do we keep the spare staples, the AA batteries, the plasters. We chase around like a family of otters and we don't mind if we can't find things. It's our dynamic. It's the way we are. It works.'

'Frankie – really.'

'No – *you* listen to *me*.' Frankie paused, suddenly aware that actually her mother hadn't said *Frankie listen to me*. 'You favouritize Peta and you favouritize her hideous offspring and I hate it. And now you're going to say that favouritize isn't a word, it's slang. Who cares! I know I've fucked up, Mother. I know my choices in men were – unwise. I know my kids are being brought up in a single-parent household much to your dismay and I can tell you, I wish they weren't.'

Frankie paused. Her mother was looking a little ashen, her hands tight on the back of a kitchen chair.

'And Scott's gone.' The constriction in Frankie's throat, so painful it felt like tonsillitis. He had gone. He had died. She would never ever see him again. 'And I know you didn't approve of me being with him. But I'm telling you something, the joy and contentment

427

he brought me, and Annabel and Sam – it was worth the wait. However long it was to last, it was worth it. Now I understand what real love is. And now it's gone.'

Frankie bowed her head and wondered how life would ever feel all right again, for any of them.

An arm around Frankie's shoulders. Another turning her slightly as she was brought against a body familiarly fragranced by Yardley.

She thought, it's my mother. I'm standing hopelessly unstable and she's ramrod straight and she's keeping me close while I cry.

The dribble and snot streamed out but Frankie was only aware of it when her racking sobs subsided and she saw how her mother's nice pully was now creased and slimed with her daughter's sorrow. She didn't object to Margaret guiding her over to the sofa, she desperately needed to sit.

And then Frankie woke up unaware that she'd slept. Her mother was looking at her with an expression Frankie wasn't sure she'd ever seen before though she found it surprisingly easy to read. Patience and pity.

'I only didn't approve of Scott because of the Canada issue,' Margaret began. 'It seemed such a preposterously long way to maintain a relationship and brought you all sorts of logistical and financial complications – you juggle so much in your life as it is.' She paused. She could see her daughter was too depleted to speak. 'And when I met him – well, when any of us met him. When one met him, darling. Well! It made perfect sense. He was just super. I liked him enormously. And he was *perfect* for you.' Her voice wavered and her eyes were soft. 'Happy,' Margaret said. 'I could see – we all

428

could – how happy you made him.' Frankie's mother always kept a handkerchief up her sleeve, and often criticized Frankie for not ensuring her children did too. Fine cotton with edging and a little embroidery. 'I'm truly sorry for your loss, Frankie,' Margaret said. 'I hate seeing you like this. Hate it! That's why I'm tidying. I'm trying to make a smooth surface wherever I can. It's all I can do. I – never had a love like yours.'

And Frankie realized just how much she wanted her mother to keep talking.

'I'm a bitter old bag, Frankie – I know I am. I've been bitter and old since your father left me – and he left me when I was younger than you are. I thought it was love – I thought that's why I hurt. It wasn't. It was rejection – and *that's* why it hurt.'

Margaret smiled a little sadly. 'I asked Scott, at Christmas, if he might come and visit when he came in February to work.'

Frankie didn't know that.

'He didn't make it. I'm sure he was very busy – commuting between London and Norfolk. But I should have liked him to have visited though.'

And then Frankie remembered Scott saying, hey baby, why don't we load up the kids and go visit your ma? And she remembered saying, are you mad?

It had been February back then. Short days, cold weather; the perfect opportunity to hunker down at home, light the fire, and not think of anyone other than the tight little unit they were.

'I was dearly hoping there'd be a next time,' Margaret was saying. She looked at Frankie levelly, drawing her daughter's eyes to hers. 'But my hopes for a next time can't be anything like yours must have been. And my sadness and shock cannot be measured against your agony and despair.'

That feeling of tonsillitis again. No tears. All dry.

'As a parent,' Margaret said, patting Frankie's leg to ensure she listened, 'we only want that our children should be happier than we've been. It's that simple. Frankie – I pray for the day when you will feel a little less raw. But don't dread that day, darling. Don't keep it at bay. It won't compromise your love for Scott – it will just signify that in your own muddled way you have accepted that your life must go on.'

The words trickled all the way through Frankie, warming her blood, steadying her heartbeat, taking the edge off that thumping headache. The beauty of her mother's words struck her, underscored as they were with so much feeling and a wisdom she had never before credited her with.

'I'm sorry,' said Frankie.

'You needn't apologize.' Margaret looked perplexed. 'You have it very wrong about Peta, darling. I'm not harder on you, I'm just rather pathetically soft on her. An expensive house with all the trimmings in Hampstead does *not* a successful life make. She's the opposite of you. She has the most alarmingly compartmentalized bits-and-bobs drawer – and I hope you know I speak metaphorically as well as literally.'

She looked out of the window. Two birds having a scatter in the birdbath, making Margaret smile.

'Peta's always been neat on the outside and a terrible mess under the surface. Her husband is a dimwit oaf – he's decent, yes, in that he provides financially. But a good husband? Is he there for her? Is he even interested in her? And those boys of hers are absolutely dreadful.

There really is no better way to describe them than hoodlums. It's not her fault, she tries her best. She's been dealt a ghastly hand and I just hope, somehow, they shape up.'

She looked straight at Frankie.

'You have courage. Your poor sister has none. You have determination and talent – you take the odds and you do battle with them. Look at what you've achieved! Not just your career – but also your children. All by yourself. How brave you were to move here, how right you were, but how difficult it must have been. All this is *yours*. And in there – in that pretty head of yours with the hair that needs a colour, cut and blow-dry – that's where your true might is. You have a strong head and a big heart – there's nothing you can't do. All your poor sister has in her life is mounds of stinking washing that her children seem to excrete, a husband who's as conversant as a doorpost and far too lardy to be attractive, and a book club once a month where frightful women gather around her and make her feel thick. Poor Peta.'

It struck Frankie then that her mother was absolutely right. She thought of Philip being as conversant as a doorpost and far too lardy to be attractive. She thought of her ungrateful and pungent feral nephews. She thought of her older sister. She considered how, since Peta was little and Frankie even smaller, Peta always tried to keep everything neat and peaceable. And Frankie wondered, how often do I actually say hey Peta, how are *you* doing? Are you OK? Are you happy?

And Frankie thought, I love my family.

See. I'm holding my mum's hand.

Ruth had Frankie on all fours; the movement was to crawl and she spoke about spirals, about muscles and bones and something or other that was quick firing. She spoke about energy and release. Frankie didn't take it in but her body was happy to oblige and, set into position by Ruth, off she went. Suddenly she thought what she must look like; crawling around at forty-one years of age struck her as so preposterous it was hilarious. In hysterics, she rolled around the floor laughing and wheezing, much as she had with Jenna when she remarked how strange Scott's house was without Buddy there. And when the laughter peeled away, Frankie just lay there, with her head in Ruth's lap, feeling raw and exposed but somehow just a little more peaceful too.

'You know,' said Ruth, 'at the moment, it's about finding what works for you. If you want to come for AT every day – I'm here.'

'And if I want to talk?' said Frankie. 'If I want to talk about Scott – repeat myself ad nauseam, tell you things I've told you a million times? Pore over photos and make you go *ooh* and *ah* over them, though you've seen them all before?'

'I'm here.'

'And if I want to fucking scream that it's not fair, it's not fair? If I want to wonder where is he? Where's he gone?'

'I'm here.'

'And what if I just want to lie in your lap, catatonically?'

'I'm here.'

'I found a receipt in his truck. I keep it with me. Here, Ruth – read this.'

Ruth looked at the receipt from Melody & Midsomer for a long time. She read the words overleaf. Shwrgel and COFFEE and Mountain & Ocean & Us. She looked at Frankie and shrugged. 'Beautiful,' she said. Then she smiled. 'But no surprise. It doesn't surprise me, not one bit.' She tipped her head to one side. 'Tomorrow – let's get out. Let's go for a walk. You look pale and pasty, Frankie. Scott was a fresh-air freak – he'd hate to see you all cooped up. Especially with what's right here on your doorstep. He loved it.'

Frankie could hear him again. *Look at where you live, Frankie. Slow down – or you'll miss the details. It's beautiful here.*

'Not tomorrow, Ruth,' said Frankie. 'I said I'd go for a walk with my mum. Before she goes home.'

Margaret watched how her daughter walked. She wasn't looking around or ahead, she was looking down. Not down at her feet, but a little way along; circumspect, as if quicksand was only a stride or two away.

'Oh good God, how monstrous!' Margaret barked as a fighter jet from Lakenheath screamed across the sky as if slicing it in two.

'You get used to them,' said Frankie. She looked up.

God knows where the jet was now. Frankie stopped, squinting up at the sky and then out to sea for a moment. 'I don't know.'

'You don't know what?'

'I don't know if this is where I should be.' She trudged on.

'We can go, if you like. Have an early lunch somewhere – I liked that place with the patio and the views. The White Horse. We could go there?'

'Not the beach, Mum. *Beyond* the beach. All of this – Norfolk. Maybe it's not my place. Maybe there's somewhere better.'

Margaret picked up her pace, marching briskly past Frankie.

'Mum?'

But still Margaret kept walking. Frankie caught up with her.

'I'm just saying – after everything that's happened – I just don't know whether it's here that I want to be.'

'Leave your troubles and your sorrow and your regret here? Leave it in the house, pack up, move and miraculously it won't have followed?' Margaret looked at her daughter sternly. 'Your children are settled, this is their home.'

Frankie turned away, stared at the shingle in a scatter over the wet sand like confetti. Maybe it was time for her mother to bugger off back home. Margaret's response unnerved her, she'd rather expected her mother to say marvellous idea darling, head to the Cotswolds.

'I wanted to move to Canada.'

'I know you did,' said Margaret.

Frankie kicked at a stone badly. It went nowhere. Yesterday's numbness today a fractious anger. At everything. 'There are too many memories of him here,' she said, 'and there.'

'In time, that will be a good thing, a comfort.'

'I *like* the thought of moving away, somewhere completely new.' Frankie paused as a dog, wet and sandy, belted past so close that her jeans were sprayed. Sod the dog. 'I know I can do it. I did it already, remember.'

'No one argued with you then,' said Margaret. 'I know I sniffed that Norfolk wasn't the Cotswolds and Peta bemoaned it wasn't Burning Bloody Markets – but the fact that the children were the age they were and your reasons were so sound, we all supported you on that front. We were – are – very proud.'

'Exactly.'

'But I'd strongly advise against moving again. It will be for all the wrong reasons.'

Margaret watched her daughter clenching her teeth, looking stonily out to the shore.

'He liked it here,' Margaret said gently. 'He liked thinking of you here when he wasn't. He thought it suited you well. We talked about that, on this very beach, over Christmas, him and me.'

'It's not about what Scott wants!'

Margaret glanced at an elderly couple startled by Frankie's sudden outburst.

'Scott doesn't matter any more,' Frankie shouted, striding ahead not wanting to be followed. 'Can't you see?'

Shut up Scott, shut up.

Frankie didn't want to hear what he had to say. She didn't want to recall a conversation that they'd had in February. She didn't want to remember him taking her hand in his while she banged on about Canada and

how she believed sometimes it's a parent's responsibility
to make decisions even if the children don't like it and
other people disapprove.

'Certainly it's your responsibility to keep your eyes
open to possibilities where your family is concerned,'
Scott had said. 'But whether we're here or there, we're
together you and me. Seems to me, right now – at this
point in your life, in my life, in your children's life, in
my child's life – this is a very good place for you. You
need to see all the possibilities that are right here on
your doorstep, baby. You're looking in the wrong direction, Frankie.'

Back on the beach today. Alone and out of sorts.
Frankie thought how the death of the one she loved
was an injustice so cruel, so abjectly wrong, so powerful,
so beyond comprehension and any known cure, she
had been left chronically injured.

I'll never properly heal, thought Frankie and she
placed her hands over her ears and walked and walked
and walked.

* * *

Keith Mawby saw Frankie standing in the lane having
a good look at her house. She had her hands on her
hips as if she was assessing something gone awry. He
thought he'd go and have a look too, see if he could
help. Not much a woman knows about clay-pantile
roofing. Not sexist, that, just a fact, he reasoned. He
stepped down from his tractor and walked along
the lane towards her.

'Hello dear.'

'Hello Mr Mawby.'

'Keith.'

'Keith. I was just – I must get going.'

'What's going on here?' He was squinting up at her roof. 'Looks well enough to me.'

'What does?'

'Your roof.'

'I wasn't – I was just. I don't know if I'm staying or going.'

Keith Mawby had a think about that one. Funny woman this, a famous author you know. Quite nice having her around, even if she likes to keep herself to herself. It was good for the house, good for the lane, having someone around most of the time, and a family at that. Not like the lot before her, holiday home it had been. Not right for an old cottage like this, he didn't think. Shocking thing about her fella though. Upset Peg no end.

'That'd be a shame, we're just about used to having you here,' was all that came out of Keith Mawby as he loped off back to his tractor.

Six weeks to the day. Bless you, my Scott. A few days without tears but today I couldn't stop. Sometimes I think I prefer the numbness or the exhaustion, but actually whether it's anger or sorrow at least I feel something, I know I'm alive.

Half term was about to start. May had brought burgeoning warmth but the sea still kept its chill. It was a special time of year; the cusp of summer. It brought birds and visitors and a steady flow to the garden centres; a time for planting up hanging baskets and window boxes and deciding what herbs would suit which pots. Summer clothes were brought out from their vacuum-sealed winter under the bed and woolly jumpers and warm coats were put away. A time of change and growth; lighter, warmer, longer days.

Frankie had been standing at the window in the kitchen, just gazing out. She didn't know how long for. Ages. She didn't want to move, though; Scott was behind her, his arms loosely around her. Oh how she could recall it! And his voice. And what he said, his cheek against hers, a kiss to her neck. *Look around you, Frankie. Look right outside your window and way beyond it. Your world is a pretty good place to be in at the moment. Embrace what you have instead of tiring yourself out, hoping for more.*

Her stomach rumbling brought her back to the day in hand and she realized she'd skipped lunch again. She cut a chunk of cheese to have with an apple. She looked in the fridge while she ate; she couldn't give the children pasta again. How about omelettes for supper. But she needed eggs. And suddenly she thought of the lady in Howell's and that day with the kindness, which seemed so long ago. And she remembered that she still hadn't paid what was owing.

Where had she put her handbag? She meandered from room to room, finally locating it slung on the back of the chair in the study. What else had she bought that day? She couldn't recall. There was money in her purse and she grabbed her car keys and left the house. She started the engine but sat in the car awhile, thinking what am I doing here? What am I thinking?

I'm going to walk. It's a beautiful day. It's only a mile there and a mile back.

When they'd moved here, she and the children had made it their mission to always walk to the village shop. That didn't last.

Today, the sky was a-squawk and a-chatter with birds. Frankie thought about Scott. Perhaps the stores sell books about local birdlife. She smiled at a memory of him vaulting the fence at the end of the garden and standing out in the fields with Sam's binoculars. Greylags, he'd told her. And Canada geese. See, he'd said, I'm not the only one from my country who likes it out here. They spend part of their year here, Frankie had told him and he'd grinned and pulled her in close and given her a kiss and Sam had said yuk! and walked off.

As she walked down the lane, Frankie thought of

the lady in the shop, her concern and kindness, her hand on Frankie's arm. The offer of tea. The shopping not charged for.

'Maybe it's not about you today, Scott,' Frankie said softly. 'Perhaps they gave me credit at the shop not out of sympathy, not for you, but because it was me. Maybe it wasn't forgetfulness or charity on Howell's part. I went home with shopping unpaid for – but it didn't matter because they know where I am, I'm just up the road.'

But Frankie forgot the eggs for the omelettes. She'd been distracted, chatting to the lady in Howell's, insisting that she paid what was owing and then realizing she'd need to jog home if she was to make the school run and not be late for Annabel.

Both children looked at their mother that evening.

'Not pasta *again*.'

'It was going to be omelettes.'

'But there are no eggs, Mummy.'

'Exactly, Annabel – that's why it's pasta again.'

'But it's half term now,' said Sam. 'And it's Friday night. Why don't we go to Wells for fish and chips?'

Though they'd been to the café many times since taking Scott here, Annabel would always privately remember the evening when Scott took her chips and the crispiest piece of batter right off her plate and under her nose. That's when we bonded, she said to herself. That was the point I decided to like him.

The staff greeted them, happy that they'd be having in, not takeaway.

'Starting to get busy, isn't it,' Frankie said to the

waiter as he led on, both of them observing how many tables had been commandeered by visitors.

'Yep,' he said. 'But what's not to like.'

The food was heavenly. The golden batter ballooning away from the fresh white fish that fell into glistening chunks as soon as the fork touched it.

'This is my absolute favourite restaurant,' said Sam.

'Actually,' said Annabel, 'I bet it's one of the top ten restaurants in the world.'

Frankie looked at her children and looked at the food on her plate. She looked outside at the busy little town welcoming locals and holidaymakers alike. And Scott said to her, see – you live in such a great place and these fries are the best I've ever tasted.

'Mummy.'

If there was something on Annabel's mind, or if she wanted something, or if she was feeling unwell, she never called Frankie 'Mum' – always Mummy. It re-established their dynamic at its most intimate. Frankie had come into her room to say goodnight. She sat on the edge of Annabel's bed and felt her forehead.

'Do you feel sick? Maybe you shouldn't have had a double 99 after such an enormous plate of fish and chips?'

'I don't feel sick – that's just you worrying about synthetic ice cream being so evil,' said Annabel. Frankie thought, is my baby really soon to finish primary school? Is she really going to get on that bus in September with her brother and enter secondary school? How will she find her way around? How will she know whom to befriend?

'Mummy.'

'Yes darling.'

'I've been thinking.' Annabel sat herself up. 'I have an idea for a story for you.'

Frankie groaned. 'Thanks for reminding me. I really must get a grip on the first *Just My Luck* book.' A credit-card statement had arrived this morning. She hadn't opened it.

'It's a different sort of story,' Annabel said. 'It's the sort of book that a child might *need*. Not every child – hopefully. But some of them, some of the time.'

Frankie couldn't imagine her agent turning cart-wheels at that. Here's a book that a few kids might read at some point.

'It would mean Alice coming back though,' Annabel said pensively. With a pang, Frankie considered how her daughter often thought of Alice as her biggest rival. Sometimes, Frankie had to admit, Alice won. 'Do you still think of Alice these days?'

'Occasionally,' said Frankie, who thought of her often.

'It would be about Scott,' Annabel said, 'but not about Scott.'

Sometimes, Frankie and the children could talk about Scott for ages. Other times the children had only to mention him and she'd have to leave for a while, go back to the downstairs loo, lock the door, press the hand towel against her face. Not tonight, though.

'Tell me?'

'For children,' Annabel explained. 'To know what it might feel like if someone special – goes. Dies. How they might react. How it might seem. Make Alice deal with what – I – did.'

Frankie thought, never would I have come up with that one.

'And Mummy – not just that book but *another* book too, another Alice. But in that one, Alice is slightly older – say, Sam's age. The same story – but for children who are—'

'Sam's age.'

Frankie sat awhile and stroked Annabel's hair.

'I think you should think about it,' said Annabel.

'I think I will.'

'Promise?'

'I promise.'

She kissed Annabel goodnight, then popped in on Sam and told him he could read for as long as he liked. As she went downstairs, Frankie thought how if there was anyone she could truly talk to, it was Alice.

Her grief would be my grief. But I don't know if she'll speak to me. I sent her packing to Canada, after all.

* * *

'Hello?'

'Frankie?'

Oh God, not Miles.

'Hi.'

'How are you Frankie?'

'I'm –'

'I wrote to you.'

He had written to Frankie when he heard about Scott; a kind letter telling her that if there was anyone such a thing should not have happened to, it was her but if there was anyone who had the strength and grace to find her way through, it was her as well.

'Thank you Miles – it meant a lot. How are you? Are you back?'

'Yes, oh yes. Bogotá can bogger off.'

'Oh.'

'I was just phoning to see if the children want to come for the weekend?'

The silence on the phone line was a studied one. Miles wondering how she'd respond. Frankie wondering what she was meant to do.

'I could meet them from the train – and if they have homework, I'll make sure they do it. Do you remember Z-beds? I bought two for my flat.'

She wondered, what would the children want to do? They'd want to go on a train just the two of them and be met in by their incorrigible father who'd probably be late, they'd want to sleep on fold-up Z-beds and have a little look at what his life was all about.

If she told Peta? If she told Sam not to hesitate to phone Peta for the slightest reason?

'OK,' Frankie said.

'You sure?' Miles sounded amazed, excited.

'Yes,' she said. 'You will be –'

'Oh I will be. *Very*.'

It was to be the first time Frankie had been in her home without her children, the first time she'd been on her own, since Scott died. Her mother had offered to come up and her sister had invited her to stay. Ruth told Frankie the spare room was at her disposal. But Ruth also knew that it was no bad thing for Frankie just to try it, to figure out where her place was in the house, how she might fit in there, with no one else about. A chance for her to listen to the silence and try and hear what it might say. We're having a curry tomorrow night, Ruth told her, you're welcome to join us.

Frankie found that she felt all right if she kept busy. She went to the bits-and-bobs drawer her mother had arranged and took out the hammer. Then she whacked at the nail in the floorboard that had been annoying her for so long. No more socks being ruined. Who'd have thought a bit of banging could be so satisfying. She went from room to room to see what else might benefit from a tap or a whack. If only the groan and gurgle of the water pipes could be solved with a bash. But she didn't dare. And, as Scott said to her at Christmas, all houses have annoying habits – but so do most people. You just learn to rub along.

Oh to hear his voice again, that soft accent, the timbre. His laugh that was in his eyes as much as his voice. And Frankie thought how the things that are hardest to bear are sometimes the sweetest to remember. She went downstairs and sat at the kitchen table with a glass of wine and a new pad of paper and, with Annabel's idea in her head, she jotted down a few notes.

It was so quiet in the house without the children. Horribly quiet. Scott would disagree. He said that music is everywhere, even in silence, one only has to listen. So she sat and she waited and, while she waited, she felt her body do something it hadn't done in a long while: it relaxed a little. She switched on the television, scanned through what was on and found a film she'd seen some years before. Since Scott had died, she hadn't been able to focus on the television, let alone books, not even magazines. But that night, she found she could concentrate; it wasn't just images and noise, it was a refreshing dip into a parallel world for a couple of hours.

In the morning she lay in bed with her scramble of thoughts and decided she'd go back to sleep. So she did. Until eleven o'clock, when she woke with a start not knowing whether to be proud or ashamed. It was T-shirt weather out there so she put on shorts and trainers and headed for Holkham. Maybe she'd run on the beach. Maybe she'd just stroll. Perhaps she wouldn't even go onto the sand at all, she'd stay within the pines and find that rope swing the children were crazy about. But Frankie loved the sea. She really loved the sea.

Walking the beach, she observed the families, the groupings, the different paces at which people moved, the different reasons they came here. A couple having a row walking stroppily. A child trying to pull her grandfather faster, Grandpa, faster, race me to the sea. Someone running after an absconding dog. An elderly man and his wife, hand in hand, eating biscuits. Frankie stood still and, against the swathe of sand and the silver mass of water, she felt suddenly flimsy and acutely on her own. How easy it would be to turn and go back to the car, scurry away and hurry home.

But what a waste of her time that would be. What a criminal thing to do on such a beautiful day.

So she put one foot in front of the other and she kept walking. Someone she passed said hello but Frankie's mumbled response came once they were out of earshot. Scott wasn't like that. You couldn't have described him as gregarious but he liked people. He'd've replied immediately with more than a mumble. He'd have said hey, how are you? and he'd've been happy to stop awhile and converse. When she'd been in Pemberton, she'd marvelled to him how everyone seemed to actively embrace where it was they lived. And he'd just shrugged and said to her but it's the same where you are Frankie, they seem to me to really appreciate it too, don't you see it? He'd gently chided her for walking in such an introverted way. Her mother had too.

One foot, then the other. Repeat. She walked on.

A woman a little younger than her was walking towards her, but just as she neared, her phone went, leaving Frankie simultaneously relieved and a little put out. She'd intended to say hello, really she had. Further on and she was approaching an elderly man, a dog lead in his hand.

'Hello,' said Frankie.

'Hello.'

'It's – nice!'

'It would be nicer if I could find Sam.' He showed her the lead, limp in his hand.

'Shall I help you?' Frankie asked.

'He's a little bugger.'

'My son's called Sam,' said Frankie. 'He can be a little bugger too.'

'Have you time, love?'

'Yes,' said Frankie. 'I'm not in a rush. One can't rush a place like this. Look at it.'

She walked with Ruth and her family the next day. Exactly the same walk.

'Around about here,' Frankie said, marking the sand by dragging an X with the toe of her trainer, 'I passed the time of day with an old chap. I helped him find his dog. Before I knew it we were walking together. He told me a legend, a ghost story about Binham – there was a secret tunnel to Walsingham and a tall figure in black robes. So Jimmy Gribbs the fiddler, and his dog, went into the tunnel after him but a landslide blocked it and Jimmy and his dog were never seen again. Now it's called Fiddler's Hill. Did you know that Ruth? Apparently, in the 1930s, workers found the bones of a man and a dog.'

Ruth giggled. 'Do you think your friend yesterday was the ghost of Jimmy Gribbs?'

'No,' said Frankie. 'His name is Robert Something, he's from Wiverton.'

Ruth linked arms with her. 'How are you doing, Frankie?'

'Who knows.'

'Please don't leave – don't go. We also see your funny little family as part of the landscape.'

Frankie looked out over the sands, back to the dunes, up to the canopy of silken blue. She looked at Ruth and she looked at Ruth's dogs. She glanced at Ruth's children and she thought of Sam and Annabel, tucking into fish 'n' chips in Wells. She looked up and down the beach at all the people she didn't know. She looked for Scott, she'd always look for Scott. And she looked at who she was yesterday and she saw who she was today.

The smell of salt and pine in the air. Sand underfoot. Breeze in her hair. Sun in her eyes.

'You know Ruth, when Scott died – those first few days, it was hard to breathe. These past weeks, I felt I couldn't even walk without help.' Frankie paused, tracing an arc in the sand with her foot. Being still. Nodding at the horizon. 'But now I've learned to limp. Day by day I see that I can go for longer distances.'

On they walked, watching the black Labs, Bessie and Alfie, rounding up Jack and Penny as the children gambolled about in the surf.

'My children find walks boring,' Frankie said. 'But they swear to me that, if we had a dog, they'd never complain. They promise me I'd never have to drag them out for a walk.'

'Dogs stink,' said Peter. 'Their breath, their farts, their food. Their shit.'

'They're a commitment,' said Ruth.

'They do like structure and boundaries,' said Peter. 'Just like children, really. Just as messy, too.'

'To have a dog, you have to open your home to them,' said Ruth.

'I know,' said Frankie.

Back at home, she thought about the morning and yesterday, about what she'd felt and all that she'd said out loud. She thought about stinking dogs and happy children. She phoned Sam who said everything was cool and that Miles had the best takeaway pizza place right on his street. She texted Jenna and a sweet conversation pinged to and fro. She thought of Buddy. And of course Frankie thought of Scott.

He'd told her not to heap so much symbolism on her move to Norfolk, not to burden the place with so much responsibility. Why don't you just slow down, Frankie, and see the details? Discover the reality of where you are. You're going to have to muddle through hassle but don't turn away from that. There's beauty in the everyday, baby. There's music in silence, remember.

Scott. At the centre of my world. Still doing home improvements to my life.

Drifts of time. School was out for the summer. Annabel was officially no longer at primary school and Sam's feet had grown a whole shoe size since Easter. Frankie's progress on the first *Just My Luck* story was slow but steady. Her new character, Tom, was a funny scrap of a boy who never had matching socks and whose hair always flopped over one eye. He was a pleasure to draw. But he wasn't Alice.

Frankie thought, this time last year I feared I couldn't write. But her current deadline wasn't so much a guillotine, it was more of a winning post. If she made it there on time, then she'd think about a dog. She'd told the children that. They were doing everything they could to facilitate her work.

'What do you want Sam? Stop hovering please. I told you – I need to work this morning and we'll go to the beach this afternoon. But hovering is just going to wind me up.'

'Mummy?' Now Annabel was loitering at the kitchen table next to her brother.

'*What?*' Frankie was irritated now. 'I'm working. Go in the garden or go and see if Mr Mawby needs any help. Here – here's a fiver, you can walk to Howell's and buy sweets. Ten. Take ten quid. Just let me work.'

But her children stood there, defiant. Sam was holding a folded piece of paper. He sat down and Annabel took a seat next to him. Frankie felt as if she was before a panel.

'It's something Scott wanted,' Sam said. 'It's something he planned to do – for you.' He unfolded the paper and read. '*I thought we could make her office a place she wants to go to*. That was when he first mentioned it, Mum. Then he wrote: *are you "in" for helping me plan the room for your Mom. Sure – we can FaceTime later if you like. When I was over in February, I snuck a bunch of stuff into the small shed. I went to the stores when she didn't know. There's some wood and shelving and a desk that we have to put together. I was going to buy paint but I thought Annabel might want to choose colors. When I'm next over, we'll go get some drapes (curtains). That's the plan!*' Sam paused. Just one word left to read, which reverberated around the room and settled back in their hearts. '*Scott*'.

Frankie just stared at Sam. He handed her the pages he'd printed off and she read them, a part of her wishing they were handwritten. Like the words on the back of the receipt. But these were Scott's words too, unmistakably.

Out by the shed, Annabel squealed on account of a very large spider. It made Sam jump too, but he brushed it away with his bare hand and Frankie stole a glance at him, the man in their house. They creaked the door open and had a good look at all the stuff that Scott had secretly bought, trying to figure out what the planks and fixings were for. The desk was flat-packed and the illustration showed drawers to one side and a cupboard to the other.

'Useful,' said Annabel. 'For bits and bobs.'

'You sound like Grandma,' Frankie said.

'So?'

Frankie thought, she's right and she gave her daughter's pony-tail a little tug.

'What are we going to do with it all?' Sam asked.

'I have no idea.'

'I'm choosing the paint colours,' said Annabel. 'Scott said so.'

'We're a long way off painting,' Frankie said.

'What about those guys who came and did the work when we first moved in?'

'Don't you remember?' said Frankie. 'They're only coming back here over my dead body.'

'Peter's always doing DIY for Ruth,' Annabel said. 'He's good at all sorts of stuff. Why don't you ask him?'

'Peter does enough for us,' Frankie said. 'But I bet Ruth knows someone else.'

'Let's ask her.'

So they did.

Frankie watched the van trundle up their drive.

If I bring Scott's plans to life, it has to be because I want to stay, that I want to live *here*, that I want to work out *there*.

She told herself, you cannot build it as a shrine.

'And the dog,' she said under her breath, as she watched the man get out of his van and take a long look at her house. 'A dog means we're staying.'

And so John Sprackett came into their lives and started to fix quite a lot. Not hearts – he was at least 102 and Annabel was convinced things lived in his beard. But he was a brilliant chippie and he had a coterie of aged but excellent plumbers, sparks and roofers. He wasn't cheap – but as he'd often say to Frankie as he sucked his tea through the gaps where once there were teeth, 'You get what you pay for.'

Annabel chose paint in gentle colours like those found on a vintage print. Dusky rose and a soft silver-grey. Frankie took the children to London, leaving them with Miles for a night while she stayed with Peta. Stan and Josh were away at cricket camp and Philip was working late, so her sister relished the company. Peta took charge, off to John Lewis they went with the colour-card Annabel had given them and together, the sisters chose a rug for the office. And drapes.

They went to IKEA too, though they swore almost as soon as they got there, never again. But Frankie bought a table lamp and a rocking chair, a throw and some storage modules. On the way out, passing through the cavernous area of items stacked in bay after bay, a scent enveloped her and she was back in the forest at the other side of One Mile Lake. From the mundane to the poetic, from indoors to outdoors, from England to Canada, from being on her own to being with Scott.

It's just the smell of pine. That's all.

She could have cried, dissolved, but instead Frankie just stood in IKEA, inhaling, having her moment with a memory so sweet she could smell it too.

John could see where Scott was going with the planks and the fixings and soon there were deep shelves running all the way around three walls. The colours worked brilliantly. He'd sanded the floor and sealed it and he'd put the desk together. He'd also fixed two of the worst windows in the house and his plumber had found a way to make the water pipes less argumentative. John told her it would be a crying shame to think of changing the clay pamment floor in the hallway.

'What do you want to do that for, duzzy? Those floors are masterous. Those floors are part of your house, like your feet are part of you.'

With the children over at Ruth's one afternoon, Frankie started to unpack. Boxes of books – her own, in the various languages she'd been translated into, but also the books which had inspired her for so many years. Children's books, photographic books, art books. An old thesaurus. An ancient Blue Peter *Look Make and Cook Book*. Poetry. And the Collins dictionary that she won at prize-giving in the fifth form.

It didn't matter that the curtains had yet to arrive and that the room was flooded with such extraordinary light that, at one point, she had to put her sunglasses on. The smell of floor wax and fresh paint didn't bother her. She could have done with buying the rug in the next size up, but it wasn't a problem. The IKEA rocking chair was comfortable and all those storage racks, pots, trays and files had a purpose already.

She sat at the desk and smoothed her hands over its surface. She thought, I'm ready to work in here. And she thought, if it doesn't work for me in here – for this book at least – then there's always the kitchen table.

Though Sam might have something to say about that. And Annabel. Ruth too. And even John.

They were back in Canada. Of course they were. They were hardly likely to ship out to France again for their holidays, that summer. The flights alone cost Frankie the same as a holiday in Europe but of course once there, they had the house. They were going for almost three weeks, with a trip to Vancouver in the middle. Jenna would join them for some of the time but at the moment, she was in Calgary staying with Kyle's family. So it would just be Frankie and the children in Pemberton at first. Only of course it wouldn't be just the three of them. Plenty of people had kept in touch and there were open invites for barbeques and kayaking, hikes and just saying hi; whatever the family felt like doing. Frankie didn't know what that might be. She wasn't sure how hard it might be either. She was last here in April. But, as she drove the Sea to Sky, she reminded herself that this time last year they were out here too.

Annabel and Sam were a little quiet in the hire car, Sam especially. Frankie asked him if he was OK, what he was thinking. He just shrugged and said nothing, Mum.

'Do you remember what that is? On the right?'

'The Chief,' said Sam, looking at the granite monolith

growling up into the sky. 'I'm so going to climb that one day and have a beer at the top.'

Frankie wanted to giggle that the apotheosis for him, a fourteen-year-old boy, was not to reach the top but the age at which he could drink beer. She glanced at him in the rear-view mirror. He was still gazing at the rock. She found herself hoping so much that one day he'd do it – climb the Stawamus Chief and have his beer at the summit.

When they finally reached Pemberton, Frankie stopped in the village. It might have been because they were hungry, or it might have been that they weren't quite ready to go straight to Scott's. The children wanted to eat at the Pony; pizza, burger, ice cream from the cart in the entrance. They wanted to see if the model train track suspended from the ceiling was working. Frankie had a craving for the hand-cut wedges and garbanzo wrap at Mile One Eating House. But the children were tired so the Pony it was, where they were greeted like old friends.

Before they got back in the car for the final twenty minutes of a very long journey, they all stood awhile and just gazed at Mount Currie, at Tśzil. As the evening light started to flow down its flanks in ribbons of pink and gold, its mass appeared to soften. It seemed as if the mountain was broadening, as if it was saying to them that they're safely here now and will be looked after by the land and its people. What was it that the Líĺwat say? Frankie tried to remember. *Pelpala7wít i ucwalmícwa múta7 ti tmícwa* – the land and the people are one.

It was time. Time to go home. Time for the children to confront how they might feel. Time for Frankie to gauge how she was doing. They drove quietly out and along. Past the road that led to the airfield. Past the

Sturdys' farm and the invitation for the children to help out at their stall at the farmers' market in Whistler that Sunday. Through the Líl̓wat reserve at Mount Currie and on to the D'Arcy road. Turning left. And then left again.

'Slow down, Mummy.'

Frankie slowed right down and, from the bottom of the drive, the three of them just gazed and gazed at Scott's house.

Rose told Frankie the house would be open and the key would be on the kitchen table. There were also fresh flowers in a jug and a note to say there was food in the fridge. It was all the same; nothing had changed since she was last here. Well, everything had, but it surprised Frankie how steady she felt about being back. The horror that first came with the concept of Scott not being here, had slowly slid into an understanding of the reality, he just isn't. She felt as close to him as ever, but a little easier with the knowledge that he's really not here. The children, though, seemed reluctant to move, as though they were waiting for something.

'You OK?' Frankie asked.

Sam didn't answer.

Annabel's face crumpled and she ran into her mother's embrace, sobbing. It's OK, poppet, it's OK. But Annabel needed to be able to miss him all over again and think that none of this was OK. And still Sam stood there, not moving, not talking, not looking at either of them.

'Sammy?'

'I was just wondering where I'm sleeping?'

Frankie could hear the crack in his voice, that he didn't want it noticed.

'In your man cave?'

'Cool,' he said. 'Is it open?'

'The key's on the hook on the side of the window frame.'

'Cool.' He fetched it. 'I'll just go and – you know – unpack.'

Frankie went over to the studio with a pile of fresh linen for the sofa bed. The music was loud and fast but harmonic and reaching – she wasn't sure who the band was. Sam was facing away from her, sitting on the Chesterton. At first, she thought he was nodding to the beat. But he was out of time. He wasn't nodding, he was crying. Frankie put the sheets down on the surface with all the knobs and switches and buttons and dials and she went and sat with Sam. He had a guitar of Scott's on his lap. She put her head on his shoulder and there they sat, their thoughts of Scott entwining while music filled the room.

Does anyone ever get used to jet lag? Frankie wondered. Travelling might be good for the soul but jet lag can't be good for the body. The family were so utterly zonked when the car came phuttering up the drive the next morning that it remained in their periphery. She'd tried making pancakes to go with the peameal bacon and fresh blueberries that Rose had left – but failed. They were like Frisbees and about as tasty. Now the three of them were watching with some alarm as four young guys walked across the porch, heading straight for the studio. Time seemed to stand still while they tried to compute the scene before suddenly scrambling into the present and out onto the deck.

'Excuse me? Oi!'

They stared at Frankie, stock-still. Perhaps because

459

she was wearing a T-shirt of Scott's emblazoned with the words Swans Buckerfields Brewery, just a pair of socks and her hair all in a tangle. Perhaps they were just staring because Scott's house was usually empty so who the heck is everyone?

'Frankie?' One of the boys stepped forward. 'We met at Scott's – at the – back in April. I'm Jonah. These are the guys – Chase, Quint and Ryan. We were all – there. Back in April.'

'We're the band,' said another, 'that Scott was, like, mentoring? We're at school together, in the village. I'm Chase – this is Ryan, this is Quint.'

'We're called Defy?' said Quint.

And Frankie wondered if they knew it sounded like Deaf Eye. Or maybe that *was* what they were called.

'Of course I know of you. Scott thought you were really talented.' How old were they? Seventeen, eighteen? Frankie sensed Sam shifting beside her. 'Are you here to – jam?' She knew it sounded clunky and she could see them bite down on smirks.

'Mum,' Sam muttered, mortified.

'If that's OK?' said Chase.

'This is my son, Sam.'

'Hey Sam.'

'He's staying in the studio,' Frankie said.

'Oh sure!' said Jonah. 'We can come back?'

'No,' said Sam and he stepped away from Frankie. 'It's cool.'

Frankie watched them assess her boy, as if they were recalling being his age and how guys their age were who they'd aspired to be.

'You OK if we play in the studio, Sam?' they asked. 'You're welcome to hang with us.'

Sam glanced at Frankie and then, barefoot and still in his jimjams, he led the way.

Frankie thought she might take them refreshments in a while. The surprise had done away with jet lag. It was time to greet the day.

'Hey you,' Frankie said warmly when Jenna came through the front door the following week, Kyle in tow.

'Hey Frankie,' she said and they held each other, releasing a little bit of Scott back out into the open. Annabel was so happy to see her, to meet Kyle too. With Jenna busy upstairs braiding her daughter's hair, Frankie asked him how she'd been.

'Well, not too bad,' he said. 'We have an appointment with her specialist next month. My dad knows Schultz. He says he's really good.'

'How are the seizures?'

Kyle shrugged. 'They come,' he said. 'And then they go. They are what they are. They don't define her – not in my eyes.'

It's OK Scott, your daughter is in very capable hands.

'So – no driving just yet?'

'She's counting the days Frankie, she's always counting the days. But you know – I like driving. I like her next to me. I like being – the strong one. So, if it doesn't happen, that's OK, right?'

'Will you come for Christmas again?' Frankie asked Jenna when she had her to herself. 'You and Kyle? Steph's coming.'

'Oh Frankie,' she said. 'I'd love to. It's just that I've been invited to Calgary – and I said yes already.'

And that's OK, thought Frankie. And she thought, Scott – you don't have to worry, your baby girl is doing just fine.

And then, two days before they were due to go home, Frankie saw her bear.

They'd been into the village for supper – the children had ganged up on Frankie and off they went to the Pony again. Driving home, the children asked to go to the airfield. Dusk was just perceptible after what had been a beautiful day. They'd been kayaking with the Eslakes and were softly sunned and deliciously tired.

Scott's truck had gone, of course. Jenna had sold it and given the proceeds to Rose. Aaron's business was up and running again, with a percentage going to Rose and the children. Annabel announced that she was going to say a prayer. She walked on ahead and it felt appropriate to give her privacy, so Sam and Frankie sat on mismatched chairs at the table on the deck outside the office. The little planes and the helicopter looked as though they were snoozing. Frankie realized that now she felt neither fear nor hatred for them.

On their way home, they popped in on Rose and the children and Buddy. They'd seen them already a couple of times, but Frankie was concerned that they might not see them again before they left.

'Frankie,' said Rose. 'I forgot – I have something for you.'

The children were watching the TV, with Buddy assuming they were watching him.

'Wait there, Frankie,' Rose said leaving Frankie in the hallway while she went into her bedroom. Frankie wondered, does she ever sleep with pillows along her back so that just occasionally, in her reverie, she might think it's Aaron?

Sometimes, she still did that.

'Here.'

Rose gave Frankie a little ceramic pot. Inside was a brown-red paste.

'It's precious to my people. It's called *temlh*,' Rose explained. 'From red ochre. It's prized and sacred – for ceremonies, for protection. You put it on your feet, it will guard you where you walk. You put it on your temples, it will take care of your thoughts. One day, Frankie, there will come a time when you'll dip your finger in and put a little over your heart.'

Frankie bowed her head.

No.

Not after Scott.

Tears she hadn't felt for a while came at her eyes in a sharp surge. She wanted to go to Rose and embrace her, but she knew Rose wasn't like that. Rose's warmth emanated from her in other ways.

'Yeah we will Frankie,' Rose said. 'We will.'

Unlike the lanes in North Norfolk, which Frankie happily belted her car down, in Canada she drove much more slowly. Early evening was a beautiful time out here so she let the car dawdle its way. The mountains appearing to slumber, their peaks and ridges just edged in sunset, the trees becoming inky, the turning sky wafting velvet across the land. And then, on the final stretch of the road home, that's when it happened, that's when they saw the bear. Only it wasn't just one bear – it was a mother and two cubs.

They walked right across the road, right in front of

the car. No more than thirty feet away, the bear family ambled by.

Frankie stopped. They stopped. No one moved. Three pairs of eyes on three pairs of eyes.

Then one cub snuck away and the other cub gambolled after him.

She looked at Frankie, the bear, absolutely directly at her. Two mothers sharing a thought. And then she was on her way. She needed to catch up with her kids.

Frankie thought about the bear a lot that evening.

There's poetry in flight – metaphors to be wrung from eagles and swallows and Steller's jays in BC, as much as from the pink-footed geese, greenshanks, redshanks, the sandpipers and Arctic waders back in Norfolk this time of year. Bears, though, are big furry galumphing creatures. But now Frankie knew how, when you see one, you learn about composure and self-containment; you note how every hair moves separately, like breeze sylphing through grasses. Bears have an energy and a dignity that fits well their huge bodies. In Northwest Coastal Native culture, a bear symbolizes family and strength and is sometimes seen as an elder or a good person who has passed on to a new life.

But Frankie had never seen a bear before, not even in a zoo. She could never have anticipated the peaceful connection she'd find with that lovely girl lumbering through life with such grace as she keeps an eye on her children.

* * *

With the children in bed, and their homeward journey starting the next morning, Frankie steps out onto the porch. She stands there, in the moment, breathing deeply, the way Ruth's taught her.

I have two homes, she realizes.

It strikes her that this part of the world is her spiritual birthplace yet it doesn't detract from the fact that she really likes her day-to-day Norfolk. There's a pace and a pattern back home that she's starting to really understand and even enjoy. There's a power and vitality here in the mountains that stays with her wherever she is. The qualities of here and there have started to combine, somehow, into contentment.

She realizes how much easier it feels now, to return to England, knowing that Scott's house is here, always here for her too.

Who's that?

Suddenly, Frankie isn't alone. She thinks, I know you, I *know* you but—?

Frankie.

Alice?

Yes – it's me.

But – you're so much older!

Yes Frankie, it happens!

Alice! How are you?

Look at me – never better. Thank you for sending me here. What a place to live.

Told you so – told you you'd love it and have a good life here.

Thank you for writing about me, Frankie – when I was little. I think about Him still – being there in the thatchety hedge at the bottom of the garden helping the children that come and go from April Cottage.

It should be me thanking you! It's down to you that I can provide for my children, that I could buy us a little patch of loveliness two miles from the sea. And anyway, it was my pleasure being your author, telling your tale for you.

I know you're busy writing that *Just My Luck* book about some boy called Tom – but I wanted to tell you something. I wanted to say how grateful I am that you're going to write those other two books – about me, about what I went through. Children need to know about death, that it's OK to feel how they feel.

I'm all set to do so. I have a contract for both – and a dreaded deadline.

And how are you doing Frankie? You?

I'm all right, Alice. I'm – learning. I still ask why. Why did it happen? Why to him? Why to me? I can have a day when I'm absolutely furious and long periods when I just feel numb. I can have a day when I feel absolutely fine, when I feel light, when I don't think about any of it. I'm still so tired. And I miss him. Still I cry. But mostly I try to live in the day that I have. There's a beauty to stillness, to enabling yourself to really experience the present, to just allow yourself to stand and sense and breathe and be. Scott taught me that.

I *hate* what happened to you.

Thank you. But it's OK, Alice. Honestly. I am working out, slowly, slowly, that actually I am far more lucky than I am unlucky. I saw a bear yesterday! I'm *here*. Look where I am!

I don't know—

No – I *do* know. I'm fortunate to have had a love that was life-changing, a love that took me to such a crucial turning point in my own life and provided me with the innate knowledge of which way I wanted to go. The same love that guides me now, that shows me how to keep on going.

Not many people have that.

You may be right but do you know something Alice, I hope that they do – I like to think that they do. Perhaps they just don't stop often enough to realize it.

Alice and Frankie, together on Scott's porch.

So you'll write those books about me?

With very great pleasure.

And after that?

Frankie thinks about her work just then. She considers how people often assume that, if her books are easy to read, they must be easy to write. But actually, every book she writes always takes her on such a journey.

Alice – I have no idea.

So Alice tells her.

Write about love, Frankie. Write a novel – not for kids this time. Write your heart out Frankie. Love is a subject you know so well because it's something you're very good at.

EPILOGUE

Early in the New Year, with the children back at school, Frankie lets Banjo the dog out into the garden for a wee. She watches him from her favourite window in the kitchen as he pokes around the flower beds and inspects his excessive selection of toys, which are lying in an unruly scatter all over the muddy lawn. He's a funny little fellow and he's slotted right into their family and their home, with only the occasional chewed shoe or mishap on the carpet these days.

'Dear God,' Frankie mutters, wiping his filthy paws with the manky towel that now lives by the back door. He pads after her as she goes through the house to the hallway.

Frankie puts on her coat and the dog looks at her expectantly. When Banjo wags his tail, his entire rump sways. A little like Buddy.

'No Banjo – you have to stay here.' She strokes his head. 'And be good, you little rascal.'

She leaves the house and backs her car out of the drive, waving at Keith Mawby, then pointing to her watch and slapping her forehead to signify sorry! in a rush as usual! Perhaps she'd pop in on Peg tomorrow.

She's off to the cinema, to the Screen-next-the-Sea in Wells. Frankie can't remember the last time she's been to a matinee, or any time that she's been to the cinema on her own. She had thought about asking Ruth to join her but she decided that she'd like to go by herself. She could have seen the film before Christmas, but she hadn't been ready. A month on, she feels OK about it.

Back Road Open.

That's the title of the movie.

It stars Jeff Bridges, perennially one of Frankie's favourite actors.

It's the film for which Scott had written the music, the film he'd been working on in Abbey Road back when they'd first met. A contemplative road movie about a man reconnecting with his past to soothe his present and make sense of his future. Wide-open vistas, spit-and-sawdust bars in the middle of Nowheresville, a beat-up truck taking a damaged man along the lonesome, winding road home. Sometimes it's not about the destination, it's purely about the journey.

Frankie remembers the music so well, not just from what she'd heard being recorded in the studio, but from when Scott hummed the melody as he read a paper or whistled the tune when he was tinkering around her house, singing it softly while he made sure the Christmas tree was stable.

Hear that? That's Scott's guitar. Those are his fingers eliciting that sweet sound. He is still playing.

As the film ends and just before the credits roll, the screen momentarily fades and then it fills with a photograph of him.

In loving memory of Scott Emerson

His dates.

Audiences will always flatten when they work out he was just forty-six years old.

Freya North

Frankie gazes and gazes at the picture. She'd been there when it had been taken, in the control room of Studio Two at Abbey Road. That easy smile and those generous eyes. And look – right next to Scott – see that arm of someone just cropped out of the photograph? That's Frankie.

Side by side.

Always there.

*   *   *

As is a tale, so is life: not how long it is, but how good it is, is what matters.

Lucius Annaeus Seneca

ACKNOWLEDGEMENTS

For me, researching and writing *The Turning Point* was a profound and unforgettable experience and there are many people to whom I am indebted.

From Vancouver to Pemberton BC, I met wonderful people along the way who were excellent company and so generous with their time. Warmest thanks to Jordan Sturdy, Barb and Dan Eslake, Beverly and Nick Smith, Delores Franz, Anne Crowley, Judith Walton, Bev Blundell – and all the sparky members of the writing group and book club in Pemberton. At Pemberton & District Chamber of Commerce & Tourism, my thanks to Shirley Henry. Thank you Andrew Fleming at the Vancouver Courier. Very special mention and heartfelt thanks to Valerie and Richard Megeney, also Christine Haebler – *mi casa, su casa*.

I feel extremely honoured to have been given the support of the Líĺwat nation – and would like to extend my sincerest gratitude to Chief Lucinda Phillips and to Elders Lois Joseph, Veronica Birkadi and Martina Pierre at the Líĺwat Culture Heritage Language Authority. Also Ruth Dick at the Úlĺus Centre and Mary Ann Narcisse for such a lovely warm and informative chat under the shade of a cedar. The Líĺwat nation are a wonderful people with fascinating traditions and an extraordinary history. I urge you to find out more. Should you be near Whistler, please visit the Squamish Líl̓wat Cultural Centre. In Pemberton, do call in at the Úlĺus Centre at Mount Currie. Any trip to Vancouver must include a visit to the stunning Museum of Anthropology at UBC.

Researching Scott's career was exciting. My deepest thanks to my treasured pal Kle Savidge, music supervisor extraordinaire, for all her help. Also, to Carolyn Manetti and the real Paul Broucek. Thank you to Colette Barber at Abbey Road Studios – also Isobel Griffiths and Richard Evans. Jesse Zubot – many thanks for such a lovely and in depth correspondence. Paul Leonard-Morgan thank you so much for one of the longest and most fun FaceTimes.

For information and details about flying light aircraft, I'm most grateful to Quint Gleza, Troy Boswall and Dan Maclean at Whistler Sky Diving in Pemberton. Also, for fact-checking and advice, sincerest thanks to Graham Elliott – and to Suzie and Stu Purser for the introduction.

In Norfolk, thank you to my very precious friends Kirsty Johnson and Tom Jones for letting me use their home as a base. In and out of the years, you have meant so much to me.

Thank you to the real Ruth Ingram – through researching this book I have become somewhat evangelical about the Alexander Technique not least because after 14 books, finally I can now sit comfortably and write without the twangs and aches I used to endure.

My research into epilepsy brought me into contact with some incredible people. I have immense respect, admiration and compassion for those who suffer themselves or have loved ones who do. I implore you to become better informed about epilepsy. I was humbled by the honesty and grateful for the level of detail so patiently related by those to whom I spoke. In no particular order, I am indebted to Leon Legge, Yvonne Harris, Dawn Glorioso, Shaz Meredith, Chelsea Best, Danielle Lewis, Debbie Fuller White, Laura Fern, Pam Herstein, Hazel Patching, Jackie Jackson, Deanna Gray, Ann Cox, Emma Murphy, Alison Sanders and Nathalie Boyle Small. Thank you to many others who responded via Facebook.

Any errors in this novel are my own.

Behind the scenes, Team North continue to do a sterling job. My fondest thanks to Jonathan Lloyd – my agent of 20 years – and Lucia Rae at Curtis Brown Ltd. Also, my new pals at HarperCollins Canada as well as my old friends at HarperCollins UK. I truly appreciate your support, energy and patience. To my lovely followers on Facebook and Twitter – it's great to be able to interact with you.

During a twelve month period when I juggled two books, two kids, two dogs, a horse, running a book festival, doing my charity work for Beating Bowel Cancer and the Campaign to Protect Rural England, the support of friends and family during frequently challenging times was crucial and much appreciated. You know who you are – take a bow...

However, my profoundest thanks of all go to my children Felix and Georgia because they put up with me day in day out and they never cease to inspire me, enabling me to see how beautiful the world is and how lucky I am. Frustratingly, there are simply no words to describe just how much I love my cubs.

Please explore these websites:

http://slcc.ca
http://www.lilwat.ca
http://www.pemberton.ca
http://www.tourismpembertonbc.com
http://www.northarmfarm.com
http://www.whistlerskydiving.ca
http://www.lillooetriverlodge.com
http://www.jessezubot.com
http://www.paulleonardmorgan.com
http://www.bcepilepsy.com
http://epilepsymatters.com
http://www.youngepilepsy.org.uk
https://www.epilepsy.org.uk
http://www.alexanderworld.co.uk

In loving memory
Liz Berney 1968–2005
and
Hannah Berry 1983–2013
www.beatingbowelcancer.org

Reading Group Questions

Could you have taken the risk, like Frankie and Scott, and tried to make a relationship work long distance?

Discuss the theme of the 'turning point' - is there more than one in the novel? Are they comparable to any you have experienced.

Do you think Frankie would have married Scott? What would their life together have looked like?

How does Scott's appearance in their life change Sam and Annabel's lives? How does Frankie affect Jenna's? Will the change last?

What's the point of Miles?

Explore the relationship between Frankie and her mother and Frankie and her sister. Compare it to Scott's relationships with Jenna and Aaron.

Alice and Buddy - how important are their roles?

What did you think about the various locations in the novel? What did they bring to the story and how did they affect the characters?

How did you feel after reading the novel? What would you say when you press it into someone else's hands?

Can you read another author's book and lose yourself in it as we do yours or do you read it with your author's insight and view it critically? *Kaz Earnshaw*

Oh yes – when I read a book, I'm immediately absorbed into its world. It's one of my favourite and most life-affirming leisure pursuits. Saying that, when I'm in full flow writing a novel, I don't tend to read fiction. Instead I'm constantly reading around the subjects in my novel. But I'm always reading. Always.

Is Frankie's journey with Alice one you have lived with your characters? *Roxanne Gray*

I journey through each story with every character. Never as their puppeteer, always as their PA ready to take dictation. To this day, I think of characters in my earlier novels like friends I haven't seen for a long time. Sometimes I'll say so Chloe, how's life treating you these days? I was absolutely stricken with writer's block writing *The Way Back Home* – for a while it was as if Oriana, Malachy and Jed were speaking a foreign language, and in whispers at that. With Frankie, I truly felt everything she felt.

Do you really believe that Frankie's story ends here? *Rachel Copeland*

No. I know it doesn't...

Which of your books would you most enjoy being turned into a film? Would you need to keep a tight control of the adaptation? *Diane Ashman*

I'd love for *The Turning Point* to make it to the screen – and I'd absolutely love to be involved in the script. It's a very different craft – only 120 pages rather than 120,000 words. I've always been an avid film fan and, of all my novels, *The Turning Point* ran across my mind's eye like a film. I watched it scene by scene and wrote down what I saw.

Do you have the Alice and the Ditch Monster books written in your head, if you do would you consider publishing them? *Amanda Tattersall*

I do! And I absolutely intend to. If you're on Twitter, follow @frankieshawnews - you heard it here first!

If you could, would you like to relocate to Pemberton, especially if Nathan the horse could go with you too? *Suzanne Porter*

In a heartbeat.

You are one of my favourite authors, who are yours? *Julie Morris*

Mary Wesley. John Irving. Maggie O'Farrell. Thomas Hardy. Laurie Graham. Rose Tremain. Frankie Shaw.

What size feet do you have? *Alison Gallagher*

I'm a size 4 – I have 14 pairs of Converse and a 'thing' for boots.

Freya, who would you most like to have a dinner date with and why? *Clare Hamilton Sneddon*

Well, I'd love to sit with my grandmothers in the late 1920s when they were 18 years old and women had just been given the vote. I'd love to know what that meant to them, what hopes and dreams they had. And I'd love to share a riotous meal with Moll Flanders – I imagine there'd be much wine and salacious gossip and I wouldn't be able to get a word in edgeways, which would be a first. As for a dinner 'date' – Keanu Reeves please.

What is your go to/favourite meal and drink? *Renée Key*

A baked potato with butter. A fat coke. A vodka lime and soda (make it a double).

How do you yourself emotionally deal with the complex emotions that your characters go through? *Karen Hockin*

It's tough. Most my novels leave me ragged, really. I am so closely bound with my characters that I find I can easily access the emotions they experience.

Whilst writing this novel, I had to take two weeks off after 'that' turning point. I grieved and I mourned and I was pretty inconsolable. Since publication, I've re-read *The Turning Point* twice – because I want to be back in the world of this novel. The characters and their stories meant so much to me – it was as if I lived it alongside them.

A letter from Freya

As an author, one of the perks of my job is research. I have always been passionate about being very thorough in my research, not just to give my stories integrity, but to do right by my characters and my readers alike.

Before writing *The Turning Point*, I had never been to Canada – and yet this main character of mine, the fictitious musician Scott Emerson, was 100% Canadian. Initially, I was a little perturbed by this – and even asked Scott if he wouldn't mind being Californian because I'd recently come home from a fabulous road trip. But, as with all my characters, before I even start writing their stories, Scott was already fully formed in my mind's eye. I knew that I needed to see where he lived and learn about his lifestyle, eat where he ate, see the view from his deck, hike his hikes, meet the people who lived around him. Had I not made the trip, the character of Aaron would not have existed because I had known so little of the Canadian First Nations.

Being a single mum, it's difficult for me to simply pack up and go. But, promising my children goodies from Roots (and with my parents house-sitting for me) off I went. Like Frankie, it was the furthest I've ever been from my kids and the longest I've ever left them – a very big deal for me. Like Frankie, I dithered at the departure gate as to whether to board the plane or not. Ocean and time zones away, that's where I was going, to a land I didn't know.

When I gazed out of the plane window at seemingly endless mountains, my heart started to soar. When finally I had landed and was looking up at those wonderful carved cedar Welcome Figures in Vancouver Airport, I experienced such a surge of excitement that I knew I'd come to the right place and that I'd be well looked after.

My trip had a profound effect on me. From exploring Vancouver and spending time at the Museum of Anthropology at UBC, to driving the Sea to Sky Highway. From speaking at the local writers' group in Pemberton, to hiking alone to Joffre lakes for 12k. From coming face to face with a black bear to trying my coffee double-double. From talking to elders of the L'íl'wat community to getting to know Pemberton village – it is truly a time I will never forget. I ate at Mile One Eating House and The Pony, I bought pastries from the Blackbird Bakery and fresh fruit from North Arm Farm. I needed the pharmacy on Frontier Street. I visited the Úlĺus Centre in Mount Currie and hung out at the tiny airfield in Pemberton. I walked in Frankie's footsteps and I felt Scott was around every corner. I made friends but I also rediscovered my own company. I loved it, all of it.

The landscape imprinted itself onto my heart. I was mesmerized by Mounts Currie, Meager, Owl, Tenquille, Camels Back and Seven o'Clock Mountain; I daydreamed by the Lillooet and Ryan rivers, I sat by the glacial lakes of Joffre and actually wept because I'd never even imagined anything so beautiful. You can see on my website the rather breathless video I took there. I slept really well, I felt healthy and so alive. I didn't want to leave.

Whilst writing *The Turning Point*, I embarked on a love affair with British Columbia that truly enriched my life and I cannot wait to return. I hope that, through *The Turning Point*, my readers will fall in love with BC too

Freya North

Ps: yes – I spent a small fortune in Roots for my children. Er – and one or two things for me...

Read on for an extract from

The Way Back Home

by

FREYA NORTH

CHAPTER ONE

Oriana

To Oriana, it seemed so small. So ridiculously and unnervingly small that she felt compelled to rub her eyes. It had to be an illusion – the truer, more sensible, more realistic proportions would surely be reinstated after a good blink. But there it was still, nestled in a fold of land which looked soft enough to be made of fabric. Like biscuit crumbs in a scrunched napkin, there was the small town outside which she'd grown up. She pulled the hire car in to the verge. She didn't want to get out, she wanted to avoid familiar smells that might make it seem real. She didn't want to hear anything that might say well! welcome back, duck. She wanted to believe that she had no history with this mini place and no need of it. It looked silly, being so small. Not worth a detour. Certainly not worth a visit. Not worthy, even, of a drive right through. This wasn't Lilliput. This wasn't romantic. This was Nowhere. Nowhere, also known as Blenthrop, Derbyshire. The worst thing about this bastard place striking Oriana as being so small was that it made the rest of the world feel so vast. And suddenly she felt isolated, acutely alone and terrifyingly far away from the place she'd called home for so many years, the place she'd left only the previous day. God Bless America, she said under her breath though she knew she'd never go back.

Driving to her mother's house was easier because she'd never lived there. There was little to recognize, nothing to flinch at; she was unknown and that was preferable to intrusive welcomes and waves, however warm and well meaning Blenthrop folk might be. The further she drove from her childhood home, the longer the space she could finally create between her ears and her shoulders. As she relaxed a little, the car seat felt more comfortable and her headache lifted. Really, jet lag had nothing to do with the tension and now that the anxiety had dissipated, Oriana let the genuine tiredness billow over her the way her mother used to waft her duvet when she was a little girl, giggling in bed waiting for it to land. They call it a comforter in the United States, she thought. My mum's gone all sheets and blankets because she says it makes the bed look 'properly made'. My mom – the all-American girl who's now as small-town English as they come.

The tiredness, the tiredness. Should she pull over? Half an hour left to Hathersage. Open the window. Turn the radio up another notch. Drink Coke. Pinch yourself awake. Pinch yourself that you really are here again, eighteen years on. Kick yourself, wondering if it's a stupid idea, really.

* * *

Oriana's mother didn't know what to do. Her daughter was sleeping and though she'd told her mother not to let her, under any circumstances, what was Rachel to do? Her daughter, wan and sunken-eyed, too thin. Rachel looked in at the front room. Oriana was curled embryonically into a corner of the sofa, her hands tucked tightly between her thighs, the tips of her socks hanging limply a little way off her toes; the heel of her right sock was twisted to her ankle, as if her shoe had wanted to cling onto her feet. Her hair looked lank and flat and her lips were chapped. She wasn't wearing earrings. She'd spilled something on her top. This wasn't jet lag, Rachel sensed. This was exhaustion.

Rachel had done that trip back to America often enough since she herself emigrated from there aged nineteen. She knew well that, though jet lag made you feel discombobulated, it didn't make you look like *that* – how Oriana had looked on arriving an hour ago. When Rachel had opened the door to her daughter, she read in half a glance all the unrevealed secrets and sadness that had slipped unnoticed between the lines of her sporadic emails. On her doorstep, Rachel saw how the crux of it all was suddenly writ large over Oriana's face, her general scrawniness. The details, however, remained concealed. She was shocked. How could she have known nothing? She was ashamed that, once again, a mother's instinct had failed her.

'I'll give her another ten minutes,' Rachel said, unsure.

'That'll make it forty winks,' Bernard said. 'I'll be

popping out now. Just round the block.' And he kissed his wife who, just then, really did love his habit of explaining life with sayings and clichés. Bernard Safely. Had ever a person had a more appropriate surname?

'Two shakes,' Bernard told her though they both knew that his walk around the block would take far longer than two shakes of a lamb's tail. She watched him through the bubbled-glass panel of the front door as he walked away. The distortion made him appear to have no bones, amorphous as jelly. Her ex-husband, Oriana's father, referred to Bernard as spineless. Through the warped glass, he did indeed look so. Rachel felt disloyal. She rarely thought about Robin these days. She supposed she'd have to, now Oriana was back, even if she didn't want to. She'd see him in her daughter's crooked smile, her high cheekbones, the way her gaze darted away while she talked but focused fixedly on whoever spoke to her. Father and daughter both had the ability, without realizing it, to make one feel simultaneously inconsequential and significant.

'Oriana Taylor,' Rachel said quietly and then, in a whisper, 'Oriana Safely.'

It didn't flow. It didn't work. It would never have worked. She'd always be Oriana Taylor, daughter of Robin. *The* Robin Taylor. Would they mention him? She and her daughter had managed for eighteen years to skirt issues as if they were dog mess on the pavement.

* * *

Malachy

An ex-girlfriend had described it as *Saturn Returns*. Malachy hadn't a clue what she meant. That dream you have, she'd said, you might not have it often but it'll always recur – like *Saturn Returns*, with similar cataclysmic fallout. It makes you introverted and horrid to be around.

He'd ended the relationship soon after. She was a bit too cosmic for Malachy and she talked too much anyway. If he had the dream, the last thing he needed was a load of astrobabble bullshit. A warm body cuddling next to him, soothing him, taking his mind off it – that's what he required. Saturn Returns. She never knew that a prog-rock band of that very name had formed in his childhood home, exploded onto the music scene for a couple of years in the late 1970s and then finally imploded back at the house in 1981. He never told her, even though the band had jammed in the very place where Malachy currently lived.

Last night, the dream had once again hijacked his sleep, apropos of nothing. In the woods, with his brother Jed, their teenage bodies of twenty years ago encasing their current souls. They were out at summer dusk, shooting rabbits. A large buck running away, stopping, turning and facing him. Delicate eyes and soft silver pelt conflicting with the anomalous fuck-you gesture of lope-long ears rigid like two-fingered abuse. Malachy pulled the trigger and smelt the saltpetre and heard the harsh crack and felt the kick and experienced the extreme pain as half his world went dark.

He'd often wondered whether the rabbit was some kind of metaphor. He'd tried to analyse why in the dream he didn't shout for help; why his brother was there only at the start. And he never knew whether he killed the rabbit, the little fucker. The pain cut the dream short, always. And he always woke up thinking, but it didn't happen like that, *it didn't happen like that*. And he'd be cranky and introverted for a good while after because he knew that he'd much rather it *had* happened like in the dream.

Stupid dream. Malachy left his bed and showered. Dressed, he snatched breakfast, yesterday's post in one hand, toast in the other. What he really wanted to do today was write his novel, not go to work. Business was slack this time of year – early March, thick frost, too cold for tourists, too close to Easter for more hardy holidaymakers; too close to Christmas and Valentine's and Mother's Day for locals to fritter any more of their money. The irony was Malachy could very well *not* open the gallery because, after all, he owned it – but the fact that he owned it compelled him to keep it open, never take time off, never get sick. Tuesday to Friday, 10 till 6. Saturday 10 till 5. Summer Sundays 11 till 2. Closed Mondays. If the gallery was as quiet as he anticipated, he'd work on his novel from there today. He left the apartment, glancing guiltily at the house. He ought to do the rounds, really. He hadn't done so for a couple of days.

Paula de la Mare waved at him, before she hopped into her car, belting down the drive. Malachy followed, absent-mindedly creating acronyms from the letters on her car's registration plate. At the bottom of the drive, she turned right, taking her girls to school. Malachy followed her a little way before joining the main road into Blenthrop.

Some idiot had dumped litter in the doorway of the White Peak Art Space; yesterday's chips lay like flaccid fingers in the scrunch of sodden paper. He rummaged in his satchel for something suitable like a plastic bag. Phone. An apple. Slim leather diary (he refused to use his phone for anything other than calls). A tin of pencils, a spiral-bound notebook and a flashdrive. He had no plastic bag. The toe of his shoe would have to do. He shoved the takeaway detritus into the gutter and opened up the gallery.

It was always the weirdest feeling. It never diminished and it engulfed Malachy the moment he entered. The immediate stillness and quiet of the space contradicted by the undeniable sensation that, up until that very moment, they'd been alive; the paintings, the sculptures. If he'd turned up a minute earlier, or sneaked in through the back, he was certain he'd have caught them at it. Now, as every day, they were just figures frozen into their canvases, others quite literally turned to stone, bronze or, in the case of Dan Markson's work, multicoloured polymer. It was like the characters in his novel – Malachy sensed they existed without him but whenever he returned to the manuscript, he found them exactly where he'd left them.

In the gallery, he straightened a couple of frames and adjusted the angle of a spotlight that was glaring off the glass of a watercolour. There were few emails to respond to and within the hour Malachy felt justified in inserting the flashdrive and clicking on the folder called 'novel', selecting from within it the file called 'novel10.doc'.

'Tenth draft in only fifteen years.'

He said it out loud, with contrived loftiness, laughed and took the piss out of himself, receiving the abuse well. All residual effects of the dream had gone, the details were forgotten. Until the next time.

* * *

Jed

None of his girlfriends knew this, but whenever Jed had sex in the morning, he always had Ian Dury playing in his head. He'd grown used to the soundtrack. It wasn't a distraction and it didn't irritate him; it was a brilliant song after all – as sexy in its funk as it was funny in its lyrics. It had started with Celine. She had been French, intense and passionate, and when she'd purred in his ear in the middle of his sleep, *wake up and make love with me*, that's what kicked it all off.

Jed knew his current relationship was on the way out; from fizz to fizzle in eight months. It had been as awkward as it had been depressing last night, to be the only non-conversing table in a packed and buzzing restaurant. They checked their phones, ate, gazed around the room, checked their phones again, eavesdropped on other people's conversations and barely looked at each other. Fiona went to bed when they arrived back at his flat. I'm tired, she'd said, as if it was Jed's fault. He'd sat up late, finishing off the red wine he'd opened the night before, even though he'd forgotten to put a stopper in it and it really didn't taste very good. Jed had thought, I'm too young to be one of those couples that go out for dinner and don't speak. And then he thought, I'm too old to be frittering away time on a relationship like this. I have a headache, he thought, collapsing into bed and drifting to sleep before he could remember to kiss her goodnight let alone check she was even there.

But he woke, horny. It was natural, chemical. Ian Dury was goading him to have a proper wriggle in the naughty, naked nude. He sidled up to Fiona, his cock finding the soft dale between her buttock cheeks to nestle in. Unlike Ian Dury, however, it wasn't lovemaking he wanted. Just a fuck. She moved a little, her breathing quickening as he ran his hand along her thigh, up her body, a squeeze of her breast before venturing downwards and between her legs. She was warm and moist and she let him manoeuvre her so that he could work his way into her from behind. No kissing. She had a thing – paranoia – about morning breath, which initially he'd found charming, then irritating but today just useful, as he didn't want kissing and eye contact. He just wanted to come because soon enough she'd be gone.

She dumped Jed in a stutteringly over-verbose phone call that lunch-time. It's not you, it's me. I just need some space. Let's just be friends. It's fine, he kept saying, I'm fine with it. I agree. If something of such little substance was finally over, it really didn't warrant this level of analysis or justifying. Don't worry, he told her, don't worry. I feel the same.

'You feel the *same*?' She sounded affronted, as if her self-esteem was dependent on him being crushed.

Jed sensed this. 'I mean,' he qualified, 'if you're *sure*. Take all the time you need.'

'I'm sure,' she said.

'OK,' he said, 'OK.' And for her benefit, he dropped his voice a tone or two. 'Take care,' he said.

'You too,' she said. 'Friends?'

'Friends.'

He had too many of these 'friends' with whom he had mercifully minimal contact. None had truly made the transition from girlfriend to friend. None had even re-formed into useful booty calls. Ultimately, none meant that much to him because none was the one who got away. He hadn't seen her for such a long time, not since she moved to America a decade and a half ago.